HE SAID,
SHE SAID

ALSO BY JOHN DECURE

Bluebird Rising

Reef Dance

HE SAID, SHE SAID

A MYSTERY

JOHN DeCURE

Skyhorse Publishing

Skyhorse Publishing books may be purchased in bulk at special discounts for sales promotion, corporate gifts, fund-raising, or educational purposes. Special editions can also be created to specifications. For details, contact the Special Sales Department, Skyhorse Publishing, 307 West 36th Street, 11th Floor, New York, NY 10018 or info@skyhorsepublishing.com.

Skyhorse® and Skyhorse Publishing® are registered trademarks of Skyhorse Publishing, Inc.®, a Delaware corporation.

Visit our website at www.skyhorsepublishing.com.

10 9 8 7 6 5 4 3 2 1

Library of Congress Cataloging-in-Publication Data is available on file.

Cover design by Laura Klynstra

Print ISBN: 978-1-63450-867-4
Ebook ISBN: 978-1-63450-868-1

Printed in the United States of America

For Steve Pico, the Sultan of Stoke.

"What's madness but nobility of soul at odds with circumstance?
The day's on fire!"

—Theodore Roethke

"They come out of nowhere, instantaneously materialize and just as quickly they break and vanish. Chasing after such fleeting mirages is a complete waste of time. That is what I choose to do with my life."

—Miki Dora

1

BRADLEE AAMES, ESQUIRE, DEPUTY ATTORNEY GENERAL

My life is an endless, all-consuming struggle with perception. Morning light fills my bedroom window because while I slept, the earth rotated away from the sun—okay, none of which I actually witnessed first-hand; but like any sane, otherwise rational person, I can accept this as true and . . . hence, I begin my day counting on a reality not seen, but known. Good start. But later, on the drive in to the office, my wind-shield becomes a sky portal, a poet's looking glass through which I spy a bank of shadows and chalk-blue autumn clouds rolling over downtown LA, hiding in plain sight as slowly, secretly, whispering—I can hear their rumbles—they organize themselves, carving arcs with godly precision as they overlap and interlock, lashing and intertwining and braiding into a mammoth atmospheric rope that, with an almighty whip-crack, threat-ens to lasso a skyscraper—but then, no. Stop it, girl, stop it, sideways tilting brain. Straighten up in your seat. Change lanes. Chew your lower lip. Anything. Snap out of it. The tears, they track roadways of fear and joy and exhaustion down my cheeks, and as I drive my LA drive with a million other silent, bereaved commuters, I forgo the urge to wipe my face in shame, instead letting the wet streaks set in, preserving the evi-dence of an event not real but experienced, and endured, just the same.

Evidence of the real—I need only describe my commute to work and you'd never guess that evidence is my professional métier. In my line of work, preserving evidence is a necessity and at times, an art. In so doing, a clear head and a good shit detector go hand-in-hand. My problem is that the latter is predicated on the former, and at times my twisted brain, like a cheating lover, will deceive me, crush my spirit, stunt my bearing, leave me doubting myself, a legal best-guesstimator tapdancing along the edge of ruin. Or some other self-important bullshit. I could write a bad country music song about getting hit by a train, but no. Instead I'll tell you about what I do. I deal.

I'm a prosecutor for the California Department of Justice, the Office of the Attorney General to be precise. In this state the AG is the top law enforcement officer, an elected official charged with enforcing the laws and protecting the public. A noble cause unfortunately intertwined with political realities such as pleasing the support base, image enhancement, and future career planning. My top boss, whom I won't describe here, is a politician. That's all the high-end job description you need. Typically, the AG wouldn't even know that a line deputy like me existed, unless I got a big case and blew it. In my storied legal career as a state employee, I've yet to reach that still very reachable milestone.

Most people would say I don't quite look the part. Women think I'm scary, and because nothing short of dynamite can move a woman off a preconceived judgment, I don't much give a rip what they think. I'm a tall girl at five ten, with long legs and a taut, angular form with which to torture men, if that's what I want to do. But usually I don't. The oddly intrigued male who comes face-to-face with me sees a pair of black eyes that glitter like distant stars as they untangle the latest jumble of disparate thoughts and images; a pile of fine, straight black hair that in sunlight, shines metallic; a thin, small nose; lips tight with a born critic's unimpressed perusal, though the mouth tends to crack open with inward-pointing curiosity; and a full complement of wet-black painted nails, their edges rounded by repeated taste-testing—this who-dat? girl ready to rock and roll or die trying. Or maybe just die. By now, it dawns on the locked-in guy that whatever he was initially feeling in his pants has either died or left the building, and perhaps he should follow via the easiest route. This one? Why wouldn't a guy want to nail her? But then, there's a certain subliminal risk-factor assessment going on that's . . . inconclusive, 'cause, Jesus, she's got it going on, but damn, she's killing the killer instinct, making it too complicated to put a man's-man, Type A, sexually dominant move on her. Screw it: this one is too dark, too racy, too intimidating.

So, screw them right back.

I prefer being alone . . . to ride bareback on rainbows and field impassioned complaints from bridges that haven't slept in years. It's easier to occupy my distorted world without a blandly lustful man looking over my shoulder, puzzling at the gargantuan indifferent nothing-to-say-or-do moment, as I stare back through the silent fire of hyperreality.

Not that I'm complaining. As I said, I deal.

The great leveler in my life is the concrete, analytic, nuts-and-bolts practice of law. My life's work is performed in the service of the sacred triumvirate of facts, law, and evidence. But it's not all deadlines and dry pragmatism; the subject matter of my cases is endlessly interesting.

My job as a deputy attorney general is to go after bad doctors, of whom there are no shortage these days. I prosecute wayward physicians on behalf of the Medical Board of California, the regulatory agency that grants doctors licenses and can also take them away. Some of the MDs I chase down in court will land on probation or be suspended from practice for a time; others are forcibly evaluated for mental and physical competency. The worst of them tend to be axed from the profession altogether. Occasionally they go to jail, and in such cases, I'll follow the matter over to the criminal courthouse to ensure the judge there knows how the medical board feels and the DA doesn't get lost in the factual details, because medical cases can get very factual and very detailed in a hurry. But that's typically not my direct order of business.

My work centers on public protection. I apply the laws of the State of California to stop the incompetent surgeon who performs only the first step of a complicated three-part procedure, because step one was the only part he was trained for twenty years ago when the surgery was a new thing; the ER doc who fails to take a wheezing fat man's family medical history or put him on a treadmill, sending him home instead to wait in isolation for the acute myocardial infarction—that is, the heart attack—that will kill him; the hoary old family practitioner that, refusing to hang it up despite his failing vision, one day confuses 10 a.m. patient Bob's chart with 10:45 a.m. patient Bob's records and prescribes a contraindicated medication to 10 a.m. Bob that stops his breathing, rendering him brain-dead in just under five minutes.

I prosecute bad psychiatrists, too, mostly shrinks who screw their patients. Not by the usual overcharging or distribution of ill advice; I mean the male shrink who *literally* screws his female Tuesday three o'clock in a cheesy motel on Ventura Boulevard or in a honeymoon suite at the Ritz Carlton on the Marina or in a two-dollar movie matinee on Melrose—so vigorously in that sad case that the projectionist dimmers up the house lights to have a better look. The last shrink I took out did the deed right there in his office atop a polished maple desk crammed with family photos, Dad's and the kids' frozen faces looking on as he put it to his patient, and them, at the same damn time. He finished the job by doing the patient's insurance plan, billing extra for critical-care "intervention services." No conscience, no shame, no soul. Took that rat bastard down, but with the wreckage strewn about, my victory felt as empty as cleanup duty. So what? He was gone and the public was a teeny bit safer. I took the win for what it was: a win. Moved right on to the next rat bastard.

Of course, the act itself is the primary focus of any sexual misconduct case because the breach of patient trust is so profound, it can, and often does, destroy the victim. But in terms of how I'll go about proving up the facts, location means a lot. Every psychiatrist knows that to admit to banging a patient is to kiss his career goodbye, because a license revocation will surely result. So he lies, denies, obscures, misdirects, and obfuscates. If the only other evidence I have to offer is the victim's retelling of the shrink's abuse, the result is a standoff. He said, she said. And that's not enough to meet my high burden of proof, which consists of clear and convincing evidence in these cases.

I need corroboration to support the victim's story. That projectionist who got a prurient eyeful during the matinee. The receptionist who heard moaning and humping noises through the door, and saw the patient stagger out of the office later with a tear in her skirt, a bra strap peeking out of her purse—and a gauge mark deep within her beating heart. A motel clerk with a good memory for faces when it comes to patrons who use movie-star aliases and pay cash for their rooms.

Whatever it takes to get to the truth.

Which is a serious challenge because sometimes patients lie. Unhappy, narcissistic, delusional, obsessive patients willing to ruin a caring professional's career just to draw attention to themselves. Those cases tend to include a victim's story rife with factual inconsistencies and bereft of solid corroboration; in other words, they just don't pass the whiff test. It's tough any time for me to walk away from such serious allegations, but bullshit never passes for real evidence, and the impossibility of meeting that high burden of proof makes the decision to close out a file a bit easier.

You can see by now why I need to have that shit detector working all the time—and imagine how, if I don't, I might land myself in a world of trouble. This is precisely what happened in the case I'm going to tell you about, but I don't want to get too far ahead of myself here. You need to know why my head wasn't on straight before I got the case.

In a word: heredity. I mean, just for starters, what kind of crazy parents would name their daughter Bradlee?

It's true: people assume I did something wrong to be a girl named after a guy, since, as you know, the sound of Bradlee rolling off the tongue doesn't exactly leave one swimming in visions of feminine enchantment. They presume I was a bad seed, undesirable. I get that; I used to think that way too, skinny and spider-limbed-freaky in front of the bathroom mirror. But in time I realized that my only sin was to come along when I did to the people I was born to, and compared to my other well-documented deviations, that one just doesn't rate.

Bradlee Aames is who I am, and like most of life's great mishaps, you can blame that one on God.

Or maybe partly on my father, John Marshall Aames, a gray-suited, stand-up federal government lawyer, a career United States Department of Justice guy who'd always wanted a son to follow in his footsteps, and wouldn't you know, he'd already picked out the perfect name which, in his view, would deftly set the bearings on his boy's moral compass. But Jack Aames was no tight-ass; despite his veteran status, he protested Vietnam when the body bags and lame rationales piled up, and his law-and-order professional orientation never quelled his interest in Tolstoy, Nietzsche, Sartre, Kerouac, and Ginsberg. In a way he enjoyed the best of both worlds—the straitlaced and the anti-establishment—as a federal prosecutor who found his niche prosecuting civil rights violators. His work made him a friend to Berkeley free-speech advocates and scabs assaulted by Teamsters, and an enemy to any cop who tried to play back-alley judge, jury, and executioner. To try emotionally loaded cases like that, you've got to truly walk the walk, especially in front of a jury box full of strangers. Having read all of the published legal decisions in which he was counsel of record, I can tell you he did. My father won every last one of those cases.

I was a child when he died, and by now, my memories of him are shifty and full of blind spots, yet there are times when I can smell the cigar in his worsted suit coat, can still hear the roar of the troll beneath the bridge during our bedtime reading. As for my name, the historical explanation is simple. During Watergate, the *Washington Post*'s editor, Ben Bradlee, had run all those infamous Woodward and Bernstein pieces without bowing before the great machine of government, taking an epic stand against an immense, immovable power my father knew oh so well. Had I been a boy, my name would be Ben. Too bad . . .

At least, this was how my mother recalled it going down. Not so long ago, when she was slowly fading out in a nursing home, she'd clutch at my sleeve and tell me all sorts of things I never knew. Big, important things that parents from Mom and Dad's era would typically whitewash. Such as, how she'd miscarried twice and was over forty and still childless when I came along. The sense that no, let's be serious here—there will be *no son*. Her body was tired of being tricked by nature, so Mom didn't much feel like fighting over the name of a baby she'd failed to produce in a manner that met expectations.

Sometimes I wish she'd been like my father and said nothing. For years, on low days, I'd hyperventilate, gagging on . . . I don't know, the guilt of having gone and spoiled Dad's plan by entering the world without a penis. I wanted to disappear, to die tragically, poetically—Bradlee Aames, the Joan of Arc of her third-grade class, her abbreviated life choked away by a wayward tetherball chain . . . . But then, my father's silence on the subject included, concomitantly, not a single complaint. And he was kind. He loved his only child, and she him. Still, I couldn't shake my feelings, however misplaced they proved to be.

I hadn't thought of my dead father much until maybe a year back or so, when Mom made her final demented sashay around the grounds of the Blessed Mary assisted living facility in Colton, a forgettable patch of smog-burned brown where strip-club billboards cast biblical shadows over abandoned minimarts. By then she was mostly gone, waltzing about in the predawn blue, feeding little colored marshmallows to the sparrows like Francis of Assisi in a bathrobe. They need their momma, she explained to the staff psychiatrist, who'd phoned me, the half-crazy daughter, describing the scene in real time, hoping I could shed some light on the situation from my apartment in Venice Beach.

My mother didn't get me, never knew what was wrong with my head: Why I'd thank the FDR statue in the park for his advice on how I should wear my hair; why I'd ruin a perfectly swell mother-daughter baking moment by hiding behind Mom's apron to keep the hot, angry oven from swallowing me whole; why I'd chuck her sewing needles into the garbage after overhearing their plot to poke my eyes out while I slept. So what if her little Bradlee was a little quirky? Who did those nosy, "deeply concerned" school counselors think they were anyway? Lots of people claim to have seen angels—the networks are always doing TV specials on the subject, for goodness' sakes. Crossing guards? Bunch of losers in their thirties still living at home, don't know what they're talking about, because no little girl would *ever* try to stop a moving car with her bare hands. And what was with that Father Lonaghan, was he hitting the sauce on the job? Such a disappointment for a man of the cloth, that Lonaghan. After all, a youngster's confused mumbling while kneeling in a dark, scary confessional should not be construed as speaking in tongues . . . .

There were other signs, too, but I won't go on; as always, the one constant was my mother's oblivious response. To her, I was just a curious, intense little girl blessed with a rich and vivid imagination.

When she died, I unexpectedly took a step closer to the thing my mother had denied about me all those years.

About a week after the funeral, a man with a heavy Middle Eastern accent called me, huffing and puffing and threatening unspecified legal action unless I either reclaimed the contents of a public storage locker Mom had rented, or paid a fee closing out her account. If I didn't agree to let the junk be put up for auction, or take it away myself, a draconian fee would be tacked onto the final bill, with interest. "No negotiate!" the man shouted before he hung up.

I politely pointed out that indeed, everything is negotiable.

"No pay up, big trouble!"

The next Saturday morning, I got up early and drove fifty miles inland until I came to a blighted row of empty lots in Pomona aglitter with broken glass and shiny springs curling out of discarded mattresses. The address was wrong, had to be, but . . . beyond the vacant lots, a storage yard was set back, hidden in a weedy culvert, and at the rusty front gate the litigious man on the phone awaited me. His name was Farhad, and his Hawaiian shirt was made of polyester and stank of sweat at ten paces. I found his speech to be crude and hard to follow, but his undisguised enthusiasm for my cleavage was never in doubt. I come in peace, I told him amiably, but the spit flew as he issued the same hardline demands as before. I did what any good attorney would do and asked for a copy of the contract binding my mother or her successors to such terms. When Mr. Farhad failed to produce, raising the specter of legal action nonetheless, my head, which had been fogbound all morning, was cleared by a jolt of indignation.

"Go ahead, try and sue me on the terms and conditions of a contract you can't produce."

"Terms and conditions?" He seemed surprised. Still staring at my chest, he asked what I did for a living.

"I sell seashells," I said, gently cupping my boobs as if they were conches.

"I take two."

"Not for sale. How about putting your eyes back in their sockets."

"Yeah, yeah." He studied a passing truck and the miniature dust storm it kicked up. "What you really do, seashell lady?"

"In my spare time, I practice law. Please think about that before you threaten me again with legal action."

"Woman lawyer. Huh."

I counted out a hundred bucks in twenties, held them out for him to see, but didn't hand them over just yet.

"One condition."

"You say terms and conditions. What happened to 'terms?'"

"Never mind. Just cut the lawsuit business. I don't like being threatened."

He folded his meaty arms, sizing me up all over again. "You don't like threats. I think to be lady lawyer, you must be tough." He leaned forward a few inches, peering into my aviators. "Right?"

I leaned in the same distance and tipped up my shades. "Better than that. I'm tough *and* crazy."

Studying my eyes, he reached the same conclusion.

"This is in full and final settlement."

"Yeah, yeah, forget lawsuit. I take money."

He growled a little for show as he took the bills. After that I followed him on a long walk to a distant row of bunkers. Farhad found my mother's unit and crouched, grumbling as he wrestled with a ring full of keys, the sweaty crack of his ass winking back at me.

"Lawyer—hah! My country, lawyer is lower than dog, we tell lawyer what to do!"

"Not in America the beautiful."

"*Woman* lawyer? Even lower than snake. My country—"

His whining was tired, but he'd lost a tussle with a lady lawyer in black aviators and a white Harley Davidson tank top, so I let him vent. At last he clicked the right key into the base of a rolled metal door that hissed like a dragon as it unfurled, and I was left alone to sift through a stack of useless old junk, most of which I would later gladly pay Farhad twenty more to toss.

But one box with a lid bearing the letters JMA—my dad's initials—got my attention. Heavy and stuffed full of old documents. Leafing through a loose stack of papers, I glimpsed several pieces of my father's history: a set of college transcripts from USC, the owner's manual for the 1957 Plymouth Belvedere Sport Coupe hardtop he'd driven for twenty years; an US Army notice to report for duty at Fort MacArthur in San Pedro on June 12, 1942, at 0700 hours; a Chase Manhattan life insurance policy—the payout of which had funded my mother's final years at Blessed Mary. There was more: a deed to a house my parents had owned in West Hollywood before I was born; a book of pristine, vastly dated Disneyland tickets, marked A through E—probably from a family outing cancelled by an emergency legal deadline; a pile of furniture and household appliance receipts from big department stores no longer in business today. A lot more random yellow paper that I wouldn't begin to categorize as useful.

Last, I came upon a thick brown file resting at the bottom of the box. Inside was a thick stack of papers secured by fat rubber bands that disintegrated the instant I dug my fingernails under them: a police report and medical chart—the officially recorded data from the hit-and-run accident that had killed my father—and a detailed coroner's report, with complete lab results. Each set of documents neatly hole-punched, tabbed, and bound.

Someone had taken care to put this file together, as if to form a complete picture of what had become of Jack Aames on the last night of his life. My mother? Doubtful—she'd always seemed so flighty and out of it. I couldn't think who else would compile such a detailed record, but that didn't matter. Finding it was what counted.

Farhad was pacing around in the inland heat when I emerged. The sun beat rudely, invading my thoughts.

"Lady lawyer, not look so happy."

I regretted having taken off my shades. My inner life is best maintained by walling off outsiders. I'm like those tribes that won't let you photograph them because they believe a photo can steal a part of their souls. I get that thinking completely. The less of my real self I put out there, the less I give away my power. Whatever that's worth, at least. Telling this dude I was crazy sounded cool in the moment, but I'd paid the price of giving him an insight.

"I read your ad. Climate and humidity controls."

"Yeah, sure, motors running now. Very quiet."

"Right. Smells like you're storing dead rodents. I ought to call the Better Business Bureau."

His palms shot up. "Hey, hey! We keep friendly!"

I offered him the tiniest of nods. He knew, now, to keep away.

"Okay, okay." Farhad sighed and pointed to the box I was juggling on my hip. "You take away?"

I nodded, handing him the cargo before he could speak again.

"Thanks. It's heavy."

Walking back beside me, he'd dropped back into studying my chest, but at least he was working for me.

"Hunh. Women lawyers."

His stubbornness amused me. "Jesus, get over it already."

"My country, woman knows her place—"

I knew mine. So I retreated to Venice Beach, where I spent the rest of the weekend on the floor of my bedroom, reading.

The accident that killed my father had happened on a Holy Thursday in late March, at 10:14 p.m., in the eastbound far right lane on Temple Avenue just short of the intersection with Main Street, a few blocks south of the federal courthouse. The officer on the scene had drawn a simple overhead diagram that reduced Jack Aames to a crumpled stick figure in the roadway, felled at a spot marked by an *X*. The culprit—nothing but a long-necked arrow running out to the edge of the drawing—seemed to stop a block away, where the paper ran out, and for a heartbeat I felt an urge to drive down there myself for a look. I pictured those east–west blocks of civic buildings downtown. Parker Center and LAPD headquarters were a scant few blocks away, so plenty of cops were in the vicinity, but no one saw a thing. No suspicious tire marks on the road, either, which meant the driver never braked. Broken headlight glass from a car made by General Motors—a detail that served only to narrow the field to about a million or so cars on the streets of LA.

In his line of work, my father had some fairly heavy-duty enemies, which is why, I supposed, an autopsy was done: in anticipation of future criminal charges against a perpetrator. But no witnesses or evidence emerged, and no murder angle was worked up beyond the stage of speculative discussion. Every lead was exhausted. His accident, or killing, was forgotten long ago.

Next, I studied the medical chart. Massive head injuries. Hematomas behind both ears. His skull had struck the pavement, partially caving in a four-inch panel along the base, just above the neck, and probably killing him on impact. The femur, the largest bone in his left leg, had been crushed beneath the wheels of the car that had just nailed him.

Last, I came to the coroner's report, which read much like the medical chart, but with greater scope and depth. Vital organs were extracted and weighed. Contusions were noted and measured. Thorough blood and chemical testing was performed. One test result, and one positive drug finding, got my full attention.

Lithium carbonate.

My father had lithium carbonate, the drug most commonly used to treat schizophrenia, in his system when he died.

Schizophrenia—a condition known to be hereditary.

I sat there for a time, eyes shut. I was at the bottom of a well, dry and caked with dirt. Dying of thirst with nothing to drink. Blinked when I felt the bedroom walls beginning to vibrate—they'd closed in tighter while I was down that well. Without thinking, I pulled a well-placed quart bottle of Jack Daniels from beneath the bedsprings, twisted it open, smelled the euphoric burn before it lined my throat with cleansing flame. One, or three, more times. The walls around me stopped shaking, at least for now. Not a single car alarm had beeped down in the street, so I knew there'd been no earthquake. I studied the black JD label—*good to see you, my friend from Tennessee, Old No. 7*—and was slapped in the forehead by a single, persistent thought.

My old friend the bottle was equally perceptive, and with an obliging Southerner's warmth that soothed my soul, it duly attested to my very thoughts: *Yes, of course, my dear. You've been self-medicating all these years and—goodness gracious, sakes alive—you hadn't even known it! Now, kiss me again, dear, one more time, lay those thirsty-girl lips right on me.*

After this belated epiphany, I resolved to delve into a course of treatment for my condition. If my father had the resolve to face it, then so would I. Anxious to embrace whatever curatives modern medicine might have in store to fix my head, I got tested, evaluated, therapeutically counseled, and so on, the sum of which disappointingly resulted in the accumulation of more unanswered questions than I'd had when I started. No formal differential diagnosis was reached, but God, the slew of equivocations and five-dollar psychological terms that were bandied about in the process? Impressive.

Possible borderline personality.

Rule out bipolar disorder.

Rule out schizophrenia.

Thank you for the referral. Subject presents as a high-functioning individual who describes a history of intermittent anxiety and even psychotic episodes, yet has excelled in school and met demands of professional life. She is also guarded, sarcastic, and exhibits a generally negative predisposition suggestive of low-level depression with concurrent lack of initiative. Personal defense mechanisms are well-developed and reportedly effective in most social situations. Subject markedly denies the effects of psychosis on her cognitive functioning.

High-level coping skills are also in evidence. Subject reports no prior history of hospitalization or medical intervention.

I did, however, emerge from this thicket of nonfindings with a fistful of prescriptions, ostensibly written to aid me in contending with the diagnosis of Onset: Whatever. I'm talking heavy-duty controlled substances, the kind that, under the right conditions, will knock you flat on your ass, and if ingested under the wrong conditions, might leave you down for the count, down and out for the rest of time.

Clozapine.

Olanzapine.

Quetiapine.

Risperidone.

Flight conditions for this ever-changing space shot? Variable! That means, I strapped in for takeoff under every possible combination—or "titration," which is the five-dollar word favored in modern pharmaceutical practice—you could imagine. It was a white-knuckle, front seat, hands-in-the-air ride, and much of the time I was either sick or disoriented, or both. Some combinations stole my appetite, while others had me lusting after anything deep fried and sprinkled with powdered sugar. For weeks I felt nothing below the waist, forgetting sex even existed. Retaining water, I blew up like a puffer fish. One night I awoke gagging and cotton-mouthed, reached for the bottle of JD under my bed and—holy shit—barely caught myself before downing in what could have been the last thirst-quenching shots of my life. Some days I was fogged in and bone-dragging tired for hours, only to lie awake half the night, studying the speech patterns of neighborhood crickets. My moods came and went, surging and receding like the winter shore pounds at the jetties. One week, I had all the emotion of a can opener, but a few titrations and a new dopamine blocker later and I was weeping over the truth about Santa Claus.

In fairness to the American pharmaceutical industry—a business built on caring, if you believe the TV ads full of pretty actors who are anything but high on meds—the chemicals were not all bad. The drugs did slow the visions. When I was legally stoned, the corner mailbox didn't duck when I thrust forth a pile of letters; the palm trees lining my block in Venice stopped snickering at my black summer outfits; and if I gazed up to study a downpour, the raindrops didn't spiral gyroscopically to earth the way they do in Van Gogh paintings, they just fell like . . . *rain*. My portrait of the world through a convex mirror was gone—I was seeing life closer to the way it apparently existed. But the trade-off was a bitch, and slowly, I came to realize that my ability to engage in critical thinking had been blunted. Flattened. Hard, without mercy or subtlety. In the practice of law, keeping that mental edge sharp is often the difference between winning and losing, but the meds I was prescribed whittled my mental edge all the way down into a pile of sawdust.

One bad case nearly got me fired. Still prisoner to the pharmaceuticals that were meant to liberate me, I was unaware of the calamity awaiting me the minute I couldn't be at full capacity. Even seriously stoned, I still knew right from wrong, but when all the details were dialed out of focus, I got lost.

It was a simple investigation against, ironically enough, a physician alleged to be mentally unstable. Philip Burgess was a general practitioner with a good heart. He had a small clinic on a busy stretch of Pacific Coast Highway in Lomita, and specialized in servicing low-income families reliant upon government assistance for their health care. Burgess maintained his hospital privileges a few miles away at Torrance Memorial hospital, where he was well-liked. He'd never generated a single patient complaint with the medical board in over twenty years.

But Philip Burgess had a sickness. Back when he was still a resident and working killer hours, he'd suffered an attack of mania and was diagnosed as bipolar. For years he took all the antianxiety meds and mood stabilizers his doctors prescribed for him to function normally again, but eventually he wearied of the drugs' harsh side effects. So he weaned himself off the pills, carefully monitoring his own condition.

Slowly his health improved; his sex drive, energy level, and appetite also revived. Life returned to normal—until changes in state medical insurance allowances for the poor doubled his patient base overnight. At the same time his practice ballooned, a New York publisher purchased his manuscript for a book, requiring him to make significant edits on a tight timeline. Burgess began pulling eighteen-hour workdays, seven days a week. He also stopped eating and sleeping regularly, lost twenty pounds, and became manic again. When his wife found him crouched near the toilet with a kitchen knife, waiting to slay the anaconda only he could hear slithering up the sewer to get him, she called the police.

Burgess fled before the cops arrived, checking into a Hilton hotel a few miles from home. He stayed in his room for a few hours, until the time came, he said, to return to his caveman roots and embark on a quest for fire. When hotel security found him hunched beneath the leaves of a large decorative fern in the lobby, holding match after match to the base of a giant green leaf, the police were called in again. This time Burgess was put on an involuntary seventy-two-hour hold for a psych evaluation—which, in California, is called a 5150, for the Welfare and Institutions Code statute authorizing the hold. By the next day, he'd stabilized, been treated, and was released. He retained a good criminal defense attorney, who directed him to cut a thousand-dollar check to the Hilton for groundskeeping restitution and promise never to return to the hotel. Those measures, and a copy of the psych eval, persuaded the deputy district attorney assigned to Burgess's indecent exposure case to drop the charges.

In the interest of public protection, the deputy DA tipped off the medical board that one of its licensed doctors may be seriously mentally ill. The board was compelled to look into the case, using statutes that allow for medical and psychological evaluation of any doctors that may be a danger to themselves or others. If you survive the process, the board will leave you alone, but if you don't, they can use the results to suspend or revoke your license. Failing to comply when the board orders you into an eval is the same as failing the testing outright.

When the board opened a case on Dr. Burgess, he quickly took the position that he had nothing to hide. He agreed to be evaluated and signed a consent form, which was obtained by the board's assigned investigator, Jerry Roggin.

The eval was set to take place a week later. In the meantime, I all but forgot about the case, slept late all weekend, had some good Thai food at a new bistro around the corner Sunday night—or was it Monday? Malibu also got a decent head-high swell, and I took my longboard out there twice in the dead of night, which is what I do when I can't sleep. Or just when I feel like getting wet. No one surfs Malibu on moonless nights. The depth of solitude I take away from those solo sessions is very calming.

But the point is: the whole time I dealt with Burgess, I was whacked out, in contemplation of Life, the Universe, and the Great Nugatory Yawn. No visions to contend with, just a punchy numbness, my work a robotic exercise, like breast-stroking through molasses. When Jerry Roggin called me and said you won't believe what "the crazy one" did last weekend, I almost snapped that he had no right to follow me around.

Jerry told me the Philip Burgess evaluation was off for the time being because the doctor had just been 5150'd again. A Hermosa Beach lifeguard had fished him out of the surf just south of the pier in an attempted suicide. Dr. Burgess, however, claimed he'd merely been walking along the sand and was overcome by the urge to play in the waves. Can you believe this guy? Jerry had asked. Well . . . yes, I can, I'd said without irony.

Jerry had already gotten the police report and the 5150 records. His supervisor had talked with the board's enforcement director, and based on the two psych holds, they wanted me to prepare an emergency petition, ASAP, asking the court for an order suspending Dr. Burgess.

Petitions for interim suspension orders—ISOs—are done on paper, with witness declarations and other attachments, to support the request to suspend. The state's primary argument is that the doctor presents such a threat to himself, the public, or both, that he must be suspended right now pending the outcome of a trial to come later.

My job was to pull together the declarations, based on the documentation and reports. The most important input would come from the expert Jerry was lining up to review the 5150 medical charts.

Jerry drove the paperwork over to the office of the board's expert. Four hours later, he emerged with a report declaring Dr. Burgess a danger to himself or others. The first 5150 hold established the fact that without medication and therapy and professional oversight, the doctor couldn't function. The second 5150 hold led to a single manifest conclusion: off his meds, Burgess was a danger to himself and his patients.

So I typed, and typed—but all in a tired loop, sometimes reworking the same sentence or phrase, over and over. Going nowhere. Words, words, words . . . but where had their meaning gone, and why did they refuse to fit together? I'm an experienced lawyer who knows her job, and I knew this kind of brain lock should not occur while working an easy ISO matter. I knew—but didn't want to believe.

Until I ran out of excuses. My problem was obvious: the drugs designed to keep me from seeing things that were not really there were also restricting my view of my own distorted self. I was useless like this.

But hey!—here's another tip of the cap to the drug industry, I must concede, because good golly, the side effects of these substances had, indeed, been thoroughly explained! These days pharmaceutical companies, and prescribing MDs, are expert at covering their asses, so good golly again, I can't say I wasn't *warned*! (Not to worry, big pharma, though I may be a lawyer, I wouldn't dream of suing you!) But side effects aside, the net result—disconnection, debilitation— was utterly unforeseen. These drugs in which I placed my faith and well-being had turned my high-level cognition into a false-starting stammer and stutter, wrecking my core ability to move from one thought to another, then another. No logical progression, no recognizable train of thought. I'd lurch forward, stagger to catch my breath, fall back without even noticing I was starting over, puzzling over the same issue again—only it was worse the second time, my self-confidence diminished, my fear of failure further distorting what was left of my judgment. And all my prescribing doctor seemed capable of doing was to query me on side effects, consult his *Physician's Desk Reference*, read more about the limitless array of wonder drugs available to the caring physician with a patient in need, and attempt yet another titration.

The next day Jerry drove around, getting signatures on the declarations, two from arresting officers and one from the board's expert. Still flagging badly on my meds, I worked all day on the ISO brief, one step up and two steps back. Got it filed and served on Dr. Burgess. Then I caught up on the work in other cases I'd neglected for days. Sometime after 10:00 p.m. I noticed that the office was quiet. I walked to my window, where eight floors below, lovely stripes of skid row asphalt shone soft orange under a searching, prison yard moon. Another time, those stripes might bend into the shapes of letters, spelling out my kindergarten teacher's name. Not tonight. Ah, night. Time to plant my feet and take it on faith that one more time, the earth has rotated away from the sun.

My desk phone rang—very strange at this hour. I answered in the usual manner, naming my employer but not myself.

"Department of *Justice*, eh? That's a hot one, young lady," Dr. Burgess said.

"You've read the ISO brief."

"I read it all right. And you've violated state and federal patient privacy laws."

"But . . . you consented to release of your records."

"The hell I did. I signed off for you to see the first 5150 records, from the hotel incident. Not the second one, though. Hermosa PD just wanted to railroad me. No mind-expanding trips into the surf allowed. One of 'em even admitted he didn't like doctors, said we acted like 'gods in white coats.'"

"But—"

"Get your facts straight. I was fine that day at the beach. In fact, I was following my psychotherapist's advice not to always be the tightly wound, uber-responsible physician and all-around serious guy, but to allow myself to *unwind*, grant myself permission to act on impulse now and then. Long as it's a healthy impulse, that is, and what's wrong with swimming in the ocean? Is that a banned act?"

My instinct as a litigator was to dig in hard against my opponent, but he sounded so . . . reasonable. In fact, everything Burgess had said had a ring of truth, an authority you typically can't fake. Even worse, his travails seemed barely once removed from my own. He was coping as best he could, breast-stroking through his own ocean of molasses—just like me. As for dipping into the ocean, he'd come close to describing my own best outlet for dealing with the stress of constant self-regulation. I should be cutting him a break.

With empathy came a fear of powerlessness that I'm not proud of, but—well, what the fuck. I'm not a perfect human being.

"I said—is that a banned—"

"I heard what you said, so back the hell off!"

"Okay, fine, you don't need to yell at me. All I was saying—"

"Just stop talking. I need a minute." While the doctor huffed, I silently searched for the release Jerry had supplied with the newest documents. Then I found it. "I'm looking at it. With your signature at the bottom."

"That can't be. It's a forgery, Ms. Aames."

"It looks pretty good."

"I'm telling you, it's wrong. I never signed on for that Hermosa Beach affair. Look closer at the document. What else do you see?"

"Descriptions of the 5150 docs we were after."

I heard a hard, bitter chuckle, followed by a long sigh. That's when he let the stoned prosecutor have it.

"Are you serious? I get it now. That Goggins character came out to my office and had me sign the thing."

You mean Gerry Roggin."

"Roggin, shmoggin, the name doesn't matter. It's what he did that's important here. Listen to me. Know what I distinctly remember? Asking him where I should put the date. Know what he said? Not to worry, he'd type it in. But all that happened earlier this month. Get it?"

"The date on this release is from yesterday."

"Course it is! Don't you see? He came around, but I was in with a patient and late to do a procedure. Not my top priority, to drop everything for you people. By the time I could spare a minute, he was gone."

"You didn't see him."

"Boy, you are quick."

"Don't be an ass."

"Okay, okay, I'm upset."

"I get that."

"Sorry. So, what else is on the form?"

My forehead pounded with exertion. Another bad sign. Thinking is labor, but Jesus, it shouldn't hurt.

"It describes, uh . . . both 5150 holds."

"I told you, it's a fraud. The Hermosa Beach thing was added onto the old consent form I signed well before I went swimming. That second 5150? A hatchet job! They looked me up and saw I was in the system recently, so they treated me like I was nuts. The evaluation was one-sided *in extremis* as a result. Pure garbage. Think I aced it anyway. So they had no objective evidence. No choice but to release me."

"The ISO hearing's tomorrow," I said.

"What that means to me is you better get your facts straight, pronto. I don't think that's asking too much. We're just talking about my life, here."

Outside my office window, a thousand crows flew in from east LA like a plague, singing like happy mariachis.

"I'll . . . work . . . on it." The words swung in the air like a rope of taffy.

"Either we've got a bad connection or you're slurring your words, miss. Forgive me for asking, but I am a doctor. Are you on something?"

I'd gotten punchy and drifted sideways again. The way he asked me, in a caring, almost fatherly voice, it pierced my chest, made me hurt inside like I hadn't hurt in a long time. My recent travels through Pharmaland had kicked up a lot of feelings I hadn't been in touch with in a long time—if ever. I came back like a prosecutor anyway.

"Don't step over the line with me."

"I think you've got that backwards. You're messing with *my* life."

My head was on backwards. I was hyperventilating from the heat of the confrontation, which to me, shouldn't have been happening. He was a good guy, but *I'm* on the side of the good guys. Usually, I'm adept at objectifying the opposition, which makes it easier to focus on what I have to do. Only now, instead of feeling nothing, I saw a big part of myself in this man, in his predicament.

"I'm doing my job."

"I'll give you that, young lady." He chuckled benignly. "One simple, well-intended request: please do it better."

My breathing took a while to return to normal. My brain was as flat as that glowing skid row asphalt outside, minus any illumination whatsoever. I wanted a drink, a shot, a line of coke, anything to dull the pain, wanted it so badly I had to dig my fingernails into my forearms to make the craving go away. In time, I sat up straighter and thought of the doctor's plea that I do my damn job. Well . . . yes, okay. I studied the consent form on my desk. My guess was that Jerry had been sloppy, forgetting to fill in the date back when Dr. Burgess had previously signed off. Then yesterday, he'd been inconvenienced out at Dr. Burgess's office—though I knew now that Burgess wouldn't have signed another consent form anyway. So Jerry took a shortcut, filling in the second 5150 description and forward-dating the document.

What I should have seen—and instantly questioned—was the use of one form for two separate 5150 records. Too convenient. But I was zonked, incapable of sustained critical thinking, paying zero attention to detail. Useless.

Screw this shit, I decided. This job isn't worth doing if I can't do it right. And I love this job.

That night, I got ready for bed, then sent the meds down the toilet. All of them.

The next morning I walked into Raul Mendibles's office, first thing, to tell him everything—that is, except the part about flushing my meds. Mendibles is my supervisor and not much of an attorney, a rumpled, mediocre testament to the Peter Principle. He's also married, which has had no apparent effect on the candle he's been burning for me since the minute I walked into this place. He stares, he hovers, he pries, he speaks in halted hiccups. The office gals make fun of him when they think I'm out of earshot, but I've heard what they say. She's a suicide pill, Raul. A hot looker with a hot mess for a head. Don't toss your heart in a Cuisinart, Mendibles.

At the moment he was on the phone with his wife, Myrna, whom he talks to about ten times a day. Motioning me to sit down, he dumped the call. I laid out what had happened with Burgess. When I was done, he asked me if I was sure—meaning: did I know my head well enough to be certain? I was stunned by his apparent lack of concern.

Mendibles is the only person in the office who knows of my internal struggles because when I started in with the meds, the insurance company paying for them had called him, without my knowledge or consent, to verify my employment. (I'd like to sue those pricks for violating my patient privacy, but that's another story.) It seemed he wouldn't be beneath holding that personal, medical information against me, a fact that rattled me further.

Again, I attempted to lay out the Burgess ISO situation. He listened quietly, without even a word, but when I told him I was going to tell the truth at the hearing and withdraw the ISO motion, he made a teepee of his hands on his desk, sighed, and said he had one question for me first.

"Are you *sure*?"

Again, I knew what he meant: Was I sure of my own mind, that this was precisely what had gone down? Could I stand by the order of events as I recalled them? Jerry Roggin's and Dr. Burgess's careers may be depending on it.

Not to mention mine.

"As sure as I need to be," I told him without further explanation.

I was spinning when I left Mendibles's office. He'd more or less shown me no support, but in a nice-guy, gutless wimp way that seemed helpful yet wasn't worth a damn. Made me want to kick the shit out of him.

I didn't find out how ill-equipped I was to deal with the ISO until I got to court. Made my stand, bore the brunt of Dr. Burgess's suitable outrage, which was amplified by his new lawyer, a woman named Marilu Edwin, who sported a blond wig and a haughty manner. What's worse, Jerry Roggin was sitting in the gallery, and he took the opportunity to look deeply offended and shake his head gravely as the administrative law judge, Henry Contreras, grumbled about how he didn't care for this, didn't like the sound of it at all. The judge asked Jerry if he wanted to explain himself, and Jerry took the opportunity to destroy my credibility in a way I should've seen coming.

Jerry said he'd been shunned when he'd gone to Dr. Burgess's office a few days ago. When the judge asked Dr. Burgess if this was true, the doctor said yes.

Then Jerry flat-out lied, said he told me he'd struck out at Dr. Burgess's office, but that I'd told him it was all fine, we'd just keep forging ahead. I had an idea that would fix everything, I said, as I took the incomplete form from him.

Jerry had no answer for how the consent form got executed, but he readily pointed the finger at me. I'd been the one to file the paperwork, not him. I'd been the one to use the consent form as an exhibit attached to a legal brief with my name and state bar number on the front page, and my signature on the last page.

"I'm not a lawyer," Jerry pointed out with feigned innocence.

My response was that it was my fault not to have caught the error. But I would never, ever alter a legal document. To the best of my recollection, this was what Investigator Roggin submitted to me.

"I did not, Judge," Jerry said.

"Sloppy work either way," the judge said. "Sloppy at best, and at worst? I don't even want to say."

He glared at me for a long time. Then he denied the motion. Though it was a loss for the board, Jerry did his best to act vindicated, stalking out of the courtroom after he thanked the judge for being so fair-minded. It wasn't until I was down on the pavement again, dragging my file cart back to the office, that I was stopped still by a question: why had Jerry Roggin even been in court when the motion was heard?

I hadn't invited him to come. The ISO brief was self-contained in the papers I'd filed. He should have been out working his other cases, which, like mine, had been neglected the last few days as he raced around on the Burgess matter.

A homeless one-legged black man in a wheelchair rolled up to me, as I'd made an easy target of myself by lingering in one spot too long. I dug down in my purse, found a crumpled dollar, and handed it to him.

I'd not gone thirty feet from the doors of the Junipero Serra Building, where the Office of Administrative Hearings has its sixth-floor courtrooms, when I gazed up at the terra cotta Italian Renaissance ornamentation, the jutting cornice way up top, the high clouds scrolling by. This building was once *the* Broadway department store, the flagship operation, the best in the west. People rode the trolley downtown, made a day of it shopping for hats and winter coats, luggage and makeup kits, vacuum cleaners and crystal vases. Times change. Now, it was the place where shaky prosecutors went to have their asses handed to them by mentally-ill doctors.

"Weather gettin' colder," the homeless guy commented with desolation familiar to my ears.

"Seems to be."

He smiled as if pleased with the dignity that my simple recognition of his presence afforded him. Or maybe he was just happy to have a dollar in hand.

"God bless you."

I certainly hope so, I was thinking. *Because I am fucking lost.*

Maybe a vagrant's benediction can work as Grace from God, because at that moment it was as if a set of gears in my head that had rusted in place beneath a hardened glaze of medications suddenly broke loose. I knew why Jerry had come to court, had been there to vindicate himself and make a fool of me; why his play was so much more sophisticated than might be expected of a cop—the cool logic, the clean chronology, the reliance upon authorship of the documents on file.

Just the way a lawyer would have broken it down. As if Jerry had been advised by a lawyer familiar with the case and its facts.

Mendibles. It had to be.

I'd always tossed off the pockmarked attorney with the junior-high crush with practiced ease. But now he had me.

All I could do was make myself a promise. If I was going down, my reputation and career shot to hell, I'd do it on my terms, with as close to a useful, high-functioning mind as I could capably maintain. No more hopeful upbeat titrations, no more soul-sapping meds. No more pharmaceutical fog.

Walking on, I stopped at the light before crossing the street at Fourth and Spring. Down the block, the original Farmers and Merchants Bank building's stone façade and stately columns shone a gold-tinged white in the late-afternoon light, like an ancient temple built in honor of the almighty dollar. Calling me to it, almost, inviting me to pay further homage to its timeless, awesome strength. I checked my watch: 4:15, and I hadn't taken my morning or lunchtime meds today.

Well, so what, no more—if it was going to be one girl's willpower against the world, I might as well start now.

The light changed. I tugged my cart into Spring Street's lanes and through the crosswalk, heading north at the Banco Popular building. Behind me came a profoundly deep thud, and another, then a third—a trio of sonic booms with the cadence of footsteps.

God's footsteps.

What else? No—what now? I asked myself. Turning back, I peeked around the corner, down Fourth toward Main, my eyes widening until I felt the lids peeling back into my skull. The thundering continued. It was the Farmers and Merchants Bank, it had torn itself from its foundation one block away and it was coming straight toward me. *For* me.

2

RAUL MENDIBLES, ESQUIRE, SUPERVISING DEPUTY ATTORNEY GENERAL

Why I ever thought my life would get better if I was promoted to supervising deputy attorney general, I do not know. Management—ha! Times like this it seems I can't even manage to get my hand out of my pants.

Not literally. I was twisting a rubber band, winding it between my fingers to create a little digits-in-bondage scene, rewinding the peeper's view I'd sneaked on Bradlee when we'd passed in the hallway twenty minutes ago. Black skirt, white silk blouse, black leather jacket trimmed with silver studs like bullet tips she'd bitten off herself—yeah, this one, she could chew bullets smiling, believe me. Swaying hips and high boots. *Ay Dios mio*, Lord have mercy. A lawyer looking like, what, like she's here to remind you you're nothing but a weak little sinner, little boy, well . . . it ought to be against the law. Typically, without even trying she gives off that air: brutally untouchable, hair swept back by the shades on her head, eyes never meeting mine, barely nodding in acknowledgment of my chirpy, gutless hello. The most soul-wrecking part of these little exchanges is that I know she's way out of my league, but again and again, I see her and desire her and—hell no—I sweat and I stew, refusing to own up to that intoxicating sense of want.

Not that I could blame her for ignoring her supervisor, the great Raul Mendibles. Since her untimely misstep on the Burgess ISO matter, she'd been relieved from handling medical board cases, doing her penance by working a case load of little-board garbage, nothing but routine legal paper-pushing. Respiratory care, acupuncture, midwifery, hearing-aid-dispenser shlock. An outright waste of her talents, but that's what happens when you try to take a moral stand that has the unpleasant side effect of making your biggest client agency look deceitful. I'd warned her—well, not quite, but she should've just let that consent form thing with Jerry Roggin slide; I mean, Dr. Burgess was a nutcase and Roggin had his pompous ass nailed, dead to rights. Try telling Bradlee that, though. No, she'd looked right through me like Justitia herself, weighting those scales in her favor with the judgment that you don't do the expedient, boss, you do what's right. Made me feel like a weenie, as usual . . . .

Ah, Mendibles, your tortured life is rife with tragedy! Every beautiful woman you've ever tried and failed to make it with has been headstrong, Mendibles. It's like they went to school for it or something.

I freed a hand and ran it through my ragged black mop. *You look ill,* Myrna had commented two hours earlier at the breakfast table, *like maybe you lost weight.*

Lot on my mind lately, I said. Then she gave me those sad-dog eyes she uses when something's on her mind. Twenty–one years of marriage, you notice those things. *Out with it,* I told her.

"You were talking in your sleep again."

"I've been working too hard."

"Raul? Baby. Who's . . . Bradlee?"

The guilt rushed up hot in my cheeks. My tongue stumbled to form the right words but never got rolling.

"Wha . . . . Who? No, nobody. I mean, we work together, yes, um, yeah, she's an actual person. But nobody really, Myrn."

Ay, abogado! There's a difference between standing accused and being guilty as charged, you dummy!

Her face was round with sad wonder.

"She? Bradlee's a *woman?"*

"Yeah, she's an attorney, on the team I supervise. At work."

"Oh. Oh. Well . . . ." Relieved—then not so relieved.

"Well, what?"

Myrna tittered. I hate that nervous-energy, babykins titter of hers.

"No. It's silly, too silly to even say."

"You made an issue of it, so follow through." I folded my arms like I was her daddy instead of her husband. "Gotta finish what you started."

"It's just me being dumb. I had this, um, crazy thought. You know . . ."

"No, I don't. I'm not clairvoyant."

She squirreled around in her chair, her big brown eyes too shy to take on anything but the tablecloth.

"It's like, Bradlee's a man's name and—I don't know. It made me think, maybe that's why you and me haven't been . . . you know . . ."

"This isn't a game show. I'm not going to guess."

"Why we haven't been uh . . . doing it. No, it's crazy. But just, like for a minute, I thought . . . maybe, you were attracted to . . . no, doesn't matter. Bradlee's a girl." She smiled as if she'd solved a problem. "Never mind. It's dumb."

"You're right, that is dumb. 'Cause I'm not gay." I tried to sound indignant, but it felt like acting, because in truth, I was picturing what Bradlee looked like at this hour, having rolled out of bed in some tight little cotton thing, her hair mussed into a perfect mess, those hourglass hips swaying on bare feet across kitchen tiles for a cup of coffee.

The wife seemed oddly relieved, but the tears were leaking faster than her pillowy palm could wipe them away. In her half-open pink bathrobe, with her curly mud-brown locks clumpy from fitful sleep, those fullback thighs crossed to look even thicker, she looked worn down, her femininity defeated by time and a slowing metabolism. Repulsive.

"I . . . you don't even have to say that, Raul, I know, know you . . . better than to think . . . I'm . . . . Not that gay men aren't fine the way they are. I mean, *Tío* Marlo, he's the best, a gem of a man—"

"Can we not discuss Marlo?" Her uncle, who broke off from the family due to a lot of perceived slights I never saw evidence of. "He likes San Antonio so much he can't come to LA, even to see his nieces, that's his business. But I don't want to talk about him."

"You're right, as usual. What I'm saying . . . forgive me, baby."

"*De nada.*"

I thought it was over, but she reached across the *LA Times* and took my hand, her boobs blotting out the lead headline.

"Raul, *mi amor*, just tell me one thing."

I was flashing back to homeroom period, Roosevelt High, the cutie with the flyaway bangs, a sophomore with the curves of a woman already, always smiling from two chairs back, chewing on her pink sparkly pencil when I turned to pass back the latest handout. Half the guys in the class hit on her daily, making plans just out of earshot to get down her pants at the game Friday night, or the dance, or wherever. Took me three months—till just before the Christmas break—to even realize that she was smiling at *me*.

"Is, um, Bradlee pretty?"

The self-imposed guilt I carried around was enough; I sure as hell didn't need my wife piling on. I needed to shut this line of questioning down before it started.

"Compared to you? Ha!" I chuckled casually, shaking off the absurdity of Myrna's query. If I had a white suit, I could have been Ricardo Montalbán pitching Chryslers. It had the desired effect.

"I'm sorry, baby, it's my hormones, or maybe this excess water weight—"

"Now, now."

I kissed her wet red face—my Myrna, *mamacita*, the mother of my two precious little girls. Then I lied like Pinocchio. Anything to make my escape.

"This Bradlee? Actually, she has a kind of tough look. Almost like a girl who wants to be a guy."

Myrna glommed right onto that bogus detail. "Oh, one of those. *Chacho.*"

"Anyway, she's been frustrating me lately, is all. Got in some trouble on a case, made mistakes."

"Will she lose her job?"

I shrugged. "Gotta stick by her side, since she's on my team."

Myrna seemed placated.

"You're so loyal."

I nodded to accept a compliment I didn't deserve.

"Caught some grief from the client agency over it," I explained. "But you know, you do what you gotta do, these situations." Like, sell out on what's left of your principals, for one thing.

"That's my Raul."

The undue praise served to cave my shoulders in a little more. *Yeah, loyal to you and nobody else, you lying sack of caca.*

Myrna wasn't done. There was something else. The tears had dissipated, but not entirely. Jesus, would I ever get to walk through that door over there to go to work? I patted her hand and urged her to speak up.

"The way you said it, said the name before, I almost . . . . No, you'd think I was silly."

"Honey, please. I wasn't even conscious."

Her eyes swelled again.

"No. Three weeks ago. You were wide awake, Raul."

She sniffled and gulped, more tears soaking her face. I cringed as a drunken memory stumbled forth, ugly and uninvited, from the back of my mind.

"You said it, said it that night, too. Her name."

"Did not."

"After we went out dancing, the night of Miguelito's baptism. When we got home, you paid the babysitter and sent her home. We were on the bed, and you were tipsy, laughing at something stupid."

"*Abuelo's* hair. That bird's nest comb-over, kept blowing sideways all night. The loose strands looked like a live electrical current. You gotta admit, it looked—"

"Then you pulled my dress up over my head and tore off my panties. Raul, we were—"

"Enough of this already—enough!"

Myrna shrank as she turned away. Then silence.

Let me cut to what matters, here. If you're a husband like me, trying to be good but not often measuring up, your adoring wife lacking the perception to note the difference, well, you know the feeling. I thoroughly blew it, ended up saying way too much, denying my guilt. With Bradlee, of course, I'd done nothing, so there was no call to be so defensive. But then, I was raised Catholic, and yes, my conscience is burdened with everything *that* morally entangled and contradictory affiliation implies, dating all the way back to grammar school. Those Dominican nuns at St. Linus, their lessons on how impure thoughts are just as bad as impure deeds? Sitting there at the breakfast table with Myrna, it all came roaring back to me. Those nuns' tales sounded questionable even then, even to a Boyle Heights third-grader who spoke shaky English and couldn't even tie his scuffed black hard-soled shoes without an assist from his *abuela*, but man, they knew how to set the hook right in your gut, for life.

I still can't shake this everyday guilt.

Defending myself, my frustration came off like passion, which led to more tears, and then. . .

"No!"

"Is that what you want? To break us up?"

"No, stop it! I love you!"

"Here—I got what you want!"

"Oh! No, Raul, no!"

The sloppy, torrid, knee-knocking make-up sex. Myrna, moaning hard, then crying softly, and when it was my turn to cry out, I made sure I knew my head this time and got off without adding a caption to the moment.

I got to the AG's office an hour late. Relieved that attendance seemed light this morning, just a few secretaries chatting about a C-list celebrity dance competition show on TV last night, who'd brought doughnuts downstairs, and where they'd be going to lunch today. God, I'd been thinking about Bradlee a lot these last few days, trying to decide what to do about her. She had her issues, no doubt, saw a shrink for medication and was overheard, from time to time, having conversations with ghosts, but her work ethic was stellar and her lawyer's intellect was a notch higher than my own, I'll admit.

I knew I couldn't keep her on small-bore, little-board cases much longer. Last week she'd done a half-day trial against a licensed hearing-aid dispenser, a guy who'd failed to return a little old lady's money when the device he sold her didn't work as advertised—such a thrilling legal battle that, according to Bradlee, the judge fell asleep twice. The week before it was an acupuncturist with dirty needles and no concept of how to spot infections. Another month of this junk and any good attorney would be looking to transfer out to another section. No way was I going to let that happen with Bradlee Aames.

I suppose I hadn't dealt with this problem before because I didn't know where I stood with Bradlee and hadn't risked finding out. She hadn't confronted me when the medical board hammered her for publicizing the mess Jerry Roggin made of the Burgess case, but her logical mind could've paced back through the events involving Roggin and the forged consent form without too much effort. She knew Roggin wasn't a mind-reader and couldn't see into the future. To cover his ass so swiftly and effectively, the way he did, someone had to have tipped him off before he'd walked into that courtroom. Someone like me, the only guy on both sides of the problem. Yet, to date she'd said not a word about it. I'd let her take a tumble in order to save Roggin— and by extension, the board—a major embarrassment. But it had cost Bradlee, and had damaged my standing with her. Probably hurt me more than I wanted to know—if only she'd say something. Anything!

So here it is: I had a hole card to play with the board. My off-the-record client contact at the board's HQ up in Sacramento owed me, big time, for cleaning up an untidy personal mess that I won't describe here, but trust me, it was ten times as bad as the Burgess case. The return favor I had in mind would be simple: put Bradlee Aames back on medical board cases. If I timed it right, couched my wish in the form of a demand, my contact would have to comply.

Only the situation was touchier than that. For one thing, I couldn't overtly take credit for her reinstatement. If she knew the shit I'd pulled on Burgess behind the scenes, I'd be nothing more than a false hero. I also wanted to maintain my good standing with the board, even enhance it. Coming on too boldly would cost me. If I could re-insert Bradlee on just the right case at just the right time in a way that would make the board think I was doing them a favor, I'd be golden.

Getting back on good terms with Bradlee might take longer, but as long as she stayed working for me, I'd have opportunities to improve on that.

The next hour I spent reviewing every new unassigned case, coming up with a whole lot of nothing. I looked at the other half-dozen attorneys' existing caseloads; there had to be something I could transfer to Bradlee, a case with conflicting dates that a stressed-out lawyer would be glad to hand off—right?

No such luck.

The phone rang: Poor, blubbering Myrna, broken up about some new imagined setback, an unforeseen defeat of startling magnitude. Something to do with a sale, these really cool designer Band-Aids, the store was out of stock, and some clerk wouldn't give her a rain check.

Did she say *designer Band-Aids*? Good God. I wanted a drink.

Of course, she was still upset about how roughly I'd handled her when we were doing it. Jesus, sometimes she was so like a child it made me want to abuse her, just wrap my hands around her neck and squeeze . . . . *No, no—bad thoughts, Raul. Unhealthy, man. If anything, she's the victim here, spun in circles by your many falsehoods.*

I promised myself that I'd take it easier on her until I worked out this situation with Bradlee. If it ever could be worked out. Myrna surprised me with some gratitude.

"You were too nice to say what was really going on, Raul."

"Hey, I just remembered, there's an unopened pack of bandages in that cabinet over the back toilet."

"But that's you, always considerate of my feelings."

"I love you, Myrn, you know I—"

"This Bradlee, she's attractive."

My silence lasted too long and ended up saying plenty.

"Well, dear, I want you to know this is a new era."

"Myrn, really, it's nothing. She's no one to—"

"I've let myself go, hon. Been too much a mom and not enough of a wife. Your woman. From here on out, I'm going to change that. Go on a diet. Exercise every day. Drop those stay-at-home-mommy pounds—"

"Myrn, stop. You're perfect just the way you are."

"—and look like a princess for my knight in shining armor."

With each bogus assurance, her knight errant merely deepened his dishonor.

"Perfect, babe. I mean it."

"Don't make me laugh, Raul, 'cause I'll probably start crying. I know how busy you are at work, so I'll go. But not before I tell you how much I love you."

What I took from the conversation wasn't anything new about my dear, hapless Myrna, for this was about her sixth personal-makeover speech I'd heard since our youngest, Lucita, went off to kindergarten. No, what Myrn got over on me was a timely reminder that sometimes you just have to let things happen. Look at it this way: All I'd done was blurt the name Bradlee, albeit at a few inopportune moments, and now the wife was bent on self-improvement. Not bad.

So then, why search so hard for the perfect medical board case for Bradlee Aames? If it was out there, maybe it would find me.

And—thank you, God—find me it did, that afternoon when the phone rang for the first time since the wife called to announce the New Myrna.

"Ray-ool, Ray-ool, the people's tool."

Major Coughlin, the board's current president and my aforementioned off-the-record client contact, barking at me to close my office door because we needed to put our heads together, pronto.

Sure, the last time we'd put our heads together was on the Burgess case, so I knew exactly what he meant. I shouldn't even be telling you this because board members are prohibited from discussing cases with prosecutors outside of a public board meeting—and the Major's phone call to me was squarely out of bounds. But the Major is the kind of man who's never let a legal nicety slow him down.

As for the gung-ho military name? Oh, please. There's nothing the least bit battle-tested about Everett Scott Coughlin, MD. Talk to him those times he calls past midnight, lonely and snockered and bemoaning the judge's latest adjustment to his alimony payments, and he'll tell you his life story. Major, my foot. He was an army field medic for about forty-five minutes in Vietnam, just long enough to figure out that he had no stomach for the kind of blood and guts Charlie was serving up daily. They'd honorably discharged his ass, but at some juncture of that brief, ignoble experience, the Army shrink who'd gifted him with the diagnosis of chronic battle fatigue that got him his walking papers confused him with someone else, mistakenly referring to young Corporal Coughlin as Major Coughlin. That was all that our squeamish medic needed to begin rebuilding his tattered psyche, and for weeks, until they shipped him stateside, they called him Major. Since then, with equal parts bluster and bullshit, he's managed to make the name stick.

The Major also frequently imbibes like a frat boy when the notion seizes him. Which is often—and which is why I know his wimpy armed forces history. The Major likes to talk when he's lit.

So yes, the good Major was rewarded for being a pussy with a ticket home from Nam and a purported rank he'd never earned. The irony is that the man sees no problem with this rosy outcome. In fact, he's shamelessly proud of how well he made out.

"Got a doozy of a problem this time, Ray-ool."

"Let's hear it," I said flatly enough to let him know I didn't care for the purposeful mispronunciation.

"Now, son, I'd like to speak with total candor."

"I'm alone in my office, behind closed doors."

"That is, with the assurance of utter confidentiality."

My tryst with Myrna had distracted me from eating breakfast, and I felt woozy, not my usual self.

"Kindly think who you're talking to, Major," I said. "Think what I already know."

That shut him up for the moment, at least. Let me explain why.

At times I hate his guts; I despise his superciliousness, the careless, condescending way he calls me "Ray-ool," the deportation cracks he makes lest I do his personal bidding. But we're tied together at the waist, the Major and I, and we've been that way ever since we met last year at a board meeting in south San Francisco.

Stars seemed to align and events to conspire in order for us to be brought together the way we did. We hadn't crossed paths at the meeting itself; no, I was there to deliver a scintillating update on proposed medical-experimentation statutes, a presentation attended by a few wandering physicians and lonesome senior citizens, but no board members. Opening the floor to questions and answers, I got not a single raised hand—a relief, as I was more than ready to race back to the airport for an early flight home. But while I'd been wowing them with my PowerPoint magic, a wall of tule fog had rolled down the Central Valley, causing pile-ups on the Interstate 5 and shutting down the airport. I was stuck for the night and a wine and cheese tasting event the board sponsored at the hotel seemed the best way to pass some time. My mistake: it was a bore, too many people talking shop instead of grapes, and when I finally had a chance to sneak out of there, I didn't look back. I'd only gone a mile or two down the road, five miles an hour through the fog, my head out the window, when I came upon the Major and his rental car, a bright red Mazda convertible, upside-down in a shallow ditch, the front wheels still spinning. The good Major was so blasted that when I tried to extract him from the scene, he climbed behind the wheel of my rental and insisted on driving so I could get some rest. Then he threw up all over the dash.

I knew who he was, what was at stake for a man of his position, and I reiterated those points as I shouted some sense into him. Wiped the puke off his mouth with his shirtsleeve. Eventually he listened, and on my advice we ditched the car and kept clear of his hotel room. Back at my less fancy, half-abandoned hotel, I ordered an extra cot and blankets from room service, camping the Major under a shower nozzle until he stopped rambling. About ten coffees later, the medical board's president was thanking me profusely, fully aware that if not for me, he'd have faced an embarrassing, high blood alcohol DUI bust and the scandal to go with it.

Of course, if not for him, an attorney of my modest capabilities and reputation would not have been promoted to supervising DAG. But it had happened, just as he'd promised it would.

The Major. Whatever—I'd call him the Lord God, Creator of Heaven and Earth if he could use his pull to recommend me for the senior assistant attorney general position about to come open when our current SAAG, Harry Albert, retires next fall.

In my office, when the issue of Albert's retirement comes up, the wags like to say "Hoary Harry needs to hurry." No one ever mentions me as a possible replacement, but I'll show the bastards, I'll show them all.

Now, back to the phone call with the Major.

"You've heard of 'Dr. Don.' The inimitable Donald Fallon, the smoking jacket smoothie psychiatrist, used to have his own TV gig?"

"Sure." Of course I'd heard of Dr. Don. Who in LA hadn't? "I've seen his show. He does this golden-throat thing that's supposed to be soothing."

"That's him. If you ask me, he sounds like he's talking underwater."

"I thought he got cancelled."

"About a year ago, but it was a time slot thing. They tried to put him on at 2:00 a.m., move him from midnight. He threatened to sue, so they didn't renew his deal. I heard he's working on something new, another show with a different channel. He's a slick operator. If there's a route to getting back on the air, he'll find it."

"I'm not much on late-night TV. I've got little kids at home."

The Major sighed. "I assure you, dear boy, my call today bears no relation to your nocturnal viewing proclivities. Let me be brutally honest. There's a sexual misconduct case bouncing around down there, Raul. I need it over and done with, quickly and quietly. And you're my man to see to that. Am I right?"

At least he'd pronounced my name right. I asked the Major straight up why he gave a damn about Donald Fallon, MD, though I really didn't care to hear the ignoble reason, whatever it was; it would just feel good to put the screws to the Major, rather than the other way around.

"Don't push it, son," he said. "I have my reasons. But he's a decent fellow."

"Yeah, a real good guy," I said. "Dr. Don, the celebrity psychiatrist best known for the cheesy exhortation to call-in patients to 'feel the love.' Myrna, my wife, she watched his show a couple of times and liked it. I watched with her. Guy was creepy. He told this caller, Betsy from Reseda, that she should think about leaving her husband if she wasn't 'feeling the love.' The man's self-confidence in telling total strangers what to do with their lives was . . . I don't know."

"Scary."

"What was even more disturbing was how ready those same strangers were willing to follow his every last word of advice."

"Well, if he's on TV, he must be right."

"Okay, Major, the show's off the air. Maybe Dr. Don still does the look-at-me laps here in LA, riding on hospital parade floats and doing ribbon-cuttings at pet hotels. Why do you care?"

"He's in trouble, charged with having intercourse with a vulnerable female patient in his own office. If charges like that are proven, no amount of celebrity status will save him." I heard the Major snap his fingers as he said, "His career's kaput."

"Who cares?"

"Dr. Don was an expert witness for the board not too long ago. A high-profile case against a San Francisco behavioral psychiatrist whose ideas on treating autistic children with medication regimens were well outside the standards recognized by the medical establishment."

"I remember that."

"Dr. Don was a sort of point man for the board, and he came through."

"So what? Since when does the board do favors for former experts?"

"For him to take a public beating in an ugly sex misconduct scrape, well, think how bad that would look."

I wasn't biting. "You still have yet to explain why I should give a crap about this guy."

The Major's reason for helping Dr. Don didn't strike me as compelling; the board uses all sorts of doctors as experts, and though they may testify for the board, they more or less speak for themselves. That's what witnesses do. There had to be something more.

"All right, you want to pester me this way, I'll tell you. In strictest confidence, though—and I want your word."

He seemed genuinely angry, which pleased me. Not that I'd tried to piss him off. All I wanted was to get Bradlee back on medical board cases, and suddenly the Major's doozy seemed to have possibilities.

"We're . . . related."

"You're too old to be his dad," I said, dicking with him.

"Very funny, Men-dibbles. He's married to my sister."

"Oh." I hadn't seen that one coming.

"What's with the gasp? Trust me, she looks nothing like me. Ever heard of the Tournament of Roses?"

"Duh," I said. "I grew up in LA."

"Not in Pasadena, I'm guessing."

"Let's not get personal, Major."

"Then don't suggest I'm thick."

I bit my lip and counted to ten.

"Still with me?"

"Dangling by the rich narrative thread you're weaving, sir."

"Smartass. In her day, my kid sister was once the Rose Queen. Beauty, brains, poise—she had it all in spades. Why she hooked up with that buffoon . . . ah, never mind. Pushing fifty by now, but she's still a head-turner. Like that French actress, Catherine Deneuve. You've heard of Catherine Deneuve, Raul?"

Holy Mother of God, I'd had *eneuve* of this insipid conversation and could not hold back.

"Think I saw one of her films at an art house in . . . where was it . . . oh yeah: Pasadena."

"*Touche,* Men-dibbly-doo. Guess I had it coming. Now, enough with the niceties."

"If these are niceties, remind me to never get on your bad side, sir."

"Ha, ha." He cleared his throat with a jagged growl. "Okay, here comes the hammer and nails, son, so listen closely. No admissions to wrongdoing, Raul. Only that he'd inappropriately engaged in touch therapy with the patient without her informed written consent. A year of probation, just long enough for Dr. Don to complete a few brush-up courses in professional boundaries and record keeping."

"What?"

"I say something wrong?"

"That's a gift. None of the board will vote yes to that deal. And you can't even vote because you've got a direct conflict of interest."

"Oh, they'll get in line, son, leave that to me. Your job is to bang out a quick filing, and Dr. Don and his lawyers will be at the first settlement conference accepting the deal. As for who you assign, just put somebody on it that won't ask questions and won't give us any headaches."

"You want a hack. We've got a few of those in the stable."

"A 'hack'? Did I suggest anything of the sort?"

"You did, indirectly. Because the settlement is a joke, Major. Why not go all the way, throw in some flowers and a letter of apology?"

I'd read the case file and didn't like this phony asshole Dr. Don, a man who'd wreck a woman's marriage—and probably, her life—just to get his cheap horny-boy jollies. On the other hand, at this stage of my career, I wasn't in a position to get too self-righteous with my sole professional benefactor. Our relationship was based on give and take.

Quid pro quo, they called it in law school.

"Stay with me on this," the Major almost pleaded. I'd probably pushed him too hard, but somehow, it had worked.

"I'll do you way better than a hack," I said. Then I rolled out my brilliant idea: Bradlee Aames.

Hmmmmmmmmm . . . .

He liked my thinking, to use a prosecutor feared for her courtroom skills, which would bring the defense closer to the table, but a gal—the Major's words—with an image problem of her own, needing to make nice with MBC management. She wouldn't be inclined to put herself through the wringer of an ugly court battle, not when the client agency would be happy with a stipulation.

And not when bringing in a signed stip will get her back in the board's good graces, I said. Paving the way for her return to working MD cases.

"I dunno about that last part, Raul. She's a loose cannon, a liability. You said so yourself, you—"

"No, Major, now it's my turn to be direct. I'm not offering Bradlee Aames as an option. I'm saying she's the one. This is nonnegotiable."

Whoa. I had to stop and take a breath. I'd never pushed my point this forcefully with the Major, not since I'd helped him sidestep that DUI.

"I hope to high heaven you know what you're doing."

"Don't worry; she'll do as I say. She has to."

The Major chuckled with decided pleasure. "Nobody has to do anything, son, not without a gun to their head. It's called free will."

"I'm aware of the concept."

"And one more thing, Mister Nonnegotiable. You scratch my back, I scratch yours, that's the arrangement the two of us enjoy."

'I'm aware of that, too."

"Good. So don't let me catch you scratching your balls instead. Got that, Ray-ool?"

Of course I was offended. Oddly enough, I found myself looking down to check the placement of my free hand, which was near my lap. Moved it away.

3

DONALD FALLON, MEDICAL DOCTOR

We were having our fun, my three lawyers and I, yessirree, we surely were, a good old time chatting it up with the court reporter. She was a young thing named Kasey or Kaylee or KC or . . . hell, I don't even know what she said it was, her elocution was so poor, her cute little tongue, which looked made-to-order for fellatio, it just swam in marbles the way so many young peoples' do today—but say, the girl surely could flash the cutest little dimples at me, perky little rosy-cheeked gal with dishwater hair and slightly spooky caterpillar eyelashes. Little walk on the wild side, there, but nice, hard, no-pantyhose bare legs and supple calves. Oh, there you go, those legs! The legs of a distance runner, like that doll at the coffee place on the corner near the office, Susanna, I wouldn't mind going the distance with that Susanna, let her gift-wrap my face with those creamy inner thighs, put that on the to-do list, Donny, yessiree. Dear little Kerry here is blushing, as she's seen me before on TV, even read one of my books, and oh, I can feel it coming, the glorious high, my loins tingling, the load building!

Now, do not begrudge me my pick-of-the-litter prowess, my top spot here above a scrum of striving male wannabes, for these legal gladiators, amassed to strike back at the ignorant forces of state bureaucracy, these men on my team, the Don Squad, they all know their place. They are paid, and paid handsomely, to do my bidding, and so they shall. As for dear, dear, supple-kneed Katie, well, let her be free to gush all she likes. I have earned my preeminence through years of perseverance and toil and professional dedication, and if I were to parlay that hard-won stature into a post-hearing *soiree* as—what? Let's say, as uh . . . the perfect complement to a young lady's deep-seated nascent emotional reactions to a high-status male. Let's just say I predict our lusty union will likely represent not only a rollicking good time, but a personal, emotional breakthrough for the young lady: win-win! That is, despite the fact that Kelsey, here, likely never even dreamed she might possess a single such feeling. Well, if that's what it comes to, the pleasure will be mine, and just as freely accepted as a debt collected.

My lead counsel, Terrence Heidegger, the original Bad Boy himself, now he is your Type-A alpha dog, and I love the job he does for me, but he was in pain. Little Miss Whatsername was laughing it up at my very worst lawyer jokes and all but ignoring his superior offerings, and yet, Heidegger had little choice but to smile a little, wince a little as my playful *bon mots* repeatedly strafed their intended target. Heidegger's right-hand briefcase-carrier, Arnie Chesterfield, was too short in stature and too used to sucking up to his boss to fully throw in behind me, so he sat there at counsel table, patting his hairpiece and grimacing to suppress his guffaws as the point total ballooned in my favor.

". . . cause they got no sole!—oh, ho, too much, Dr. Fallon!"

Arnie had choked that one out a few jokes back, tossing me the home run ball I was waiting for the instant he said my name.

Dr. Fallon.

"Donald Fallon? *The* Donald Fallon?"

"Why, yes, I am."

"Ohmigod! You're 'Doctor Don'?"

"Guilty as charged."

Crack! Home run, straight over the centerfield wall.

By the way, women love that line, "guilty as charged." And no, of course I wouldn't mind signing her book, but since it was at home, I said I'd be glad to mail her another copy, my compliments, and oh no, it's no trouble, I've got a few lying around—a few thousand remaindered copies on a pallet in the garage to be exact, but she'd never know the difference—so if she wouldn't mind providing me an address—

Which, of course, she didn't mind providing.

Oh, Donny, you are incorrigible! the old gang in my high school chemistry club would be saying if they could see me now. Donny the horny but hopeless perpetual virgin; Donny, whose mom dropped him off to volunteer at the prom, bathroom duty two years in a row; Donny whose pubic hair didn't really come in until he was in second-year medical at USC, as if it made a difference by then; Donny, who married a refined, connected, beautiful young lady about a hundred points above his batting average, an all-time catch. She was someone with whom he could slowly gain experience in bed, build up his confidence, and enjoy a steady love life—only to find, as the years rolled by and they found that they could not procreate, that like a cruel cosmic joke involving extinction of a species, she secretly harbored an almost pathological aversion to sex. Which eventually played itself out, a real-life horror show without end.

I will not digress on the topic of Hilary, the delicate flower I so luckily plucked in marriage. You need not know the depths of human degradation she endured at the hands of every opportunistic fertility doctor in the state; these men should have been prosecuted, then taken out and shot for what they did to her, such was her suffering. But suffice it to say that the aftermath of our failures was to yield no further pleasure in the bedroom, only workmanlike grit, and tears, and raw shouts of recrimination, my only call to action brute force and domination.

Which is perhaps not much of an explanation as to why I'm trying to put the moves on a court reporter while here, in court, defending myself on charges brought by the medical board against my license to practice psychiatry, my very right to ply my trade! I mean, they're saying I exploited a female patient, committed sexual misconduct upon her person under the guise of professional care and treatment . . . and I'm thrilling to the fact that yes—Yes! A sexual connection is there, I can feel it. Oh, to slurp up the view of little Kaydee, those round mounds almost bursting from her furry white sweater, those bare creamy thighs parted just enough, like a special invitation just for me, an invitation to nuzzle my face in there until the rest of the world just . . . fades away into nothing.

Two of my hired guns appear ready to go off half-cocked, so over-heated with envy are they when the pretty young thing hands me a business card with her e-mail address and phone number handwritten on the back. I turn the card over once more. Kathy Jones. Kathy? About as utterly bland a name as there is!

I liked KC better. God, I hope the fooling around is a whole lot more exciting than her name. Better throw in a fetish or two to spice things up. . . .

Even Vance Mooney, the walking cadaver that Heidegger insisted I bring on as Lawyer Number Three because Mooney had prosecuted a few sex cases ages ago for the state and therefore supposedly knew the ropes? Even old Vance Mooney himself, his veins rounded like speed-bumps—even he extracted his face from his file long enough to crack a grin. I'd like to think all three of my lawyers, including Mr. Walking Dead, were hoping I'd kiss and tell, say, a week or so down the line, maybe the next time we met in court for this silly case, tell them about Kathy Jones and what they could only dream about, those healthy calves spiked in the air until her ankles were pinned behind those wet, wet ears, as she gasped and panted, a new wave of passion washing over her at the sound of her pure words of praise: Oh, Dr. Don, Dr. Don! Cure me again!

Mastery is what I'm used to, the personal standard by which I live, and I was glad to feel it, that familiar sense of complete control, that certain "it factor" the TV people all say I've got—by the square foot, Donnie baby, what they want, you could sell by the square foot—the charisma I'd grown used to trading on, my own special currency. But then . . .

The courtroom door opens and this Latino Joe Schmo in a bulky suit slides in with a woman in black, she who looks askance at the out-of-place court reporter, hears the laughter among my trio of over-paid defenders, punctures my who-are-you stare and pierces my façade with a high-powered, frigging nail-gun stare-down of her own—a steely sureness, a focus, a hint of . . . fury that, holy shit, made me completely leave my body, pushed me right outside my zone until I forgot myself and was instantly stripped naked of my stature.

The court reporter, Kathy, said nothing, but her face was a shade whiter and those dazzling thighs were clammed up tight, like a chilling wind had blown the door shut. I was transfixed.

Judas Priest! Who is that?

Tall and lean, with a model's insouciance, standoffish toward the subservient stutter-stepping congeniality of every man in the room now taken hostage by her mere presence; and that face, a face carved by God's hand in his image of feminine power, a face that made me forget all about the court reporter's business card that fluttered now from my fingers to the floor.

Jesus F. Christ . . .

They take their seats opposite our table, all business, no greetings, the Latino, who looks like a dishwasher in a department store suit, opening a file and sliding it in front of the woman in black. Ho—wait! The dishwasher and Heidegger exchange a furtive glance, stand, and shake hands. The dark one's none too pleased, but she follows suit—and I thrust my palm forth for just a touch, surprising her. Hoo!

Jesus F. Christ, the dominatrix is a lawyer! The dark vixen shall be my adversary!

Now, as the array of legal talent surrounding me attests, I am not a man to be trifled with, and though this entire court matter resulted from a colossal misunderstanding, I assure you—a mere miscalculation of personal aims between myself and a former patient—well, for a man like me to stand accused in a place like this simply . . . it simply will not do. Cancelled appointments, a slow drive downtown, parking in a public lot that stank of urine, this charade of servitude to the medical board when it is they who owe me no end of gratitude for what I've done for them. And thus, in the event of such a baseless, misdirected legal challenge, a man of means and friends in high places must press both to advantage, if necessary, to extricate himself from circumstances not befitting his professional stature, his station in life. To that end, not only had I bankrolled Team Heidegger, but I'd reached out to a professional colleague affiliated with the board who might ensure that I received the fairest treatment possible. Indeed, that colleague, whose name I am not at liberty to mention here, assured me that the most equitable due process of law available to me would be forthcoming. In particular, a certain quid pro quo was in the offer, one which would swiftly deliver me from further public displays of servitude such as today's "Hearing on motion," whatever that meant.

Until this moment, all was well, and according to the Heidegger Trio, the secretly bartered quid pro quo was smoothly taking shape. But, although I may be many things, as God as my witness, I am nobody's fool; and, as a licensed psychiatrist, I like to think that I possess a uniquely keen insight into the human character. What unnerved me now, made my palms sweat and the hair on my neck tingle with electricity, was the sight of this woman in black and the way she so plainly, blatantly stood outside and beyond the reach of my considerable means, personal magnetism, and professional stature. Her eyes? Curious, somehow. Oddly off-balance, but hard and resolute, and when, from across the courtroom, I show her the results of a revolutionary new teeth-bleaching process my publicist swore was the best in the world, she . . . looks right past the Dr. Don surface and taps into a vein of fear I didn't even know I had, her unspoken disdain scuttling the offering, leaving it for dead before it even reaches the table.

Much as my care and treatment of the patient in question in this case had suddenly gone awry, distorted in a funhouse mirror of unmitigated impulses and desires, I can feel in my bones this medical board case also taking a sharp detour into the unknown and unexpected. The experience is scary, yet exhilarating, as if in confirmation that this life, my life, is indeed worth living. I am, after all, Dr. Don.

A judge walks in and the lawyers' spines stiffen. He's in a black robe, a tall man of over six feet, but the face is twinkly and impish like a gnome's. A gentle giant who tilts his frame to regard us politely with a nearly blank expression, but those blue eyes fix on me and tighten, as if I'm the butt of a joke he hasn't yet told. Court reporter Kathy's legs are still slammed shut as she gushes a good morning to the judge—*Your Honor*—her display of deference like a kick to my crotch.

Then the woman in black takes command. Standing twenty feet from the bench, Mrs. Mojo rises, going toe-to-toe with the judge. Toe-to-toe, baby.

"Good morning, Your Honor." That voice hums like a Ferrari in low gear feeling out the roadway. Ready, steady—go, go, go. "Bradlee Aames, Department of Justice, Office of the Attorney General. Representing the Complainant, Medical Board of California."

My default home base is domination. Well, conquest ain't all bad, but ultimately, the conquest leads to domination and control. Dominion. It is an irrefutable, irresistible force within, and I'm not always proud of the things it makes me do—hey, hey, let's not forget, I'm still Dr. Don, beloved by the vast, anonymous masses. But I own the driver's seat, I thrive when I'm in complete command. Yet, this Bradlee-side-winding-bullwhip-beauty-Aames-I'll-cause-you-pain-just-to-look-at-me, God! It is as if she materialized from another dimension with a cosmic two-by-four on her shoulder, with which she has just rather righteously smacked Dr. Donnie right upside the head. She da boss, the commandant, and I, the submissive accused doc-on-the-run-from-the-Law-and-Judgment-Day, I am upside-down! Hoo-wee, baby, I can hardly breathe . . .

The judge's slow but smart and seeing eyes, they take their sweet, sweet time with the Dark Angel. Oh, those eyes, I can see they grieve the near-forgotten but unmistakably sorrowful loss of young, pure love.

"Morning, Counsel," the judge says, the court reporter tapping his anguish into her little black keys.

Upside-down, I fight for balance, secretly reveling in the challenge this grievously alluring opponent represents. Oh, this will *not* be the "cakewalk" as previously advertised by my crack team of overpaid yes-men. So what? Nothing worthwhile is easy. In time I will best her, and then—and only then—I will possess her, swallowing whole her venge-ful pride, reclaiming the mine-is-bigger-than-yours swagger she has already stolen from every man in this room. Even the sad-eyed judge.

I am scared and exhilarated and more alive times ten and it's a new day, indeed, Donnie boy! Beneath the table my manhood stands at glorious attention . . .

4

BRADLEE AAMES

Times when my head is jingle-jangled but I can't muffle the noise with a shot of JD or haven't concocted the right pharmaceutical boost to hold steady, I'll simply bear down hard as I can, hard as humanly possible, like my eyes will break a sweat and my ears will spurt blood if I push myself any harder, you know. I overcompensate with sheer willpower, purse my lips, and quell the brassy clatter until I am safe from the enemy inside me, but awfully, terribly alone. Then, the quiet I've willed into being rounds into a monster all its own, a stifling, smiting, suffocating fog, dissolving my very being, as if I, too, along with the world surrounding me, am lost, disappeared, erased. So, why battle to overcome the noise with quiet when the quiet merely isolates and erases? Why bother?

This is only an approach, a tactic borne of an awareness that not a single better option exists. But it's not all futile. For a spell, a peculiar thing can happen: perhaps as a product of these monumental mental exertions, the will to slow down, brake, and freeze the kaleidoscopic mind's-eye view to a single manageable frame I stagger through, blinded—my little world of the silent scream—the fragmented view will indeed hold still, snapping more sharply into focus. Only for a moment, that's all I can hope to achieve, but it's as if my eyes had been straining so hard to make something out in the haze, that now, when a shape emerges from a thousand flickering shadows, it clicks into place with such true clarity, I have to look away or risk burning the image into my brain permanently. In that moment I tend to forget myself and my self-conscious doubts, and despite the hum inside my head, the tremor of carotid arteries and manic brain stem howl, yes, yes—a higher level of thought process follows.

All of which sounds like batshit crazy-woman talk, unless a picture of something worth looking at, worth studying, comes into view.

That higher plane was within my reach as I sailed up the elevator shaft upstairs to court with Mendibles, my ball-of-mush supervisor. He was mumbling something about liking my shoes, which—Jesus Christ, Mendibles—are *boots*, by the way. We arrived on the sixth floor and those boots just kept on walking, depositing me at the end of the hall. Department 8, to be precise, where I would find not one, but three overly solicitous attorneys for the defense awaiting our arrival like long-lost, wish-they'd-stayed-lost, gap-toothed hillbilly relatives camped on the front porch without a hotel booking. Leering at me with beady eyes and slimy mouths. I wanted to be ill. Those boots Mendibles admired were asking me, now, for permission to kick the shit out of someone, a damned fine suggestion that was nonetheless out of the question.

I enjoy myself so much more when opposing lawyers are jonesing for a street fight. A head-on, killed-on-impact collision outcome clarifies my mind that much more. Winning is a pure drug with very few side effects, a natural high I cannot get enough of.

Of course, this was my first appearance in the matter of the Medical Board of California, Department of Consumer Affairs, versus Donald Fallon, MD, but that wasn't how lead counsel, a gray-haired, sweaty-handed tool with a military crew cut named Heidegger, was playing this meeting, his two co-counsels bowing and nodding behind him like marionettes. I ignored the three Fallon apologists as best I could, but Mendibles caved quickly, shaking hands like a practiced politician as he made proper introductions all around. Then, a nod toward their oily-haired, oily-brained client, the great Donald Fallon, MD, who rushed in and gobbled up my hand with his greasy touch before I could recoil. I was glad I'd skipped breakfast, because the touch of that squinty reptile made me sick. We went inside.

My hand, still traumatized, tried to lodge a complaint, but I blocked that bitter dialogue before it could begin, wiped my palm on my skirt back and forth to muffle any sound. With a handshake, a touch, Mr. Innocence had sought to claim me as his own. Bastard—the picture of complacent, transparent innocence was he, settled in at the far end of the defense counsel table, the skilled, hollow-hearted exploiter who couldn't find it to keep his pecker in his pants when his job was to provide psychological care and treatment to a woman tormented by multiple demons. I looked at the tip of my boots and they right back at me, beseeching me to give the order. Oh, if only . . .

Enough with the pleasantries. Like his client, this head lawyer, this Clarence Heidegger, he was an emboldened one, already pushing in on Mendibles as to whether we had a copy of the proposed stipulated settlement, and whether he could read it. Mendibles looked like his head was ready to cave in. He wanted a nod of agreement from me, but I wasn't in a giving mood.

"Not now," I whispered to Mendibles. "Let me argue this motion first. It'll give us more leverage."

My boss was about to object for the third time this morning, so I put a hand on his shoulder and whispered for him to trust me. He responded to my gesture the way I expected: with silly, secret gratitude. Sometimes he is such a child.

Why the rush? I thought. This Dr. Don might be known to viewers who frequent the late-night TV world of mattress hawkers and home-gym sweet-talkers and purveyors of ninja warrior potato-peelers, but so what? He had a private practice just like other shrinks, and I was not persuaded that any sexual misconduct case should move so fast to settlement. Every sex case I've ever tried ended in revocation, or jail, or both for the offending cretin. Yet, too expectant by half were Dr. Donnie's three hired suits, and what was it about Mendibles—this fetid, overripe people-pleasing mode that extended beyond his usual spineless demeanor—that had my radar alarming?

Just why did he have to be here, anyway, at a routine settlement conference, parked at my elbow and pinching my space? If I was not to be trusted alone just yet, couldn't he do his meltdown watch from the gallery? I reviewed the surprise, herky-jerky exchange of handshakes, the way I'd seen Heidegger receive and regard Mendibles, how he'd hung on Mendibles's every word as if awaiting a cue, that scuzz-bucket Dr. Don hanging back too casually, too confidently for a man on the verge of losing his livelihood. I felt like the only player who didn't know the rules, or even the game. This settlement process reeked.

Numbed up on Oxy, I'd have missed all the little signs. Talking boots and protesting palms aside, once again I had to admit that the prescription parade had done nothing to help me practice law competently.

In terms of deception, Dr. Don was not so skilled at the game. He'd been memorizing my physical details, probably casting me now in the new X-rated movie playing in his head. I stared back, wondering how any self-respecting woman could pay a loser like him a few hundred bucks an hour to listen to her problems. Of course, all he did was keep enjoying the movie, not even bothering to hide his fangs.

We were early for the hearing, so I decided to test Mendibles, see if the fix was in. I led him back outside and down the hallway, tucked my arms closer to my sides to let him confront my cleavage, and quietly asked him why he'd just offered a deal prior to the motion even being heard. He stuttered out a denial, but my harsh appraisal convinced him that I'd heard something whispered that I hadn't heard at all.

"Bradlee, listen. The motion is irrelevant if we settle."

I told him that wasn't true, that I may not have written the opposition but I did read it.

He seemed ready to soak in a compliment. "What did you think?"

"Even with the bare-bones job you did, Mendibles, it's obvious they can't get hold of the victim's new shrink's records. What she talks about with a subsequent doctor is her own damn business. It's a fishing expedition, designed to harass the victim. The judge will know it."

Mendibles diverted his eyes as if to break the Bradlee spell. *(God, why can't I be myself and still have men take me seriously?)* Then he demanded to know what arguing the motion would prove, other than how tough and smart I was. I was thrown by how quickly he'd gone personal, and had to remind him that this was my job.

"Our client is the Medical Board," he said. "We don't go out of our way to defy the client's wishes. You know that."

"How could they possibly want such a shitty deal?"

"It's not . . . that bad."

"Right, it's worse. So who did this Doctor Don know—or blow?"

Mendibles's neck puffed up as he swayed back in his wingtips. He leaned in closer to deliver a stern, whispered directive.

"Kindly get off your high horse, Bradlee."

"I'll gladly execute a dismount as soon as you explain why I'm wrong. Preferably not while you're staring at my boobs."

That one backed him up again, pink-faced. I could hear him switch to breathing through his nose in an attempt to settle down.

"You want to be relegated forever to doing dinky-ass hearing-aid-dispenser and respiratory-care-board cases? You want more midwife and acupuncture cases? Say the word."

"I'd rather slit my wrists."

"Open your eyes and stop fighting this. I am trying to *help* you here."

The words clattered at my feet and sank into the dull brown carpet. My supervisor was a prosecutor for the Department of Justice, like me, but that face! He had that same weepy, pretty-please face the homeless panhandlers put on down on the sidewalks. Shit—at least the damn panhandlers could claim a noble purpose: they were trying to survive. Mendibles had no such excuse, which made him pathetic. I felt my stomach roll and turned away when he asked me what was the matter.

"Letting me preside over this ridiculous little giveaway. This is part of your rehabilitation plan for me?"

"Bradlee—"

"You saw the way Doctor Don was taking my measure."

Mendibles about-faced dramatically, as if Dr. Don were standing behind us in the empty hallway.

"No, I missed that."

"He's a predator."

"Oh, really?"

My boots requested permission to kick the shit out of him. I closed my eyes and fired off a response: permission denied.

"Yes. Really."

"Well, proving it's something else, and this case has holes. Look, don't complicate this unnecessarily. Just get back in there and talk with them, see if they'll take the deal. I can assure you, the board will be forever grateful."

I was tired of this tap dance.

"Soon as you clue me in."

"I have no idea—"

"Bullshit. What's behind door number three?"

Mendibles sighed, but it was for show. I stood tall and straight and inescapably in his path. My show of strength seemed to clear my head, and I took note of it.

He reached into his briefcase, which was so beat up it could have been cobbled together from old tire treads. He fished around until he pulled out the proposed stip, then handed it to me. I appreciated the fact that he refrained from another sales pitch, but he was too much a disappointment to me to be handing him any compliments. I leaned back, against the wall, crossed my legs and read.

Flipping back through the pages, I could scarcely believe what they outlined: a year of probation, a course in record-keeping, another in prescribing; an agreement that if the board put on its case, it could establish a *prima facie* factual basis for discipline, but no actual admissions to wrongdoing.

"I'm arguing the motion first," I said when I was done.

"No way. There's not one good reason to do that."

"Here's one. I'll win, which will give us an advantage. That way we can ask for something more than probation, which you know is damn near nothing. Maybe a year's suspension from practice, at least."

"Bradlee." His tone was paternal and I did not care for it.

"Raul."

"This deal was approved by the board's chief of enforcement."

"I don't care if the Pope blessed it. It's garbage."

"It's perfectly appropriate based on what we can prove—"

"It's a giveaway. Fallon doesn't even have to admit what he did."

Mendibles's chest heaved as if he were going to explode on me, which would have been a first. But he merely paused.

"You seem to be forgetting something."

In that instant my head ached. Suddenly, and badly. Pinprick little spots appeared before my eyes and I thought my ears would bleed. *And oh—forsaken girl, you've got no meds, or booze, with which to deal.* I rallied hard to hang in, to hang on to the conversation at hand.

"You all right? You look a little tired."

"Okay," I said, "don't make me guess."

"The victim's not cooperating. Without her, we can't prove anything."

Shit. That was a point I couldn't argue and he knew it.

I stayed stuck, leaning harder against the wall, spent by my herculean efforts at sustaining concentration. I was pretty sure I had an Oxy or two buried in the glove box of my Chevelle, and now I wanted them both as badly as I needed to breathe.

"We'll talk settlement," I conceded, "if that would make the board happy. Just talk. See if they bite on the concept. No specific parameters. Maybe we can get more than that shitty bottom line."

My supervisor offered me a careful smile. "That's a plan."

"But if there's no deal, I'm arguing that motion," I added with an edge of defiance.

Mendibles closed his eyes as if he were the one needing meds.

"They'll take the deal I showed you, Bradlee."

He studied my sad expression.

"What?"

"I'm disappointed. In this job."

No, that was a lie.

"I'm disappointed in myself. For signing on for this . . . bullshit. And you, Mendibles."

"Don't look at me, I enjoy my work. It's very rewarding."

"How could you do this?"

"Bradlee—"

His phony caring tone further clarified my thoughts—and I took note of it.

"Don't deny it."

"Sometimes we have to . . ."

Blah, blah, blah . . . . I tuned the rest of his necessary evils speech out. A deal was to be struck outside the courtroom, where lawyers would peek and whisper and pace before reentering the courtroom with smiles and winks for the court reporter and good news, wouldn't you know, for a settlement judge who just wanted to go home anyway.

Inside my head I was getting wobbly, the fog creeping back in. I shut my eyes, saw a fresh swirl of candy-colored rainbow dots that seemed close up and then were far, far away, like a painting, a portrait of an ancient galaxy. I pictured myself floating away to that galaxy to live in stark isolation as a mercenary for hire, but there was no work, no one there to fight, no foe except a stinging, all-consuming loneliness . . . . Sighing, I breathed inside the welcome blackness until I heard footsteps.

Behind Mendibles, down the hall in the direction of the elevators, a tall, sandy-haired young man in a wrinkled tweed sport coat was coming down the still-empty corridor, headed toward us. The man's voice was deep but soft when he stopped beside Mendibles and me.

"Can you tell me where the case involving Dr. Donald Fallon is being heard?"

I guessed this was Dr. Craig Weaver, the psychiatrist and subsequent doctor to our victim, Rue Loberg. Weaver, the new therapist who'd no doubt inherited the shitstorm of problems Dr. Don's bad behavior had caused. The defense wanted his records so they could find out what she'd talked with Weaver about: whether she'd been devastated by what

Dr. Don did to her, or whether—the defense was hoping—she'd barely mentioned anything of the sort.

Mendibles and I introduced ourselves. When Weaver asked about the status of the motion to compel his patient's records, I said nothing, thinking: *Not my swamp to swim in, Mendibles. You tell the guy.*

Mendibles soft-pedaled the situation, explaining that the fight over the records may not have been necessary, not now. Though he couldn't discuss the details, the case looked like it may be reaching a resolution. Maybe I'm judging, but when I heard my boss use that word—resolution—I really despised him for saying it so easily. It was a fraud, a travesty, a grievous blow to the basic notion of fairness and due process of law. Fundamentally good doctors routinely got worse than this deal for making honest mistakes in difficult medical situations. *Oh, Mendibles, with your goddamned resolution! Lightning should have struck your ass down for using that word.*

Weaver didn't mask his bewilderment, and when Mendibles offered no further justification, Weaver turned to me. I must have looked like I wanted to take a hot shower to wash away the "resolution's" lingering stench, because Weaver's face had fallen. I decided that, in a case where there was already so much wrong, it would be a further injustice for me to support the deal in any way. I could, however, discuss the more practical problems that a trial in this matter would present.

So I told the doctor how cases like this sometimes are settled due to evidentiary hurdles that can't be overcome. How our burden of proof, which is clear and convincing evidence, is very high. How the burden cannot be met without solid evidence and testimony across the board.

"Without the victim," I said, catching myself. "I mean, without Mrs. Loberg's testimony, we wouldn't be able to meet our high burden of proof, and since she's unavailable—"

So much for my clarifying focus; as I rambled on, a woman had slipped in behind Weaver. She was pretty, maybe forty-five years old, with a round, girlish face and blond bangs sprung from darker roots. Her gray pantsuit was prim, like an outfit she'd laid out with a court appearance in mind. I was impressed with the preparation on display.

"Excuse me, please, miss," she said. "But, uh, I *will* testify. That is, if you still want me to."

My head cleared again, the outline of a courtroom battle springing into shape. And I took note. My smile for Mendibles told him the settlement he'd been pimping was all but dead. I held out my hand to my new star witness.

"Mrs. Loberg. Thank you so much for coming."

"Sure. You're welcome and . . . h-hi."

"I'm Bradlee Aames." Then I introduced Mendibles as if he were the trash collector. He took it lying down, and my head cleared a tad more.

"I'm in time to testify, right?"

"Your timing is fine, ma'am, but you won't be a witness today. We're just arguing a pre-trial motion. Soon, though, when we come back for trial. You'll tell your story to a judge, and I'll be there to take you through the process."

"That is, if the case can't be resolved before trial," Mendibles said. "There's a possibility of settlement."

Jesus, he sounded like a sideline water boy warning the quarterback to keep an eye out for hailstorms.

"Is that likely?" Dr. Weaver asked.

"Anything's possible," I said. "But I'm not counting on it."

My comment had Mendibles shuffling and agitated. By now, he had to be regretting his decision to bring me in on this case, big time. Well, that was just tragic. I didn't care if I had to be the one supplying the conscience on this case. In a face-off with a victimizer like Fallon, my attempt to do the right thing would hardly qualify as a heroic gesture.

"I can't imagine him giving up without a fight," Weaver said. I loved Weaver's thinking: he'd assumed our deal was to force Dr. Don to resign. Loved his thinking so much that I shot Mendibles a little told-you-so wink.

"You can count on me, Miss Aames," Rue Loberg said.

Jesus, she was earnest. Almost too much so. But that was okay; on the stand, her sincerity would play well.

"That's good to know," I said. "Thank you."

And so, I thought, the unreliable, written-off Rue Loberg rises from the ashes. Well, well, well . . . . Maybe she was tough, tougher than anyone might have imagined.

Mendibles was a cheap second-rate little bottle-rocket of pent-up dismay, about to blow, but I could not have cared less. Come to think of it, he always seems pent-up around me, another thought that cleared my head a touch. I took note. Then I invited Weaver and Rue Loberg into Department 8, to watch us argue the defense's motion to obtain Dr. Weaver's records.

"Should be good theater," I said. "Three defense attorneys."

"Oh my," Rue Loberg said.

Damn—my show of casual confidence had been at her expense. I reached out and touched her hand, which for me, is something I don't do with any kind of ease.

"Just know, we're gonna win."

They both seemed genuinely thrilled as I led them inside.

"Well, aren't we in charge?" Mendibles muttered behind me.

"So much for door number three," I whispered back.

The bottled-rocket shook his head, whispered so quietly I could tell he didn't intend me to hear him. But my mind was clear with purpose and control and pre-fight adrenaline and . . . dominance. I heard what the bottle-rocket said:

"What you don't know, Bradlee. What you don't even know . . ."

5

RUE LOBERG

Scared—frightened right down to my socks is what I was, going in there, in to this . . . gosh, pretty small courtroom with Dr. Weaver. First off, I'm not much when it comes to confrontations; and secondly, I tend to get nervous in new situations, so I was already zero for two walking in the place. (Wow, the floors were carpeted and instead of feeling like a court of law, the place was more like a . . . this big living room.) But then, Dr. Weaver, he knows these things about me and I trust him. I've been talking to Dr. Weaver ever since I lost it all: Andrew and the kids, my marriage, and my dignity—pretty much everything, the sum total of what I am, or at least what I used to be. That's true: ever since I hit bottom, I've been a patient of Dr. Weaver's. If I'm ever gonna get back out of the hole I dug for myself, it'll be with his careful guidance.

You might think that's nuts, considering my track record when it comes to trusting men in authority positions. That may be true, all right. But I'm leaving the issue of the future up to the Lord at this point in time. What will be, it's God's will from here on out. I've been such a bad judge of people my whole life I don't see any other choice now but to give it up to Him, let Him decide my fate. I know, it sounds stupid, but there you go.

And one more thing on the subject of fate: I do believe Dr. Weaver was heaven-sent.

It's hard for me to even think I was that jumpy, vulnerable person before; I mean, Dr. Weaver's helped me see it so much more clearly than ever before, see myself. Six months ago he started me off in my first session by asking me to tell about my family, my childhood growing up, and I still can't even believe what I told him. What came flying right out of my mouth.

Normal, I said. Nothing really out of the ordinary.

Mom, Dad, my big brother Hiram, and baby Crystal.

Why, Dr. Weaver asked like a good listener would—why would you call your sister a baby, when by now, she's all grown-up?

Well, I told him, she probably is all grown-up, so you're right. Then I started to cry and didn't stop for a long, long time. When I finally did bring myself to stop—had to use up a whole box of tissues to do it—I told Dr. Weaver she'd only be a grown-up if she were alive, and only God or Crystal or the man who took her would know that. So baby Crystal, that's how I think of her since that's how old she was when she was taken, taken away that day in the park, right off the swing-set next to mine.

Then I told him what my parents told me, what they knew to be true: that it was all my fault.

Evil girl.

Evil Rue.

Same thing Father McManus said, which made me feel so low, hearing that from a priest, that the so-called acts of absolution, those things he did to my body to cast out the demons, acts he performed for me, on me, when nobody was around to see—not even God, he said—well, even that couldn't make me feel any lower.

I give Dr. Weaver a lot of credit for not barring the door after that first session to keep me out. He got me to face a lot of my troubles, though, past and present. Got me sold on the idea that if I face my problems, it may hurt and hurt a lot, but in time the pain does go away.

I'm still in a world of hurt, waiting for that going away part to kick in.

So then, how does a woman whose last therapist put the big scare in her, then used and abused her for his personal, sexual pleasure—how does she wind up seeing another male therapist? What is she, stupid or something? What—was she, *asking* for it? Is she asking for it now?

I know that's what any reasonable person would think, and really, it's all right, I get it. I'm fair game for that kind of criticizing. All I can say is what Dr. Weaver said, which is: I've got some issues to work on having to do with men in positions of power and authority. Fair enough.

Now, Dr. Weaver is a by-the-book kinda guy, and when I told him all about my problems with Dr. Don, he did offer to refer me to a female therapist, a colleague, in the event that it might cause me discomfort, you know, discussing personal, sexual issues with a man. But then, the colleague of his I went to see, nice enough woman with a nose like a hawk's beak, she all but referred me right back to Dr. Weaver. It was my decision, she told me, but he's very, very good. A college professor, a scholar in medical ethics, lots of expertise dealing with tough stuff like depression, addictions of every stripe, suicide prevention, and sexual exploitation; so apparently, they don't come any better equipped than he is. I'd be lucky to work with him, she said.

Lucky usually doesn't describe me or my situation, but in this case, I believed her. She was nice. Kept the tissues coming when I needed them and threw the used ones away without blinking an eye. When someone is nice to me, I take notice. Not that I'm feeling sorry for myself or anything, but being treated nicely qualifies as an occasion.

But lucky I was: Dr. Weaver probably saved my life. I was so deep in that hole of my own making I couldn't have ever climbed out of it alone, yet he helped pull me out, got me into detox and Al-Anon right off, never bothering with my many colorful excuses for why I truly did need five prescriptions for narcotics, antianxiety meds, and painkillers; why three glasses of cabernet a night were just good for the circulation, a health fact the French have been wised up on for decades. We talked it through, getting at the root causes for why I've made myself a human welcome mat for thirty-nine odd years. It hurts, and it's scary, and I still cry a lot and see a loser and an idiot victim staring back at me from the mirror, but at least I'm not a substance-abusing idiot victim, drinking up to improve the old cardiovascular health but not a darn thing else.

My weak stabs at humor aside, I do think my treatment's working. Lately, at night I keep having this dream that I'm coming out of this old brick well that's deep as a canyon and pitch dark. I come out and I'm at the foot of this huge mountain, and I start climbing, climbing all the way up, so high I'm almost up in the clouds and finally, when I reach the top, all sweaty and panting, I find a dragon. And he talks to me—yes, a talking dragon in my dream. His name is Iago, and he's one fearsome beast with huge veiny silver wings and a forked tongue that spits fire and these claws like hooked knives, and he likes me, so much that he even asks if he can be my buddy, my pet. So I say sure, yes, of course, and I climb upon his scaly black neck and hold on tight and back down the mountain we go, swooping down through parks and churchyards and alleyways, saving damsels in distress from the pimps and muggers and rapists and kidnappers that never met a soul they didn't want to rob blind. And in the end, I'm looking for someone, that one last damsel I can't find, and I know that she is looking for me because she wants to save me, which makes her distinct from all the others, and I know it's right, it's important, to keep on searching for her. I try and I try, but she's not there. I can't find her, then the dream ends, which, the sting of failure I feel, it hurts so bad it wakes me up, every time. Crying over my failure—but wait, what I do find is that I now have something more than when I went to sleep: hope. As if I'm about to be a part of something bigger than this measly, ruined life. Awake, I gasp for that first conscious gulp of air as the dream fades, and then all I want to do is take another breath, and another.

Still glad I'm alive. And thankful for that much.

Dr. Weaver is making me address the traits that allowed others to take so much away from me. It's terrible, and it hurts like death. But he's also helping me find reasons to push on, to want to see my kids again, reach out, get on speaking terms with them at least. Maybe go back to school, do some training in crisis intervention, get a job counseling abused women. I don't know if anyone would ever see fit to hire me, but I've been volunteering at a shelter for Christian women lately, learning to be a good listener, and that seems to add up to be a lot when it comes to helping those who need a calm, quiet port in the storm. If my wreck of a life has taught me one thing so far, it's that if people with problems will ever overcome them, they've got to talk, and somebody's gotta listen. Another benefit for me is when I listen, I can't think of my own problems, so it's like a vacation from myself. Sounds kooky but it's true.

So when Dr. Weaver said we should both go to court I didn't really question his judgment. Still, that doesn't mean I couldn't question my own judgment. I was nervous and shaking and practically peeing my pants over seeing Dr. Don again, had no idea what I'd say if he tried to approach me, come up and talk to me, tried any of that v-neck-sweater, saddle-shoe, I'm-so-accomplished-but-still-I'm just-a-charming-guy-at-heart bullshit—excuse my French, but I swear, I can't think of a better word—of his on me. But Dr. Weaver has always told me to trust him, bless his heart, and I have, and that trust has continued to pay off.

Because when I got there, I realized I had interpreted the dragon dream all wrong. Turns out the dream didn't involve my failed quest to save a damsel in distress. Turns out *I* was the damsel in distress. The dream? It was but a premonition of what was to come, a tap on the shoulder from the hand of God.

Now, I'm not much of a complainer, but by any measure I'm a person who has had her share of trials and tribulations. The forgiving view might reveal that neither luck, nor other human beings, have been kind to me. The harsher view is that I should have seen a lot of the ill will that's leveled me coming, and I should have done something, any-thing, to get out of the way. Some would even call me a loser, a charge that I would be hard-pressed to deny. So, let them, I guess; can't stop the doubters anyway.

I wept, right there in the hallway outside the courtroom, got all teary in front of strangers. Please forgive me for getting emotional, I wanted to tell them, especially the one who introduced herself as

Bradlee Aames. Because today my dream came alive. Today I met my real-life dragon.

Bradlee Aames. A lawyer for the state, a black-haired young woman with a body and a face that reminded me that life isn't fair, and these tiny silver orbs shaped like . . . skulls? Wow—dangling from her ears, a death image, but on her, it was shaped into something definite and powerful and lovely. Meeting her, shaking her hand, I recognized instantly her key feature, a pair of big dark eyes full-up with trepidation, but an equal complement of courage. Slow-lidded eyes, with a tired, damaged look I've seen so many times sitting on a plastic chair across from me among a circle of strangers, everybody dying for a cigarette amid familiar tales of woe. Battle weary, resisting demons she can't see, her arms tired from swinging but she can't stop, lest she lose the fight.

But oh, to know she's fighting for me now! It's hard to explain, but in that moment I followed her into the courtroom, I saw the faces of the men lined up to defend my tormentor, and I knew they had underestimated her, like mice ignoring the shadow gliding overhead until it's too late. Meal time, boys! I almost shouted as their smug faces tightened a turn or two at the sight of me, the one witness that could sink their lying, jackass of a client. And yes, I was scared to death but exhilarated that in this moment. I had located an unexpected source of power: the spoken word, the truth to be told. And yes, I would tell my story as the only person on Earth who could tell it. I was scared as hell, but that bastard shrink should be even more so.

Bradlee Aames? For her part she saw what I saw, too, and she turned to me and smiled as if to show me she knew we were together in this, and no man could pull us down. God, what a moment—pure electricity.

A judge came out, a towering but hunched-over gentleman with a little white beard and probing eyes who was formal the way you'd expect a judge to be, but he didn't appear too happy to be there and quickly made a study of the wall clock. Dr. Weaver sat next to me, rubbing his facial scruff as he whispered asides about what was happening. The lead defense lawyer was that piece of work, Mr. Heidegger, a sour man who'd stolen a week of my life last summer, dragging out my deposition in Andrew's—that is, my ex's—lawsuit against Dr. Don. Heidegger argued first, and to me he sounded just as long-winded as before, pausing every five seconds or so like he was Abe Lincoln giving the Gettysburg Address. According to him, I'd supposedly waived my privacy rights to Dr. Weaver's records of my treatment when Andrew filed the civil suit against Dr. Don. Once I made the sexual misconduct allegations public, "that was that," and Heidegger claimed it was open season now to find what I'd been talking about with Dr. Weaver in our sessions.

At first all this talk made my head spin, since I don't know the law and could barely remember what my name was the first time I stumbled into Dr. Weaver's office.

Boy, was I ever a mess when I found Dr. Craig. Living on a gin-and-oj starter or three in the morning, switching to red wine in the afternoons, and whatever I could get my hands on from there on out. Skin and bones, no appetite for real food. About the only nourishment I could find was from those court shows on TV where every case gets wrapped up with a bow just before the next commercial break. Those shows were my little stab at finding some truth and justice in a mean, mean world that had shown me none. Lying around in a bathrobe till all hours, watching reality shows where the contestants eat worms and roaches and belly flop from helicopters into shallow water, none of which made me feel any better about myself, though I always wished it would. The pain and degradation seemed to draw me in. I sorely wished I could be a contestant so I could lose. Spectacularly.

I must admit, Heidegger's ploy, his hot-stuff air of overconfidence, it delivered quite a jolt. They were coming after me. But it didn't make sense why they'd want the chart notes in the first place. As I said, Dr. Weaver and I have been steadily confronting what happened. I've told him everything, one sorry story after another, and of course, what Dr. Don did to me sits like a bullseye at the center of my shame. Wouldn't Dr. Weaver's records show I was telling the truth?

Well, maybe, but that Heidegger could get down-and-dirty nasty, and he'd have fun taking every last word in those records out of context, confusing me, embarrassing me. For now he was playing nice, suggesting that I was, perhaps, concealing something important, significant even, and all he wanted now was to know what I was afraid of, if I was honest with Dr. Weaver. Then he turned and looked right at me as if I were supposed to answer him, right there in court.

That's when Bradlee Aames stepped in—I mean literally, smack-dab between Heidegger and me. She told Heidegger to cool it, I was her witness, and nobody messed with her witnesses, not ever. He'd have his chances to question me at trial, but that was later and for now, he had nothing. With that, Ms. Aames succeeded at sucking the air right outta the courtroom. Heidegger wasn't used to pushback, especially from a young woman looking like the lead singer in a rock band and he sputtered something tired about being well within his rights. Bradlee Aames, she just shook her head like she couldn't believe the crap he was spouting, and said, "That's fine and dandy but it's not your rights I'm concerned about, Counsel, it's the patient's rights I'm here to protect."

And just like that, he was irrelevant. Fine and dandy, indeed. Good God, I wanted to pump a fist or shake a pom-pom, shout out a hallelujah. If I could out-talk a bold, pushy man just once in my life, leave him as flustered and perturbed as Mr. Heidegger was right now, I'd die a happy girl.

The judge, he was quietly enjoying the show, and when Heidegger shrunk back down to size, Bradlee Aames was given the floor. First off, she gave the judge a sketch of the laws of confidentiality. Then she tore apart Heidegger's civil-case exception, which she said did not extend to anything outside the very same civil case. In other words, if I claimed in Andrew's lawsuit that Dr. Don had wronged me as a patient, I couldn't very well keep my patient records from coming into that same case, because I'd made an issue of the same care he provided in the lawsuit. That would be unfair, to cast allegations against the doctor and then refuse to let anyone look at my chart.

But the state case here was like apples and oranges. The medical board was the party taking action against Dr. Don, and all that had gotten started when Dr. Don's insurance company paid the settlement in Andrew's lawsuit, because the insurance company had to report it to the board on account of some law that requires reporting settlements. Dr. Weaver's sessions with me? They had nothing to do with this case, no connection, and because Andrew and I weren't the ones behind the state's case, you couldn't say I'd waived any rights to privacy. Not here, not now.

Wow. The way Ms. Aames laid it all out made me feel a lot better, and the judge was typing so fast into his laptop he had no time to check the clock anymore. I took that as a good sign.

The judge didn't take long in telling Dr. Don and his lawyers that they'd lost their motion and couldn't get their grabbing hands on Dr. Weaver's records. I thought we were done at that point, but that's precisely when everything got bizarre.

That's also when the good feelings I'd been building up began to fade away, and just like that, I was that scurrying mouse with the shadow of death bearing down on me.

6

BRADLEE AAMES

Shelby Drummond is a good judge, if you can get his attention. He lives way out of town in Calabasas, about halfway to Santa Barbara, and he's obsessed with the timing of his ridiculously long commute, so he's always counting the minutes before he can make tracks and hit the freeway. But this time, I was the distracted one.

I'd just finished drafting an argument and was thinking about clicking my way through a few good turns on an open wave-face, preferably at Malibu, way after the sundown. No moon, just the weak glow of streetlamps and streaking headlights on PCH. No one but me, like a loner freak Gidget: just a girl and her board. I thought back, tried to calculate how long it had been since the last time I'd ridden a wave. Tried to channel that sensation of glide, the speed beneath my feet. Strange—the walls on each side shifted and I felt a vision pushing into my head, so I closed my eyes; it's a little trick I use to hold everything in place, like psychic Duct Tape. My thoughts went to Malibu at night, a band of swell rolling up beneath me as I swing my longboard into position and swiftly stroke into the steepening line . . . but then, behind me, a splash of whitewater, a whiff of sunbaked seaweed and dank Malibu lagoon—in the courtroom.

I open my eyes. The attorneys, and the judge, they're all in place. The seal of the State of California hovers with ceremonious benevolence behind the bench. Those ocean scents still linger, so I turn and barely glimpse him—blink—like when you're fast-lane hauling down the freeway and blow by a tiny scene, look sideways for a second or you'll miss it: he, a dark-haired, deeply tanned, handsome young man in shorts and a Mexican peasant shirt hanging out behind the gallery, a pair of black Ray Bans hiding his eyes. Then he's half out of the court-room door and he turns and smirks at me as if he knows we're both way too far inland for our own good, just before the door closes and he's rear-view-mirror gone, leaving me squinting, questioning what I just . . . saw? Or imagined. A surfer, I'm sure, and familiar to me, but not quite of the here or the now. In the past, like a classic photo I know and cherish, a moment in time. A surefooted, stylish talent, I sense, if only by the way he so confidently slipped through that door. A good surfer, maybe even a great one, fleeing through a tear in the cosmic canopy toward another, better place I know, where I want to be, if only I can remember where . . .

I'm sounding looped but not feeling unstable. No drugs or alcohol, just the weight of holding back my illness pressing down on my shoul-ders, as terrible a pressure as being buried alive.

The hearing marched on, dragging me behind. I hadn't spoken in a while and wondered if my rusted jaw would ever work again. No sensa-tions to recapture, no good vibe to reclaim. A little mind-surfing might have eased me through this internal battle, but all I could conjure was a mystery man who didn't bother to stick around. I'd been out of the water too long to detail a good ride in my head, though an open-faced screamer or two was what I needed most.

The judge, he knows I surf. One time a few years ago, when we were stuck in a two-week trial together and got into a discussion with a court reporter who was living on a boat in Ventura Harbor, I let slip some knowledge about a localized beach in Oxnard with a misnomer: Hollywood by the Sea. Misleading, because there's nothing flash or dash about the place, just hollow, unforgiving beach break peaks up and down a half mile of sandbars, and slashed tires or a broken wind-shield to greet you when you get back to your car. The hoodlums who live there and, by extension, think they own the fucking place, wouldn't stoop so low as to punch a girl at least, and I've never been hassled in the water. But they'd have no qualms about creeping my Chevelle. So when I go there, I park as far away from the shore as possible and keep it very incognito.

Judge Drummond and I had talked about passion that day in court. He's got a few acres and raises horses, and as he rhapsodized, we both sort of related on the healthy buzz of having a particular pursuit, a love, outside of one's everyday occupation. To his credit, the judge didn't mention a single sun-kissed surfer girl cliché when I waxed poetic on surfing, but I could tell he couldn't reconcile me with the image of a girl in the curl.

I mention this now because as I sat down and he ruled in my favor from the bench, I saw in his eyes an expression I'd seen when he found out about my love of wave-riding. Mildly puzzled. Not sure what to make of it all, or of me.

My hands fluttered, fingers tingling. I thought the pulse in my temples would explode my head if it beat any harder. Time had begun to slow down, way down. No air in my lungs, and was that a desert wind whistling through the ceiling vents? I felt my breathing stall, had to think to suck in another breath, had to fend off an irrational fear that my lungs were filling with sand.

Gag reflex, throat constricted, lips crackly dry. Choking, then suffocation, would not be far off. Panic: which way were the elevators? I couldn't run, though, not from court, from this, unless I wanted to lose my job. *Lose the mind, maybe, all in good time, perhaps; but for now, please, girl, let's not lose the job.*

I shut my eyes and gave the time-travel trick another try, saw a green, poured-glass wave spinning at a spot north of Acapulco, peeling along before a track of cobble-rocks lining the point, wet black rocks just like those at Malibu on a minus tide. Later tonight, the other side of midnight, when all the burnouts and crazies were in hiding, Malibu was surely where I'd be . . .

Oh, hell!—the judge is asking me a question, but my lips are rubber and free-floating, my teeth cold and useless. He is tall, like a former basketball player, and even seated, his words floated toward me on a downward slant, only to turn in on themselves, sliding back down his throat as if afraid to feel the greedy touch of my awaiting ears. I could hear the faint scream of each word dying.

Dear Jesus, I prayed as He was standing behind me, mercifully walking in the shoes of another lost one. *You watch over the flock; so watch over me.* But I only half believed, because in a glance, he was gone. Even the cynical surfer had stuck around longer. Cynical? Yes, it sounded right to me. Yet, like Jesus, the surfer was gone, baby, gone, and I? Well, baby, I'd never felt more alone.

My steely-resolve, no-meds plan to stay sharp and somehow hold it together was disintegrating, along with my vaunted laser-beam focus. My bag of tricks had a hole in the bottom. With all the grace I could manage, I sat down and pushed a bent paperclip into the palm of my hand under the table until it bled. The judge's words stopped bending back and found their mark.

"Did you wish to have a settlement judge called in for settlement discussions, Ms. Aames?"

I wanted to run: the Seal of the State of California on the wall behind Judge Drummond now resembled the business end of a locomotive—and oh Jesus, no, it was jumping the tracks to crash through the station. I shut my eyes, hard, a second before impact, and prayed again. When I opened them, the train was gone. But what it left behind was a moment in time that lingered like a freeze-frame, and what I saw now was a portrait of all that had happened since I'd stepped into the building an hour ago, the blood of my ancestors sprinkling a trail behind me through the lobby.

I prayed for clarity.

Mendibles rescued me, unwittingly taking the squeeze off with a whisper of his sour breath.

"Say yes to the settlement conference, Bradlee."

Against my will and better judgment, I did.

He was helping himself, Mendibles, having a gaze at me close up that he wouldn't dare try in the office. Bold for a shy man who shuffled and ruffled about behind me like a stalker every time I took a stroll to the printer or went looking for a file. My mind fixated on a thought, which was good, which would pull me out of this spin; the thought: why so confident, Mendibles?

Because he knew I was on the board's list and would be in no position to get creative with this case. The deal the board was offering was too good to be true, a get-out-of-jail-free card for a man who'd laid waste to his patient, her marriage, and her family. Who you know, who you blow—such was the principle in play, the driving force, the unwritten law governing how this was all supposed to go down, no doubt, the dirty details of which were not to be known to the semi-psychotic prosecutor who would only too compliantly sign off, for this was what was best for her, too. But I knew a thing or two about the sorry depths of human behavior, the lowdown scum suckers who hide behind their titles and positions waiting to pounce, the wolves in sheep's clothing. Dr. Don used the secrets he'd drawn out of Rue Loberg in therapy, used his position of trust to exploit her, to burrow his way into her pants. And now he'd take an official slap on the wrist? Mendibles was using me.

The locomotive had passed, and I was intact. *Thank you, Raul, with your apologetic grin, your sniveling act has brought me back.* I peeked around his muffin of a chin and spied the defense.

And thank you too, Dr. Don Fallon, you, who have been studying me the way a hungry fat man eyes a steak, since the minute I walked in here.

He was no dummy, Dr. Don—he had to know this was no way to greet the state prosecutor looking to end his career. But of course, this was his problem: the man could not control himself. If he saw something he wanted, he had to have it.

I asked for a moment, and Judge Drummond gave it to me. I took a few steps back into the gallery and motioned to Mendibles, who followed. By now he'd lost his feeble veneer of cool and was wiping the sweat from his forehead, his eyes darting between the judge, Heidegger, and me. If I had any Oxy on me I'd have offered him one right then.

"The offer of settlement still stands," he wheezed.

He was going to pay for screwing with me.

"This isn't right. We won the motion, and the 'no-show witness' showed."

I took out my cell phone.

"What do you think you're you doing?"

"We can get a lot more. I'm going to talk Joanna Poliak into a better offer."

Joanna is the board's enforcement coordinator, our day-to-day settlement contact up in Sacramento. Mendibles was choking on her name.

"No, no—don't. It won't work."

He reached for my cell phone.

"Excuse me!"

"Joanna's . . . she's in a meeting."

"What the hell, you're clairvoyant now? She's in Sacramento."

Mendibles wiped his forehead. "She's busy."

"Well, then." I dropped my phone back into my bag. My face had feeling again, and I became aware that I was frowning.

"Why are you doing this?" Mendibles said, as if I'd hurt his feelings.

"This isn't about me. Our witness came back from the dead. And even though you mailed in that motion, we won. I couldn't have predicted this little upswing." I shrugged innocently. "Case just turned out this way. We're rolling. In control. No way should we be giving it all back."

His jaw was rigid and he panted with exasperation as he began to whisper. I was secretly reveling in his discomfort.

"We had a plan."

"Exactly, we *had* one, past tense, which is where that shitty deal needs to stay."

"It'll still work."

I hooked my thumb toward the door. "Should I go now? The board already thinks I'm incompetent. My name goes on a sweetheart deal for a sexual predator now, I'll be off their cases for good. I can't be a part of this." I turned to go.

"That's it?"

I thought before answering. "No. It's also wrong."

"Wait." His eyes met the carpet as he kneaded his hands. "Don't go."

My eyes slammed shut from the strain that came with clinging to reality. "Give me a reason to stay."

"We can fix this."

"I'll talk to Joanna. You know, when her meeting's—"

"No. Don't do that."

"But we need her okay to—"

"I said no!"

The others had stopped what they were doing. The court reporter, a tootsie who shot me dirty looks whenever she thought I wasn't look-ing, tilted her head toward us as she adjusted her sweater. Rue Loberg and her handsome young shrink—well, I didn't look behind me to check on them, but I hoped Mendibles and I weren't freaking them out with our public display of cohesiveness. The judge looked unen-thused to be presiding over a prosecution team that wasn't even on the same side.

"What's got your panties in a bunch?" I whispered.

"I can't say. Just leave it alone."

Huh—maybe this mental clarity I'm after is overrated, I was think-ing. I knew I'd just glimpsed a situation I didn't quite understand, like seeing the outline of a picture but not the picture itself. But Rue Loberg was here, and that fact made going to trial a reality. And a hell of a threat, when you're talking settlement. So enough with Mendibles. I slid into the gallery to talk to my witness. If she and her bearded therapist were rattled by what they'd just seen, they weren't showing it.

"I'm ready to proceed to trial," I whispered as they leaned in. "If you can testify to what happened, Mrs. Loberg, we've got a shot at winning."

"I . . . wanna put all this behind me, Ms. Aames. I think . . ."

The victim conferred with her shrink with no more than a glance, which he returned with a nod of approval.

"I know I can do it."

Fine. There would be no settlement conference this afternoon. I shuffled back to Mendibles and whispered that Rue Loberg was good to go.

"And so am I, boss," I added helpfully, "in case you're wondering."

"You're not going to call Joanna," he said.

"You're still stuck on that, even when I'm thinking about the trial." I surveyed him as if I were working out a puzzle. Then I acted like I'd solved it, just to see what I could find. "I know what you're afraid of."

"Hah! You know absolutely nothing."

"Afraid, because when I call Joanna about your sweet deal? She won't know what I'm talking about."

It was a calculated guess, but a good one, and he didn't deny it.

"Fuck it. You're on your own," Mendibles whispered bitterly. He got up and left. An alarmed Heidegger excused himself to follow Raul out.

A few minutes later, Heidegger returned. Team Dr. Don huddled up, got the news, and harrumphed their asses right out of the courtroom, their cheeks puckered, as if they'd been royally cheated but couldn't say why and that fact was killing them. I was lapping up this delicious scene, so I packed up slowly, giving Dr. Don a good look at a woman he'd never, ever possess, and letting the defense get a good head start so I wouldn't come across them again downstairs on my way out. I still wanted those pills, but at least I was feeling stable. Outside in the hall, the young shrink, Dr. Weaver, was leaning against a wall, reading a paperback, waiting for me.

I thanked him for coming and for bringing Rue Loberg with him. He graciously gave all the credit to her and to me for so eloquently defending those psych records on the motion. Eloquently? Without warning, I blushed.

The man had big shoulders and a fresh smile but bland clothes—navy slacks, a rumpled blue shirt and a repp tie combination that resembled a schoolboy's uniform. But I liked the red highlights in his short-trimmed beard and his voice was deep and so well measured he could've been a radio announcer. I could picture sitting on a couch, telling him my problems. Except I wouldn't know where to start. Instead, to my surprise I pictured myself kissing him.

It was time to go and I had to get something into my bloodstream to steady myself. My forehead was bricking up. Without a chemical or alcohol infusion, a crash was sure to come.

We took the elevator downstairs and walked through the double doors out onto Fourth, which was blaring with stop-and-go traffic. The sun had prevailed over the gray overcast, and working people were out and about. I bade the victim, Rue, and her bearded guardian farewell, but before I could walk away, he caught up with me, said he needed to ask me a personal question. I was surprised, and for a second I hoped he would ask me on a date. But his face was dead set on business, not flattery.

"How long have you been fighting your illness?" he asked, his voice gentle and liquid smooth.

Oh, God, I thought, *I'm sinking . . .*

A pair of options leaped to mind. I could step into a lane of traffic on Fourth and avoid having to answer Weaver's question for today or maybe all of time. Or I could stay on the sidewalk and melt into a puddle right where I stood, wait for a street sweeper or an early-season rain to wash me away.

Before I could decide what to do, this Dr. Weaver showed me his powers of perception, sidestepping my little bubble of gloom and doom, my downcast alternate zone of space and time, of time not recorded in my head. He came around, a hand outstretched, detouring me from the grip of a creeping panic, coaxing me straight back into the here and now.

Willing the moment to be solid enough to grab hold of and hang on to, I met him there, halfway—or perhaps all the way, I don't know; but I found him, found him warm and kind-eyed and offering me a handkerchief as I set down my bag, my aching hand levitating to stay above a fire-red plateau of pure pain.

"You're still bleeding."

Shit—he'd seen me doing my no pain, no gain self-mutilation routine under the table. And if he saw it, from back in the gallery,

Mendibles may have, too, though Mendibles lacked the balls to say so. Embarrassed, I shuddered, retracting my hand. This guy was probably scared shitless to have his shaky victim of a patient relying on me to take care of her when she testified. *Here comes the lecture*, I told myself.

Instead, he smiled the way a good guy should smile, I guess. Patient. Kind. Pressed the hankie's cool white folds into the palm of my hand, holding it there, firmly but not so tightly as to make me wince; just both hands over mine, the perfect level of pressure to stop the bleeding.

And I thought: *how long has it been since I let anyone take care of me?* Too long, girl.

7

CRAIG P. WEAVER, MEDICAL DOCTOR

There's much to be said for proactive psychiatry, the central idea being that at times, a more case-sensitive, innovative mode of treatment may be found outside the traditional realm of one-on-one, couch-and-notepad, doctor-patient therapy. I, myself, am a believer. I've visited an ICU with a mom to say good-bye to her teenaged son when life-support was turned off; flown coach beside an aviophobic patient in-flight to San Francisco; stood by as a widow pounded the gravestone of her cheating husband, and helped her find a seasoned estate-planning lawyer after the dead husband's executor announced an out-of-state mistress as the sole beneficiary. When proactive intervention works, it really works, but the standard of practice requires meticulous planning and discussion. The patient has to understand beforehand what will happen, what the objectives are. And, of course, the risks involved. None of this is as easy as sitting in a chair, asking a patient how her week is going.

I wished I was doing exactly that right now, reclining in the friendly confines of my study, my father's collection of hardbound books lining the shelves, the two lamps on opposite ends of the overstuffed leather couch casting a golden glow over the room, providing just the right measure of light—and cover—to foster steady two-way conversation.

Indeed, this was the controlled, ambient setting for my latest break-through moment of insight, at which time I assured my patient, the fragile, oft-violated Rue Loberg, that in order to move ahead she had to be brave enough to confront her demons head-on. Little did I know that our trip to court today, which for all intents seemed to go well enough for Rue, would leave me doubtful about my line of thinking in the first damned place concerning my role in this unfolding drama. But walking double-speed down a urine-soaked sidewalk in downtown LA, heading straight for skid row, shadowing—or giving chase to—a young lawyer with a man's name and a ballsy unpredictability that was beginning to frighten me, I couldn't help but laugh at myself, the great, cutting-edge clinical slayer of fears: scared shitless.

She seemed bound and determined to test me, to lure me down the darkest, dankest alley, where I might unwittingly tread, lily-white and painfully overdressed, on the ragged nerves of some snarling denizen of these parts. Whose turf might I invade with a miscast glance or an ill-timed stumble? If this were a test, my nerves were failing already. Bradlee Aames was her name, and she strode not unlike a man in pur-pose and intent, but with hips slim and feline in the way they smoothly swayed. Mesmerizing, even at half a block's distance, yet quick in step. I hastened to keep pace, holding steady a few dozen clicks behind.

My breath was quick, but not from exertion; to my shame, I was still afraid. How could I be so easily out of my element? And in broad daylight? My spirit had lost its adventurous side, if ever one existed. Slow down, Bradlee Aames, slow down.

A woman in jeans and a fouled pink ski jacket loitered among the shadows, mumbling against a towering wall of antique brick. As I passed, she reached out with a trembling hand and whispered some-thing I took to be a prayer. I hoofed it even faster, thinking: *What are you so afraid of, Doctor?* I stopped, found a quarter in my pocket, and slapped it into her grubby hand. Hustled on, my shame turning to righteous anger.

How do people scrape by in such squalor? Well then, it's a free country, I reassured myself. But then, a chord of truth resonated inside me until it rattled my teeth, and I felt like that brief exchange had exposed me for what I am: a pampered, highly credentialed phony. Turning back, I dug a five from my wallet, but I had no time or I'd lose Bradlee Aames; instead, I whistled at the woman, holding the fiver over my head before I set it on the pavement for her. Some gesture—I'd just treated a mentally infirm adult like a begging dog. The hell with Bradlee Aames, I'd either catch her or I wouldn't. I picked up the bill and headed back.

Two blocks of running at a half skip had me feeling out of my element all over again. The end of the long alley was deserted, but I saw her turn right as I jogged to catch up. How is it that I've become so smug in my views on the plight of the homeless—so uninterested in adequate funding for the mentally ill? How did this insulating sense of superiority become so effective in sheltering me from real life? I reached the sidewalk, a bus roaring past a few feet from the gutter. *The Wall Street Journal*'s editorial page seemed like a dispatch from another planet just now. Some things you think you know, you just don't know.

Took a right, panting; couldn't see the lawyer up the block, but she had to have gone that way. *Breathe, Doctor Greg!* a smarty-pants chorus sang out in my head, like the many patients of mine who would surely be vastly entertained to see me sucked into a little life's-rich-tapestry moment (yeah—that's a phrase I admit to overusing and should quietly retire from the therapist-patient repartee). A legless panhandler, black with grime, pumped his wheelchair toward me with a hungry, no-teeth smile. No time; no change—so much for my newfound sense of altruism. Ignoring the man as if to deny his very existence—God, the liberal guilt these streets brought out in me!—I trucked on, spotting the elusive Ms. Aames as she ducked down yet another alley.

Oh, the human mind is such a mystery! I say this because despite my sudden attack of conscience, I could now only fix on vivid memories of . . . the New Haven café where I had my first cup of coffee . . . of footballs tossed on deep-green lawns . . . of arches and colonnades and all the bricks-and-mortar reassurance only a Yale education could offer a pimply geek from a respectable but humdrum corner of the San Fernando Valley. Then, an insight struck me—and in a flash I saw what was happening. Today I'd taken what I believed was bold action, accompanying my patient to court to witness a legal battle over her right to privacy. But, like the pilot who drops the paratroopers into a night sky over enemy territory, then returns to a hot meal, a shower, and a warm bed back at the air base, I'd done little, acting as no more than a glib insider, a supposedly knowing observer who in truth was merely a voyeur. Rue Loberg had borne the impact of that confrontation, whereas I'd barely registered a presence.

As a therapist I'd failed.

But then I'd seen disturbing signs in the state lawyer's demeanor. She was offbeat, with a strong individual presence, no doubt, but something in the modulation and rhythm of her speech and affect was . . . off. She'd been tough and maybe even fearless in court, successfully defending my patient's privacy, and in a rare moment of bravery myself, I'd . . . rewarded her valor by confronting her about her condition. Without warning. To my chagrin—no, make that shame—I'd made her bolt.

If I knew anything as a professional, it was that she was in some kind of trouble. So okay: I'd followed her into this hellhole, for once trusting my instincts. And this was how my mind protected me: a gush of collegiate reverie, of gauzy memories, an idyll long past if indeed, it ever even existed.

I envied Bradlee Aames, she burned with a sense of . . . sheer want, such that my eyes filled with tears. The here and now—that's where she chose to reside. But there was no time to cry for my wounded ego. Catching up at last, I saw her fifty feet ahead, leaning against the painted white brick of an old office building, her back shielding what I guessed was a drug transaction in progress with a tall man in a black beanie. When the man straightened up, his dreadlocked hair spilling off his shoulder, I thought he'd spotted me. But that wasn't it—not at all. The dealer was backing away because just above Bradlee Aames, on an old metal fire escape, a crouched figure prepared to leap.

There is a cry that those of us who study the human mind call the primal scream. It comes from a place deep within, encoded in that part of our DNA we share with our cave-man ancestors, a visceral reaction that springs entirely from the moment. Quite without warning I locked in with that lineage and faced the tiger with a banshee wail, startling the attacker so badly that he fell from his crouch and hit the pavement sideways. Wow!—but what now? I froze up. For her part, Bradlee instantly saw what was happening and backpedaled over the fallen man, kicking him square in the face when he lunged for her leg. *Run!* my brain commanded my legs. *Not that way! Run away!* But as I came to her side, I had no clue what I would do if the attacker went for me. And yet, I didn't care. I'm not a fighter, but maybe I could muster a punch from the same place from which my roar had sprung. And what of the dealer? Not to worry—he'd jumped on a rusty bicycle and was already pedaling away with such fury he had to keep a hand on his beanie so it wouldn't fly off.

Bradlee Aames nodded for me to back off.

"That's the wrong way anyway, doc." Her hand, the bloodied one from before, came forth, the touch reorienting me. "Here; come with me."

She was right. We scooted back out to shafts of direct sunlight and the big noisy boulevard—Los Angeles Street, I think it was—with street vendors and squealing brake sounds and an entirely new set of heartbreaking panhandlers to guiltily sidle past. Almost immediately a police cruiser drove by, and as I raised my hand to flag it down, Bradlee Aames dug her fingernails into my forearm until I yelped.

Technically I'd rescued her, so this was not the sort of gratitude I'd expected. I asked her what was wrong.

Her eyes were well hidden by a sleek pair of aviator sunglasses.

"You can't be serious."

Her sense of disgust with my cluelessness was plain, but as she turned her back on the black-and-white, she stood close to me as if we were a couple, placing her hand in mine and whispering for me to just be cool. For an instant, I felt young and free and—wow, boy—way more cool than any of my high school buddies in Advanced Calculus would've ever dreamed I could be. Yet I knew she was only using me to hide from the cops.

We watched the cruiser round the corner and disappear. Bradlee Aames shrugged.

I was still shaking.

"Sorry. I feel safer in their presence."

She nodded. "You're white, so you can say that."

We started back up the street, north, toward Fourth Street and the court, but before she let my hand go, she abruptly stopped as if she'd forgotten something important. That's when she kissed me on the cheek, setting off an electric tingle that traveled down to my toes.

Okay; even if she was using me, this wasn't so bad . . .

I knew she'd been scoring drugs. A prosecutor who probably worked in that big Ronald Reagan government complex a few blocks away, so in need that she'd been willing to risk her career. And her neck. I'd read the names on the proof of service that came with the subpoena for Rue Loberg's records. Spring Street, I think. We'd crossed Spring just before heading down that first alley containing the woman in the pink ski jacket. Of course Bradlee wouldn't want to flag down a cop; the dealer she'd been seeking had probably sold to her before, which is what he'd say when questioned.

"Thank you," she said very softly. "You're a kind man."

Then she smiled. I felt green, out-of-step. But alive—so alive I wanted to sing. Wow. I skipped a little to catch up with her.

At the corner of Fourth and Main, she slowed to look up at the stone columns of one of those marvelous old bank buildings sprinkled throughout the neighborhood. I gazed upon it with her, not sure what we were doing. Was this a test?

"This building," she said. "What if I told you it chased me down the block?"

I folded my arms, said I didn't do street corner diagnoses. Made her laugh.

"Don't be such a tight-ass. I'm not your patient."

My face got warm and my throat constricted. "No, I guess not."

The bank's façade was gray and angular and wonderfully stout in its proportions, classic in its solidity, the kind of structure that exudes strength and imperviousness. But mobility? Definitely zero.

"I'd say you may have been hallucinating. Having a vision."

She arched a black eyebrow. "*May* have? Really sticking your neck out, aren't you, doc?"

"I'm not your doctor," I said. "So you can call me Craig."

We turned the corner onto Fourth, walking slowly west, back toward the old Broadway building and courthouse. The stone buildings lining both sides of the street created a canyon of shadows, reminding me of New York and the charming city blocks around NYU, to be precise. Once again, my thoughts returned to college.

I'd come into Grand Central on the New Haven Line to visit my cousin Stuart, an NYU sophomore with a spirit of adventure that far outstripped his life experience. Made the trip a couple or three times on weekends, lured by the promise of private parties with hot co-eds and endless kegs. Stu was a pot-smoking econ major and his pitch was way better than the payoff; but after another grinding week of logic, statistics, and Kant, I hardly cared. Nonetheless, I'd end up sleeping on a couch that smelled like a gym locker and invariably getting stuck with the check all weekend until I'd limp back onto my northbound train Sunday afternoon, just as awkward and reserved as when I'd arrived.

It wasn't my cousin's fault that I'd always struck out, though; I was a terrible conversationalist with females, always analyzing their words for meaning that often wasn't there, while never revealing a thing about myself in return. I took with no concept of how to give back. Was it any surprise that I'd ended up like this, lonely and listening to peoples' problems for a living?

Bradlee Aames had stopped walking.

"Did you just say you're lonely?" she asked.

"I, uh . . . no. Did I?"

"Okay, Craig. Here's an observation of my own. You look a little zapped."

"It's . . . these buildings. Guess I was someplace else."

She nodded, my tense reflection staring back at me from inside her shades.

"Happens to me all the time."

Her comment was revealing. I could sense her suffering back in the courtroom, the way she'd seemed to hold herself together by clinging to every well-chosen word she'd offered in argument. And the drug-scoring foray? She was not paying close attention to her environment, to say the least. We were both lucky to have gotten out of that alley in one piece.

She looked up at a row of lions' heads jutting from a shaded cornice a dozen floors above us. "They're so beautiful. Each one tells its own story about how people lived in this city, what—a hundred years ago. Seeing what they saw, admiring the details, it makes me feel . . . connected to something bigger than myself."

Huh—she was far more thoughtful than distracted. Admiring the local architecture while I was still jumpy with fear. Maybe this was not the time to psychoanalyze.

You want adventure, Craig? Then easy does it with the clinical patter—you haven't crashed on Stu's couch in ten years; just be yourself. Time to let a real adventure unfold.

I liked her. Found her very attractive, I admit. But I had to think of why I'd come here, had to put my priorities straight.

"You aren't well," I said, putting it out there for better or worse. "And self-medicating isn't any kind of solution." So much for adventure.

She pursed her lips bitterly. "No shit. But then, be honest. You're not worried about me."

I knew what she was getting at. "Okay, fair enough. So then, you tell me, what's going to happen to Rue when she testifies?"

Bradlee Aames stepped back as if to appraise me.

"I get it. Today was supposed to be therapeutic, a feel-good field trip. But now that you've met the crazy, fucked-up lawyer for the state, you're wondering why you ever brought her around here. I'm freaking you out."

"I'm . . . concerned for my patient's welfare."

"So am I, doctor."

"I didn't mean—"

"I know my damn job. Hers is to tell the truth, her story. She does that, she'll be fine."

Then she tilted her shades up, her black eyes studying my face.

"As for you, Craig, you still look iffy."

As far out of my element as I was at that moment, I was compelled to be professional. Or at least act the part. That much I owed Rue Loberg.

"I think you need a doctor."

She bent at the waist, lowering her chin to assess me, close enough to land a kiss. Suddenly, Rue Loberg's welfare was the furthest thing from my mind.

"Seems you're the doc with all the answers. So . . . write me a scrip to quell this thunder running between my ears."

Whatever I had to say on the subject remained hidden. My tongue was like a slab of rubber.

"Right, I thought so."

She walked away, and I let her. *I let her!* Oh, God—oh, damn, damn, damn!

I might as well have gone back to my old dorm room, cracked open a behaviorist tome, and howled at the moon all by my lonesome. Still now—still now! That was where I belonged.

8

RAUL MENDIBLES

"No deal," I said just a tick too loudly into the phone.

Myrna misunderstood me from halfway across the room, holding up a flimsy white teddy that looked like a see-through scarf.

"What? This one don't float your boat, honey?"

I hate it when she uses terms of endearment in front of others.

"What the—did I just hear you correctly?" the Major barked from the other end of the line. "This case was supposed to be over by now. Whatever do you mean, 'no deal'?"

I'd surprised myself by coming right out and saying it, just like that. No attempt at artful dodging. This whole mess—putting Bradlee back in action, and all the ambivalent feelings that came with that decision; seeing that patient in court, looking so sad and stepped-on; knowing that I was aiding Dr. Don, an exploitative weasel if ever there was one—which, by logical extension, made me an exploitative weasel as well—it was working me over, grating my insides raw. And so, emboldened by the need to escape my misery, I'd set myself free, if only for a moment.

"Here, baby, loosen up," Myrna said, handing me a glass of white wine. "Isn't this fun?"

She trickled her index finger under my chin suggestively.

"Sure," I whispered, though a guttural scream would've been the more honest response.

"And a little naughty, too."

More like a knot in the head, a big, fat, rock-hard one, right on my forehead. Naughty? Not the word I'd be inclined to use.

"Edge city, Myrn."

Eight Latina housewives buzzing around my living room on a weeknight was neither fun nor naughty. But Myrna had asked me if her friend, Lupe Borbon, who had bought into a negligee franchisee operation called Sex E Grrl, could do an in-home sales party tonight, and I'd said yes. Myrna had been laying off the Mexican sweet breads and chile rellenos of late, and she'd lost eight pounds already. I figured I had to show support somehow. I just wish it hadn't been tonight.

"I know it's shitty, man," the Major fairly shouted, thoroughly misconstruing my comment to the wife. "I am awaiting your explanation with bated breath, son!" he said as I stifled a chuckle. I thought the Major was going to pop a major artery, and I'd just sit back on the couch, sipping white wine, listen to him flop around on the floor like . . . I don't know, a beached baby whale? Anyway, I'd monitor his whale gasps until whatever scant remnant of conscience or duty left in me took over and I dialed 9-1-1. But he was just warming up.

"Dammit, Mendibles, you made assurances!"

"The settlement conference didn't proceed the way I thought it would, Major."

"Of what value were those assurances?"

One of the invited moms, Consuela Lopez from around the block, pirouetted with a gauzy pink thing on her chest that, to me, looked like a bib for eating spareribs. The women went wild.

"Turn down the TV set, would you, Raw-ool? Sounds like that crazy bitch Oprah's giving away cars again, and everyone's screaming."

"I like Oprah," I said reflexively.

"Another reason you're a nimrod."

Myrna sashayed over to me with enough white fishnet in her hands to snare a sperm whale.

"Ooh, Raul, feast your eyes!"

Or maybe hide them.

"I ask you to secure a written settlement, and you give me used toilet paper, Raw-ool. That's what you gave me."

"It's not that bleak."

"You can wipe your keister with the 'deal' you worked out. We got zippo!"

"Who knows? Maybe Fallon will voluntarily resign."

"Don't you get sassy with me, young man! You led me on. Led me to believe the situation was in hand, when in fact, it was completely, totally out of hand."

Out of hand—the phrase gave me pause. Okay, so we hadn't settled, the case was still pending, the matter was still public—conceded, this thing *was* out of hand. But why? Because of a rogue lawyer, a sketchy pill-popper. Bradlee Aames, not a stinky rich talk show host handing out cars to a studio of strangers, but a true crazy bitch, the real damn deal. Bradlee Aames, the Lady in Black, dominatrix of my dreams. Out of hand? Could be, because obviously, I wasn't thinking clearly about her. Bradlee has that spin-your-head effect on me—and my guess is probably a lot of other men, too.

But . . . this was not truly out of hand yet, not if I could simply fix the problem and analyze the situation better. Tame my feelings long enough to look at her coldly, as an opponent, a legal adversary.

In her condition, Bradlee could be outsmarted. Outmaneuvered. Defeated.

Lupe Borbon held up a wineglass in one hand and a fistful of what appeared to be colored slingshots in the other.

"Two for one on these buttless beauties, ladies!"

"What's crackin,' girl?"

"Whoo—the floss is the boss!"

"This one's white and goin' outta sight!"

"Where's the coverage, Lupe?" another mom shouted amid much laughter.

"That's the point, *m'ija,* the less coverage, the better," Lupe said. "Am I right, Raul?"

They turned toward me. I raised my wineglass in salute.

"You're right and it's tight."

The ladies fairly came unhinged by my borderline double entendre.

"The hell're you talking about, Mendibles?" the Major shouted. "Fallon wouldn't surrender a popsicle in an ice age! Get your head in the game, son!"

Time to think fast. I could squeeze Bradlee again to make a deal; but no . . . she already suspected plenty. So . . . I could reassign the case. No—people would notice. I'd look positively desperate dumping a sex case this close to trial. As a supervisor, nothing was stopping me from diverting the file elsewhere, but the unlucky recipient would size up this clusterfuck in no time, bitch and moan long and vigorously enough to get everyone in the office's attention, then demand to know what they ever did to deserve such a pile of grief. And that pile would be funnelled into a tiresome, winnable union grievance I'd be stuck defending for years.

Generally, no good could come with bringing further attention to the case. Because Bradlee Aames was right: if you considered what Dr. Don did to that patient of his and her family, this sweep-it-under-the-rug resolution was indefensible.

"Just put the previous package back on the table," the Major said.

"Secret weapon time!" Lupe cried. A collective howl went up among the ladies as Lupe held aloft an electric-blue device the size and shape of a prize-winning cucumber.

"Good god! What is going on there, a cheerleader convention?"

"Settlement is no longer a viable option," I said when the noise level dipped to something closer to a drunken slumber party. "Almost half the board is made up of new members."

"You just let me handle them."

"They won't be persuaded, Major. You know how the newbies always start out, wanting to show everybody how tough they can be, how they won't play favorites, especially among their medical brethren."

"Not to worry."

"Only one of them needs to vote 'non-adopt' to the stip. One. Then it'll get kicked over to the board's next meeting for decision."

"So what? We can massage that process when the time comes."

"This free giveaway? I don't see how."

"Don't be such a naysayer, Mendibles."

Just then I felt a shaft the size of a billy club on my shoulder. Lupe, with an evil grin.

"Don't worry, cowboy, I got your back!"

The other ladies hooted and whooped as I pushed aside the projectile of pleasure, my hand cupping the phone.

"You didn't care for my assurances before," I told the Major.

"You blow smoke up my ass, I'll call you on it. Every time. Just be straight with me, son."

"I did not blow smoke up . . . at any rate, I'm through making promises. You got your inside track, know what the board would do with Dr. Don. Fine. I can't calculate what they'd do from my remove. But if anyone bothers to closely read the allegations, they'll sit on that stip, hold it over. They do that, we're dead."

"*Hola, papazote!*" Hortencia Ramos, the crossing guard at Lucita's school, exhorted as she waved an illuminated see-through yellow dildo like a light saber.

"Look, its Princess Leia!"

"Hey, Jabba, get off the phone! It's a party!"

The Major grumbled. "Hell's bells. What kind of a madhouse do you live in?"

"It's a lingerie party. Like Tupperware, where an enterprising lady brings her wares over and shows them off for sale. They've just moved from lingerie into the toy department."

"Hell's bells."

"You wanted it straight."

"Good God. Now listen closely. East LA? We've got a problem. Focus, dammit!"

Across the living room, Lupe sent me a gift, for in that moment, she reached into her pink shopping bag full of goodies, pulled out a new cordless wonder, set her shoulders back and straightened her spine for her next breathless presentation. Her black hair was wiry and not as long as Bradlee's, but the image stuck in my mind.

"Actually, there's a better way. It's staring us right in our faces."

"I'm all ears, son."

"We let Bradlee Aames try the case, let her put on her evidence."

The idea made sense: I'd seen her stagger out of the Serra building downtown as if she'd been sucked through a wind tunnel. I was confident that if she pursued Dr. Don and his pack of sharks to trial, they'd make chum out of her.

These things I told the Major.

"You know the band 'Steely Dan'?" Myrna asked the group. I cringed. This bunch of barrio babes would have no idea where she was going with this. I wished I'd never dragged her to that reunion tour show, pumping her with trivia. "Know how they got their name?" No one cared. And by the way, it wasn't how they got their name, it's the name they themselves, the band's two co-founders, selected. Jesus, sometimes Myrna's stupid comments really wore me out.

I answered Myrna's trivia question before it completely died on the vine.

"I don't like it," the Major said.

"Even with the patient's unexpected cooperation, the case will be unwinnable."

"Better hope so, Raw-ool."

"A shaky psych patient pitted against her semi-famous former shrink? He's got the smooth patter, she's terrified. Think how that'll play."

He was mulling it over, I could sense that much. I thought I heard the clink of ice in a glass. Was he drinking—while we talked business?

"I see."

I didn't care if he was sauced. I was going to sell this concept because it was our best option—and the best way to keep Bradlee close to me, until I could find my way out of my own shadow and make a move. Let her know how I felt about her.

Jesus. You're such an immature, unrealistic idiot. She'd laugh in your face!

"And only those two can tell the story of what happened between them? It's a standoff."

"He said, she said. Indeed."

"To break the impasse and prove her case, Bradlee will need corroboration."

"You mean hard evidence. Other witnesses."

"Right again. But this case won't have any."

"Hmm. I like it, Ray-ool. Long as it works. Better say your prayers."

The Major hung up without further notice or fanfare. Sighing, I studied my free hand and found that during the call I'd chugged my glass of wine dry. The living room bubbled with sweaty energy, the pastels of Mexican bullfighters and troubadours on the walls standing by like befuddled spectators that had wandered into the wrong house. Uncle Ray with his glass eye, pumping out one awful swap-meet painting after another in that rest home off Eastern—Jesus, just because he gave them away every time we visited him didn't mean we had to bring them home and hang them up. I'd have to talk to Myrna about upgrading the living room décor. Not now. She was seated by the coffee table with Lupe, eyeing a lush purple implement that could have been stolen from a missile silo. Myrna glanced at me.

"Don't blame me, Raul," Lupe called out happily. "I'm just the conduit!"

Oh yeah? I got a conduit right here for you, I was thinking. Mental note: no more lingerie parties, ever.

The other women tossed back their heads and sang out their exuberant support for my wife's freedom to choose.

What I hadn't acknowledged to myself, until now, was that I'd foreseen the Dr. Don deal unraveling well before it had. Bradlee Aames was precisely that unpredictable. Putting her on the case had seemed, at first, like an act of self-loathing on my part. An invitation to chaos.

Now, by letting her proceed to trial, I'd simply invited more chaos into a rule-oriented arena that tolerated little else than the highly controlled, carefully orchestrated marshalling of facts, law, and evidence.

"Do what you want," I said to my wife.

So, too, could Bradlee do as she damn well pleased. No matter: at worst, she would lose at trial, then wish she hadn't fought me on settling this thing.

After that, everything would fall neatly into place. Bradlee would appreciate me for not having stood in her way, for letting her take her shot. Her valiant, if unsuccessful, effort would nonetheless prove that she should be back in action for the medical board, not handling left-over, dinky-board garbage. I'd see to it that her regular case load was reinstated, further burnishing my image in her eyes.

As for the Major, he would be quite happy—make that ecstatic—with a dismissal. And with the Major's influence, that might put me in line for the senior assistant AG's job, once old Inglechook finally fades away.

What could go wrong?

Yeah, yeah . . . very funny.

With some effort I extracted myself from the depths of the easy chair I'd been molded into the last half hour. Across the room Lupe reached up under Myrna, whose hands were clasping the purple sex toy like a baseball bat, and flipped a button. The object hummed to life, the women erupting, paper plates of tortilla chips and veggies tilting in their laps.

Then just as abruptly, the violet orb died.

9

BRADLEE AAMES

My roommate, Reevesy, was lying on the couch—my couch—eating premium banana fudge walnut cream—my premium banana fudge walnut ice cream—when I got home. His first name is David, which is pronounced Dah-veed, because he's got an overbearing French Canadian mother who did her damnedest to make her mark on her only boy. He's also blonde, as handsome as Richard Burton without the mileage, and as gay, as he put it when we first met, as a furry pink mascot in an Easter parade.

I threw my car keys on the counter and eyed his dessert. Or mine, depending on how you look at it.

"No, really. Help yourself."

Like a well-kept cat, Reevesy seemed to have all the time in the world, though he didn't swallow all of his latest bite before he spoke.

"Thanks, doll."

He was in his usual faded jeans and white v-neck tee, barefoot, which is all the uniform required of him to do computer-programming work from home. When I met Reevesy six months ago at Pete's, a downtown restaurant around the corner from work, I was on a bit of a personal downswing, having dreamed vividly the night before that I'd drowned in an underwater canyon beneath the surface of my bathtub.

Because I lived alone, in the dream I'd died with the unpleasant knowledge that no one would find my body until it had devolved into a jaundiced puffer fish. A silly dream, I know, because when you're dead and gone, what difference does the aftermath have anyway? But after that night, I pushed away the ice water every time the waiter brought a pitcher to my table; and now, here was this well-educated looker of a man buying me vodka martinis and telling me he'd hoped to find a place to live, now that his boyfriend had left him for a soccer team in Barcelona. It seemed meant to be, the timing of our meeting.

And David had been a good roommate, keeping his stuff tidied up, the kitchen sano, and the rent paid on time. Even better, last month he'd met Franco, a bartender who lived and worked in Venice and had a condo two blocks from the boardwalk. So now I had my apartment to myself two or three nights a week, which was nice when I wanted to retreat into myself. Like most gays I've known, David was an astute observer of human nature, and in the first few days we were together, he'd sensed my withdrawals into an inward landscape replete with blind chutes, nocturnal forests, and abandoned mineshafts. Then again, a lengthy conversation I'd had with God in the form of David's pet goldfish, Miss Molly, also may have tipped off David, but he'd been too polite to say.

"You look more tan," I said.

His straight jaw was grizzled with two or three days' growth.

"Franco wanted to go roller-blading today and the sun was fierce."

He sized me up.

"What?"

"Nothing. Just, you look like hell."

"Well, aren't we speaking frankly, Mr. Shankly." I tossed it off, but he watched me intently as I went to the kitchen cabinet, took out the Jack Daniels, and poured myself a three-finger shot.

"Aren't you the optimist? Your glass is way more than—"

"Half-full? And your humor's half-empty, guy."

He finished his ice cream as I sipped, my hold-it-together hurt marinating in the bourbon.

"Girlfriend," he asked more gently, "let's start again. What troubles thee?"

"Me?" I was not in the mood for personal revelations.

"I'm not talking to Miss Molly."

I eyed his goldfish swimming placidly in the same counterclock-wise direction she always preferred.

"Look at that little girl go," I said. "Against the grain, just like me."

"She's a true original."

"More power to you, Molly." I toasted Reevesy's goldfish with a single, slow-burning pull.

Without making a conscious decision, I poured myself another. My roommate seemed to follow my movements with studied interest.

"So, what's jumping at the old saw mill?"

"That's confidential."

"C'mon, Brad, I watch those TV lawyers all the time. You change the names to protect the innocent, no worries."

Oh, hell. What was I afraid of, having a little human contact with my nonthreatening, mostly nonjudgmental roomie? It's this sense of not knowing my mind, a mild embarrassment that hangs over me, all the time, like an upcoming jail sentence. I have to admit, it wears me out.

"Pour you a glass?"

He raised an eyebrow at my offer.

"I've got work to do later, but just a nip won't hurt." As I poured he eyed his goldfish. "I know, darling, Daddy's a lush."

I dropped four ice cubes into his glass and poured a generous shot.

"I'm working on a case against this TV psychiatrist who couldn't keep it in his pants with a vulnerable patient."

"Doctor Don. So I've heard."

"How?"

"Five o'clock news, dear."

"You're kidding."

Reevesy looked at me sideways.

"The fact that he was once a TV talking head himself must make him newsworthy, I guess."

"Channel Six?"

"Yup. Same studio, so maybe they knew him back in the day and didn't much care for him."

I liked the sound of that. "Schadenfreude."

"They ran some footage with the story, the doc with a headset, taking calls in front of a big hanging microphone. Odd little self-satisfied grin, a little madcap, if you ask me."

"He looked like that in court, too."

"Anyone who'd call a TV shrink to talk about their problems on air? Have to be a bit mad as well, eh?"

"Amen. I might be crazy, but not dumb-as-a-rock crazy."

The buzz was working to hush the background noise in my head. David studied my face with the kind of wonderment one reserves for roadside crash sites.

"Girl, you just downed two triple shots."

"How about this weather."

He frowned. "Cheers."

"It's one of your business. I mean, none of your business."

"You're wording your slurs, doll."

A sour mash cloud floated up from the base of my throat, but I gulped it back down with everything I had.

"Ha ha. I'm under control."

Reevesy made a show of studying his fingernails, as if averting his eyes from the spectacle I'd made of myself.

"If you say so. I'm certainly convinced."

He sighed heavily and closed his eyes.

"You don't look so hot yourself," I said.

"Why, thank you, dear."

"Franco working tonight?"

He glared at me.

"Don't get bitchy, girlfriend."

"What?"

David rubbed his elbows absently and shrugged me off.

"It's not you. Franco and I . . . we had a little spat."

I took a seat next to him on the couch. "Hey, I'm sorry."

"I saw him having coffee with someone just down the street, same guy I'd seen lavishing attention on him last week at a pool party. Got all emotional and possessive, fired off an accusation I pretty much pulled out of my arse, and damned if he didn't admit it."

"Ooh."

"Well, easy come, easy go, hon, right?"

"He'll come to his senses."

"Least I hope so. A Canadian mama's-boy software-geek who doesn't have a driver's license—in LA? What would you call me?"

"A catch."

He looked as if he might burst into tears. Instead, he hugged me. Hard. For me, it was almost like an out-of-body experience, and I yearned for all the previous years I'd lived in the safety of my isolation, alone, no roommate to gauge my weirdness. This kind of intimacy was foreign to me, not my thing. Through all the instability my mind had tripped me with, I'd convinced myself that I could never achieve the Normal, could never bring it off. So I'd quit trying. But then I'd met Reevesy, his sexual orientation providing a natural buffer between us. Bullshitting myself that he could help with the rent, when I could afford it anyway, I let him in. Now, I'd even reached out to him with just a few well-laced words. Shown him I cared. And . . . holy shit, I *did* care.

A gutful of JD did nothing to obscure the revelation that my carefully maintained dividing lines were fading. Maybe meeting Reevesy was not at all happenstance. Maybe I was sick of being alone and consciously didn't know it. Sick to death, until my unconscious took over and guided me to him.

He hugged me harder. I shocked myself by hugging him back.

"I'm gonna get you behind the wheel of my Chevelle this weekend," I told him.

He chuckled. "Can't picture myself driving a big, bad American beefcake-mobile."

"I do it every day."

"But, girlfriend, you are exceptional in every way."

In my head I sensed a single black, beady-eyed crow landing on my car and perching like a hood ornament, as if he owned it. The crow was followed by ten others, then a hundred, then a thousand, all cawing the word "mine," because they owned it now. Then they dug their beaks into every crease and crevasse until they lifted the car up and flew it down the block like a hovercraft. I fought the impulse to run to the window for a better look—and that internal tussle must have registered in my eyes because my roommate . . . who knows? Hard to tell what he saw; that is, what was in my head versus concrete reality.

I looked away.

"It's so smooth, it drives itself. You'll see."

It took effort to turn toward the sink, but I made it there and dumped my shot glass. Shut my eyes and simmered in the blackness.

"Brad," he said behind me.

I staggered a half step and put a hand on the kitchen counter to steady myself, my head ringing from the day's exertions. The drive home tonight had been particularly rugged, as a row of tall palm trees along Crenshaw bent over, dipping almost into the roadway to get a better look at me. Then after sunset, my vision in one eye blurred as if I were looking through wax paper. The only thing that worked to click myself back into focus was to squint through my good eye like a demented pirate. And—oh yeah—sing old punk tunes from memory, screeching choruses out my open window as the cool salt air rushed in.

White riot, I want a riot, white riot, a riot all my own.

"You're not well, dear."

"Please, no lecture tonight, Reevesy."

"My concern for you is real. And I fear you don't understand what's happening."

He rose as gracefully as a dancer from his spot on the couch, his legs unfolding as his bare feet found the floor and gained traction. Gliding by me, he set the pint down on the counter with the spoon still in it, as if it were empty.

"Know why I'm eating your ice cream?" he said over his shoulder.

"'Cause you're too damn cheap to buy your own," I said, following him to the hallway.

"Ha. You make me laugh, girlfriend. But, no, it's because I'm disturbed, upset. And when I get like this, I eat comfort food to calm my nerves."

"Franco's a weenie. Forget him."

He pointed his finger with a snap of the wrist.

"I agree, but this isn't about him. Follow me."

Pacing slowly and deliberately, David proceeded down the hall, poking his head into the bathroom on the left and his own room on the right before making a wide left at the end, straight into my bedroom. It's a decent master with enough space for my queen-sized bed, a free-standing antique armoire, and the large oak desk my father used to have in his study, which I've stuck in the far corner. Aside from the usual small piles of clothing I leave almost everywhere, nothing looked out of place. But then, the screen to the second-story window had been removed and was leaning against the wall just below the windowsill. I was confused by that last detail.

"You did this?"

Reevesy responded with his patented diva lip-snarl.

"Darling, don't be silly. Not now."

He paused as dramatically as an illusionist introducing a featured trick, then sauntered over to the window.

"I was just back from the boardwalk," he declared in a lower octave. "When I heard a noise, from back here! Thought it was you, but I said your name through the door, and all was silent. Yet I could hear breathing, so I thought, well, if she's in trouble, at least she's still alive."

I flashed again on my bathtub dream.

"At least. Thanks, Reevesy, I'm touched."

"Well, excuse me, but do I look like Chuck Norris to you?"

"So, you heard breathing."

His eyes widened. "Yes. Then, 'boom!' This loud, sudden clatter, and then? More silence." He fanned out his hand with an airborne sweep. "Like, like a big . . . bird flapped its wings and flew out the window!"

Or a thousand crows. The JD shots were pooling at the base of my brain, sweet and golden and numbing. The room was faintly fluttering, like an old movie, only this one was in color. My thoughts slowed down, way down, slowed to the point where it felt as if Reevesy's words, and the details of the scene I was taking in, were coming and going, lapping me. To make matters worse, the tub began talking at me, declaring, in the voice of Wally Wadsworth, a smartass kid who used to taunt me on the bus in grade school, that no, I was not at all fit to occupy that tub unless I gave it a good scouring now and then.

"A bird," I said to Reevesy, repeating his words in an attempt to find my place in the conversation again.

"It all happened so fast."

"That's one talented bird, to be able to remove a screen from a window."

"Oh, stop it. That was just the way it sounded to me. I'm a little dramatic now and then, so sue me."

"You also have an active imagination."

He grinned. "Look who's talking to my goldfish, babe."

Obviously there had been a break-in. I sat on the bed, tired and drunk and exasperated.

"I thought about calling the police," Reevesy went on, still buzzing. "But I didn't like the idea of having to show some burly blockhead all my US visa papers half an hour after the fact. So I went across the hall and rang the elderly gent, what's his name—"

"Mr. Sturges."

"Right. Rang his bell and good thing he was home, what a fine bloke, too, that Sturges! We're going out for fish and chips, Sturges and me, soon as he can break free of the old ball and chain."

I was so sure my forehead was cracking open that I reached up to run my finger along the fissure. But I couldn't find a thing.

"So, you and Sturges."

"Right-o. Anyhow, I got him to stand vigil while I came back down the hall. By the time I got my nuts up to sound a harsh warning and bust on in here, the window was half-open and . . . well, all too late."

I studied my room's rather standard state of dishevelment once again. Nothing seemed amiss.

"Reevesy, if this is the kind of bullshit you need to resort to just to mask a wicked ice-cream craving, then—"

"You can't be serious, girl!"

I winked at him.

"I'm not."

Then I leaned over and gave him a hug. *Second one of the night between us*, I thought. *What is happening to me?* This was unfamiliar territory, but it wasn't the first time my life felt upside-down, and at least . . . fuck, I don't know.

No—that's a lie.

At least you're not alone, girl . . .

"Cheers," he said. "What was that for?"

"Didn't know I was rooming with a superhero."

He looked about my room. "Nothing's missing?"

"I don't think so."

Then, as if the logical and paranoid synapses in my brain fired simultaneously, I was knocked flat by a strange, dreadful thought—a recognition, more like, the way you dream of waking up in a crowd and suddenly realize you're bare-assed naked. There was one object in the entire apartment the significance of which I alone held dear.

I stepped inside the accordion closet doors, crouching into the left corner. I'd put the box from the private storage place here, behind the leather jackets, black jeans, a low-cut sequined job I forgot I even owned, and a moth-eaten pair of leggings that needed to go and a floor rack stuffed with shoes smelling of gum and tar and LA streets in need of a good rain once in a while.

"Everything a-ok?"

"There was a cardboard file box," I said.

"Valuables?"

"Just some documents from forever ago. But yeah, valuable to me."

"Gone?"

"Ah, shit."

"Brad. Darling, talk to me."

A spinning drillbit noise echoed inside my cranium. The closet space seemed to close in around me.

"Autopsy report."

"What report? Who died?"

Just then the whiskey in me took a whack at the laws of gravity. Backing out of the closet, I fell onto the bed and stared up at the ceiling.

"My father. A long time ago."

"Oh dear, bugger that."

"Lithium carbonate."

"Lithium . . . what?"

The bed springs creaked as he sat down, and I felt his fingertips brushing my forehead. The handful of times he's seen me melt down, I've got to say, old Reevesy has always had a soothing bedside manner. His touch somehow did the trick of easing my pain just enough to make it tolerable, but I still couldn't lift my head.

"Not sure I'm following you, dear," he said so sincerely I had no choice but to screw with him.

"How can that be? You eat my ice cream. In some cultures, that's as bad as nonconsensual sex."

"'Dessert rape?' No such thing in Venice, California, doll."

"How would you know? You're Canadian."

"Don't ask me how, I just know. And don't change the subject. What's this about your father and an autopsy report?"

"Doctor Don. He's got three lawyers. The lead guy, I'm breaking his balls in court and the whole time he's smiling at me like an executioner. Like, go ahead, hit me with your best shot, it doesn't even matter."

"They did this?"

"Who else would possibly give a shit about a box of my personal stuff? A prick like Dr. Don is used to getting his way. I know the type."

"This is burglary. It's a crime."

"Only if you get caught. They'll find ways to discredit me, seize an advantage. Freak me out."

Reevesy nodded. "Mission accomplished."

"They only care about winning. Whatever it takes."

My roommate's face had a faraway gaze. "I'm scared, Brad."

"Don't be. He's on the way out. What this creep did to the patient? Let me tell you."

"He broke into her place?"

I shook my head no. "What he did was sit in a chair opposite her every week, and listen. Ask his questions. Listen some more. Unearthed all her weaknesses, every last one. Then he went to work exploiting them."

I'd shut my eyes to picture the scene, Dr. Don and Rue Loberg, the lion and the lamb, behind closed doors. Civilized slaughter. Pausing to inhale the breath of the sea streaming in the window, I slowly coiled into a fists-up, legs-spread, training horse battle stance, ready to strike. But my opponents had fled.

Unclenching, I saw Reevesy's big green eyes straining to keep up with my movements. I patted his hand.

"Don't mind me. My thoughts are like meteors. They streak across the sky, then burn out."

"Darling, you don't look so well."

Whoosh: my addled thoughts suddenly coalesced brilliantly. Meteor-like.

"Doctor Don, Mendibles, Craig Weaver, and now you, Reevesy."

"What's that, dear?"

"Every man I know, including you, wants me off this case."

His hand came out as if to halt my words. "Wait just a minute. I didn't say—"

"No, it's all right. I know you're on my side. Aren't you?"

Reevesy put his hands on his hips. "I'll never touch your blessed ice cream again. That's a promise."

I stood up and went to my closet, found a full wetsuit. Reevesy watched as I gathered up a beach towel and hooded sweatshirt.

"So, it's you against the world," he said.

"Something like that."

"And where might you be off to at this late hour?"

"It's been two weeks. I'll lose my mind if I don't paddle out."

Scooping up my pile of clothes and neoprene, I headed for the door.

"Ah, surfing," Reevesy said, his tone wistfully ironic. "Sport of kings. And apparently, the last great bastion of sanity."

10

Bradlee Aames

No moon to glaze the empty lanes on Pacific Coast Highway, no packs of synchronized cyclists, no earth mothers in decrepit VW vans full of herbs grown in Topanga, no tourists in compact cars swerving in lanes to glimpse a famous resident—or was that just a very good-looking local doppelganger? Nothing to divert my attention or distract me from this color-purple mood or lift me from the hunkering drilled-down low I'm dwelling on.

They want me off this case they want me off this case they want me off this case, I think, half laughing. Incredulous. *Gentlemen, I think not. The more you push the girl, the harder the girl will push back. Nice shot— too bad you missed. . . .*

Windows down, the Chevy's growl announces me to the lyrical liquid sweep of coastline, the front seat vibrating with bass drum authority, a thousand crickets' eyes jumping in the hilly scrub. I check the rearview mirror, but for what?—a drunken frat boy with a sports car and an ego that needs bruising? A Westside Division cycle cop lucky enough to draw the graveyard-shift Grand Prix patrol? Nothing—not a soul out tonight; PCH is mine. The Nova barely clears its throat at seventy-two miles per hour, a set of Thompson ET Street Radials spinning silently, the yellow lines in the road straining to stay ahead, as if pressed to reach the classic, fabled, perfectly foiled, most rat-fucked overworked point break on the planet before I did.

Malibu. The California Dream. No longer visible in the monotonous yellow glare, that hide-your-eyes cheerful bleating too-much-of-a-good-thing sunshine that has so effectively, tragically welcomed the masses to pile in and pile on and keep on coming to this place, every guy and his brother with a get-out-of-Dodge dream. Hell, why not bring their cousin and an aunt and her two dogs, too? Why not leave the divorce and its aftermath and that abysmal Midwest deep-freeze winter weather behind, dear? And how about that lovable ex-con with a fistful of potential to go with those forged letters of recommendation? Every Maria from her high school's production of *West Side Story* because, obviously, with her pipes and a face like that she is going places—twenty-eight in the audition line to be precise, give or take a few hopeful sure-thing stars in the making? Come on down! And let's not forget, let us make ample room for every last fresh-start loser and washout wannabe, all of them! Everybody, just hurry up and come on out to the coast because the romance inherent in "coming on out to the coast" is so undeniable, all you've gotta do is turn on the radio and you'll hear it captured in a song, or channel-surf your way right onto the beach and in no time flat, a dreamy lifeguard will save a swimmer and save your future in one swift gesture! And when you get here, just look look look up in the sky at that towering sunshine, feel its coddling welcoming embrace, and oh, God, they're gonna love you here! You'll soon be dictating your impending success to the folks back home—such is the rejuvenating effect of so much sunshine on the brain, but please, be careful not to count your chickens before they die of heat stroke and dehydration. This place can be monstrously large and impersonal and seem preoccupied with everything but your presence and render you nothing more than an anonymous abstraction, and should you take an ill-timed dip in the ocean, there's no handsome lifeguard to save you. Oh, and did anybody warn you about skin cancer and melanoma and wrinkles and liver spots? So please, do not forget the sunscreen, bring a big tube and lather it on, just bathe in it and everything's gonna be all right, there's a canon full of pop songs that says so, which means you know it's gotta be true.

The greatest bumper sticker ever: Welcome to California. Now go home. God help this place.

My apologies for ranting; I'm just another bitter California native, one of a great many. But man oh man oh man, how do I explain the sad, weird gloom that hangs over me daily amid all this bombarding sunlight? Even at 2:00 a.m., I'm casting shadows. But the point at Malibu awaits. Better, I think, to come face-to-face with a cherished dream at night, especially if that dream is hopeless and shattered.

Hendrix wails, serenading the lone surfer girl, his Voodoo Child. PCH twists and teases her, colossal blasts of feedback ricocheting between her ears and lingering on even after the music stops playing.

Meet you on the other side, and don't be late.

I surely hope so, but not just yet . . .

See how this famed strip of paved glory feels at ninety-five, the Chevy coiled and barreling. *Okay, okay, point taken! Don't become a statistic, Drama Queen!* I ease off Jimi, ease off the gas, stare out the window at flashes of mega-dollar beachfront pads, wave a hand into the screaming wind, laugh at my stupid vanity, my utter insignificance geographically laid bare as I ride along the rim of this limitless black sea that plays hide-and-seek with me now behind an endless string of boxy, overblown architectural crimes.

Jimi's deal is nothing more than fabulous crunching guitar work sprinkled with a stock rock-n'-roll sentiment, a typical male phallus-grabbing gesture.

Not for me. Not tonight.

Return to the real—the now—girl. What brought you out here in the dispassionate stillness, thrilling to the chill embrace of night? A chance to breathe, to sort out the jumble of pieces banging around inside your skull. Ride a few waves as a bonus. So cut the operatic flourishes, write up your California Tragicomedy review another time, and get on with it.

This case should be a winner; the facts, law, and evidence militate against that smarm Dr. Don. But the civil lawyers who first smoked him out from under his slimy little rock got what they wanted, got the filthy lucre and moved on, leaving the victim—and now me—behind. I'll be lucky to find a single cooperative witness. The medical board should boot Fallon's ass right out of the profession, yet they seem to want to keep him in the club, for reasons I can't begin to discern from my oblique, outsider's perspective.

Mendibles, betraying my trust with a single leer from those soul-sucking licentious brown eyes that do nothing but zip in and out, stealing snapshot views of me to be hoarded away for future carnal reveries. Mendibles, alone in a toilet stall, reviewing those snapshots with the same glazed pie face he reserves for his little come-to-papa managerial chats with me.

Mendibles has got to know why this thing is rigged in Dr. Don's favor. He's been too eager to stuff me into that courtroom, to jam me into signing off on a pre-ordained gift-wrapped settlement that's embarrassingly lightweight. Mendibles knows the story.

Does no one care about the truth anymore? To my father the truth was everything—and look how his life turned out.

Lithium carbonate.

Maybe his mind had let him down at some point in his quest. I sincerely hope not. As his biological offspring, I am as chemically, genetically flawed as he was. Meaning I can no longer rely on willpower and meds and alcohol and every on-the-make combo I can cook up to get me by. This is my nod to truth, to the real, for now.

I help those who help themselves, God says to me through every gorgeous, empty, roaming bend in this deserted highway. *Combat the motion sickness you feel from swinging back and forth between the real and unreal. Quell your queasiness with my gift to your sanity.*

Ride a wave tonight.

* * *

Paradise lost, I can't help thinking every time I pull up at Malibu. But in the middle of the night, a lone rider can take refuge from the shit storm.

I paddle over black water in sweet anticipation. Probably 2:30 a.m. by now, though I can't see the face of my waterproof watch. A wake-up chill jars my bones as I duck the first oncoming line of whitewash, thinking, for the first time in weeks: *Yes, I am glad to be alive. Thank you, God.*

In that brief moment of hope and renewal comes a meteorological shift, as the Crazy Wind creeps up from behind, huffs and puffs right out of the hulking hills and ruffles my wet hair, laying down a whispering salty kiss on my ear.

Mad girl, the breeze insists. *Mad to be surfing alone on the rim of a city of killers and pedophiles and rapists and gangbangers none of whom give a damn about beauty sleep.* Mad girl, the crazy wind's lone dance partner . . .

I mimic a few Hendrix power chords to quiet the wind's voice. Paddle on, steering my attention back toward surfing.

Nighttime forays require a thoughtful approach. Observe. Process. Digest. Wind. Swell. Tide. Time those swells, their intervals.

I haven't slept well in so, so long. A sickly exhaustion creeps into my joints as I paddle, my thoughts inanimate and out of reach, drifting like burned-out chunks of rocket floating in space. The offshore breeze is picking up. There goes my false calm, blown straight out to sea, replaced by a tension in my gut that grasps and releases simultaneously.

The offshore breeze tickles and teases my neck. I sit outside, in repose on my nine-two Harbour longboard, a classic Trestles Special model I'd found at a garage sale eighty miles inland on a weekend visit to see my mom. A region not known for its secondhand surfboard market, but there it was, the forgotten, neglected Special, amid a pile of rusty welding tools well past their prime. Dust-caked, rotted surf wax applied a hundred times over for traction now merely obscured the board's deck like nasty storm clouds, but when I scraped off a chunk with a car key, underneath lay a pristine fiberglass finish. Silently noting the multiple stringers and handmade wood-laminate fin, I knew I was looking at a board worth a few grand in mint condition, but the hayseed selling it wanted a hundred bucks.

Lil' ole surfer girl, eh, sis?

Guilty as charged.

Heh heh.

I dickered with him just for fun, talking him down to eighty.

He'd followed me across the dirt-patch yard on down to the curb, watched me strap my purchase onto the surf racks, wanting to know what year was that there vintage Chevy.

Seventy-two.

What I thought.

He rubbed his chin. *Borrowed it from your daddy or boyfriend, dintcha?* he said with a knowingness he hadn't earned.

I didn't dignify his inane question with a response. Instead, I settled for dumping the clutch and leaving a little cloud of smoking rubber for him to remember me by.

The point at Malibu is utterly inert at the moment. I thrum my fingertips across the deck, legs dangling off the Harbour's rails like shark bait in the inky Pacific abyss, my back turned from three thousand miles of sleeping continent. Watching and waiting.

If you surf, you know it's mostly a waiting game, a test of patience and wave-knowledge and timing and sometimes sheer luck, looking for an open face that will offer you a shot of speed, a sliver of self-expression. If you don't surf and you'd happen to see a girl like me out here in the night, a wetsuited figure poised and motionless in the recessed orange glare of PCH, staring into the brink of nothing, well, who knows what bad thoughts you might think. But you could not be blamed for thinking them.

A flat calm settles onto Third Point. Mother Ocean is dawdling, toying with her lone admirer's patience. I'm jonesing for the freedom quest, for the one wave that will change me, transport me, fuel my sagging spirits, make sense of everything. Sure—just a friendly, happy-go-lucky little session, no pressure at all.

Your approach is all wrong. Freedom is not about marshalling force. Relax.

Yet nothing is rolling in, nothing, at least, to compare with the modest three-wave set that zippered toward the cove while I was suiting up by my car. I squint harder, but there is not a thing to see, on this, the most intensely studied and stared-at patch of water on earth.

First Point Malibu: hallowed ground, the epicenter of California surfing. But that was half a century ago when the place was still rural ranchland, before Gidget and the beach blanket movies came along and the hordes descended. Before my time. Now if I want a wave to myself out here I have to wait for a black-lacquer night like this.

My eyes are still adjusting to the absence of light, and slowly the crude shapes began to morph into lines of swell. Up close, the surf seemed a shakier proposition than it had appeared from shore: waist-high shadows running too fast along the glowing ribbon of exposed cobblestones that give the point its classic form. But that Crazy Wind, the Santa Ana, is picking up, gusting, whipping my hair into my eyes and passing a steady, grooming hand over the ocean's surface, commanding order.

Reluctantly, I let a too-small set of perfectly shaped swells roll by beneath while ruminating on this fierce desert wind, how it will kick up more dust and dirt and inland filth than you can imagine and blast it all the way out to sea for days, making your throat itch, your eyes squint, the skin around your private parts tighten up, just the way mine used to when I'd interview a witness in lockup.

Cops like to say Santa Anas make people do bad things, the way a full moon supposedly brings out the werewolves.

You know that's bullshit.

Of the many bad-people-who-do-bad-things I've had the distinct misfortune to know, they all seemed to share a common affinity for conjuring lame excuses for their misdeeds. The devil-wind made me do it. That song on the radio reminded me of my ex, and hell, I just went nuts. Damn pizza-pie moon followed me all the way home. Swear to God it was mocking me.

Self-serving drivel. Look—are you another one of those weekenders who sit around philosophizing and never even take off, or do you actually surf?

Another gust of offshore, intent on pushing me around. I shiver, drop to my deck and paddle farther up the point. When they're not chattering at me, the Santa Anas—the official meteorological term for the Crazy Wind—are busy polishing the ocean's surface into a fine mill grain. At last a set comes down the rocks, each wave peeling thin and ruler-straight with a white-rocket trail of foam building and zippering through the black maw of space, mesmerizing little crystal-spinner lips exploding into delicate roostertails. I paddle chin up, my head happily tilted sideways, choose the third wave, streaking high through three or four tight sections, jiving and arching with the pitching lip, guided more by sense than sight. It is a good ride by objective standards, a fine one by my own. By some miracle my head clears and I realize full well what I'm doing out here: reclaiming my sanity, no less. The ride ends and I consider going in, but the thought of lying awake in bed two hours before dawn, staring at shapes on the ceiling to the sound of Reevesy's snores humming through the walls provides zero impetus.

I've kicked out well inside, almost to the pier, and the light shining down on the pilings makes it harder to see back up the point from where I'd come, like standing under a porch light staring into solid night. I drop prone to begin the paddle back out, hair breezing across my eyes, and as I pause to wipe clear my vision, a strange thing happens. There, up the point—a flash of movement, a shadow, a streak of white slicing across the last wave to roll through. A rough form, an outline.

A surfer.

Another shadow rider, unfazed by darkness, come to join you. Can it be? See? You're not so original after all . . .

No, not in these near-blackout conditions. Not likely.

But yes—there he is, and he's very, very good! Perched on a classic nose-rider, stalling and stomping the tail, fluidly cross-stepping back up to the tip to accelerate, whipping a cutback, then back off the bottom again, raging through another critical section in an easy, confident crouch. More details emerge as he comes nearer: black trunks, black hair, a lithe, muscled torso. I'm not seeing this, except I am.

To me, he is instantly recognizable: Miki Dora, the original Black Knight. Malibu's greatest surfer ever. In his prime.

I don't know those fluid moves firsthand, but from studying the rider in grainy snippets of a half-dozen old surf movies, memorizing the limp, controlled disdain, the bullfighter's casual defiance.

But this is impossible. He'd taken his leave of this place in the sixties, declaring the scene dead and buried, a farce. Traveled the world to search for the perfect wave, always on someone else's dime. Went to jail for credit card fraud, got out, and went surfing again. Never, ever returned to Malibu, though his name is perpetually spray-painted on the wall just below the parking lot.

Dora Lives.

That's just a saying, a connotation, something to do with the rebel spirit of surfing, or what's left of it. Not much more than a pose anymore, but surfers can be sentimental that way.

Dora doesn't live, not literally. We'd crossed paths briefly in Jeffrey's Bay, South Africa, where I'd gone to decompress from law school and the bar exam. He was in his sixties then and going gray, drove a four-door beater with broken window handles, and was worried about his upcoming cataract surgery. Hardly the dashing figure of surf lore, but he was lonely, like me, and starved for good conversation—which I supplied—about the law, politics, film, World War II, and a hundred other subjects. There was tennis, a trip to a farmer's market one rainy Saturday, and afternoon tea at the B-and-B straight uphill from Supertubes, where I was renting the servant's quarters for two weeks. I saw Miki out in the water only once, though; he was waiting way, way outside, at Boneyards, anticipating the arrival of a bigger wave that no one else had the patience to wait for. When I paddled over and said hi, he acted like he didn't know me. If his aloofness hadn't reminded me so much of myself, I'd have been hurt. So I told myself I wasn't. I stroked back down toward the point, but before I reached the takeoff spot, a head-high beauty popped up out of nowhere and shot me all the way through Supers and down into Impossibles. It was the best wave of my life. I called it a session and bellied in on a line of whitewater. Sat on the sand for an hour, maybe more, waiting for Dora to rip one to shore. Yet his wave never came. My flight to Capetown left at ten the next morning, so I had to be up early to catch a bus to the airport. Walked down to Supers one last time. The swell had dropped overnight and the point was deserted. No Miki.

Good-bye, friend. And thank you for that wave yesterday. . . .

He fell terminally ill a few years ago and finally came home to California—Santa Barbara—to spend his last days with a father he rarely saw. I'd read every word I could find on the subject of his demise in newspapers and surf mags, because Dora always had meaning for me beyond just his prowess as a surfer. His rejection of what surfing had become—which, of course, was inevitable because surfing is so damn cool, so damn fun, it just *had* to come to ruin—was to me almost poetic, as I lived daily with the same nagging hollow sense of disappointment. But his love and devotion to the pursuit of perfection, the act, the dance . . . well, in my hopes and dreams and prayers and secret aspirations, I could relate.

He also had his imperfections and contradictions. His staunch opposition to the commercialization of surfing never slowed him from making a buck on the side, if the price was right. Dora's noble, unwavering pursuit of perfection plays less virtuously upon closer inspection as well, if you factor in the reports of scamming and fleecing of friends and admirers that helped fund his extended sojourns. Always swift to excoriate the surfing press as exploitative, he'd just as quickly publicly trade on his fame to gain an advantage.

Yeah? So what?

His flaws only made him more compellingly human to me. Like Malibu and California and surfing itself, Dora was flawed and complicated and not easily definable while also capable of great beauty and complex originality.

Special—very special.

The offshore blows PCH car sounds into the lineup. Some unlucky delivery driver, gripping his steering wheel against the gusts. I stop stroking, content to wait forever for one more wave, if that's what it takes. Just being out here is a gift. Within seconds a wave rolls in, right to me—God, or Poseidon, showing his sense of humor.

Don't take yourself so seriously . . .

I swing around, hook into the lift and surge, track an inside rail high in the face, and go, turning and burning, baby, tenderly caressing the hook, my toes and the memory of ten thousand other rides guiding the way.

Miki Dora is dead.

But I just saw him!

The Crazy Wind has claimed me.

Coming in over rocks sharp and slippery, the buzz of that final ride makes the traverse less arduous. My eyes have better adjusted to the night, and as I walk up the sand, I turn back toward Second and Third, hoping to glimpse him but sighting nothing.

Just like South Africa.

A crunch of shells sounds behind me; a repulsive stink of body odor taints the desert breeze. The tail of my board bucks sideways under my arm. I screech wildly, hoping to rattle my attacker.

He grunts when I whack the board back into his ribs, lets go just as I spin forward, my own momentum knocking me off balance. Resist, then remove the resistance—like pulling out the chair from under your opponent. An old trick, but it works, landing me facedown, my gums tasting a million cold gritty granules.

A kick to my ribs, then another. No air in my lungs—

Breathe!

No shit, but I can't inhale without screaming pain!

Scrunching fingers, I make a grab at two big handfuls of sand and—ssflllattt!—fling them just as the third kick should land between my teeth. Surprise: another explosion of pain, this time in my breastbone.

Boot? Fist? Board? Oh, what's the difference? Scream again, as if this is what dying's like and it ain't happenin', no matter what.

Aaaarrrrhhhh!

No apparent effect. No air in my lungs. Should I be taking notes on my demise?

Kick! Not air, goddammit—kick something hard and solid! Oh, fuck . . .

Then . . . lightheaded, eyes closed, and the view inside my eyelids is quite pretty, like a star-shower, the stars, how they pop and chirp, and a white light floods in through my ears, filling my head with . . .

11

CRAIG WEAVER, MEDICAL DOCTOR

I'm on call twenty-four hours for my patients, but the truth is, the phone almost never rings. Tonight it did. A young man with a deep, lilting voice, disturbed about his roommate and friend, Bradlee Aames.

Oh boy.

She'd just left their apartment.

At this hour?

He knew it sounded crazy, but hey, that was Bradlee. She'd done it before, but tonight, for some reason he'd felt compelled to watch her taillights recede down their congested little Venice Beach block. That was how he'd noticed another car, an American sedan, he thought, pulling out behind her. He'd found my business card sitting on her bed and figured I was her psychiatrist.

"Least I was hoping," the roommate said. "'Cause, uh, maybe she could use one, eh?"

"I'm not her doctor," I said. "Or her therapist. We're acquaintances. We just met."

"If I might say, you don't sound too broken up about the present intrusion. Thanks for that."

The concerned roommate probably thought I was trying to get into her pants, but at this hour, I didn't really care.

"Okay. Call me Craig."

"David. My pleasure. Sorry to have to ring you like this."

"Never mind. So, where could she be headed in the middle of the . . . sorry, I don't know what time it is." I reached for my wristwatch on the nightstand.

"I'm on it—spot on. Malibu point."

"It's the middle of the night."

"Sure is, Craig. She likes to surf there."

The fear and loathing aspect of my downtown LA adventure rushed back to me. My eyes swept the unlit bedroom. The dim outlines of rogues and miscreants crouched in the darkest corners, ready to leap. I flipped on the lamp by the bed, the phantasms fading away. My breath rate increased. Exhaling slowly, I steadied myself.

"Of course."

"You sound like an insightful bloke. Bet it makes you a good psychiatrist."

Moments like this, I honestly have no idea what I'm projecting. Insight? Not hardly.

"I hope so, David."

That qualified as big-time hedging. My comprehension of the situation was a full step behind. Still barely awake, I robotically dressed and found my car keys. I wasn't entirely over the scare I'd gotten in that downtown alley, so before I ventured through the door, I took a peek outside the side window. Nothing—just an indistinct view past my apartment's front walk. Parched brown crabgrass fizzing up through the cracked pavement; a dirty white soccer ball left out by the kid next door; garbage cans lining the street curb.

No scary monsters to greet me when I stepped outside. (Yes, I've got an active imagination.) The first thing I noticed was the calm. No boom box crackling on the apartment stoop across the way, no freeway whine humming through the treetops. The Toyota's seat was crackly cold and the interior reeked of a week's dirty laundry, which I'd stuffed into a duffle bag to take to Mom's but forgotten about completely after my LA adventure. I felt a stab of remorse, realizing how effortlessly I'd faded Mom into obscurity. She'd cooked my favorite, beef stroganoff with white rice instead of noodles, then sat there, alone, watching the sauce congeal from across the dining table while on the TV in the corner, the national news gave way to tabloid shlock, final *Jeopardy,* and Pat and Vanna showing a star-struck ex-Navy goofball what he'd just won. Mom, with no greater ambition than to study the void that Dad left, to sit for hours, pressed into that outdated brown captain-of-the-ship recliner, the lone oddball piece of furniture in an otherwise impeccably tasteful home, slowly twirling the stem of her wineglass. Last week, she'd upset herself when she tried to recall the sound of his voice but couldn't. I made matters worse when I pointed out that it was just as well. Dad rarely had anything very nice to say anyway; more often than not, his intellectual bent was about as cool as my uneaten stroganoff.

At the first stop sign, I jumped out and stuck the duffel in the trunk. Then I rolled down the windows to get rid of the stink.

Dinner with Mom tonight; her peace offering to the son that hadn't come around since the last Dad argument. And I hadn't even called her to beg off. . . .

But this is too much emphasis on my mother—Jung would certainly disapprove.

How it goes, I guess—because the truth is, by the time I picked up David Reeves, the concerned roommate, by the curb on a street called Superba a few blocks west of Washington, the thought of going after Bradlee Aames tonight had faded Mom right out of my conscience anyway. In court, in the hallway, in that alley; the half-smile, those wary, appraising, bold eyes. It was like she exerted her own gravitational force.

The roommate, a handsome chap, wore tight jeans and a v-neck sweater over a tee. His hair was short on the sides and in back, but a thick sandy wave spilled over his forehead. The silver wristwatch was either a Rolex or a damn good copy. I thought he was nuts to be standing alone on a dark street in Venice sporting the thing.

Apparently everybody called Mr. David—did he say "Daw-veed?" I'd missed that detail on the phone—Reevesy, so he invited me to, as well. He thought maybe he was overreacting tonight, so I rid him of that notion by telling him about Bradlee's little escapade downtown.

"You must like her," he said when I wrapped up my narrative. "I mean, to come out so soon for another fun adventure."

"I'm the helping type," I said as coolly as I could manage. "It's sort of my business."

But secretly I felt nicked by the suggestion that she meant more to me than I might admit. Bottom line, it bugged me to know I could be so quick to objectify a mentally compromised female; and yet, the truth: I just couldn't help but picture her naked. Sure, I'd studied Freud in a core survey course, sharing my professor's smirking condescension toward the Father of Psychotherapy's vastly overreaching central premise that sexual desires dominate our consciousness. Well, that was fifteen years ago, and a lot of TV dinners and nighttime soaps had come and gone since then, enjoyed by yours truly in the company of none. I no longer dismissed Freud, don't you know. Women were my patients, God's most wonderful, complex, vexing creatures, in need of guidance and support, which I was none too glad to supply. Yet I also coveted them, lusting after the splayed forms of exploited strangers in dirty mags and blue films; grunting, alone with my shame, my face taut with empty pleasure.

The carnival lights on the Santa Monica pier caught my eye as my Toyota piped through the tunnel and onto the coast highway. I craned behind me for a view.

"There's a fun spot," I said to Reevesy. "My dad used to take me there."

"Oh, really?"

"This one time, on a Boy Scout outing, I ate way too much ice cream and hot dogs and peanuts and cotton candy to hold it together on the Ferris wheel. Staggered off the thing and barfed all over the ticket lady just as she reached out to steady me. My dad had to take me to the . . ."

"The what?"

"No."

I was wrestling with a false memory.

"I'm sorry. That's not how it happened. It was . . . Bobby Dennison's dad, another kid's dad, he rescued me. My father . . . shit—he wasn't even there."

"Quite a story, Craig."

Apparently I was making David squirm. But I couldn't stop talking. Driving down a dark highway to Malibu, revealing an unpleasant chunk of my past I'd effectively buried till it was forgotten—how had I come to this point so quickly? Where was the control the modulation, the pre-planning, the safety that wrapped me up so comfortably? I had no clue, and couldn't stop talking, my throat rank with bitterness.

"What else is new? He couldn't make it. A lecture on campus, or maybe a meeting with colleagues on the thesis committee. Details. Bullshit anyway. Pick an excuse, he had a million."

Embarrassed I'd brought it up, I shook my head. "True confessions on PCH." I shouldn't have missed that dinner with Mom.

"Whatever gets you through the night, doc. All right by me."

"Thanks."

Reevesy sat silently across from me for a time. The marching streetlights flared orange across our faces, but nothing could sway us.

"You're a shrink."

I nodded.

"You analyze dreams?"

"Yes. Sometimes even against my better judgment."

He chuckled faintly. "Got it. If you don't want to . . ."

"We're here," I said, "and it's dreamtime for about ten million others who wisely, are home in bed right now. What the hell."

He tightened his fingers around his knee before flexing them loose. Sat up straight.

"All right, here goes. It's always the same. I'm out and about, on the town, walking in sunshine and all that, living life, a click in my step. Don't know exactly where I'm headed, but my mood's sky high, I'm owning that big, wide sidewalk, everything's gonna be lovely. Then I turn a corner, and there's this storefront with a huge glass display window. Inside the window, there's a tuba. For sale. And I get this overwhelming sense that I'm out walking today not just to soak in the vibe, enjoy myself, but instead, for the sole purpose of walking into that store and buying that bloody tuba."

We took the next Coast Highway curve in silence as I waited.

"So, I don't go in. I keep walking, but now I'm tired, feet of clay. Glum. The whole day, my mood, it's all gone to shit."

This time he waited. "Know any tuba players?" I asked.

We both grinned. "Why didn't I think of that?" he said. "You *are* good."

"Think about music in general. Whatever comes to mind, just let it happen."

"Well. Dunno. Used to play the violin, there you go."

"How long?"

"Forever. Least, it felt like it at the time. Grade school all the way through high school orchestra. Stuffed it back in the case after graduation. Haven't played it since."

"Why not?"

"It was always a blasted chore. Practice, lessons, rehearsal. Did it to please the peeps, you know, but I never had the passion." A patch of darkness—in this light, a mere suggestion of the Pacific Ocean—opened up on our left, and he stared into the space briefly. "Not like Luke. My older brother."

"Tell me about Luke."

"Didn't know him all that well, in all honesty. He was nine years my senior."

"You said he had passion."

"Oh yeah, he had it, and the talent. Talent to burn. 'Lucky Lukey.'"

"Why was he lucky?"

"I played my arse off and never made one sound as pure and clean as Lukey could. I'd practice and the neighborhood cats would scatter. When he played, people passing by would stop and stand outside to listen, even in the dead of winter."

"Tell me the rest," I asked when Reevesy went silent again.

"Luke aspired to be a jazz musician. Went to New York 'cause that's where a trumpet player goes if he's serious about playing jazz. So he did, for a time. Cut a record or two, got some press. It's here nor there. He didn't play the tuba, never touched one, far as I know. Dead end, eh."

"Tell me anyway."

"He wasn't so lucky after all. Had some down times. Got hooked on heroin, somewhere along the line. Died on a bench in Central Park. In February. Cops who found him said he was frozen solid. He'd been living in the park a while. No one knew the depths he'd sunk to. Went through all his money, sold off his stuff, even his horn, anything and everything to make the next buy. My mum refused to accept the fact that he was gone. At Christmas, she'd put presents under the tree for him. His birthday, she'd bake a cake and sit by the window."

"I'm sorry."

Reevesy sniffed. "And to think, I'm the black sheep, the big disappointment 'cause I'm queer. Bloody Luke pisses his life away, and Mum canonizes him. But the gay one? Forget about it."

"Your parents, were they religious?"

"French Catholic. It's how I was raised. My father the Brit converted from Protestantism to marry Mum."

I eased off the gas a tad, lost myself in a zone I fall into when I'm analyzing by feel, letting my instincts take over. I can't explain it, but this is what it must feel like to tap into an underground well with a divining rod. It's why I love what I do, I guess.

"You know the story of the Prodigal Son."

"Of course."

"He's Luke."

Reevesy sat up straighter. "Okay, I'll bite. That part's easy enough to see, except in the parable, the Prodigal Son goes away and is presumed dead, but he returns. Lukey's dead-dead."

Jesus, I felt so alive I thought I would burst.

"He sold his horn for heroin."

"Right. The sorry bastard . . ."

"He pawned it. That store you're walking by in your dream, it's a pawn shop."

"But it's a tuba, doc, not a trumpet."

"I know. That's the unconscious mind for you. It's not always tidy. What it does symbolize, what I think it's telling you, is that there's a brass wind instrument in the window, for sale. A tuba. So big you can't possibly miss it walking by."

"But I *do* keep walking by." He paused. "Oh—there you go. Right. Crashing down in the dumps every time I do pass by. That's the problem. So, if I stop, go in the store, then what?"

"You tell me."

Reevesy gazed up into the hillside shadows this time, as if he'd had enough black ocean for one night.

"I buy back his horn. Reclaim it, the best part of him."

"That's right. And how do you do that?"

We passed the next mile like we were floating in slow motion, just us and the night.

"Forgive the poor bastard," Reevesy said at last. Then he sat back, and as he did, he made a slight whistling sound. "There's no other way, is there?"

"You tell me."

"Spot on, Doctor Craig." Then he whistled again. "How'd you do that?"

"Do what? You more or less talked yourself through it."

"Nah, you're brilliant, man."

I thanked him for the compliment and shut up, sensing there was more.

"And Mum—you wanna know what's ironic? She never even knew the true circumstances of his death. We shielded her from the truth. Pops insisted on that. I always thought it was too damn hypocritical for words, and . . . here's the thing: I'm not proud of this, but I can't count how many times I wanted to burst her little bubble, fill her in on a few dirty details." He sighed. "The gay little brother, jealous to the end."

"But you didn't, David. That's what matters."

"How the hell could I? She'd have gone to pieces."

"She lost her son. That was enough loss for a lifetime. You knew that."

My unspoken suggestion was that David forgive himself. As the family outcast, he'd acted honorably, and with great generosity, toward a mother who'd been unfair and unkind to him. But self-love is a sensitive subject. What I hoped for David was too private a notion to put into words, and I wanted him to reach that place of recognition on his own.

"Funny. All this was ancient history before tonight. Same old shit, different day, you know? But right now, it's all staring me in the face, brand new."

"You're giving this a fresh take."

"Gotta say, it feels good, but . . ."

"Scary?"

"Yeah—yeah!"

"What you're doing? It takes balls."

More silence. We passed the spot where Topanga Canyon Boulevard dead-ends into PCH. A blackened, empty beach lot blended with the night sky. Beyond the lot was a cobblestone point where surfers rode waves, but tonight, it was all in my imagination. Zero visibility.

David snapped his fingers. "You see? It's fate. This is it, this is why I'm rooming with a looney tunes lawyer who rushes off to surf alone in the grip of night. So I can have my tuba dream interpreted by the amazing Doctor Craig Weaver."

He reached across with an open palm and shook my right hand heartily. Then we fell into silence. Enough personal breakthroughs for one night. Where a moment ago I was exhilarated, now I was simply dragging ass. A sign that told us Malibu was three miles ahead flew past. Raking my hair through my fingers, I glared at myself in the dark of the rearview mirror. The clock in the dash read 2:17. Glad to assist David Reeves, but this at the core, this still felt like a fool's errand, a wellness check on a woman who was not even my patient and who, by my best guess, suffered from depression or psychosis or an anxiety disorder or perhaps all three. A lawyer with a flair for confrontation, a thing for leather, and this . . . wild, black, amazing hair. God, she made my head spin. Probably was done with me the minute she walked away downtown. What would I even say to her tonight?

By comparison, analyzing a dream never seemed so easy.

Just past the Malibu Pier sign Reevesy pointed, at a dark shiny Chevy muscle car with surf racks on it parked on the ocean side of PCH. I swung a U-turn across the empty roadway and pulled up behind it.

"She's out there." David pointed toward the ocean, which could be heard much better than seen. I locked up and we trudged down onto the beach, my flip-flops sinking and bogging down instantly in the cold sand. I took them off and carried them in one hand. It was too dark and we had to wait for our eyes to adjust.

"Look," I said.

A rider on a wave, a figure at least, tall and perfect as a Greek statue, near the pier. Or . . . no. Was I seeing things?

David was peering in a different direction, toward the point of land to our right. "Let's cut down, get closer to the rocks, and have a better look."

We made our way down to the edge of a field of shiny cobble-stones, rounded but as black as lava. The sand abutting the rocks was gritty and bit at my soles as we trudged along. Reevesy stubbed his toe and grunted. I kept checking over my shoulder for the surfer I'd seen by the pier, but the reflections under the pilings were oily and smooth. No one there. If my feet didn't hurt so badly, I could've been dreaming.

Fifty or sixty yards farther up the point we found her, lying on her side, a great plank of a surfboard a few feet away.

"Stay away, get back or I'll kill you!" she screamed.

Reevesy and I stayed put, but only for a heartbeat or two.

"Brad, darling, it's me. And your friend, Doctor Weaver."

"He . . . he jumped me!"

I looked up and down the beach, behind us, even toward the water. No sign of an attacker. No sign of any living thing.

"We're here," I said. "Just us. You're safe."

She laughed. "Says who? Just because you can't see him doesn't mean he's not out there."

"Let's get you warm and dry, doll, eh." Reevesy helped her to her feet.

Bradlee tried to stand, but stayed half-bent.

"My ribs . . . are sore. I suppose that's a figment of my very colorful imagination too, Doctor Weaver?"

I was way beyond my comfort zone as a clinician, and as a man.

"I'll get the board," I said.

"Knock yourself out."

She seemed thrown by my presence. Confused, I decided to ignore her hostility. Reevesy removed his v-neck and wrapped it around her shoulders. They started up the sand. When I hefted the surfboard, I was shocked at how heavy it was. Jesus, I had a good sixty pounds on Bradlee; so how was it that a twig like her could hoist this tank off those roof racks and lug it down here all by herself? The damned thing was so wide, I couldn't trudge more than a few feet before dropping one of my shoes. Had to set the board down, panting. Dropped the other shoe another fifty feet up the sand and had to stop again. I went this way—panting, dropping, and stopping—all the way back, and by the time I made it to a broken-down old wall separating the beach from the parking lot, I was way behind.

Suddenly, I felt a powerful urge to relieve myself, as in my haste to blaze out my front door, I'd forgotten to pee. Alone, I set the board down for the eighth time and did my business, the old wall glowing an eerie gray beside me. I stared at the facade, which, in the near darkness, had a certain purity of form and placement, a brilliant utility—like a mythic barrier built to hold the entire mundane world at bay.

My pupils had slowly dilated, and I could make out more details. Bradlee's hulking plank of a surfboard was actually a very glossy, attractive item, finished in a deep purple or red, with a carefully centered triangular logo and a slash of white racing stripe from nose to tail. The sound of surf breaking also got my attention, and I turned and stared down my leaden tracks in the sand. Out on the water, what I took earlier to be odd puffs of smoke were not smoke, but the tops of waves blown back by this warm, almost summerish breeze. The kind of wind that brings out the pyromaniacs. Wow, best of luck to their psychotherapists; I guess you'd try to focus the patient on impulse control and take it from there . . . .

Reevesy called out after me. Taking up the board again like a cross I had to bear, I took a cue from my burning biceps and held the nose up, letting the tail drag gently in the sand. Put it back down after banging along a bit farther—Bradlee might get upset if I damaged the rails. Better to give my arms a brief rest and take it from there.

I squinted as shapes emerged upon the wall facing me: spray-painted graffiti, crudely formed letters adorning the wind-blasted brick-like modern cave paintings. One nearby message, not five feet from my head, stood out bigger and bolder than the scrawl surrounding it:

DORA LIVES

So they say.

Following an impulse I did not understand, I looked south, toward the pier with its thin glaze of light on the water below, the place where I thought I'd seen the rider—a surfing shadow man, posing like a god.

A wave swished up the shore and spilled nearby and the rocks chattered a California song, like shaking a pan of fool's gold. A dry sudden gust of wind nearly flipping the surfboard up into my shins, mocking my inexperience. The beach is a spooky place at night, an abandoned fun house. Another gust of breeze laughed in my ears. With a grunt I hoisted the board and was out of there without looking back.

12

BRADLEE AAMES

Men—they can beat me, but they can't stop me. Analyze me, patronize me, simplify me, sanctify me, vilify me, brutalize me, criticize me, categorize me, underestimate me, overprescribe me, anesthetize me, scrutinize me, defy me, decry me, despise me, objectify me, ostracize me.

Burglarize me.

Even jump me on the sand at Malibu. Like I said: beat me.

A girl. From behind! Cowardly, cowardly, cowardly, cowardly!

And I know that was you, Mr. Heidegger, you and your co-coward, Dr. Don. A break-in and a beat-down in one day? Even in my giant chess set of a life, that's two moves too many against this White Pawn.

It will not work. I will beat you. I will stop you.

But to do that I need evidence. Witnesses. At the top of my witness list, the victim's ex. A man.

Too bad for you, Andrew Loberg. Nothing personal, of course, but too bad for you . . .

* * *

ANDREW LOBERG

Women. They just can't be trusted. If my customers—and about 98 percent of them are guys—knew this simple truth, I'd be out of business.

See, I deal in the sales and service of custom street motorcycles, mostly brand-new Harley Davidsons right out of the crate which my crew modifies in the shop out back; plus the odd classic chopped hog, barely legal Triumph or vintage Indian I might take on consignment from a hard-luck seller here and there. No rice burners, please—I almost didn't see my eighteenth birthday when I gave a Kawi 900 too much clutch in that tunnel that swoops left before pointing you north on the 405 freeway, coming out of Seal Beach. I may not be the smartest guy around, but my brains aren't gonna be ant food splattered on the roadway, that's for sure; I'll leave the crotch rockets to the kids, the helmetless punks who twirl around the showroom, spinning throttles and lies like the fearless dumbasses they are.

But wait, I was talking about women, and I do have a notable history with the ladies in my business. Ten years ago I was in the red, strictly month-to-month, chewed up by the competition of two bigger Harley shops not far from my place, slowly dying from shitty advertising no one seemed to take notice of and nonexistent foot traffic in my neck of the woods. By chance, I hired a gal, Ophelia, a tattooed beauty-school dropout who happened to waltz into my place in my darkest hour, looking for work. Turned out, one of my competitors was hiring and she'd misread the ad, but we got to talking. That Ophelia, she knew her bikes. Also had her own set of tools. I had a backlog of flat tires, oil changes, tune-ups, and a lot of pissed-off customers. Ophelia cut through the workload like a hot knife through butter. She was good, but even better to look at—a hot knife in her own right, if you know what I mean—and just like that, half my crew's productivity went straight to hell. When my best lacquer guy stared at her so long he ended up sending a fifteen-hundred-dollar flame job up in smoke, it was the last straw—I stuck her out in the showroom with a price sheet and a ballpoint pen.

And then, it happened: magic, baby, pure magic. Ophelia was a natural. I marveled at my managerial luck—or hey, maybe it was genius, I told myself once or twice—as our sales doubled in a month's time.

Here's the thing about her instant success, which you might've already guessed. Now, I know I told you women couldn't be trusted, but I'm not saying here that Ophelia is an untrustworthy individual or anything. In fact, she's a straight shooter all the way. But when I put that girl on the sales floor, I also put her on commission; so all of a sudden, there she was without a set monthly paycheck, no safety net at all. She was freaked out that if she couldn't make a sale she'd be broke. Ophelia was concerned, put herself through two or three days of pure torture, nervously pitter-pattering about the bikes' features and pricing, and sweating like a pig in a new navy pantsuit she'd got off the rack at Macy's. For their part, the cavemen that comprise our usual walk-in public administered some hard knocks to her pretty little head—telling her: hey, babe, cut the class specifications crap, what do I look like? You think I don't know my bikes? Oh, so you're some kinda expert 'cause you work here? What you know about bikes I could put in a thimble—that kind of stuff. By the third day, she hadn't sold a thing and was talking about resuming her grease monkey job. I found her hiding behind the fuel additive rack, crying her eyes out. She asked me what was wrong with her. Why couldn't she do this? She knew bikes, loved bikes. This should be easy and even fun, but it was neither.

That's the very moment I lucked into what has to be the best managerial moment a goof like me will probably ever muster.

In all honesty, I was staring at her rack as she sniffled and sobbed, wishing I could see more of that fabulous set of lungs. Maybe she took note of my friendly gaze, or maybe it was what I said—which, in all honesty, I pulled right out of my ass, 'cause I was stumped. But here's what I told her, my lone pearl of wisdom.

Just be yourself, honey.

That message, coupled with my prying gaze, must've sunk in on her. After that, Ophelia figured out what she really needed to do to get those tires over the curb. Next day, and all that week, she came in a changed woman: killer heels; low-cut tank tops; hip-hugging skirts. No panty lines that these curious eyes could decipher. Wow. Now, she did engage in the usual cycle-talk as needed, but more importantly, she'd laugh at every dumb joke the cavemen told, took all the gee-whiz-yer-quite-a-doll compliments in stride, and smiled till I was afraid her gums would start bleeding.

All of it was an act, and all of it did the trick.

It's like a chain reaction. Men keep buying bikes from Ophelia 'cause they think they're scoring points with a hot young lady. That makes them feel empowered, enough to picture themselves riding out of here on a bike they only cautiously imagined owning before. Enough to bust out the checkbook in front of the lovely young lady, because what kind of man are you if you can't back your word?

Of course, it's a con. Not just the usual flim-flammy high-pressure-salesy kind of con. You see, Ophelia's one of those gals who isn't into men.

Not that I see anything wrong with that kind of lifestyle. In fact, I've got five gals on my current sales force of seven, all of them capable of giving Ophelia a run for her money in the looks department, and only one of them is married. To a man, I mean. Hey—their private lives are their business, is how I choose to see it.

But isn't that just too perfect for words?

So please forgive me for a touch of crudity, here, but yes, sir, I for one know the power of the pussy. It's made my business the success that it is.

Thing is, I just don't like having that same power brought to bear upon me.

Which is exactly what happened this afternoon, during that slow time between lunch and about the time my early crew knocks off for the day; well after two, but not quite three p.m. Siesta time.

So, this young woman strides into the showroom and asks for me, which isn't exactly an everyday occurrence. I was sitting around, doing nothing other than making sure all the people on my payroll were doing something, or at least making it look good, which is a big part of sales psychology as well, you know, looking like a busy shop, a convention of winners and all that bullshit. Here I am, managing Team Winner, wondering if I should make everyone clear their leftovers out of the lunchroom fridge so I could defrost it, 'cause something had been smelling damn funky in there, and oh boy, I didn't need anybody filing a worker's comp claim against me due to ingestion of mold spores or some other kind of legal bullcrap employees dream up these days to skip work and make some easy money in recompense.

Not to complain here, but owning your own business these days is no picnic. People think you got it made 'cause you can call the shots, and I admit, I do like that aspect. But having authority can be a damn tiring prospect; it never lets up. Sometimes, I wish someone else would whiff something rank in that fridge, grab a trash can liner, and just yank the plug out of the wall, start emptying out that sucker. Take some initiative, for God's sake.

But getting back to the young woman coming in asking for me—wait a minute, I should actually back up a little more, cause all of this is related to the woman's visit.

First, I have to tell you a few things about my ex-wife, Rue.

What can I say without sounding like a critical jerk, a complete horse's ass? I don't know if it's even possible. Let me just start by saying that when we met nearly twenty-five years ago, LaRue Harrigian was the girl of my dreams. Pretty, a skosh dainty and refined, but not too much the little dolly. Good general attitude about life, a good kid, never full of herself. Always well turned out, nice hair and fingernails, clean teeth. And oh boy, we're talking great in the sack. Fabuloso. On the flipside, let's just say that Rue is not the sharpest tack in the box, but she worked hard, cooked dinner every night, kept the place spic-n'-span, and made pretty decent money part-time as a loan processor at a savings and loan on Atlantic. Best of all, she was a Holy Advent of Christ member, which is why both our parents signed off instantly on our union. You see, in our church, you can't marry outside the congregation, period. If I stopped describing me and Rue right now, it'd be what you'd call a good fit.

But there's more. Being that I was still living with my folks when Rue and I first met, and that my old man came from a freight-shipping family back east that, for a century or so, practically minted its own supply of money, I still hoped to have an inheritance when the folks passed on, and marrying right—that is, right in my folks' eyes, at least—was a pretty big deal at the time. Rue definitely fit the profile, and a few years later, my old man passed and I came into my money, not even a quarter of what I expected by the way. But it was plenty enough to buy the mortgage on our house from the bank outright, take a ridiculously overpriced Great Wall of China motor-cycling trip, and start this business up with a down payment on the shop and sales floor and forty grand toward a base of inventory. But I should've known that any god who demanded people from a crazy little religion had to get hitched to others from the same crazy little religion lest he damn them to hell for all eternity, well, I should've known that that kind of god would probably have a pretty good sense of humor.

Which He did, 'cause sooner or later our marriage turned into a nightmare.

That's because LaRue Harrigian, the perfect wife to end all perfect wives, had what the folks in the head-shrinking business call "issues." And I mean big ones. Turns out Daddy Harrigian, who was a Holy Advent pastor in the branch over in Norwalk—you can see the cross sticking up from that ugly glass job just off the Santa Ana freeway at Pioneer? Turns out he wasn't the pillar of the community he'd been passing himself off to be for the better part of forever. Wasn't really "Daddy" either, just a stepfather that married Rue's mom when Rue was still a toddler. Now, when I come along and marry Daddy's daughter like I did, I had to kowtow to the big-stuff minister in the usual ways you'd expect, and a few times I actually even attended services with Rue. Which means I heard some of the old man's Sunday sermons, and if I recall correctly, he used to talk about true Christians, counting himself as one, of course, while separating them out from what he called the fad followers.

Well, I may not be very spiritual, knowing what I do about God and His epic sense of fun and classic, comic timing; and no, I would not lay serious claim to being a true Christian, whatever such a claim may truly entail in terms of possessing actual faith as opposed to an affinity for spouting sanctimonious tripe. But lo and behold, I surely can say with certainty that no man who calls himself a Christian, or a father for that matter, should ever, ever lay a finger on a child for his private, personal gratification.

And when it came to Rue and her stepdad, fingers were not even the half of it, if you know what I'm saying.

Poor Rue. I say poor Rue because, you see, that isn't even the worst of it. That unspeakable nasty stuff with the stepdad went on for a couple years, I think, from middle school till she was in the ninth grade. She couldn't sleep and had stopped eating by the time she started trying to kill herself. Patches of hair were falling out of her scalp; either that, or she was pulling them out in her sleep without even knowing it. When she finally broke down and told her mama what was going on, Daddy Harrigian came unglued, the spit flying as he called her out before God himself, before the Lord God almighty, as a liar. A liar, he boomed, a heathen sinner. And so on and so forth, the shameless jerk. Beat the crap out of Rue that night, then talked his way out of it when the worthless police came around for a halfhearted round of interviews. Predictably, he blew smoke up everyone's skirts while tearing his daughter apart, blamed her wild imagination on TV and rock-and-roll music and too many Hostess Twinkies—that's right, an original spin on the Twinkie Defense, I kid you not.

Apparently, the cops were only too eager to buy in. Back then, the Catholic Church had not yet imploded from the weight of all those scandals with the molesting priests. Back then, a scared kid's word generally didn't hold up against that of a holy man. And even though he'd won, stepdaddy God Boy wasn't yet done with little Rue.

What he did was wait to make sure things had cooled down, because evil people tend to be careful people. Meantime, according to Rue, another phony local pastor might've took a crack at her, too, but I never heard those details. Anyway, God Boy sent her to this Pastor Molek at their central church over in Bellflower for some intervention. Molek, he was cut from the same fouled oily cloth as Harrigian, though. He so-called "counseled" Rue, privately, gave her special guidance on how to master the temptations of the flesh. That's right—in private, meaning the hands-on demonstrations came included.

You can let your imagination fill in the rest on that scum Molek and his ministrations to a young girl fearing familial abandonment and institutional excommunication. A couple years I paid a private investigator to look up Molek, and he found him easily enough, comfortably retired in a planned community in Palm Desert. Has a place right on a golf course, backed up to the fairway on the fourteenth hole.

Fourteen—about the same age Rue was when old Molek used her twice-misplaced trust to further degrade her.

Not long ago I played the course, just to get a peek of Molek's little retreat. A short hole, so I used a three-iron off the tee. Sliced it badly, which got me a nice view of the man himself, sitting in the morning sun as he read a book. I got so close to him I had to wave, and he waved back, the only thing between us a flimsy chain-link fence, maybe a head high. I seriously considered leaping over the thing and throttling him right then, feeling my fingers dig into his neck as he pleaded for mercy—any likes of which he'd long ago failed to impart in any way on my future bride. Then a nurse came out and gave him a handful of pills, staring me down through the chain link till I turned back to the links and my meaningless game. One day in the not too distant future I'll be visiting Molek again, when that nurse gets an emergency phone call and has to leave work early to tend to some personal business. Just Molek and me, having a private chat. I promise you, I'll have that three-iron in hand again, and my swing'll be in fine form, I swear it.

Poor Rue. I don't even know how she survived into adulthood, but she's a tough gal, I guess. Time went by and she held a lot of stuff in, kept the demons at bay, because it wasn't till we'd been married seventeen years and had a son and a daughter of our own that a lot of these so-called issues started popping up like horror-movie zombies coming out of the grave. One minute, she's too shy to show herself to me naked in our own bedroom; the next, she's dressing like a hooker to go out to the supermarket. Sometimes in the bedroom, I was banned from even touching her; other times, she couldn't keep her hands off me. Rivers of tears would flow one morning, out of the blue; but that night, she'd be as silent as a monk. Rue could be the world's greatest mom to our little girl, Mindy, one day, helping with homework, baking cookies together, fixing their hair. Next day, she'd be throwing Mindy's clothes all over the front lawn, screaming that Mindy was a slut, because . . . Mindy had gone and talked to a boy at Sunday school, or something like that.

Still, I loved Rue. But Holy Jesus, she was a wreck.

And to think now, looking back, that I was the genius who got her a referral to that quack Donald Fallon out in Beverly Hills. He diagnosed her with borderline personality disorder, sounded very official when me and Mindy would come in for conjoint sessions with Rue. His office impressed me, too, what with the dark green carpet and duck-hunting oil paintings on the walls, the brass knickknacks, live ferns, the jailbait receptionist. I didn't object to paying for the conjoint sessions, or paying for Dr. Don's individual sessions with Mindy, which he insisted on conducting, even though I couldn't see any appreciable results. My girls still seemed pretty unhappy about any number of things in their lives. So when Rue got creeped out by Dr. Don on account of the private sessions he had with her, I didn't really much listen. Life was hard, and talking about it never seemed like such a hot way to fix it, to me. Plus with Rue's history, how could I blame her for getting the willies from another male authority figure? It seemed apropos, the kind of thing her damaged mind would conjure up even if it weren't there, and I thought it was enough that she stopped going to see him at her regular time. Maybe she was learning to stand on her own two feet better, I thought. Good for her.

So yes, I was surprised when a year or so later she started going out every Saturday afternoon, late, for a hair appointment, or to shop. She never paid that kind of attention to her hair, never liked shopping much. I was still paying for Mindy's sessions with Dr. Fallon, but Rue had sworn him off a long time ago. And Rue was taking better care of herself suddenly. I thought maybe she was having an affair, or joined a cult. I really didn't know what to think, to be honest.

So I hired a private eye, a good one, black guy who'd helped me years before when my parts manager was stealing inventory and altering our bookkeeping to cover it up. That investigator did a hell of a job for me, so I engaged his services again, told him to tail Rue on her Saturday afternoon outings. Could not believe it when he told me where Rue was going.

To Dr. Don's office.

Imagine: I was still writing the pompous jerk a big check every month for Mindy's sessions, some of them which were conjoint with Rue. Which means that he was fucking my wife behind my back and billing me for it. (I know, I know: *now* who's the jerk?).

The first thing I did was tell Mindy she was never going back there. If Dr. Don would do that to Rue, who could know whether he'd try something with Mindy? She immediately got disgusted and told me I was nuts; the guy was repulsive to her and had too high an opinion of himself, and besides, he seemed more interested in Mom when she came in for conjoint. So I was relieved—at least it hadn't come to that with my little girl, who was now a legal adult and living with her boyfriend, by the way. Mindy could take care of herself, thank God.

When I confronted Rue, she completely fell apart. It was like she was a china doll and I was the ball peen hammer that smashed her to bits. Now, Fallon, he's the one who primed her downfall, hurt her, even—creepy stuff where he'd try to physically dominate her, stuff he'd worked in over a period of time, like he was conditioning Rue to be his slave. And I swore I'd make him pay, but that was no consolation for Rue and the condition he left her in. Night after night, she'd curl herself into a ball on the closet floor and just sit there in the dark, rocking back and forth against the back wall, thump, thump, thump. I was mad as hell at her for what she'd done, but I knew most of her history and Mother of Jesus, she was in such obvious pain it was hard not to feel for her.

Within a few days of the big reveal, Rue started drinking. First it was a couple glasses of wine at night, then the whole bottle. Then two a night. I had to stop stocking our wine cellar, but by that time she was spending heavy time in the poolside gazebo out back, running through the bottles I kept in my little bar by the barbecue. For a week or so she made herself margaritas, and when the tequila was all gone, she switched to martinis. I came out there late one night 'cause I heard a splash and didn't want her to drown, found her lying sideways on the step in the shallow end, staring up at the stars, rocking an empty quart bottle of Chivas like a newborn in her forearm. *I'm not a person*, she said to me. *I am less than a person.*

By then I knew the damage was done and we were finished. So I hired a lawyer. Actually, two lawyers. One for the divorce. The other to sue the shit out of Donald Fallon, MD.

Which brings me back to what I was saying about women, how you can't really trust them.

Take my daughter Mindy. Like a good dad, I warned her off Dr. Don, enough said—am I right? But now, since the divorce, the girl she barely speaks to me.

Our son, who is over eighteen now and a legal adult, is a bit of a mess himself and even he got some counseling from Dr. Don. But he wasn't directly involved in this fiasco, so forgive my bluntness, but he's none of your damn business.

Back to Rue. She cheats on our marriage, blows up the family, but today she swears she was a victim and says I'm the one who let it happen by ignoring her when she was in the pits for so long? Man, oh man, that's a lot to digest.

Okay. Thinking back, maybe I did. But then, she lied. I'm her husband, and she betrayed my trust.

Hey, Andy? Stop the rambling. You sound like a knucklehead.

It's all too sad and confusing to think about for very long.

Now, back to the Harley showroom today, this woman who comes into the shop between two and three, timing the afternoon lull perfectly. Asking for me. Insisting to see me.

I can tell you, I may own this place but I'm more of a behind-the-scenes kind of guy, and I don't cut the most dashing figure with the ladies, so customers pretty much never ask for me. But here she is, this tall but seriously curvy gal with all this wavy black hair, man-eater shades, a tank top and torn jeans practically painted onto her, and she's "looking for Andy?" Oh, man oh man oh man!

The first five minutes I spent showing her around this temple of rubber, metal, and chrome, giving her a nickel tour she seemed to be lapping up, I was thinking: *what are the odds here, Andy, of you doing the horizontal mambo with this lovely lass?* You know, realizing how long it had been since I last got some and how that dry spell had to end sometime.

Never even thought about what she was doing here in the first place. Guess I'm not much of a salesman.

She stopped in front of one of my favorites, a '67 Triumph T120 Bonneville with chrome fenders, front and back, and a violet lacquer metal flake tank that was museum-worthy.

"We call this one 'Smoke on the Water,'" I explained.

She walked around it.

"Right—Deep Purple. That's cute. I'd like a test drive."

I pictured myself out where the rubber meets the road, flicking my wrist and torqueing up this baby as the lovely lady wrapped herself tighter than ever around my waist.

"Sure. Let me get my helmet. You need one too?"

She looked at me as if I were stupid.

"I brought one. But the test ride's for me alone."

"I dunno, that's a lot of bike, miss."

"Six hundred and fifty ccs. I know."

"Well, the lady knows her cycles. You sure it's not too heavy?"

She glanced over at the row of Harley 1200s that lined the front window.

"It's nothing like those beasts. I've got good balance. I can keep it between my legs. I'm a lot stronger than I look."

Wow—I loved the way she said that. She hadn't even asked about the price tag, which would've given her about seventeen thousand reasons to look at something, oh, about thirty-five years newer. She took out her driver's license. I studied it.

"Bradlee Aames." Odd name for a chick. M-1 DMV status, though. That was all I needed to know. "You're good to go. Now, to take her out, you'll have to leave a credit card here and—"

"I don't have time for that," she said, shaking that luxurious head of hair, which had the effect of exposing a pair of golden brown shoulders.

"It's sort of our store policy to—"

"You can come with me. Don't worry, I won't break any laws."

Man oh man oh man, I was blushing like a nervous kid.

"Well hey," I said, "the customer's always right."

No idea—I had no idea where this was going, but at the very least it might result in the sale of one of our most expensive bikes, and I wouldn't have to shell out any commission to one of my reps. What the hell—I went behind the reception desk and grabbed the keys to the Bonnie for the lady, and the ones to the '62 Harley with the Panhead on a hardtail frame, a chopper just like the one Peter Fonda rode in Easy Rider. That's a bike I've intentionally priced too high, to make sure it's around for me to take a spin on it every now and again. Just sitting on a badass rig like that will shave ten years off your life, I swear. Riding it, you can subtract another ten. That bike is freedom incarnate, like dreaming when you're wide awake, a middle finger salute to all the statutes and laws and rules and regulations, noise ordinances and moving violations and exhibition of speed prohibitions in the whole entire world. Makes me feel like Captain America.

Yeah, well this middle-aged road rebel might've known he was in trouble when the lady tooled straight downtown and did a loop on Shoreline Village, which is roughly the same course they use for the Long Beach Grand Prix. The Harley I was motoring naturally sits up in the wind when you ride it, so I was fighting to keep up with her, but when she looped back onto the 710 freeway north, it was a whole different ballgame. She took that Triumph up to about ninety like it was nothing, leaving me well behind and flapping in the breeze like a sheet on a clothesline in a damn hurricane. *Not so fast*, I was thinking. When I saw her taillights blink up ahead, I knew she was playing a game of catch-me-if-you-can.

I scrunched down, my head even with the handle grips, and got serious, blazing up past a red Nissan Z-car like it wasn't even there and earning a sustained blast from the Z's horn in salute to my audacity. When the lady hit the 405 southbound transition, I was starting to lose my cool. In all my years, I'd never seen a test ride go this far north, this fast. She more or less cruised the next few miles, with me barely managing to stay on her flank. Still haulin' ass, but staying way right so she could take the hilly on-and-off ramps along Orange and Cherry avenues like they were part of a wonderfully engineered obstacle course built just for her motoring pleasure. Gotta say, although we were way off the usual test-driving map, it felt downright fabulous traversing those ramps, like riding a giant freewheeling roller coaster. When she exited on Spring Street and headed left, I had an idea what she had in mind. She wanted the stereophonic sound experience next, 'cause there's nothing like the scream of a high performance cycle bouncing off a concrete wall or two or three.

The best two tunnels in the city lay straight ahead: the first, a nice little shorty on Spring, tucked under the southwest corner of the Long Beach airport; and then, just down the road, a stretch of Lakewood Boulevard shaped like a half-mile piece of unbending pipe.

She hit the Spring Street tunnel at speed, but not pushing it too hard, and we enjoyed the double roar of the bikes and sparkling strings of overhead lights more or less together. By the time that Bonneville hit Lakewood, though, she'd found another gear, and Smoke on the Water plain smoked old Captain America like an after-dinner cigar.

I limped back toward the shop a good quarter-mile behind her, not even caring that I'd lost track of my own would-be customer on a rare, very expensive bike with a tank full of gas I'd paid for. Then I hit the traffic circle at Lakewood and PCH and she flew up in the lane next to mine. The smile and one-handed thumbs-up she flashed was a peace offering, I guessed, and I nodded as if hell, this was all part of my usual afternoon routine. But the fact is, I still had my jockey shorts around my neck and my balls in my throat from that bit of tunnel fun, and my eyes stayed glued to the highway.

Ophelia was the first to observe my blanched face.

"Welcome back, Captain America."

I shot Ophelia a look that said *don't push my buttons*.

"Hardy har."

Still grinning, she wisely retreated to her sales desk and picked up the phone.

The lady named Bradlee took off her helmet, shaking that full head of hair.

"Penny for your thoughts," I said as casually as I could.

"Thank you," she said. "That was a total gas."

"We did have fun, didn't we, though?"

She nodded, but pensively, as if her mind was no longer on the open road.

"Sorry, but I'm not going to buy a motorcycle today. I might be back for one soon, though. Seriously." She'd shut her eyes. "I'm picturing it, just not completely yet."

Huh. That was odd.

I was about to say something flat-footed about our Try-It-You'll-Like-It demo program, but then . . . I noticed how her legs were crossed, how she'd also wrapped her arms up around herself, tight. Made me recall how Rue, after the whole Dr. Don disaster, would twist herself up like a pretzel, hide out in a closet like that, when the grief loaded up too heavy in her head. Straitjacketed as if for self-protection.

Now *that* was a weird flashback I didn't at all get. What the hell? This wasn't adding up. Not knowing what to make of her, I asked her point blank what she wanted.

She'd told me she wanted to talk to me. To talk about Rue and Dr. Don. She wanted me to testify in court, to help get Dr. Don's license revoked, put him out of business.

My confusion was compounded.

"Say what?"

She handed me a card: Bradlee Aames, Deputy Attorney General, Department of Justice, Office of the Attorney General. That card read like ice water straight down my back.

Numbly, I said: "You can't be serious, miss. You must be joking."

"This is no joke."

She was a prosecutor for the state, all right, and she was sorry about the foreplay—yeah, that's what she called it. But I hadn't returned her phone calls. Which was true, a fact that didn't help stoke my righteous indignation at the moment.

"The civil case settled already, miss," I pointed out. "Sorry, but there's a gag order not to talk about the case. I couldn't talk to you if I wanted. Same goes for Rue."

"That's garbage," she said.

"But the lawyers, they—"

"It's an illegal side deal."

"That's not what they said."

"Civil litigators cook up all kinds of oddball contingencies that don't mean anything."

"It was an important contingency. We had to agree in order to, you know, get the money."

This Bradlee Aames seemed to find me amusing, and I watched her black eyes dance around the showroom.

"Listen to me," she said. "What if those lawyers told you that this month you didn't have to charge sales tax? Would you do it?"

"Okay, I see your point. But still—"

She went into her black purse and came out with a subpoena, which she handed to me.

"I could say no, you know."

"But you won't. I can tell you're a good citizen."

"I don't have to cooperate with you, Miss . . . Aames."

Her eyes disappeared behind her dark shades. If she was twisted up and straining against something a minute ago, her womanly poise was by now back in spades.

"See you in court."

"I mean it. I put this behind me. Behind me it's gonna stay."

"You've been served."

My arm held out the piece of paper and dropped it at her feet.

"Not anymore."

It felt good to take a stand, and I heard a murmur from Ophelia and Bitsy, my second-best sales gal, a petite, Latina babe-next-door who grew up around bikes and can blow minds reciting Harley nomenclature from memory. My chest got a little fuller knowing my staff was taking this in, seeing their boss stand up to the state of California, not taking it.

The attorney named Bradlee Aames flipped her shades off her face and stepped right into my grill. Up close, her beauty had an instant effect on me, the way a double shot of Bacardi 151 will just erase your every thought and intention until all you can see, all that exists, is the bottle and the glass in front of you.

"Let me tell you what you think you're leaving behind," she said. "Donald Fallon used his status as a medical doctor and psychiatrist to exploit your wife. He's a sadomasochist masquerading as a trusted professional. Excuse my bluntness, but he fucked her and forgot her. Blew up your family."

"Jesus, you're a brassy one, talking to me this way. Now you listen to me—what's done is done. It's no good talking about it now. And Rue is my ex, so don't call her my wife."

"You think this is done, in the past?" she said. "Well, what really got done? He committed a criminal sexual assault, but your wife—"

"I told you not to call her that!"

"I say that because the victim, Rue Loberg, was your *wife* at the time. She was so torn apart from what the great Doctor Don did to her, the DA couldn't possibly stick her in front of twelve jurors. So Fallon walked away from a crime. A violent felony."

"Guess that's on the DA's office. They could've took a shot, but they didn't."

"Right," she said with disgust. "So you put your crack civil litigation team together and wheedled a money settlement out of him, but so what? He didn't make a single admission of wrongdoing and—"

"Hey, don't look at me! That was another one of those contingencies the lawyers insisted on."

"Yeah, sure, blame the lawyers. It didn't involve you."

Man, she was glaring daggers into my eyes. So were my salesgirls.

"What it means, Mister Loberg, is that patients still have no clue what he's capable of doing. No warning. They're vulnerable."

"Listen, Miss Aames, I admire your passion, and by the way, you are one hell of a rider. But this case of yours is not my problem."

"Wanna know what Doctor Don's saying now? That your—wait, let me get the verbiage straight for you—that your *ex-wife* is a liar, not a victim. To hear him tell it, *he's* the victim."

The whole thing, I mean how I was reacting, was just a mystery to me. It was like my face was hot and my eyes were tearing up, like a girl. And to think, this . . . humiliation was going down in my showroom, in front of my own staff, my people.

"Well, that surely isn't right," I said. "Not my problem, though. Nope."

This lawyer, she was no dummy, and I could almost see the shift in her consciousness. Instead of staring right through me, those intense black eyes softened, the seek-and-destroy look gone out of them. She bent down to pick up the subpoena and her voice dropped with her, almost an octave as she slowed her breathing, reasoning with me now.

"Without your testimony, Donald Fallon is going to move on to the next victim, and the next. You of all people know he will."

"Wouldn't doubt it."

"I need you," she said, very much like she meant it.

"Please, Miss—"

"And Rue needs you, to bolster her position. To stand by her as only you can."

She'd located my bottom line, and nothing that I thought I'd successfully pushed out of my life and left behind stayed there. The guilt, the pain, the anger and embarrassment, the whole bag of rocks—it all came crashing back onto my head, and I could barely breathe.

"Don't say that about Rue," I sputtered. "I'll come in and be a witness, but please, don't say she needs me."

"All right," she said, not quite understanding. "I won't."

How to explain my show of emotion? I wondered. Who knew?

The cycles stood in perfect rows like soldiers awaiting orders. Behind them, through the big glass windows, traffic on PCH clashed against a bland blue sky. An overhang of gray marine layer was closing in, casting patchy shadows on the tire store across the way. Pillars of colored balloons whipped against the breeze, as did a big white banner announcing a huge sale—50 to 80% off—at the tire place across the street. Those Iranian dudes who own it are always trying something new to attract business, but today it was to no avail. The place was empty.

"See," I said. "I know something about what that woman's been through in her lifetime. And the thing is, I've got nothing, nothing at all on Rue."

The lady lawyer said she understood. And by God, I wanted to believe her.

13

DESHAUN FELLOWS, CERTIFIED PRIVATE INVESTIGATOR, FELLOWS AND ASSOCIATES, PRIVATE INVESTIGATIONS

My back's been hurting since probably around midnight, 1:00 a.m. Must've thrown it out helping Sadie move her furniture outta her little apartment. Yeah—jus' another rescue mission in the dead of night. Sadie, she's my stepdaughter from my second marriage to Ida Mae Wade, Ida Mae being the one seeking my impromptu furniture-moving services. Being that Ida Mae's my personal secretary, bookkeeper, and wife going on ten years now, and she's also the one writing my investigation reports, when Ida Mae asks me Can ya help, Deshaun, honey? The asking part's jus' a formality.

Truth is, I never should've tried to get that sofa down those second-story stairs myself, but we were in a big hurry to get outta there before Sadie's no-good bum of a fiancé, Lester Buggs, a.k.a. Bulldog—'cause of his mashed-up face and mashed-up demeanor—came home from his nightly drinking and carousing and assorted no-good whatnot he's always getting into. Bulldog, he's a mean one for sure. I checked him out back when he first started comin' around calling on Sadie, and let me tell you, the war vets, parolees, and street hustlers I check in with around Central and 125th, to a man they all says he a smooth operator, always working somethin,' but he get mad, he get personal, boy's temper turn him into some kind of Jeckyll-and-Hyde stone cold killer, shoot first, ask questions later, sleep like a baby that night. To a man, that was the word on Bulldog.

Anyhow, I set one side of the sofa up on the metal railing, run over to the other side, get the sofa sliding on down, nice n' easy does it, sliding along okey-dokey 'bout halfway down, with me underneath the damn thing scrambling like a cockroach, one eye peeled jus' in case Bulldog might've run through his drinking money early and popped on home. *Jus' get me outta here, Lord*, I'm praying, n' right about then that damn sofa starts tilting like its about to flip right over onto the patio down below. Should've jus' let it go, let her rip, 'cause that saggy-ass sofa?—It's about as valuable as ole Lester, you know? Not worth the trouble n' no damn good anyhow. Damn near let it go, too, let it crash on down n' bust into a hundred pieces, but it weren't my sofa, n' I recall thinking: *It ain't right for me to decide to junk the thing. Not my call, even if it's the right one.*

That's the problem with me, my momma used to say; *Boy, sometime you jus' think too much.*

Can you believe that? Helluva thing to say to a child, *you think too much!* But there she is.

So I'm thinking plenty anyhow because that's jus' me, I'm thinking about Sadie n' what she's gonna do about Bulldog, and I'm thinking how my momma was all things considered, a pretty wise woman, 'cause in this case, all my thinking wasn't helping Sadie a damn. And I realize, these are kids, and sometimes kids, they gotta learn on their own. How I was when I were young and headstrong. How I still am, at times, to this very day. Gotta take my knocks, you know. Nothing worth a damn in my life has come easy. Sadie? Aside from her current taste in men, she's a good kid. Maybe one of these here days she may learn something, you never know . . .

Right about then, as I'm deep in thought—well, miracle of miracles, somehow I get that sofa on down off the railing without it crushing me, and wrestle it into the truck. Doing the same thing with

Sadie, too. No Bulldog around, coast is clear, so we vamoose it on outta there, but I know it ain't enough, jus' moving her outta there, I'm still considering how I can help this girl, a girl who can't seem to help herself. So I buy Sadie breakfast at Denny's, sit through the latest hard-luck story about the latest ton o' bricks been landing on the poor girl's head these days. Worse than I imagined, too; the poor girl, she's jus' babbling like her head's gonna roll off her shoulders and land right on her stack o' flapjacks.

Turns out Lester wasn't jus' mean and a bit violent when he was drinking, which she says is pretty much whenever he feel like it, but he'd been working something steep on little Sadie, getting up close and personal with her about her job at the savings and loan. So, I ask some questions like I usually do when I'm working an investigation, jus' trying to establish the basics. Turns out ole Bulldog, he's been pushing Sadie to get him copies of these keys, keys to safe deposit boxes at the savings and loan. Got this idea, told Sadie he'd done his homework on this deal and it's surefire, cannot fail.

Homework? Call it what it is, he's plotting a felony, a federal crime! May the Lord have mercy!

He's gonna have copies of the keys made, Sadie says. Keys these wealthy bank customers are using at the bank for their safety deposit boxes, where they stash their jewels and cash and documents and assorted valuables of unestimable value?

I mean, *inestimable*. Please excuse me. When I want, I can speak with perfect clarity and diction. At times, my job depends on that, so I proceed accordingly.

Anyhow, jus' three, maybe four customers, ones come in all the time, old white ladies dripping in jewels, carrying poofy little dogs under their arms. Checking on their valuables 'cause they got time on their hands and nothing better to do but go visit with their wealth.

That's all Sadie's gotta do, i.d. some rich customers, get the box numbers they're using, then find an excuse to get into the place where the bank keeps the duplicates, a safe box in a anteroom just outside the big safe.

Damn, I jus' about spit out my silver-dollars and sausage listening to that last part.

"'Duplicates,' huh? The guy's a dummy! They probably have a master key."

"There's more, Uncle D. Don't be mad."

"Lord have mercy."

Good ole' Uncle D, he's been listening the whole time, smoking a cigar he hadn't lit since Tom Bradley became the mayor of Los Angeles. He's been pretty quiet till now, happy to watch the waitress, an old pro, slinging hash behind the counter. But Uncle D must've looked like he couldn't take it anymore.

"You want to hear this or not? I can stop if you want."

My appetite takes a nosedive, listening to all this, so I stick with my coffee.

"Go on, let's hear the whole sorry thing."

"He wanted me to return the dupes once he made copies," says Sadie. "So no one's suspecting a thing."

"Yeah, right. Bulldog, he'll jus' stroll in like a new customer, sign up to get his own safe deposit box from the bank. So he can get inside the vault, just walk on in, of course!"

"How'd you know that, Uncle D?"

"Then when he's inside, he jus' whips out the copied keys and you guessed it, Lester Buggs is going on a miniature crime spree!"

I thought Sadie would be impressed with my acumen. Thought wrong.

"Why'd I need to bother telling you, you already got all the answers?"

Typical young black man, that Bulldog, I'm thinking. Always trying too hard to find a shortcut, the lazy man's way to riches. But at what price? A federal crime? This plan was so dumb I didn't have the words. And Sadie, she's eyeing me like I'm a dartboard and she's a dart. Like this is *my* fault. I was not getting through, so I put on my investigator's hat for a minute.

"Young lady," I tell her, "that fool Lester never even thought about all the security measures at a bank like that, all they already got in the works, in place, designed for all the dumbasses of the world like him to come along, try and rip them off."

"Security measures."

"Oh, yeah. Such as, they don't let you into the vault at banks to see your deposit box, not unless you got special clearance. Otherwise, they bring it out. Also, the box has gotta get opened with two sets of keys, a bank master and the customer's key. How it's done, I'm pretty sure. Point is, nowadays, a bank's all over the process."

"Yeah, that's right, Uncle D. I never even thought of half those things till you mentioned it."

"That's because you're not a criminal. That boy must've eaten some paint chips as a kid. I can't explain it."

She pauses like an idea hit her, making me want to hide my eyes and shield my ears.

"What? Say it, girl."

"You won't get upset?"

I must be twice her size, and I was leaning too far forward over the table. *Okay, okay, time to ease off the intensity, boss.*

"Here? And disrupt this fine dining experience? I won't make a scene, darling."

She smiled, then shrugged her shoulders. "The plan, how stupid it is—I agree with you, Uncle."

"Amen to that!"

"Uncle." She shook her head like to say, *Please, just listen.* So I shut up and waited.

"The truth is, I dunno . . . bad as it may be, he surprised me with this. I mean, don't be mad, but . . . it's not like Lester."

She stirred a bite of pancake in the pool of syrup on her plate. Honestly, I was getting ready with another Uncle Knows Best piece of timely advice, lay some philosophical wood on her about the evil in men's hearts and all that. But I spared her—and myself—from that blast of hot air because it was right then, before the next lecture, that it hit me: I'd been looking at this wrong. All wrong.

"Good point, young lady," I admitted. "In fact, it's worse than it looks."

"What do you mean?"

"Bulldog, he's got a street rep' for being a smart one, always working the angles. He landed you as a girlfriend, and that took some doing. But this plan of his? Tell you what: He knows it's no good, knows it's bound to fail. But here's the thing, if he can get you to buy in, get you to commit—"

"Like, get him some keys—"

"Then he's got you under his thumb. In a very bad way."

"And I can't leave him."

"Lord have mercy."

"He probably knows the deposit box rip-off won't work."

"That's my guess."

"So tonight," she says. "My leaving like I did, I'm not so brave after all. He didn't give me a choice, did he?"

"You did good tonight," I say. "What you did took some guts."

I laid off her from there. Should've seen all this myself. It's not like some other damn fools hadn't tried that tired old deposit box plan, I don't know, twenty or thirty years ago. I remember a few heists on the west side, two in Culver City, one over by the airport, this bank right on Century Boulevard by that big strip-club sign. All those geniuses got was free room and board in a federal penitentiary for their trouble. Banks caught on and made changes as they saw fit. Security is like life. It keeps on evolving all the time. Bulldog? He's got his finger in a lot of pies around town, must've heard of the scam, figured he could use it to spin a little web around Sadie.

Know what? I need to stop looking down on young black men in general long enough to see the person standing in front of me . . . . The view from Deshaun's soapbox? It's not as good as I think. Better to have both my feet planted on the ground.

"Thanks, Uncle D," Sadie says. Relieved, but sad, like she'd been through a meat grinder. "Sometimes I forget you got lots of experience with things I don't know a thing about."

I say: Hey, no problem. I tell her, in my best authoritative voice, about the world being full of good men. Good black men, too.

"You've only got to find one, darlin.' Don't give up."

Sadie's nodding along, like, yeah, uh-huh, good advice, point taken, but she's hardly touching her food. So, I back off even more, paying a bit better attention to her needs, now. Next thing, I'm holding her hand.

"I'm scared."

"It's gonna be all right, child."

Though with Bulldog out there looking for her, that pretty surely qualifies as wishful thinking. I was honest with her about that, too. Had to be.

"What about you, Uncle D? He's gonna be real upset. Aren't you afraid?"

"Me? Nah."

Thing is, I *was* worrying about him now. Went and made a big racket moving that sofa, saw some curtains part in people's windows. People had to see me. Bulldog talks to them, they tell him about me, tell him fast, just to get rid of him? Not good. *Should've left the damn sofa, bought her a new one!* Don't know what I was thinking.

But I don't say a thing to my niece.

Good thing I've got a permit to carry a concealed weapon. Might need it when Bulldog catches up with me.

And yes, he will. Some things you jus' know. It's like, you can feel it in the air. The way a bird know it's time to fly south for the winter. I've been around enough dangerous characters in my line of work to know these things. My time to face Bulldog will come. I've jus' gotta be ready when the moment arrives.

*   *   *

That was all last night, though. Now, here at the office, my back's jus' killing me as I recollect the story of Bulldog. Even though all I'm doing is sitting on my ass.

Postman comes by, wrinkled little Asian fellow with a scowl on his face and a pile of bills in his hand, and like a polite fool, I thank the man. That's how I was raised as a black child, the great-grandson of slaves, grandson of cotton-pickers, son of a maid and a chauffeur. Too damn polite at times for my own damn good.

Sitting in a metal lawn chair under the tiny awning out front of my office, back hurting, squinting through my sunglasses though the sun isn't even out yet and it's pushing up on noon. Oh, my tired eyes and aching back! Gotta be the trip down those stairs with the sofa riding down on me like a giant's shoe about to stamp me like a cockroach. I've got some tough years on this body, for sure, but I still pump iron and hit the speed bag over at City of Angels gym at least once a week, jog three miles often as I can, so I'm holding my own, can't think of anything else would make me ache like this. Weather could be a factor, too, I guess—look at this fog and rusty brown sky out there, same thing day after day! Typical of what we get here in Inglewood, a mix o' these morning clouds come creeping on in all the time off the ocean not four, five miles away, and that sea mist, you cross that shit with a million tailpipes on the 405 freeway chugging on by, heading somewhere, anywhere other than here—well, what you get is this brownish morning sky you could cut with a knife.

So there you go. Blame it on the sofa and the weather, I guess. I shift in the chair and moan like a old man, look around, hoping nobody heard me, but there isn't a soul out and about today, sidewalk's empty.

In my kind of business you don't get a lot of walk-ins anyhow, especially on a no-name stretch of La Brea like this one. It's quiet, though, peaceful even. Jus' next door to me is Villareal's, a beauty supply place run by a Mexican woman, Miss Maria, she been here years, now, still doesn't speak much English. Nice lady, don't get me wrong, Miss Maria, she brings me homemade food all the time, tamales at Christmas, always says hello. I helped her out a few years back when she had to find a man who stole a delivery truck from a friend of hers, illegal immigrant so he couldn't go to the cops, but that truck was his whole business, his whole life. Located the truck pretty easily, in jus' two days using some damn shaky *Español* I learned a while back, working on a brick-laying crew, before I got my investigator license. Miss Maria, she wanted to pay me the going rate, but I jus' couldn't take it, knowing her business was as slow as it was at the time. Today, she's still bringing me food, paying me a couple dollars here and there, though I tell her every time she doesn't owe me a thing.

On the other side of my office is a Jewish bail bondsman, Bert Pink—and you guessed it, he's got a storefront painted about the hottest of hot pinks, jus' in case you might drive by, wonder if a man named Pink who owns a business posting bond has got a sense a humor. Or, is that what they call irony? I don't know, but that color pink will make your eyes bleed, you look at it long enough on a summer day.

Old Bert's got a different kind of clientele, but it turns out we refer some clients back and forth, some business opportunities popping up for both of us. Some tough-guy types might make fun of Bert's name and all, but Bert doesn't care, he's glad to let them have a laugh on him, especially when they're forking over the cash into the palm of his hand—which, come to think of it, is pink, too.

Anyhow, you might probably guess marketing's not exactly my cup of tea. Doesn't really have to be, though, 'cause I do my business almost entirely from referrals, word of mouth. People happy with the work I've done and willing to tell someone else about it? They're buttering my bread for me. Which isn't always the case because a lot of what I do, folks I'm working for don't wanna be tied in very close to it, you know, at least not in an attention-getting kind of way.

My specialty is simple: I dig up dirt.

Cheating spouses, people filing phony lawsuits, claiming this injury or that when the truth is, they fit as a fiddle; employees got a hand in the till when they think no one's looking. I've done all kinds of jobs, always getting hired by and paid by those folks who've been cheated on, ripped off, bamboozled. Confidential services, nothing illegal, results guaranteed, no questions asked. My clients, they like things kept on the hush hush. It's jus' how the job works.

Think about it: Nobody stuck in a jam is ever fond of broadcasting it, saying Hey, y'all, look at me, I totally fell asleep! My brain went dead! I got played for a dupe! Been drop-kicked hard, right upside the head! No, what they say is very, very little, as little as possible, and quietly. But I'm good at what I do, and Ida Mae, she writes a damn fine report, so you combine our skills, and okay, its all right for business. I get more than my share of referrals.

Wow—hold the phone, here! Today, I think I've got a rare one, a walk-in. My back's still killing me, but I straighten up, try to look presentable. Shiny black Lincoln, jus' cruises up out of nowhere and stops not ten feet from my door. Man in a dark suit gets out slowly, looking at my sign, then at me. Smiles with these small, straight teeth, nodding like yeah, this is it, this is the place. Definitely not a friend of Miss Maria's—too dressed up. Maybe a little out of Bert Pink's class of clientele as well.

Which gets me wondering: Why this empty street in Inglewood? Why me?

No good answer for either question. Something tells me this one's not gonna be a surprise walk-in . . .

Honestly, I was this close to kissing off the entire day, after the night I jus' survived playing midnight moving-man for Sadie. When the man in the suit walks in to have a chat, I take a seat in the big oak chair behind the desk, today's Hollywood Park race card spread out in front of me. And it hits me, jus' how *tired* I am. But that race card also gets me thinking how all in all, life's pretty good. Sadie is safe, it's all that matters for now. And Ida Mae? She can give me her best dirty looks, now that I'm inside my office with a stranger who may want to hire me, and I'm staring at that race card like it's my ticket to freedom. Can't help it. Ida Mae can draw her own conclusions about what I intend to do with the afternoon, that's okay. Still, I had no real designs on the day. Another hour or two jotting notes on the thoroughbreds I like in each race, maybe make a few phone calls on a missing person case, I'll be ready to clock out. It's my show, I can call it quits when I want.

And then surprise—this man wants to see Deshaun. Looks familiar, but I can't say from where, which bothers me. Anyhow, the man looks like he's coming straight from a board of directors meeting, first-class dressy suit and tie combo, expensive duds, suit as black as coal up close, the tie a burning red. A lawyer, most probably, though not the kind of lawyer any of Bert Pink's clients could ever afford.

"May I call you Deshaun?" he says, getting settled in now.

Fine, if I knew who he was. I gear up and played along with him anyway, though.

He says his name is Leyes. Gives me his card. Beverly Hills address, office high-rise on Wilshire. Starts talking me up jus' as easy as that, like we're old friends from way back. I smile and nod, sure that something's coming. He says, don't I remember him from that case I'd done work on, well known psychiatrist, Dr. Don, 'cause he sure does remember me!

I lie that yes, I do remember, but no, I don't.

Next thing you know, we're discussing the Lakers, USC football, where you can go for good barbecue in these parts, and so on, but for the life of me I can't recall his face. Small, tight nose and lips, like you might find on a possum.

"Hey, Deshaun, I've got some Kings hockey tickets for tonight that I can't use, and I'd like you to have them."

Hah! Real slick operator, I'm thinking, as if a black man has much use for hockey tickets. I'll just give them to that kid who mows my lawn, lives around the corner, Miles Davis Saunders the Third. Fine boy. He can ride his motor-scooter over to the SC campus, find a few white kids with trust fund money burning a hole in their pockets, and scalp them for a discount.

"Thank you, Mr. Leyes. That's very kind."

By this point I know for certain he isn't the man who hired me before, back when. No, the man who hired me, he was talking to a lawyer about a lawsuit, about suing his wife's doctor, her shrink. Not a lawyer, the man who hired me, not a slick operator like this one. No . . . the man was involved, in deep. He was . . . the husband, that's right!

Sad and still in shock and talking too much, telling me all about his wife, and she sounded like a head case to me. To make matters worse, her shrink was putting it to her, doing the dirty deed—right there in the shrink's own office, right on the couch. Saturday afternoons, the late late shift, I guess, right as the sun was going down. This husband who hired me, he wanted his, uh, suspicions confirmed, was what he said, but what he really wanted, even if he didn't come out and say it, was to get the goods on his wife, who sounded to me like a lost cause, you know, a real basket case. But he wanted me to get the goods on the well-known Doctor Don, Doctor Do-Ya, or whatever the doc's name was—the last name, it escapes me, now—so he could confront his wife, deal with her, then sue the doc six ways to Sunday.

"Doctor Don. You remember Donald Fallon, MD, of course?" Mr. Leyes asks me.

There went the suspense of piecing this together.

"Sure, I remember." And I did.

Dr. Don. Big shot TV shrink, supposed to help people with their problems when they called in. Think he even had his own show—I can't recall that detail for sure—but the man? I did not like the man. Donald Fallon. The kind of man who looks at you, sizing you up?—it can make your skin go cold. Like Bulldog—and I'm not just saying that. I mean, they're both the kind of person who gets weird pleasure out of someone else's pain. Torturers. Tormenters. Cruel damn people.

I remember more, now. The man who hired me, the husband, he put up a good front when he was hiring me but cried like a baby just ten feet outside the door. Ida Mae saw it, saw his legs crumple on the sidewalk, so I brought him back in, gave him a glass of water, sat him on down for another half-hour, gave him another glass a water, just let him get it off his chest. The grief and pain, I mean.

As usual, I got the dirt for this husband that hired me. Damn shrink, he may be a big-shot MD everybody's heard of, and even Ida Mae said she'd seen him on TV, but he turned out to be either wildly careless, or have a self-destructive streak in him, or both, leaving the blinds to his second-story office window tilted open, I figure so they could catch the late-afternoon light just so, catch the sunset. Well, that's not the only thing that got caught through those blinds. Mind you, I thought about asking the husband for a bigger budget, considered renting a cherry-picker, using it to get right up there into position with a camera, catch the doc on film. But it turns out I didn't need any custom set-up like that, not with that window-blind view. Instead, I go up in the parking structure across the lot from the shrink's building, went for a simple set-up, Nikon, six-hundred telephoto, stuck right on a tripod, ready to point n' shoot. Couldn't see a thing at first, but then the minute the sun started going down, sinking behind the top of that same parking structure, the shade comes creeping over the shrink's window and it is Lights! Cameras! Action! After that, I just waited to see what'd happen. Half hour or so they're just talking, nothing but sitting and talking. Then next thing you know, in the time it takes to rub my tired eyes a little, I look back in the lens and he's on her, grabbing hard, like he's wrestling an animal, tearing her clothes off, then takes her over to the couch and he's on top of her, going at it. Man moves fast, like time's a wasting.

I moved fast, too, shot three rolls in a matter of minutes. Got everything I needed. Aside from the obvious impropriety of what was going down, there was . . . an aggression about it, the way that man cornered my client's wife, like a wild animal taking down helpless prey. Left my stomach turning and churning, long after I'd stashed the camera equipment and headed back to the office.

Loberg, that's the husband's name, the man who hired me. Arnold, or Andrew. Yeah, Andrew.

He liked my work one time before, another, earlier job when he had this problem down at his chopper shop in Long Beach—inventory problem, he called it. A bike was stolen off a loading dock, turned up for sale by one of his employee's cousins? Yeah, now I remember. I did good work on that, moved fast on that one, too quick to get to know the client. Well, I did the job for him one more time on the Dr. Don thing, not that it made me feel good, to see the look on Loberg's face when I showed him the evidence. That day, he was so upset he couldn't drive. Taxi had to come and get him. After that, we had to wheel his big, expensive Harley Davidson into the office for the night.

Paid me everything and took all the pictures and negatives, didn't ask for a report. In fact, he told me not to write one.

So, why was the possum-faced lawyer here now?

Mr. Leyes, he thought we were getting along fine, but I was playing along, nothing more.

"I've heard you've got an interesting background, Deshaun. Tell me a little about it."

People usually ask this before they hire me, so I complied with Mr. Leyes's request.

"I've been doing this twenty-eight years, Mr. Leyes, since I left the Marine Corps, came home after Nam to no-job, long-hairs spitting on me outside the VA. My first wife, she left me for a man who owned two car washes on Imperial, the neighborhood honcho, or so he thought."

"That's tough," Mr. Leyes says. "Some thanks for serving your country."

There was nothing tough about the man, so how would he know to comment? But I let it go.

"I had to fall back on the skills I learned as an MP, sir."

"Please, call me Mitch."

"Okay, Mitch. It took a long time and lots of moonlighting penny-ante little side jobs till I built up the business, but I did it."

"Very nice," he says—or he might've said that. Don't know for sure; I was mighty distracted, thinking about the times I've had to sit down to sift through the piles of dirt I've found, showing a man the mess his wife had made of their marriage. Or vice versa, more often than not. No matter how many times I've done it, it never gets any easier to do. Mr. Loberg was a decent fellow, and I felt bad for him, same as all the others. Truly I did.

By now I was getting tired of talking with Mitch Leyes, who now wanted to chat about basketball and the Late Show, to be precise. He was getting on my nerves a little, wouldn't have known Kobe Bryant from a Kobe burger or Magic Johnson from magic beans. So I put a question to him outright, asked him what was his precise connection to my client.

That stopped the bullshit on a dime.

He didn't say anything the least bit specific. Claimed to be a friend, an interested party who wished to remain in the background.

"My client is Mister Andrew Loberg," I tell him, "and—"

"Deshaun—"

"—you're not him. You've heard of confidentiality with clients and their business? The way I see it, that means I've got no business to discuss with you. None at all."

"That's all in the past," he says, like I'm the one who doesn't get it. "You and I need to discuss the results of your investigation. But only in the abstract. The fact that you gathered evidence, and that evidence exists. That's all."

"You're not the client."

"No, I'm not but we both want the same thing. We both want the results to remain very, very confidential."

"Confidentiality doesn't have a shelf life on it. Once a secret, always a secret. But that starts here. I don't take orders from you, sir."

He almost snickers, looks around at my place as if we're in a pigsty and he isn't about to get dirty.

"What? I say something funny to you?"

"This is so . . . unnecessary. Really, if money is what you want, rest assured—"

"Sir, I've got half a mind to throw your ass outta here."

Then he cuts to the chase—hard.

"No, you'll hear me. I will talk and you will listen."

"I'm asking you politely to leave. You refuse, it's at your own risk."

Mr. Leyes just keeps smiling. "You're not the only investigator here. I know things."

"Such as?"

"Oh, that you've got family back in Louisiana." He takes a tiny stroll in a circle, appraising my office again. "And I know something about all the hardship they've been facing. You're a kind man,

Deshaun. A generous spirit. You've been sending money to them ever since Katrina, to help them get back on their feet. Very commendable of you, Deshaun. Very . . . noble."

"You getting into my personal business is not, sir. That's crossing a line."

The phony smile is gone. "Nobility is not one of my strong suits in life. I dare say I'm jealous."

"What do you want?"

He takes his time, letting me know he's in control. "Go and see them," he says finally. "Help them out the way you only wished you could before. Show them a good time. Make it a vacation."

Then he hands me a blank white envelope, thick and heavy. I don't need to peek inside to know what's in there. If it's twenties, maybe a couple grand. If it's hundreds, maybe five or ten times that. Leyes's black-as-night suit is lined with tiny white pinstripes. I hadn't noticed that detail until now. That suit probably costs more than every suit I own put together. To my private shame, he has me thinking.

"A vacation."

"Yes. An extended vacation."

"Just how extended are we talking about?"

He tells me Dr. Don's medical license is in trouble. Tells me how long he wants me to visit the kinfolk. When I say nothing in return, he smiles as if he just purchased my soul, and I want to slap that grin right off his possum face. But I don't. That envelope is too heavy.

The Lincoln pulls out onto La Brea and is gone.

I don't have to open that envelope to know what's inside. But I look. Hundreds, with bands binding them. First thing I'm thinking about is counting, thinking how maybe I can break some off, a little Hollywood Park fund jus' for today. Next, I'm wondering how I'm gonna break it to Ida Mae that we've gotta scoot, and right now, in the midst of Sadie's time of need, what with her situation with Bulldog. But then I stick my thumb farther into that envelope and see there's more than a few stacks, but three, no four, each of them shaped like slender, perfect bricks. Machine probably did the binding—something a supposed expert on bank operations like the great Uncle D should know. Man oh man, I said too much at breakfast with the girl, pontificating like I'm the last word on relationships. Now, I've gotta live with the regret of knowing I went too far. But then I thumb back those perfect stacks of Franklins, and like that, I see Sadie's situation is no problem, we can jus' bring her right along with us. Girl's got no real prospects at that bank, anyhow.

A reasonable solution, but before I can congratulate myself on solving the Sadie Problem . . . holy Jesus and the Lord have mercy—I've got another visitor! *And whoa, boy, hold on to your hat, Deshaun, this one's not a walk-in, either.*

"Mr. Fellows?" says this tall, black-haired, very fine white woman.

"Yes, ma'am," I say like my face is rubber.

Sounded like I said "it's ham." Trying not to stare, but she's got a special look. Nice tan, slipping off her shades with one hand, other one stretched out for a handshake. Wow, coming in closer she looks like she's from a rock band or something with her black eye makeup and long eyelashes, a chiseled body to go with a chiseled face. And attitude, too, like she's not afraid to kick ass and take names if it comes to that. But wait, something . . . I dunno, a little off about those eyes, though, as if she's in two places at one time. I shake her hand and she gives me a card.

"Department of Justice, Office of the Attorney General," I say. "How nice of you to drop in."

"You gave me no choice, Mr. Fellows. I've tried you by phone, but you haven't returned any of my calls."

"Oh, right, well, I'm very sorry about that. Been very, uh, busy lately."

She watches me as I roll up the Hollywood Park race card, and damn, I could feel my hind-end puckering. Like all that money sitting in the envelope I was still holding was stolen or something.

Damn, gotta plan your retirement soon, 'cause this kind of shit's gonna give you a heart attack one of these days!

When she comes straight out and asks about the investigation I did for Andrew Loberg, the one involving Dr. Donald Fallon, I damn near fall out of my chair.

Naturally, I play dumb, but she reads my face. Smart girl. Instantly she wants to know about why I didn't cooperate with the Medical Board of California when they investigated the matter.

I tell her I'm sorry, but my investigations are confidential, I couldn't say anything even if I wanted to. She says sure, that's fine, but she needs me to know what this is about. She's going after the doc who took advantage of his patient, Rue Loberg. Sexual misconduct, she calls it. Gross negligence. Doctor Don, a hot-stuff shrink. A man who hurts women. A man who has to be stopped or he'll just do it again to someone else, and I could take that to the bank.

Bank. She says the word and boom! My brain is stuck on that money again, no helping it.

"Love to assist you, Miss Aames, but I'm retiring this month. Twenty-eight years and I realize I've finally had enough."

"How nice," she says through tight lips.

"Going back to Louisiana, ma'am, got family there."

"Just like that."

"Yes, ma'am, just like that."

"I need to call you as a witness," she says, handing me a paper. "Testify for me. Then you can retire."

"I told you, Miss Aames, what I did on that old case was confidential."

She shrugs, brushing off my logic. "Rue Loberg and her husband sued Doctor Fallon. They waived that confidentiality when they made public their allegations back in the civil case. You were hired by Mister Loberg, which means your client signed that waiver."

Why I take the paper she gave me, I do not know. Maybe because she seems like the kind of woman you don't defy. Of course, it was a subpoena. Witness. Medical Board. Matter of the Accusation against Donald Fallon, MD. A court date coming up fast on the calendar. A Fourth Street address, downtown LA, sixth floor.

I hand it back. "Like I say, I'm retiring, ma'am, going to Louisiana."

"You have been served. Be there or be square."

By this point my boxer shorts are chapping. First that snake Mr. Leyes, and now, this pushy young woman with her precious case for the state.

"I will be in Louisiana," I say firmly. "This piece of paper can't touch me there."

"You don't get it, do you?"

"Go to hell."

"Watch me go," she says, real calm. "First, I'll go to Superior Court, get a judge to issue an order of contempt due to your failure to appear. Then he'll issue a warrant for your arrest."

"That's just fine and dandy," I say. "But a warrant won't reach out of state."

"Well, guess what? The governor of California is my former boss, the Attorney General. He gets along swimmingly with the governor of Louisiana, who, when he hears about you, won't like the idea of a California law-breaker hiding out in his state. You'll be expedited, sir. And you'll foot the bill, which will be enormous."

This young lady seems to know her stuff, leaving me with nothing to say in response.

This is some kind of battle shaping up. The visit from the possum-face lawyer with all that cash—no coincidence. The state of California wanted Dr. Don's ass, and his hired hacks weren't rolling over. It all made sense. But my next move? It wasn't shaping up so quickly here.

A beer-delivery truck snorts out on La Brea, prompting the lawyer lady to peek her head inside the open door to my office. She looks about, seems to be noticing everything in its usual place, right down to the ceiling fan that needs dusting, the pencils in an Auto Club can, the Jackie Robinson bobblehead on the shelf.

"You don't look like you're going anywhere, Mister Fellows. What changed so suddenly?"

I wanna fire off a powerful comeback, but before I even open my mouth to speak, I remember the money—and like a dead bang idiot I stare right down on the envelope in my lap.

She's staring down there, too, and now at my head, her eyes like laser beams. She laughs quietly, like whistling.

"They bought you off."

"This?" I say like the world's worst actor. "No, no, this is rent money!"

"You're a coward."

Right then, I didn't know what I might do, but I was tired from last night and confused from my visit with Mr. Leyes being followed so quickly by the State of California, attorney general and all, n' that tiredness and confusion was makin' a bad brew inside me. 'Cause I gotta say, jus' physically throwing her ass into the gutter did come to mind—and then, like that I was moving toward her, and she looked scared, still a little crazy and setting herself to make a stand, but scared, and I could see the fear and conflict in those black eyes of her.

"I've had about enough of you."

Then I hear a scream.

"Deshaun Fellows!"

Ida Mae, of course.

"Not now! I will speak to you in just one minute!" I tell the wife.

The woman is half my size, Ida Mae, but when she puts her hands on those sweet little hips? It's like she doubles in height.

"Stand back, Deshaun," she orders me. "Give her some breathing room, for goodness sakes."

I do jus' that. Try to say something to both of them to explain, but instead I just sputter like my lawnmower when the plugs need to be changed out. That Mr. Big Stuff advice I handed down to Sadie last night about being realistic? Well, it's hanging over my head now, pressing down—as if I could just run away to Louisiana, and not look back.

As if! You are so much smarter than that, man!

Life just doesn't work that way, not in my experience. Nothing is ever that neat and easy. Nothing good, at least, nothing right. I let go of the whole idea of the money right then and there. Snapped out of my funk.

"I didn't mean to scare you, ma'am. I apologize if I did."

"Thank you for your time, Mr. Fellows," the prosecutor Bradley Aames says, calmer but with an edge, a hidden advantage, like she's holding an invisible hammer.

"Uh-huh," I say, still holding the subpoena.

"I'll be sure to touch base with you before you testify. And thank you, ma'am." She nods at Ida Mae.

Then smooth as silk, she glides out the door. Had to know how good she looked in the eyes of any man who could see. That would include me, and I couldn't help but watch her go, skipping across La Brea to a midnight-blue, very fine Chevy muscle car, a Chevelle that sounds like a row of bass drums in a parade when she starts it up.

"Crazy day," I say lightly, turning back inside, already working on formulating the words I'll need to soothe the wife's nerves. Gotta come up with something firm and believable, I tell myself, a fresh game plan that'll make everything alright. It better be damn good, too.

"Un-hmm." Ida Mae's jus' standing there, cross-armed, not budging, and instantly I know she's way, way beyond any convenient explanations I may cook up. Too smart, and who knows how much she's heard between me and both of my visitors? That rear door to her office was open the whole time, and she's nobody's fool, my Ida Mae.

No, you may as well ease off the fast-talking formulations. Maybe you could try playing it straight, genius.

And . . . oh my, it's even worse than that! Ida Mae? She's jus' checking what's . . . in my hand.

"What's in the envelope, honey?"

Nothing to say, man—when she calls me honey, I know I'm under her thumb.

14

CRAIG WEAVER, MD

Change is good, I like to tell patients. A sign of life, of growth. Hope.

This time when I went to Malibu, it was different from the last time. This time, I wasn't responding to a phone call from a breathless apologetic stranger asking if I could help his roommate—well, his friend—*well, her name is Bradlee Aames and she's got your business card Dr. Weaver, so I just figured . . .*

This time, the call came from Bradlee herself, and she sounded not the least bit excited. So this time, I had a better idea what to expect. Okay, so that was the little lie I was telling myself.

The phone woke me out of a dream. I was in a grassy meadow, peacefully flying a kite, but then a gust of wind picked me up, tore me off the ground, and thrust me high up into the clouds until suddenly, the kite was gone and I was falling, straight down, fast and hard and bracing for impact. But there was nothing beneath me, just the sensation of descending forever, into nothingness . . .

"Hey, what are you doing?"

"Uh, sleep. I mean, sleeping. What time is it?"

"Oh, yeah, sorry. Hey, you sound a little out of breath."

"I was . . . having a dream."

"Huh. This is quite a moment. I just woke a shrink from a dream. I mean, how many people can say that?"

"No big thing," I said. "One time I was out driving and saw a guy stuck on the side of the road, no one around, so I pulled over to help. The guy? My mechanic."

She laughed. "I love it."

Jesus—if you could catch me coming out of a deep sleep, I was quite the charming bastard, it seemed.

We were supposed to talk when she needed it, when her stress-level rose and it seemed her mind was slipping into instability. My idea, my friendly offer. All part of the plan. Although the hour was absurdly late once again she wasn't having an emergency; apparently she'd effectively anticipated one coming. Or so I surmised. So, okay then, we were meeting in the absolute dead of night; so what? She's a quirky girl.

Despite my misgivings about the trial and Rue Loberg testifying for the board, I was impressed with Bradlee's judgment. Her discretion.

Maybe this can work, I told myself. Whatever *this* is.

Of course, past-midnight meetings with a woman that probably suffers from depression or psychosis or an anxiety disorder or even all three—well, you could search through every medical journal in the land and never find a methodology quite like this one. So hey, I'm an original, half-asleep charming bastard.

Rumbling up Pacific Coast Highway, smooth and pale with streetlit glare, as devoid of life as a dry riverbed on the moon. I tried to review a mental checklist of things to say, of how to proceed; yet, despite my best efforts, my mind kept fixing on what might be termed nonclinical observations.

Female objectification. Or would one term it personal infatuation?

A wedge in the dark hillside to my right flashes by, and I think of full breasts; two trees in silhouette bring to mind a heart-shaped der-riere. Deep thoughts from a guy with my training and experience. I knew that on an elemental level I wanted to help as a clinician, but on another level, I was kidding myself.

I pulled into the lot of the all-night diner she'd chosen, rolling my passenger window down so I could hear the gravel crunching beneath my tires. The damp air swiped across my face like a wet rag. *Yeah, guy,* the voice inside me said, *that rag's going to be wrapped around your heart in no time. You're out of your depth, Craiggy.*

My jeans felt starched and a half-size too small. Or maybe I just hadn't worn them in a while. Should I unzip the jacket to show off the surf wear-label tee I'd so carefully selected? Ah, crap—the logo was on the back; it wouldn't even matter. Unless I took my jacket off and . . . walked in backward? Brilliant.

Clinical observation: Craig Weaver lacks confidence with women.

Acknowledging this deficiency, I paused by the door to the joint and said a simple prayer before entering.

God, please allow me to summon my best self, from wherever that self may be stashed. Make it available to me, God, make it apparent. If only for an hour.

The café was the kind that trades in nostalgia: white vinyl, black and red trim, lots of chrome. An old-style fifties counter. Lots of seats in a row, but no customers. Jukebox music: a bygone classic about a little runaway playing softly.

She waved me over to a corner booth. A bucket seat curved around her snugly, a scene suggesting Fay Wray wrapped in King Kong's giant open hand. My psychological training rendered an instant interpretation of the image: Bradlee was attractive, an object of desire, while Kong symbolized her psychosis, holding her captive in its dangerous, powerful grip. Was I about to battle Kong for her sanity? Beauty and the beast, and Dr. Craig to the rescue. Oh, please. What an overanalyzed overdramatization.

We studied our menus but only came up with an order of two coffees and ice waters with lemon, which plainly would not do. I tacked on an apple pie a la mode to appease our waitress, a grumbling older gal who eyeballed me as if I were up to no good just by being in the place, in this female company, at this hour. The fact that we were the only customers amplified my every move.

"I like your take-control style, Craig," Bradlee remarked as I stacked our menus behind the vintage song-selector in our booth. I couldn't tell if she was serious or mocking me.

Bradlee told me she'd been out surfing Malibu. I asked her if she thought such a thing was safe, considering what happened the last time. She pointed out the fact that she'd done it a hundred other times without a problem. And that I wasn't her dad. I said I wasn't trying to be, and that she was being rude for suggesting that I was. She shrugged.

"Sorry. Guess I have trouble opening up sometimes."

"How can I help?" I said, which sounded so forced I wanted to kick myself.

"No need to psychoanalyze me. Not yet, at least."

I told her I had no intention of doing that. We could talk, that was all.

As seems to be the norm in every restaurant in America, just as we seemed on the edge of something real passing between us—a spark of truth, a meeting of the minds—that goddamned waitress materialized at my elbow with our coffee and pie. When she said she'd be right back with our ice waters, I told her to take her time. Matched her dirty look with something approaching white-hot hatred.

"You look a little tense," Bradlee said.

My next line of zippy patter was dissolved by the acid on my tongue. "Aren't you the astute observer."

"Okay. Maybe you should've met me earlier to slide a few," she said with an eye-roll.

I hoisted my coffee and drank. First for the heat, then for the act of it, the sheer distraction. My hands were grateful for something to do. Half a cup later, the stuff hit my nervous system. I retracted all my vicious thoughts directed toward our waitress, the wonderful caffeine goddess who'd just transported me.

"Good coffee?"

"Not good, the best."

"Feeling better?"

"Not fully awake, but I'll get there."

The ice waters were delivered, along with the check. "Anything else, just holler," the waitress told us.

"More coffee soon," I said. "It's spectacular."

But she'd walked away and didn't hear me. Or acted like she didn't.

"Great ambience, this place," I said lightly.

"You're adding a lot to that bottom line, Doctor."

The waitress returned and dutifully refilled me, for which I offered my profuse thanks as she groaned and went away.

"Well, I do want to tell you about tonight," Bradlee said. "But I feel a little odd doing so. A little . . . raw."

"Why do you think that is?"

She drummed her fingertips on the tabletop.

"What?" I asked.

"You sound like a therapist again."

"Sorry, it's what I do. I'm just used to asking questions."

She swirled a spoon in her coffee but didn't take a drink. "Maybe you could tell me a few things about yourself, you know, to even things up in the revelations department."

I asked her what she wanted to know.

"Another question, Craig."

"Sorry. Instinct, I guess."

"Okay, fine," she said. "I'll answer your question with a question. I want to know why you look at me that way, but you don't do anything."

Then she sat back a little, nestling into the booth. Right in King Kong's grasp.

I looked around. All the empty booths looked right back. White speckled tabletop—why the hell did I order apple pie? I despise apple pie. I should've given our waitress, the Hover Queen, a twenty just to leave us alone, that would have done the trick. Just keep the coffee coming, but only if I raise my cup. The rest of the time? Stay away. The Hover Queen would understand the stay-away bribe for what it was, would appreciate my honesty.

"More coffee?"

"Sure," I said, holding out my cup.

"Anything else—"

"—I'll be sure to alert you." I slapped a twenty on the table. "This is for you to leave us alone, unless I give you the signal."

"I'd like to give you a signal all right, but fine, have it your way!"

The waitress stalked off muttering unkind things about her ungrateful customer as that same customer got busy flipping her off dually, with both hands from beneath the table and with great feeling. Bradlee seemed entertained by my discomfort, which I thought I was hiding better than I was.

"Next time we'll find someplace more intimate to talk," I said. "Like, in line at the movies."

"You mean, on a date."

I slurped at my coffee without accounting for the refill. Too hot; it burned the roof of my mouth.

"You okay, doc?"

"More cream." I gasped, clutching at my water glass.

For her part, Bradlee Aames simply sat there, looking smart and lovely and well above my station in the human sexual pecking order. "You don't want to talk about yourself, it's okay," she said.

"No, no. For starters, a date would, uh, be great," I said, rubbing my smoldering gums.

"Try not to sound so enthusiastic. I'll get a big head."

I was making this way too difficult. Harpooning my chances. The key to getting through this, I knew, was to be brutally honest with myself, to remove my desire. Beginning with a simple premise.

Face it, dude, you've got no shot with this girl, no shot whatsoever.

That tack actually worked; having nothing to lose, as I had nothing really to gain, I felt my man-on-the-move persona crumble, and along with it any pressure I'd been under to impress Bradlee Aames, to make her want me. But the problem is, what follows a complete dissolution of personal want or need, what comes after like a latent side effect, is a void. Feeling left behind. Empty. Hollow. A leftover ache.

"Hey, Craig Weaver. Still with me?"

Her hand came out and touched mine.

"My do-gooder inclinations are not noble, not in the least," I said.

She seemed amused with my confession. "So? Join the club."

She wanted to hear me talk about me. "Don't tell me about your favorite color, or whether you thought the moon landing was faked. You're a handsome, young, educated professional. What I'd like to know is why you're still single."

To be sure, she was only being playful, and I appreciated the gesture. But it took me in a different direction altogether, on a course that for better or worse, seemed inevitable. While I can't remember the exact words I spoke—what was it? Perhaps the hour of night, the coffee, the attention coming from this odd and intimidating but quirky and very beautiful woman, and a sense of nothing-to-lose, what-the-hell insecurity swamping me—I can't say for certain. Perhaps these factors coalesced, all at once, into a potent bullshit antidote, and I found myself talking straight and true and without the usual cloak of distance and intellectual density. This is more or less what I told her.

Back in the day, I was a hot-shit guy with plans: A year in the Peace Corps after graduating from Berkeley with honors; medical school, preferably Harvard, my father's alma mater; and what the hell, with my stellar grades I'd be attending on a scholarship; a well-timed, glibly self-satisfied marriage proposal to my blonde-haired, blue-eyed cutie of a sweetheart Deb, maybe springing it on her while cruising the Grand Canal in a Venice gondola or as the helicopter hovered over the fiery maw of Mauna Kea. *My life is hands-down fabulous*, I used to think. *All I've gotta do is show up every day and I'm set.*

Turns out my self-satisfied attendance wasn't enough, not by a mile. It all took an epic nosedive when Deb got a part-time job waitressing at an upscale steakhouse and fell in love with the owner—the married-with-three-kids owner, who was actually insane enough to reciprocate. In my rage at being dumped, I had my own moment of insanity, ringing the manager's wife's doorbell one afternoon when she was home alone and telling her the name of the motel two miles away where her husband could be found at that precise hour with the object of his affections. Thought I was pretty slick, too, until the police came to campus the next morning and plucked me out of pre-med chemistry to interview me. It seemed my actions had set off a chain of events. Deb made it to an ICU still alive but with six bullets in her. The crime-scene photos they showed me were horrific, like a form of latent punishment. The one I remember best was like a top-down portrait, husband and wife hastily reunited and posing for eternal posterity. Both of them staring face-up at the ceiling on an unmade queen, their stiff limbs stacked end over end, like kindling awaiting a hot match.

You could say that incident changed me. Forever. By a single instance of acting on impulse, I'd orphaned three innocent children and essentially murdered their parents. Deb dropped out of school; the bullet that nicked the base of her spine caused her left side to droop, requiring multiple surgeries, and the cheerleader's glow that was her most visible feature drained out of her cheeks for good. I dropped out of the human race for a while, kissing off med school. My father stopped talking to me; I was such a "grave disappointment," Mr. Everything just didn't have it in him to shoulder that burden. I left home, got a job working for the Southern Pacific railroad, overslept, and came in work late several times, which got me fired. Didn't even realize that the disrupted sleep patterns were a symptom of major depression, but the boss who canned me walked me to my car, gave me an extra hundred bucks of his own, and made me promise to get evaluated. Got some treatment through my dad's insurance plan—which painfully indentured me to him at the time, but I didn't want to live anyway, so what was a little more pain? It's a miracle I ever made it back, but fixing on med school and studying hard for my entrance exams provided the best distraction I could find at the time, and really, pursuing my education was what saved me.

"So, for me," I said, "impulse control is a personal challenge I take very seriously."

Bradlee smiled as if she knew I wanted to kiss her—and that the fabulous internal braking system I'd just touted would halt any such spontaneous gesture dead in its tracks.

Like a good sport, I smiled back.

"Thanks," she said. "For the backstory. I just thought you'd say you were too busy to get out much."

I slapped my forehead like I'd forgot. "That too."

"You're funny."

How was the surfing tonight? I asked.

"Not bad. Not good, though. Inconsistent."

"What's it feel like, being out there in the dark, all by yourself in that limitless space?"

A noisy sports car downshifted on PCH as it blew by the diner. Bradlee watched it go before turning back to me.

"I wasn't alone."

"Miki Dora."

She nodded. "Tearing it up."

"If you want to, um talk . . . ."

She picked up a fork and took a stab at my slice of pie, the blob of ice cream slipping away like a melting polar cap. "Not really. Although I wouldn't mind knowing what a psychiatrist thinks. Just not right this minute. Not yet."

"So, how's the Doctor Don case going?"

"Shitty. No one's cooperating. The witnesses, I mean. And I just found out my expert's in Vienna."

"Vienna?"

"Yeah. At some big medical conference."

"I know the one. It has to do with developing standards of practice for newer medications. But that's not until next month."

At that Bradlee looked steamed. A raw sense of agitation came over her, and her eyes darted as she checked behind us. Nothing much to see: a row of empty booths, a lot of black pavement beyond the huge panes of glass, occasional bursts of car lights streaking by, gearboxes grunting out on PCH. My guess was she was fighting a delusion, but I didn't dare to suggest as much.

"You're looking at me funny," she said, putting me on the spot.

"Sorry. You seem upset."

"That doesn't mean I'm crazy."

"I never—"

"Want to know what I think?" she blurted. "My expert? He got paid to disappear for awhile. That worm Heidegger probably bought his airline tickets, booked the hotel, and threw in a Viennese call girl to keep him busy."

"That's terrible."

She stared up at the dull white ceiling and a fan that wasn't moving. I thought I saw her lip quiver, as if she were conversing with someone only she could see. Next thing, she glared at me.

"Very insightful, doctor."

"So, uh, does that mean the case is over?"

She took another bite of my pie as if to stave off starvation. I began to think that when she reached a certain plateau of stress, her mind might go sideways.

"What else can I do but get another expert." She swallowed her bite. "Keep putting the case together. Or die trying."

I took a bite of pie, which tasted like spiced rubber. The ice cream was better, and I thought of Mom, fast asleep, the shock she'd register to know I was up now, in the middle of the night, sorting through my excitement with a court case and the exotic, unpredictable company I was keeping.

"So," I said. "This is why you're out surfing in the night. The case is falling apart, you're feeling the strain. Naturally, you go surfing."

"That's your analysis."

"Just a small series of observations."

"Glad I'm not paying for this."

Her defiance struck me as a defense mechanism. *Do what you're good at,* I told myself. *Do what you came here for. Do your damn job.*

"There's more," I said.

"I'd certainly hope so."

"I've done some research on Miki Dora. I know about his place in the surf world. The Dark Knight, the bad boy, the ultimate iconoclast who never had a real job, who bailed out when he felt Malibu was ruined. Miki Dora didn't surf Malibu tonight. You know that."

He coffee cup clanked when she set it on the table between us. "You don't believe me."

"I wasn't there, so I can't argue facts. But I have no doubt that you believe you saw him. What's important is to understand what this means to you."

"I'm not wired up, I see things."

"You're not self-medicating."

She wiped a pile of hair off her forehead and studied the window glare.

"No." Bradlee wrapped her arms around herself and squeezed her shoulders. "In case you haven't noticed, sometimes I don't know my own mind, doc."

"Craig."

She sighed. "Sorry. Craig. If you'd tell me what you think it means, I'd be grateful to you."

I told her that as she knew, Dora was a romantic figure, a symbol of an idealized time gone by, a rebel revered by surfers because he never knuckled under and joined straight society, never bowed to the system. But he was also a canny individual who played up his own myth whenever it was to his advantage to do so. A fast-talker and a scammer, if the situation presented. There was a duality to his persona, a real side, and an imagined side to him. He seemed to have little trouble switching back and forth. Eventually, he fled to exotic, faraway places, perpetually searching for the perfect wave. At one point in his life, though, he was merely evading charges of credit card fraud in a California court. He was extradited, placed in custody, took a plea, and did time for his crime. Took up The Search again.

"So why would he want to come back here, and surf with me?"

"I think you have it the other way around."

Her arms wrapped herself even tighter.

"For you, it's like this," I said. "To surf Malibu in the middle of the night, the one time when the place is abandoned, just like in the old days, is an attempt to go back in time to an earlier era when the place, and the whole surfing experience, was still unspoiled. I think you want to go someplace else, the way Dora did."

Bradlee stirred her coffee with a spoon in a slow circle, but didn't drink. "Escape. Leave the whole stinking dung heap behind."

"Something like that."

"Makes sense, the way this case is going."

"You seemed pretty committed to the outcome, the last time I saw you."

She raised the spoon and licked it, cocking her head. "Yeah, well since then I've gotten my brains beaten in by an army of gutless men who got what they wanted and don't give a shit about what the esteemed Doctor Don did to an innocent patient."

"But Rue was there. She'll testify."

"Fine, but she'll be on her own. I've got no corroboration."

"She's telling the truth."

"Dr. Don will deny anything happened. It'll be his word against hers, the sum total of which will fall well below the clear-and-convincing-evidence standard I've gotta meet."

"But—"

"He'll skate."

We sat there sullenly until Bradlee dug into her purse and pulled out a baggie full of pretty blue capsule-shaped pills bearing the letters OC.

"Oxycontin," I said, not quite picturing how my patient, the ever-fragile Rue, would survive a bout on the witness stand with Dr. Don's team of lawyers. Not with Bradlee Aames fighting off psychotic episodes as the pressures of trial slowly cracked open her skull. What had I been thinking, encouraging Rue to face down her demons? They'd destroy her in court, and then I'd carry the guilt of her demise on my back for all time.

But no—I don't want the weight, can't take the weight. Whatever Rue Loberg decides, she'll have to own it, live with it.

She nodded. "Like a rusty safety valve that doesn't always open. Shouldn't have gone to the baggie."

"Tonight?"

"After my session. Without any Oxy? Hey, you never know, Dora might've followed me right up the sand and swept me away from all this"—she waved a hand at the empty rows of bucket seats—"uphol-stered splendor."

The waitress, thinking Bradlee had motioned for her, hobbled over, eyeing the check, which was still on a tray. Then she noted the baggie of drugs and frowned.

"We're good," I said.

Bradlee clutched the baggie proprietarily. "Perfecta-mundo, thanks."

The waitress hardened, her wrinkles contorting on her forehead. "Okay, you two, pay up and go."

Not what I had in mind. I raised my cup and asked for a refill.

"And another piece of pie," Bradlee said, picking up my vibe. "I've eaten most of his."

The waitress scowled. "We don't serve dopers. You can take your business elsewhere."

"They're prescription meds," Bradlee said.

"And I've got some real estate here in my bag," the waitress countered.

My opportunity to pay the woman to simply leave us alone had arrived, though later and not quite as planned. I stood up, slapped a twenty on the table, and took Bradlee by the hand to guide her out of that hideous booth.

"Got half a mind to call the cops," the waitress said as we strode past a row of empty swivel chairs along the counter. Bradlee turned on her heel.

"This man is an MD. A psychiatrist."

I held up a hand as if I was ready to swear to it. "All true."

"That means he can prescribe drugs legally. He came here to dis-pense advice, though, not drugs, and I was lucky enough to be the beneficiary of that advice. That is, when you weren't interrupting us with your inane entreaties."

The woman blinked at Bradlee. "I'll entreaty you right out that door."

Bradlee flicked her hand toward the kitchen. "Thank you for a splendid time. Your unique brand of tough love represents a true breakthrough in food services."

"Get out."

We kept going, but at our own unhurried pace. As we cruised past the big metal cash register with the toothpick dispenser and complementary mints perched up top, I stopped to scoop some of both.

I gave one last tip of an invisible hat. "Ma'am."

The woman returned the gesture. "Doctor Smartass."

She fired another grumbled parting shot, but the words of consternation seemed to fade in our wake, splattering against the double-paned glass doors that clipped shut behind us as we reentered the night. Like that, the diner experience was done and the cool salt air rushed our senses and it was as if we were shooting through a portal into another plane of experience. A gathering roar: the droning wails of a delivery truck blasting one way and an RV barreling along the other way rose and rose until—with a screaming wah!-wah!—they briefly crossed paths, then slipped off again into the quiet. A denouement: the highway sighing, then going pleasantly dark and dead. But then, there was more—like a lover's cooing tease you could hear the faint steady hush and kiss of surf on sand. Climactically, a star-bright sky threw a canopy of pulsing glitter over our heads when we weren't looking.

That sky had our attention now. Standing spellbound beside her car, our backs arched, we were hushed—no need to speak, nothing to say; just let this infinite billion-mile vista of cosmos roll on up for our viewing pleasure and roll right over our shabby wants and needs and petty concerns.

"You're smiling," Bradlee said, her eyes trained close to vertical, just like mine.

"Well . . . God is smiling back."

"I love the night."

She squeezed my hand and leaned her shoulder into mine. My thoughts were clear and I was pierced by a vision of my future, of the spotless beauty of giving love selflessly. It was all I wanted to do, and that recognition alone made for one of the most perfect moments of my life. I had not seen any of this coming.

"I have to tell you something," I said, "but first, please know that I'm not saying this now because I want to kiss you."

"Wouldn't dream of it."

"Really, I'm serious."

"About what—killing the moment? Jesus, Craig, whatever the hell it is, kindly spit it out before the moment passes."

"You're right. Sorry. I just . . . well . . ."

"I'm waiting, Doctor Smartass."

"Okay, okay. It's . . . about Dora."

She turned a little to face me better.

"You saw him that night you and Reevesy came out."

"Wait. I don't know what I saw. Over by the pier, there's this kind of surreal glow coming off the water under the lights, and it's really hard to make out—"

"What was he doing?"

I was miffed that she'd cut me off. "Crocheting a new sweater. What do you think?"

"I knew it!" She paused, gently rubbing her forehead. "So . . . I don't know what this means."

"Me neither. I don't even know what I saw, to be honest. It was just a figure."

"Stop being so honest, it's overrated. You saw Dora."

"I didn't say that."

"You're not alone. Next time you're at Malibu, read the message on the wall."

"It's just an expression."

She shrugged, then gave a tiny laugh as she came up on her tiptoes and kissed me on the lips. "So is this."

I was about to say something perfectly arcane and byzantine, but a don't-be-a-complete-horse's-ass-Craig override deep in my brain's social circuitry took immediate effect, locking down my overeager mug.

"I like you, Doctor Smartass. Even if your eyesight's not so hot."

Bathed in blue-white starshine, I clenched her tight against my body as if to taunt an indifferent universe. "So who's crazy now?" she whispered.

15

WENDY GLICK, MEDICAL DOCTOR

Subleasing a medical suite with other medical practitioners has its pluses and minuses. The obvious upside: you get to share expenses for the cost of the office space itself, a common lobby, and a receptionist. I, for one, certainly need to be economical; when I first tried going solo seven years ago around here—a good Jewish psychiatrist in a good Jewish neighborhood just west of Fairfax practically bursting with video-game-addicted kids; obsessive-compulsive tiger moms; and type-A Hollywood dealmakers with the commensurate array of ulcers, drinking problems, hair-loss issues, and Napoleon complexes—you'd have thought the walk-in business would have more than covered the rent, which was astronomical even on the four-hundred-square-foot cracker box I was squeezed into. But the walk-ins, they walked on by and kept on going, leaving me with malpractice premiums, utilities, CPA fees, and professional association and licensing dues that quickly devoured what little balance was left in my general account each month. Either I could cut my overhead or file for bankruptcy; that is, eat, or starve.

And yes, I do like to eat—way too much, in fact. So two years ago I moved in here.

But playing in the sandbox with professional colleagues can also be a pain in the patootie, as I catch more lingering looks and snarky remarks from my own brethren than I ever would if I hung out my shingle in a dodgy little strip-mall space on Pico or Olympic. Wendy, my dear, a far more successful shrink on my floor told me just last week, you don't network enough. You've got to reach out to the community, get out there and mingle. Press the flesh.

Let's just get this out of the way. For me, networking is a problem. People don't want to come close enough to me to let me press their flesh, or vice versa. I'm diabetic. Due to my abiding love of food and a thyroid condition I've had since childhood, I weigh over three hundred pounds. My vision is 20–200, and because my eyes are too dry for contact lenses, I wear glasses with lenses so thick people call me "Wendy the spot welder" or the "coke bottle kid." For years a chronic overbite had me chewing up my gums at night and waking up the next morning to a bloody pillow, so last year I got orthodontia.

Oh—and I was born with moles, groves of them, on my face, neck, and body. Benign and nonthreatening, but the way people look at me, you'd wonder if I had the plague.

In case you haven't been keeping score up until this point, let me tally it up: I'm a fat, four-eyed, thirty-six-year-old MD with a tin grin and enough spots to rival a leopard, only you'll never find a handbag or pair of boots resembling the Wendy Glick Mole Farm.

So I have to say I was pretty damned stunned when Malcolm Flaherty came to me late this afternoon with a business proposition. Malcolm is a silver-haired smoothie who smiles too much and will say all the right, empty things until you're bored so completely stiff you'd pay him just to shut up, so the blood flow to your brain stem can once again commence; he's also the helpful colleague who thinks I should get out and network. I've never liked his brand of psychiatry, which goes light on attacking root problems and heavy on prescribing pharmaceuticals, and I was surprised to see him in the anteroom just outside my one-room office. I'd just wrapped my four o'clock with Toby F, a frustrated music producer on his third marriage who couldn't seem to shake an irrational fear of African American men—a bit of an inconvenience when you work exclusively with rap and hip-hop acts—and I was still scribbling patient notes as Flaherty knocked on the slightly ajar door.

"Wendy, my dear, so glad I caught you in today."

"Hey, Malcolm, you know me, not one to get out a heckuva lot."

My subtle dig at his business advice went undetected. Catching his breath, he looked older and whiter-domed than the last time I'd seen him, maybe a month ago heating a cup of coffee in the lunchroom. His spiffy older-man-about-town look was sure going strong, with a cotton button-down shirt, a herringbone tweed jacket, black slacks, and Italian loafers. Big, well-shaped head, with nary a useful thought inside, it, but his blue eyes, blocky jaw, and dimples were undeniably authoritative. Like all handsome men, Malcolm kept a safe physical distance from me, as if I might snatch him in my chubby arms and gobble him up with saliva-drenched fangs, pausing only to belch.

"Wendy, dear, I'd uh, like to ask you a favor."

The slick jackass had a voice descended from Moses: low and strong, the kind that allows a lesser clinician to burst out in front of the pack and head up a department or peer review panel. That's a sad fact about my profession, that how you say something is often more significant than what you say.

"Shoot, Malcolm," I croaked in response.

He slid the door to my office closed behind him and eyed the couch and overstuffed chair that my patients use. But he didn't make a move. Just as I was about to ask him what in hell was going on, there came a knock on the door.

"Might I be frank with you?" he asked. "About a case?"

My confusion was reaching its peak. This man was barely good for a quick hello in the hallway, and though we're both psychiatrists, he'd never discussed a patient issue with me. Come to think of it, in two years, Malcolm Flaherty had never even acknowledged that I was his medical peer. That realization iced me a tad, and made it easier for me to snap out of my usual fat-Jewish-reject-girl mode of schmucky passivity.

"Why don't you start by telling me who's on the other side of that door, Malcolm."

"Uh, sure, sure, you betcha," he said, followed by no explanation.

I motioned him to sit down but stayed stuck by the door anyway. I leaned past him to have a peek myself, but saw nothing.

"What, Malcolm?—is it the Big Bad Wolf?"

"Huh! Oh, Wendy, you're funny. No, no, no, may I just—level with you?"

"I wish you would."

"So, ha! See, I've got this . . . this dependence and addiction conference in Vienna, and—"

Sure. Of course he did. I thought of his bright orange Lamborghini parked downstairs in the underground lot, four slots over from my pockmarked Volvo wagon. Shrinks like Malcolm Flaherty do conferences in places like Vienna all the time. I get a prison board referral, I'm jumping for joy that the state will pay me fifty cents a gallon to drive up to San Luis Obispo and back. Guys like Malcolm sport snazzy caps and ascots tableside in the cafes of Europe while some cash-strapped medical department back home foots the bill.

"I know the one, Malcolm."

"—you do?"

"Sure. I saw the ads in the journals. You know, even though I don't get out as much as I should, as you're well aware, I do keep up with advancements in the profession."

"Right, Wendy. Yes, yes, of course you do!"

"I've always wanted to see that part of the world. The beer gardens, alpine villages, concentration camps."

"Yes, yes . . . ." Malcolm's over-affability slowly ground its way down to a stunned silence.

"Sorry," I said. "Just a little gallows humor. My tribe tends to use it as a shield. But Vienna? Hey, that should be great. 'Yoda-le-hi-hoo' to you."

"Uh-what?"

I gave him a tinny smile. "Little *Sound of Music* reference."

"Oh, right—right. Ah, Wendy. You are *such* a funny lady." Had he not been stiffer than a wooden Indian when he said it, I'd have appreciated the compliment.

Much as I shouldn't have cared what Malcolm thought of me, my insecurity barked a plain message at me: *You are bombing, girl!* At least he decided, rather abruptly, to stick around, closing the door as we stepped further into my suite. Just as soon, there was a rap on the door. Malcolm dropped his gaze as if I'd put him on the spot, and put up a finger to signal a whisper.

"I have a case. They thought it would settle, but the state's prosecutor was, uh . . ."

"Hello?"

He leaned forward to whisper. "Apparently most unreasonable!"

I may be no picnic to look at, but I'm far from stupid.

"Let me guess," I said in a plain, screw-this-whispering-nonsense voice. "That's him outside."

Another knock thudded against the door. Flaherty nodded.

"Uh, her."

I was disgusted by his cowardice.

"Well, let her in. Maybe she can shed some light on this situation sooner rather than later."

Malcolm sank back against the nearest wall as if his charming-guy inner tube had sprung a leak. I looked at the digital clock that faced my side of the desk.

"Wendy—dear Wendy."

"I don't have time to play hide and seek, Malcolm. I've got another session in twenty minutes."

He swallowed and looked away, toward the window blinds. Outside, the faint roar of homeward-bound commuter traffic on Robertson rose and faded and rose again. I asked him to open the door, but he didn't seem to hear me, so I did it myself.

Oy vey—not what I was expecting. A woman in black who looked like she was all business—but not necessary the law business.

"Hiya, Big Bad Wolf."

"Excuse me?" she said.

"I'm Wendy Glick."

"Bradlee Aames. May I come in?"

"I'd be delighted."

I told her to have a seat as we stared at each other with equal curiosity. She was younger-looking than I thought a state prosecutor would be, with black eyes that seemed to pulse when she spoke and a beautifully unkempt head of dark hair, but she was gripping at something unseen, or edging away from it, I couldn't tell. Just . . . her look reminded me of a manic patient I'd treated some time ago who'd show up semi-glazed, as if she'd forgotten her appointment time but knew she was in the right place. This chick was a real looker, though, with very fine angles to her face, chin, jaw, and nose that were both soft and clean at once—the kind of face cold cream companies use to sell their products. As for her figure I will pause only to observe, for the millionth time in my life, that life ain't fair—*oy!* Black mid-length dress, black sweater, black leggings and boots; it all went together nicely, adding a touch of formidability to her presence, and when she sized me up it was with a predatory cunning.

I had a delicious thought: now here's a gal who could *really* eat Malcolm Flaherty for lunch.

I offered her an ice water, which she declined. Then I turned to my first surprise guest of the afternoon. Poor Malcolm was standing half hidden behind a vertical brown file cabinet in the corner of the room, looking deflated because he'd failed to locate a trap door as yet.

"And this is—"

"—the enigmatic, ever-elusive Doctor Flaherty," Bradlee Aames said.

Malcolm was as flat and pale as the paint-by-numbers duck pond sunset hanging on my wall.

"I'm s-sorry, young lady. But I told you on the phone—"

"Hung up on me, is more like it, Doctor—"

"I must attend a conference in—"

"Vienna, yes, I know—"

"Y-you've heard? Why, I—"

"My spineless excuse for a supervisor told me."

"—wouldn't know who you're referring—"

"Don't make me laugh," she said. "You guys are all in bed together on this."

"Ms. Aames?" I said. "I only work in the building with Doctor Flaherty."

"Sorry, I didn't mean to implicate you, Doctor. Or to barge in on your practice."

"No, no, you're welcome here." I grinned at Malcolm to leave no doubt about how much fun I was having. Bradlee Aames took her time to breathe—in, out, in, out—though her black eyes reflected a mind on hyperdrive.

"You wouldn't believe the week I've had," she said. "Everybody hiding out, ducking me. No one returning my calls." She glared at Malcolm. "Gotta give you credit where credit is due, because—"

"Young lady, as I tried to explain—"

"Vienna? You're easily this case's most ambitious sell-out yet. I mean, one witness is just saying no, another's talking Louisiana, but doctor, you take the prize."

She went into a black leather purse and came out with a white envelope with a government seal on it, flipped the thing at Malcolm, who caught it belatedly.

"What's this?"

"The prize!" I piped in, unable to resist. I was loving every minute of this.

"Most people only leave the state to avoid my subpoenas," she said. "But you went global. You've got a special flair for shirking your public duty."

"This could not be avoided," Malcolm said as if he was lecturing her. "I assure you. I want nothing more—"

"Stop with the transparent little justifications about why you've gotta go. You filled in the expert questionnaire? Funny you—"

"—nothing more, I tell you, than to aid the medical board in its efforts to—"

"—didn't say boo about being unavailable this month."

"—protect the public! I . . . I'm truly sorry, but the scheduling of this conference—"

"Stop it already."

"—wholly precludes me from—"

"Stop!"

Using her palm, she'd rubbed her forehead as if his words had smacked her just above the eyes. Without knowing this young woman enough to truly care about her yet, I was nonetheless concerned for her general well-being and felt a pang of protectiveness—just like when Lady Jane, my Chihuahua, comes unhinged at the sight of that German shepherd from across the street when he bounds up to our front porch for a peek through our screen door.

"You won't do it," she said quietly. "So there. Whatever. Just don't lie to me, I can't stand the lying."

Malcolm fumbled with his big veiny hands, which failed to conjure a convincing gesture of reasonableness.

"Miss, I assure you—"

"No! Let me assure you, your assurances are worthless, Doctor. Worthless!"

One of the big veiny hands pointed at her face as he huffed, his loafers creaking on my carpet.

"Now . . . just a minute, young lady, I have been a medical board expert for going on twenty years and I have never, ever—"

I barely heard Malcolm's bluster, so fixed was my attention on the way Bradlee Aames was now using her hands as earmuffs, as if she wanted to tear the sound of the offending words back out of her head.

"Quit lying, you're going two weeks early," she said. Two weeks!"

She'd stopped him cold. Malcolm looked at me beseechingly, as if I might rescue him somehow. I had to work hard to keep a delighted grin from forming.

"Well, now . . . . H-how . . . how did you—"

"You're ditching your responsibilities. You're ditching the patient."

"Former patient."

"You're an ass for even saying that. And her name is Rue Loberg. She's a person. A victim."

"W-who told you I was going?"

"Nobody told me."

"But—"

"I'm a lawyer. I'm very good at looking things up, Doctor. That's what competent lawyers do. You're ditching me."

The exchange seemed over. The lawyer seemed to be mildly hyperventilating, and I wished I could reach out and give her a big mamabear hug, but I hardly knew her and didn't want to take that risk. Yet my contempt for Malcolm was red-hot, and even though he seemed seriously diminished, I had an impulse to take him down a notch.

So—what the hay? I piled on a little.

"Skipping out on a trial, Doctor?"

Malcolm had never been on the receiving end of criticism from me; in fact, he'd always been smugly superior in every respect. He was somebody; I was . . . not. As if to correct such a cosmic imbalance that had found him eye-to-eye with fat, moley Wendy Glick, the office joke, he growlingly revved up a comeback or two.

"N-now you—"

"Like the young lady said, save it."

"Listen to me! It's not—"

All he could do was mumble on like a cartoon of a real man.

"Sit," I ordered him, motioning at the cracked leather couch. To my astonishment he obeyed. The attorney was still agitated but had brought her shaky hands down from her face. She told me in so many words that she was screwed, as trial was only a few days away. The whole thing had gone like this, she said, no one standing up against this Dr. Don, people taking the easy way out, leaving town as if they'd been bought off. Even the victim, a shaky, vulnerable middle-aged divorcee Dr. Don had easily exploited, was now failing to return phone calls. The case was looking like a total loss.

"I'm sorry," Malcolm said, checking his watch. "But I've got a supervision meeting with an intern, and—"

"Yeah, yeah, please, just go," Bradlee Aames told him. "In five minutes' time I've gone from desperate to see you, to desperate to get you the hell out of my sight."

"Give my regards to the Von Trapps," I said as Malcolm shuffled to the door. The joke wasn't funny but it made Bradlee Aames smile.

"Right. And don't choke on those teenie weenies while you're there."

"The big weenie," I said under my breath. We shared a chuckle as the door closed behind him.

Her hands continued to quiver, and I had a therapist's instinct to make a commiserative gesture. Not to mention, I still felt dirtied by the oily manipulations of my compromised colleague. Sliding open my desk drawer, I found the box of See's Candies, the finest chocolates in town, which I keep for emergencies.

"Here. It's pick-me-up time."

Bradlee Aames seemed grateful. I watched her select a cherry cordial, which half-exploded as she bit into it. I handed her a napkin as she sopped up the rest. For my part I went right for the mocha truffle in the corner.

"Oh, God," I mumbled. "I'm in heaven. Have another."

"I probably shouldn't."

"With that body? Please, girl, do not patronize me."

"Okay. Thanks."

"So, who's this putz, Dr. Don?" I held out the box again like a tray.

Bradlee Aames made the safe choice by going for the pair of English toffee sticks.

"He's an exploiter."

"Banged a patient?"

"Right in his office."

"Oy!"

"Some of the things the victim's told me . . . I dunno. He may be a sadomasochist."

We ate two more candies apiece. My next patient was less than five minutes away when, following an impulse, I told her I wanted to help. Sex with patients was an overt no-no, and I knew the standard of practice on therapist/patient boundaries inside out.

"The money sucks," she warned me. "One-fifty an hour."

"This doesn't strike me as like the kind of thing one would do for the money. I mean, primarily."

"No, I guess not."

"Course, I've never testified."

"I can help you with that. Prep you."

"It'll be good," I said.

"Well, challenging is more like it. He's got three lawyers. Between them, they have no morals."

"Well hey, they're lawyers, what did you expect?"

"Ha-ha."

"I'm just sayin' . . ."

"There are plenty of good guys in the law."

"And good girls. I can tell you're one of them."

She shook her head. "I'm just trying to put a case together with a decent shot at winning."

I was enjoying the candy—a dark chocolate caramel marshmallow, to be precise—and the company with equal pleasure.

"Anyway," I said. "It'll be good to test myself."

"It's not a test. You'd just tell the truth. Review the evidence, and give your professional opinion."

"No, dear," I said. "You heard enough bullshit from my esteemed colleague for one day; the least I can do is be straight with you."

"You don't have a medical license?"

"No, I'm licensed. My resume's solid, too. SC undergrad, UCLA med school. Internship and residency at Cedar Sinai. I know my stuff."

"Great. So, *what*? You're a convicted felon? An axe-murderer?"

Not quite believing my good luck, I found a milk chocolate almond cluster, lying upside-down and lonely in the corner of the box. Rescued it posthaste.

"I've been off my antianxiety meds for two years and—no, no, it's okay. Don't look at me that way."

"Sorry," Bradlee Aames said. "I just wouldn't want you to wind up in a bad place. I mean, this trial's gonna be a fight, and you could—"

"I'm fine without them, I swear. It's just a thing I had, a problem I had about accepting my personal appearance. Actually, it was more about other people not accepting how I looked, and about me learning how not to care."

"What comes out of your mouth is all that matters. No posturing or preplanning. Just the truth. That's the only way you'll be judged."

The way she said it gave me chills. The way the young lady cut to the chase. Thrilled as I was, at the same time, in my mind, a voice was cautioning me.

Hey, Wendy, fat girl, anxiety-prone fat girl Wendy? Are you bonkers? Stoned? 'Cause you probably will be stoned—that is, pummeled with big, fat rocks—when you walk into court. One look at you, fat girl Wendy, and the rocks will surely fly . . .

"So, may I see the case file?" I said.

"Don't you want to check your schedule first?"

"Nah—Vienna can wait, right?"

Bradlee Aames laughed. I lifted the box of See's one last time, balancing it like an hors d'oeuvres tray.

"But first! One more for the road."

"God," she said, successfully persuaded. "If chocolate isn't the best drug on the planet—"

16

RAUL MENDIBLES

The Major knows just how to push my buttons. Though he was on the phone, I could easily picture his self-satisfied smirk as he drew out the vowels in my name.

"So, Raw-ool, you'll be there to watch the trial, to monitor the little wild thing, of course."

"Of course."

"She'll not prevail, I dare say."

"No, she will not."

"That's my boy."

But his oily cloak of superiority could not hide a mistimed, nervous chuckle he let slip as the general unpredictability of courtroom confrontations was assessed. Then he made a too-strenuous complaint about the unfairly heavy-handed effect of subpoenas on witness availability, to which I politely listened, expertly hiding my incredulity. Jesus, I was thinking, we're the government—what did he expect laypeople to do when the Department of Justice issued them a personal love letter? Blow it off?

What I sensed about the Major was that, despite his usual big-dog pretensions, his air of control was not absolute. As a master manipulator, he'd lost some traction, and he was deeply bugged that the Dr. Don case was going to trial.

So was I.

Yet, what else could we have done? Bradlee Aames was lawyering this thing relentlessly, like a zombie, the unkillable, undead prosecutor, and try as we might, we couldn't keep her from putting on her damned case. According to the Major's well-placed—yet to me, unnamed—sources, the state's witnesses had been vigorously discouraged from testifying, persuaded that in this instance, the performance of civic duty was not an act of honor or good conscience, but an invitation to chaos and pointlessness. Private favors had been granted, secret benefits conferred. Nevertheless, Bradlee's subpoenas had been issued, a fact I'd verified personally by fishing through her master file while she was out in the field, hoofing it. Made me feel like a sneak, a loser, having to slink past the secretaries outside Bradlee's door with a cheesy grin and a wobbly, concocted tale about a mislaid attendance sheet that needed retrieving. Had I simply waited till five, they'd have all been gone home, but the Major had called twice and I couldn't stand his insinuations about the case turning into a train wreck. Rooting against Bradlee, wishing and hoping she hadn't done her job, I'd leafed through a file which did nothing but hammer home the fact that we'd failed to dissuade her from her purpose. By all appearances, she seemed ready to go forward, and all I could hope for now was that she'd not be in her right mind to pull off a win.

On that count she was hard to read of late, but she certainly didn't lack confidence. When I'd ask her—vaguely, casually—about the shape of things to come, she'd deflect my entreaties like shooing a fly, jokingly neither confirming nor denying a thing. *We'll see who's there when I start calling names*, she told me, breezing a hand through that fabulous mop of hair. *And those who fail to answer the call will have hell to pay, won't they?*

The last time I checked in with her, I'd uttered something lamely encouraging, if for no other reason than to show her I was, indeed, on her side as her supervisor. But she'd gone silent, her tight-lipped amusement at my weak efforts damnation enough.

"Never should've gone this far, Raw-ool," the Major lamented.

I had to agree. We even took away her medical expert—the major had dispatched the guy on an extended European vacation, for God's sake—and somehow she'd conjured up another expert, the same damned day. Proud of how she'd done it, too, confiding in me that maybe this was a sign this case was about to go right.

Ay, Dios mio! The same damned day!

I could hear too well the major's chunky breathing, pictured him sitting in his black-leather swivel chair behind that big walnut desk in his study, his protruding middle inflating and deflating, up, down, up, down . . . . I waited, reminded of a pregnant Myrna, her abdomen big as an igloo, all lubed up for the ultrasound. Holding her hand, trying to love her despite my revulsion at the sight of what my sperm had wrought. Half a decade has since gone by. Seems like a long time ago, when she was young and pretty and exciting to me . . . seems like so very long ago. Her figure never quite recovered, the so-called baby weight becoming permanent, like a vat of concrete hardening in a wheelbarrow. My attraction for her had gone missing ever since.

Staring at the wall, at the Los Lobos concert poster above the file cabinet, I was thinking about the lonely wolf and his plight, yearning for that kind of roaming freedom . . . but the major, he was barking at me again, jerking me back to the problem at hand.

"Can't spin it for you anymore, son. This case has got to resolve. Conclude. Settle."

"We tried that."

"Obviously you did not try hard enough, so dammit, try again!"

"It won't work."

"You don't know that."

"I know her. Listen to me. Bradlee Aames won't win. She's off her head. And that patient, Loberg, she looked like a nervous wreck at the settlement conf—"

"Don't tell me about the patient, whatever you do, dammit!"

"What?"

"It . . . makes me think about all the other patients out there!"

"Excuse me?"

He was snorting like a bull. "Oh, come on! Don't you see that's what this is about? Damn it to hell, Raw-ool, are you blind?"

"You lost me."

Half my desk blotter baked white in sunlight. Wishing I was anywhere else at this moment, I leaned forward tiredly and spun the gold wedding ring on my finger, tried to conjure a quicksilver reflection but couldn't find the right angle.

"All right, then, Raul," the Major said, his pronunciation spot on. "Truth is, it's my fault."

"Well, I wouldn't say—"

"Just button it, stop talking! Listen to me, son. Just listen. You probably think Donald Fallon's just an old pal I'm lending a helping hand to, I'll bet. That about right?"

"No, sir, you'd mentioned your family's link—"

"Cat's out of the bag already."

He belched quietly, as if he was holding the phone away from his big fat pie hole. But I heard it. He'd been drinking.

"I guess so is the bullfrog," I said, just to mess with his head. "Out of the bag."

"Son, any time you need to supply a roadmap for a joke, it wasn't funny in the first place. But I digress. Now, tell me something, what's the weather like down in LA?"

"The weather?"

"Stand up and go to the window. Then take a look, a really good look. I'll hold."

I didn't move. "What about the weather?"

"Check the weather, dammit. Get cracking."

Bastard. I hated the way he pushed me around, but I set down the receiver and got up to take a peek. The last time I'd glanced out my window, I'd not noticed a thing, so lost was I in the riddle of what to do about Bradlee; a hailstorm wouldn't even have raised an eyebrow. For now, the bright, cloudless, midday sun-scorched blanch of yellows and blues I expected to see seemed to have receded. Instead, ruffled high clouds had formed a ridge over East LA, dappled with the colors of rainbow sherbet.

The air evaporated from my lungs, and I felt my heart knocking against my rib cage.

Oh, pale sky, deafening street, roar on, in mourning and majestic grief!

Ancient poetry, setting the scene eight stories up. Lightheaded, I had the sensation of falling. So much I'd wanted from this life, and what was so wrong with trying to take it? My father, his brown-leather face—I spied a hint of it in my unsmiling reflection in the window. *Papi!*

He'd tended fields in Mexico, washed dishes in Calexico, dug ditches in Pacoima. Died trying to give his children more. What else could I do, but reach higher?

Sin verguenza, Raul. Sin verguenza.

No, no, there's no shame in striving for a better life, no shame in having ambition. . . .

Wiping a coil of hair from my forehead, I left the window and my father's judging eyes, remembering the major's stupid objective. I sat back down, feeling vaguely defeated.

"The weather's sunny and beautiful, sir. Some high clouds, but otherwise, typically perfect."

"Well, let me tell you a little story about a man who's out there, enjoying that perfect afternoon somewhere not so far from you. Let me tell you what's on that man's mind, and I assure you, Raul, his thoughts don't match your description of the weather."

So he told me about Donald Fallon, the promising neuro-psych resident who, thirty years ago, had wowed the Major's only sister, Hilary, a lovely, quiet RN who didn't get out much, with his witty patter, his seemingly vast social contacts around town, and the supreme ease with which he could order fine wines from menus written in foreign languages.

"Still," the major said, "he was marrying a Coughlin."

"Marrying up," I said.

"My point exactly, Raul. Something of the confidence man, that Fallon, the way he operated. My father met him once, called the estate lawyer right after, to put Hilary's inheritance into a trust. But Hilary couldn't be persuaded. We didn't have any evidence, just a gut feeling that old Donnie wasn't the innocent charmer he professed to be."

They were wed on a beach on Maui a mere three months after they'd met. I asked the Major if he'd attended.

"No one was invited."

Life went on. Eight years later the couple had a big Spanish house in Hancock Park with red-tile roofs and a pool. Maybe the Coughlin family had been wrong, too hasty to look down upon an outsider. Maybe in Hilary's case, true love had won out.

But no. Despite the mundane domestic trappings, Hilary couldn't help but notice her husband's increasingly odd work hours. He seemed always to be rushing off to rescue a patient, particularly late at night. As a former nurse, she knew how doctor's worked. Knew he couldn't possibly be on call that often.

"Cheating," I said.

"She didn't know for certain, Raul. But yes, she suspected. Tried to talk to him, reason with him, but every time he'd shut her down. His hours got stranger, and when she'd object, he'd go from annoyance to rage, breaking stuff, the neighbors calling the police. When she told him he had to go with her to counseling, he threatened to kill her, then himself."

The major laughed tiredly. "Eventually she came to me, the big brother."

"Last resort, I said.

He was silent for a while. I studied that wolf on the wall, saluting his nobility.

"You're a bright young man, Raul, you can figure out the rest."

"The patients. This isn't the first time."

"Bingo. Bango."

"You've known this . . . for what, years now?"

"Bongo. Should've acted a long time ago to rein him in, but I couldn't figure out a way."

"So, if this case settles with a term of probation, you won't be putting him out of business."

"How could I go that far? Think about it."

"Your sister—"

"I hope you're not judging me, Raul. I had a probation monitor all picked out, Dr. Hans Kupferman. Heard of him?"

I hadn't.

"Doesn't matter. He's tops. Knows little Donnie's backstory. Kupferman was gonna be my eyes and ears."

The Major's purported containment plan was so asinine, I involuntarily issued a snort.

"Oh, so you *are* judging me, my friend."

"Come on, major, he rips into another patient, I guarantee a probation monitor's not going to be around for it."

"Don't think you're so superior, Raul, because you aren't."

"Had I known, I'd—"

"You'd have done nothing different, son. You question my judgment? Look at you! That little wild one, she's defying your authority. Your feelings for her have clouded your judgment, son."

"That's not true."

The Major chuckled malevolently.

"Let me put it in plainer terms for you, counselor. Had you not been thinking with your johnson, you'd have assigned this case to a worthless hack, like say, that Ravola character."

The Major was referring to Dirk Ravola, a Deputy AG better known to his many detractors as Dork Revoltya. To the worthless hack description I would add only the words lazy and unprincipled.

"But you didn't," the Major said louder. "You let your selfish interests get in your way."

"My selfish interests? You should talk."

"Yeah, yeah, yeah, so I'm a deeply flawed individual, Raul, so help me God. But you're the one who didn't do your job, here."

That was it for me. "Know what, Major? You don't even know what you're talking about. It's true, I thought Bradlee Aames would've imploded by now—"

"We're screwed, son. Both of us. Not to mention the next little patient Dr. Donnie gets in his—"

"No, it's your turn to listen, Major. I'm gonna let you in on something, because even though you roll out the slick little backstory on this creep, and now you play the injured party 'cause I didn't sweep this entire pile of crap case under the rug for you, it's you who don't know what your interests are. You don't even know what we're dealing with, here."

"Okay, Mendibles, I may have been a little harsh, and if so—"

"I don't want an apology from you, I just want you to see how fucked up this whole thing has become."

I heard another quiet belch, followed by more heavy breathing. I pictured the major fortifying himself with his juice of choice, studying his portly outline in a window reflection just before his head was about to spin off his shoulders.

"What you get with Bradlee Aames is not just a mentally ill problem child. She's a very good attorney. I've seen her case file, took a peek at it to keep up with what she was doing. There are more bad facts than we alleged in the Accusation. Things Dr. Don did to the victim."

"Hell, he nailed her in his office under the guise of therapy. I know that. What more do you need to know?"

"The victim, Rue Loberg. He abused her. Degraded her."

"Hell's bells."

"He's got the characteristics of a sadomasochist. What he does is charm, woo, make a victim feel special. Wins her over. Then slowly, he introduces a new dynamic. Undermines her sense of normalcy. Gets her to do things she knows are outside the norm. It's like, the sadomasochist conditions his victim to be a 'bad' girl. Then once he's accomplished that, when she does something 'bad' again, he's got to punish her."

"Man's a public menace."

"You know why I'm telling you this. You should talk to your sister, Hilary."

The Major took a swig, or a slurp, I couldn't tell. "Jesus. And say what?"

I was already swimming in deeper water than I'd ever attempted. My usual work routine involved carefully remaining uninvolved. The major was an unsavory ally to be cautiously cultivated and maintained, not a friend to reach out to with concern. This was not how to get ahead.

"You're right. Never mind."

"Mendibles," he said after another half minute of throat burn and heavy breathing. "You did good. So should I, believe you me. Problem is, we're not programmed to be do-gooders. We're fixers. Don't deny it—it's how you met me. I like you, believe it or not, I like you because you remind me of myself. So okay, my brother-in-law is a sick puppy. I'll follow up with Hil, soon as I figure out what to say to her. Meantime, let us reassess. Come up with a new containment strategy."

"In all honesty, I don't see it. He's a menace, you said so yourself."

"Containment, son. Gotta put our heads together on this."

He was half in the bag. I hung up the phone and put my head into my hands instead.

The stench of Dr. Don lingered long into the afternoon. I sat at my desk as if pinned to my chair, like a puppet—his puppet.

Over a slow, indeterminate spell of self-pitying stewing, I simply didn't budge, and in time the motion sensor shut the lights off automatically. I sat there, in my energy-saving government office, watching the sunlight angle down, more sideways now. Blocks of shadow crept up the sides of the brick bank district buildings, an inky plague slowly blotting out the elaborate wedding cake facades. When I fell asleep or lost consciousness, I can't say, but . . .

On the wall the Los Lobos wolf detects the scent . . . of my wishful raw ambition, responding with a yellow-eyed, feral proud howl that stokes my soul. Where to? Does it even matter? Untamed fearless wide-open roaming awaits! A pathological yearning to join the wolf swells my tired spirit. My raw eyes and crooked spine and overstuffed inbox say no to this . . . sheer preposterousness, Mendibles, but . . . follow, I will follow. . . .

A sundown breeze cools my neck amid green fields of budding corn and mud drying hard on the state capitol's riverbanks, where old-town planks moan with rot beneath the tourists' feet. I ruffle the fur on your back, Lobo; it's just you and me and nothing but highway ahead. But then . . . it can't be! No—anywhere but here, I know this place, Lobo, I've been here before and it's not worth stopping, not for anything. But you can't hear me, and so you slow to peer down into a gully beside the road, down a slope of wet grass, where an upended car lies, a front wheel still spinning. Inside is a man, passed-out drunk, hanging from a strap like a pig in a butcher shop window—and if I had words to tell you to keep moving, to quietly light-foot it on by, I would; but predictably, I find that I'm present . . . but not quite here, and I fail you. So you approach, dip your head to investigate, paw a button until it clicks, and the man slumps free, his shirt collar clamped in your jaws as you tug him, snorting with supreme effort, to safety. He awakens, his head jerking up at the sight of you, and he recoils in fear, scrambling backward.

I stand at a safe distance, a self-involved witness to what for you was merely an instinctive act. How I wish this scene would end; but over my avid objections, the laws of the universe assert themselves and impose another moment on us. You move on, padding down the road as would suit your spirit, but the unheroic impostor stays behind and very much alone, hatching a surefire plan . . .

17

RUE LOBERG

It wasn't hard to understand why Dr. Craig was worried about me. I mean, I'm not the most stable, reliable person. And I could see a lot of myself in Ms. Aames, too, the way she seemed to be fighting off things only she could see, only with her, she kept going no matter what, win or lose. Ms. Aames just had that certain fire, like a wild animal that knew it was wounded but would fight to the death anyway. It's hard to pin it down any better than that, but what she had, by instinct I wanted it for myself, too. So, with this trial coming, I was looking up to her. It was like, by believing in her, I was casting a vote of confidence in myself. Hope that makes sense.

Not that I'm anywhere near her level in life—a successful lawyer and such a head-turner, and all. But we share one thing. Men? They look upon her as an object of pleasure; you can see it in those sweaty stares, hear it when they laugh along with her simplest comments, even when nothing's remotely funny. And boy, the men have done this to me, too. I know what it feels like, to be seen as an object, not a person.

Ms. Aames, though, she's nobody's toy. She opens her mouth and out comes a lick of fire. She can make them pay. But Ms. Aames, she's also burdened with a kind of tiredness of spirit that hangs about her like a shawl made of lead. A kind of exhaustion that chews at you all the time, a weariness that comes from fighting the world, but also yourself inside your mind, all the time. She promised that when I took the witness stand to tell my story, she'd be there to protect me, and though I didn't think it possible for me to say my piece without getting plastered, I believed her anyway. Believing in Ms. Aames seemed to be on par with her believing in the epic, bad girl, screw-up-turned-state's witness Rue. So what the hell.

Dr. Craig didn't see it that way, though. He wanted what was best for me, didn't want to see Dr. Don's lawyers destroy me. But all I had to do was tell the truth, and I prayed to God that if I did, well, He would shine His light on me. In the Last Judgment, with the many mistakes I've made, a sinner of my advanced level of achievement, well . . . one day I know I'll need God on my side, so just maybe this would be a start.

All I wanted was to get in there and say my piece, but when we got to court, one look at Ms. Aames and you could tell she'd been fighting herself and . . . maybe losing the battle.

She came down the hallway as we approached the courtroom. Out of the corner of my eye, I thought I saw her chatting with someone who wasn't there.

"Rehearsing my lines," she said when Dr. Craig inquired. He didn't look convinced, to me.

"Ready to go?" she asked me head-on.

I was about to say yes, I was about as ready as I'd ever be, though the truth is, I was terrified. But Dr. Craig leaned closer to Ms. Aames with a question.

"How much sleep did you get last night?"

"Enough. Trial work is demanding, doc."

"Just how is it that Miki Dora figures into your opening statement?"

"I didn't . . . he doesn't. What I just said . . . oh, forget it."

She lost me on that one. They both looked concerned, and that scared me a little.

"Who's Miki Dora? Is he testifying for Dr. Don?"

Ms. Aames turned and really looked me in the eye for the first time today, and there was kindness in her eyes.

"No. He's just a friend of ours," she said. Dr. Craig nodded like he agreed.

"Sorry. I'm dangling off a high ledge, trying not to look down."

She told me that was normal, and not to worry. She looked great in a gray dress that went past the knee, black stockings and a long black sweater, but to me, her face seemed a tad blotto and her eyes had that little bit of frantic in them. 8:40 in the morning, and you'd think she'd been through a war already.

Dr. Craig was shaking his head, hands in the pockets. He'd worn a blazer and nice slacks, had that professor look going—which is what I told him when he came to pick me up. A nice look for the ladies, I'd said, and I'm pretty sure, he blushed when I said it. He could try and hide it all he wanted, but there was a spark going back and forth between him and Ms. Aames. That spark was not in evidence at this juncture. In fact, they looked like they wanted to kill each other.

Not quite out of my earshot, I heard Ms. Aames deny she said the name Miki Dora—whoever that is. Dr. Craig said no, he just heard her. They went back and forth a while, whispering, but not quietly enough so I couldn't hear them going at it. Dr. Craig's point was that my welfare should come first, and if Ms. Aames couldn't protect me sufficiently in court, then this thing was going backward, two wrongs not making a right, and so on. Ms. Aames, she told Dr. Craig she'd been a trial attorney a long time, and testifying's no picnic for anybody, but she was on top of her gig.

"So, what if you start having visions?" he asked her. That I heard for sure.

Good Lord! I said to myself. *She's mentally ill!* The eyes; that intensity. Why hadn't I put it together sooner? I was torn right in half, loyal to her on one hand, but scared stiff on the other.

She told him she had a system, kept two lists up-to-the-minute. What's real, versus what isn't. Easy to tell the difference, she said, she'd had a lifetime of practice.

"That's it?" he whispered, but hard.

"I was talking to my father a little while ago," she hissed under her breath. "He's dead, but he was a good trial lawyer. I was trying out a few phrases in my opening statement. The words were real. My father wasn't. I know the difference. Satisfied?"

"How can I be?"

"Craig, back the hell off!"

That last part was above a whisper.

They fought one last round after that, neither of them seeming to care when I retreated a few paces and found a window to a dull white room, a little spot designated for witnesses like me. Nice place to stew in your juices, I thought, sitting down at a fake-wood table. Prayer seemed apropos, but before I could compose a new way to beg for God's mercy, my dueling protectors both came in together, looking pretty winded.

"Here's the thing, Rue: it's up to you," Dr. Craig told me.

Ms. Aames kept her arms folded. "Your call, Mrs. Loberg. I won't make you testify unless you think you can do it."

Glad it was finally settled, I said thanks to them both.

"Just know, the case is over without your testimony," Ms. Aames added.

"Well, no pressure there," Dr. Craig shot back.

"I was just—"

"Get off her back—"

"Don't fight," I told them. "It's all right. I've been wanting to do this for a while now. I'll be fine."

Dr. Craig probably didn't look too happy, but to be honest, I can barely recall. It was like a white light fell on me, and I was blind with fear, too terrified and nervous to think straight anymore. What I didn't know was Ms. Aames, whatever her troubles may be, was able to see that I'd been blinded. As she led me down that hallway to the court-room, she turned to pause, taking a motherly hold of my wrist.

"Fear not," she said. "You've been through far worse already than anything these clowns can throw at you. You lived through it, body and spirit, once before, and you survived. You were strong enough. Now all you've got to do is experience it one more time, but merely in words. Be strong again."

"Th-thanks."

At the door, she put her jumpy gaze to rest by closing her black eyes. When she opened them she was a foot away, her hand coming up to rest on my shoulder.

"We can do this."

I floated up to that witness stand in a haze of doubt.

They asked me to state my name, and I smiled because I wanted to make a joke and say *Joan of Arc—and which one of you, by the way, remembered to bring the matches?* Instead I said my name, took an oath, and was asked to tell the truth. When I said I would, the sound of my words seemed to turn tail the instant they left my lips and tuck back into my mouth. I'd been praying a lot, nonstop for days, and I thought maybe this was a sign. Just the way my whole life has gone, I thought: *promise to tell the truth, but no one cares to hear it.*

In that moment of dark revelation, I felt God's presence—recognized that He had been there, just outside the courtroom, speaking to me through Ms. Aames a minute ago. Encouraging me. Now, on the stand, Jesus whispered to me.

Say your piece anyway, My sister, say it for all to hear.

Dr. Don, he was over at the table beside his lawyers, in a dark suit that, to me, made him look like a boy in his father's Sunday clothes. Of course, I'd seen his penis before, so it was easy to think of him as a kid. Men and their penises—acting like children.

He was scribbling notes and being careful not to catch my eye. I wanted to say: go ahead, try to act like a man, but you never will be. Never.

The judge had a nice smile when he welcomed me, but I wished he hadn't. The thing is, I'm too much of a people-pleaser, it's one of my many weaknesses, and when someone's nice, I automatically try too hard to be nice right back. Probably he was just trying to put me at ease, which is fine, I guess. But no, I was not here to satisfy him.

My hands were sweaty and fidgeting like crazy, and my insides were rolling like snakes were crawling around in them. My blue pantsuit fit me tighter than when I'd bought it for that Harley dealers' convention in Laughlin me and Andy attended two, three years ago. It made me look like an office temp, but it was my only outfit that would do for court, I figured, so I wore it anyway. Now I could hardly breathe and the bobby pins just behind my ears were pinching my skull every time I moved. I hadn't even started, but I was doing a fine job showing them all what a loser I am . . .

Here's what I remember saying, not the exact words, but close. Including the highlights—or I guess, the lowlights, depending on how you might judge a person like me.

I was born and raised in Carson, California, the armpit of the Los Angeles Harbor. (Ooh—no one laughed.) My dad had an auto parts store in Artesia, and in the summer I used to work there, sweeping up and cleaning the glass doors and doing odd jobs for fifty cents an hour. Except Daddy never got around to paying me because *what would a foolish girl do with money except spend it on foolish things?* he'd say. He was a big-time Holy Advent of Christ follower, he and my mom, but he had no problem stiffing me for my work. That's a pretty good example of the man's sense of fairness and right and wrong.

Mom, she was a happy housewife back when you could find happy housewives all up and down the block. But she wasn't ever happy about much anything I did. One time I brought home a spelling test with a hundred percent mark and a gold-star sticker from the teacher. All my mom could see was that my handwriting on one word, remonstrate, deviated from the line it was written on. She tore up the test; then she tore up my backside with a switch.

My mother beat me even harder the year I grew breasts, because a girl my age, to grow breasts already, must've had impure thoughts and then, you see, the Devil read them and brought on this unnatural change. Yeah, a whole lot of what I went through growing up had that kind of loose connection to God and the Devil, though I was always one step behind, getting smacked.

About that time my dad got lucky with his business. There was a new freeway coming through, and his store was sitting right in the way. Normally the state would've taken the land and paid him what they wanted to pay, and he'd have been stuck with the deal, but there was an old oil well out back, and it caused a lot of complications because those drilling rights were written into the deed. There were supposed to be geological studies to sort out how the well was going to be capped, and how much my dad could've expected in projected revenues from the well that he'd never see, now that the state was buying him out. If Dad wanted to fight it, he could tie up that whole freeway project for years to come, so they settled by overpaying him six ways to Sunday, as he put it, and he quitclaimed them back.

Suddenly we were rich by normal-people standards. I figured we'd move to a bigger house, in a nicer neighborhood, my mom would buy some jewelry, my dad, a fancy car. But they didn't change, not at all. My dad no longer had to work, so he started hanging around the local Holy Advent church in our area, doing charitable stuff like paper drives and collecting canned goods for the poor. That first summer after he sold his business, I couldn't work in the store anymore so I helped around the church. Right after Fourth of July, Dad paired me up with the new minister, Pastor Jim. He and Dad were both in the Army when they were younger, and they liked each other. Late afternoons, I'd see them sitting in Pastor Jim's office, their hands down at their sides, so they could hide the whiskey they drank in little white paper cups. Telling stories and laughing, always quieting down when I walked by, then laughing and giggling like schoolgirls as I went away.

But like I said, I got paired up with Pastor Jim, helping him set up the hall for bingo night. Thirty folding tables that bit like snapping turtles when you tried to open them, and five times as many chairs that had to be spread all around them. The first time I did the job, Pastor Jim bought me a soda. The second time, he gave me a gold locket, but made me promise to keep it a secret. By August he was stroking my hair down to the tips, right above my nipples. It was always late afternoon, and by then, Dad was drunk and sleeping on a couch in the rec room. The first time Pastor Jim made a move on me, he came up behind me in the storage room, clicked off the light, kissed me on the neck, and tore my panties right off. Said if I told anyone, he'd kill me, and my soul would rot in hell. I'd been asking him to do this, inviting him, by letting him touch me those times before. I was evil, did bad things. Not him, he was just a man, he was just responding. He was a minister, I thought, so he must have that kind of power.

That went on till the next summer, when my dad woke up from one of his naps and stumbled over to Pastor Jim's office, looking for that hidden bottle of booze, I guess. What he saw was his daughter bent over the table and Pastor Jim saying something from the Book of Revelation that he liked to say whenever he reached, you know, that . . . point of no return.

I guess I was getting silent and crying, because Ms. Aames asked the judge if she could approach, and when she did, she offered me a tissue. I blew my nose with an embarrassing honk, then told her and the judge I was fine.

"Pastor Jim," Bradlee Aames asked me.

"Oh, right."

That day with my dad, it's like, I can still see it as if it was yesterday. He was hurting me with his . . . well, he was being very rough. What he said, every word of it I recall: *And the ten horns which thou sawest upon the beast, these shall hate the whore, and shall make her desolate and naked, and shall eat her flesh, and burn her with fire.*

"What did your father do?" the judge asked me.

My dad, he looked like he'd been hit across the face with a baseball bat. He jumped at Pastor Jim, got on him and they started to tussle, but Dad was the smaller man, and he was still pretty lit up, and then Pastor Jim started getting the better of him and just laughing, uncontrollably laughing, his pants still around his ankles. It was a horrible sight. My dad, he was in tears and could barely breathe, I think from getting choked. Didn't say a word, but you could tell something inside him had died like a part of him had snapped off now, broken. He gave up with the fight and leaned on the floor against the wall. Then he threw up into a fake potted plant. Pastor Jim came over to offer him water in one of those little white paper cups they were so fond of using. That's when it got really ugly.

Turns out, I *was* the whore. Though I didn't even know what the word "seduced" meant, I had caused all this when I seduced Pastor Jim. My soul had been commandeered by Satan. You get the picture. Next thing I got sent to the church over in Bellflower for counseling from a supervising minister named Pastor Molek. Same result.

"You were raped again?"

I nodded and tried to say yes, but no sound came out. Everybody just sat there quietly until I got myself together again.

Anyway, the rest of that summer I stayed home, in my room, grounded. My father acted like he didn't know me. My mom wouldn't speak to me, but she found lots of stuff I did wrong, lots of reasons to hit me. Again and again.

My body kept changing, getting curvier. Boys kept noticing. I didn't know how to deal with the attention. I was a whore with a ruined soul. My junior year in high school, my drama teacher, Mr. Chambliss? He got in my pants twice in his car when he offered me rides home in the rain—my parents not caring to pick me up, of course. Another time I got caught shoplifting a two-dollar bottle of nail polish at Woolworths, which honestly, I forgot I even had in my hand. I was carrying it around the store for so long, just feeling low. The manager, he put me in a back room for questioning, and he kept me there all afternoon. I had to, you know, put my hand on his thing, or he wouldn't have let me out of there.

Dr. Don? Oh, he started out nice enough, but he had this way of looking at me that I knew meant trouble ahead. You know, complimenting me on my dress, my hair, letting his eyeballs roam. We came in, Andy and I, on account of our two teenagers, Mindy and, well, my son's got nothing to do with this, so I'm not going to mention him. They were seeing Dr. Don for some fairly serious problems. What kind? Well, drug use, ditching school, running away from home. Andy and I were supposed to do conjoint therapy, and we did that now and then; you know, come in and talk about the kids' problems with them.

Mostly though, those sessions, we all just sat around and listened to what Dr. Don had to say. He was kind of long-winded. After about six months, he started telling me I needed individual therapy, because of some of the, uh, skeletons in my closet that kept popping out during sessions. I knew he had a point. I mean, Andy, my ex-husband? He knows about the problems I had with my stepfather, but I don't think he even knows about the Pastor Jim stuff.

Stepfather problems? Yeah. I know I call him "Dad," but he's not my real father. Yeah, it took years to face the facts, I'd pushed them down so far for so long, but he did things to me too. Man-woman things to a young girl who didn't understand what was happening to her. Maybe Pastor Jim was wise to that somehow. I don't know. I don't want to even think about it.

Anyway, I saw Dr. Don alone for several sessions, and he heard my whole history. A diagnosis? Yes, he made one. Borderline personality disorder. Not that I think he's wrong. I know I've got a lot of problems. It's just, he was creeping me out in our sessions. Asking these really personal questions about my marriage. You know, how often my husband and I had sex. Did I think about it a lot? What did I like? What made me have . . . you know, an orgasm. I just thought it was weird, like, I couldn't see how this was supposed to help me. It seemed more like he was helping himself. My husband and I, we were having our troubles, just not getting along, and in bed, as well. I couldn't talk to my own kids. Was drinking too much, which seemed the only way to hold back the pain I was suffering day and night. So I quit seeing him, until about six months later, when he offered to see me in his office at no charge. Made a pitch that he'd been studying my problem and had a new therapy he thought could help me.

What he did, though, was help himself. Called the new treatment, um, touch therapy. I know . . . I'm embarrassed to even say it. Said it had to do with building up trust, enough to supposedly free me from my repressions about the past. Good touches, safe touches, then next thing I know, he's giving me the horny touch. I didn't know what to do. My life was such a mess. I was overwhelmed. The first time he took my dress off, we were on his office couch, this brown sectional. I was in shock, like I was watching a movie and starring in it at the same time. Dr. Don told me I'd been teasing him, egging him on with my bad behavior. Now, I was going to reap what I'd sown. Had me by the wrists, pushed me down. It was the same old script, even when he put his hand over my mouth and threatened to stop me for all time, as how he put it, because . . . yeah, I was a bad seed.

By now, you know all the rest.

The whole experience just froze my insides. So much bad, mixed-up feeling was just getting raked up, dredged right up from somewhere way, way down below.

Andy? He knew something was up, you know, the way a husband not getting any would know. Just by looking at me. So in time he hired a private investigator, and not long after that, filed for divorce. I started drinking more. Some afternoons I was alone at home with nothing but the TV to keep me company. Pretty soon I was in an apartment, by myself; my whole life went upside-down. By the time I pulled out of the tailspin I went into, I had an ex-husband who claimed I sabotaged his happiness, which I guess I can't deny, and two kids so mad at me they wouldn't even return my calls.

The judge called for a recess. I wanted to melt into my chair, just hide from everybody. Even the court reporter couldn't look at me. She knew I was a freak, and though people like to stare at freaks when they can get away with it, it's not something they do as easy out in the open. I had to pee, but I stayed put.

*   *   *

Ms. Aames asked me about some of the things I'd done since, to rebuild my life a little. I said something about school, my criminology studies, working part-time as a dispatcher for the local police department. Therapy I was doing with Dr. Weaver, which was working well enough for me to at least talk about my life like I did here today.

The nice judge asked me if I wanted to take another break, before Dr. Fallon's attorney asked me some questions. Put that way, it didn't sound like a bad experience, getting questioned by the other side. But Ms. Aames did her best to warn me, told me to just answer each question, one by one, clear and direct and short—like, the fewer words the better. And I should pause before answering in case she needed to make an objection. And I should try not to take anything personal, just duck if they start throwing mud, 'cause no question ever killed anybody. I told the nice judge no thanks.

This part of my time on the stand I don't remember so well at all. I recall precious little about Andy's lawsuit against Dr. Don, but his lawyer, Mister Hydigger? He made quite an impression in that case by trying to wear me down. For two whole days he strung out my deposition. Attorney Hydigger, with the sharp chin and crooked way of looking at you, cold gray naughty-boy eyes stuck in an older man's bony face. Seeing him now, taking a second crack at me, it didn't scare me much because I figured I'd been there and done that. But when he started in on me today, his every jab hit me fresh and hard, like a sock in the jaw. What I forgot was that back when the civil suit was going on, I was still a basket case. Now, though, I'd been in therapy and was more in touch with my problems and with myself. Which meant I was more vulnerable. That's probably why this part of the medical board's trial is so fuzzy to me now. Dr. Weaver says that as a natural coping mechanism, my mind will throw up a mental block on certain memories that are too painful. Maybe so, but this much I will carry with me to my grave:

"Your sexual liaisons with Pastor Jim were consensual, were they not?"

"No. He forced himself on me."

"But you didn't call the police; you didn't file rape charges, did you?"

"I was a dumb kid, sir."

"Your stepfather didn't either, did he?"

"My stepfather was a drunk. And a coward."

"Please answer the question, your stepfather—"

"No! He didn't."

"Isn't it true that you seduced Pastor Jim?"

"Not true."

"Isn't that why he referred to you as a whore? Because—"

"Objection," Ms. Aames said. "Argumentative. Calls for speculation."

The judge nodded, and said: "Sustained."

Not that it mattered. That Hydigger, he just went right back after me.

"You like to play that role, though, don't you?"

"No. Never."

"Well, Ms. Loberg, your ex-husband, Andrew, gave sworn testimony in a civil lawsuit that one of his favorite role-playing games with you was when you played the role of lady of the night. Is that true?"

"No, sir. Andy, he's a gentle person. He just had an active imagination in the bedroom, and it was his idea to—"

"Did you play the role of a whore or not?"

"Maybe one or two times. Yes. But it was for fun, not—"

"And isn't it true that you did that to control your husband?"

"No. That's ridiculous. Andy wouldn't even let me work. He was the one controlling me."

"And Pastor Jim. You used your body as a weapon, didn't you, to turn him away from his chosen vocation?"

"Objection!" Ms. Aames shouted, and the judge agreed, but I was too angry to keep my mouth shut, so I told Hydigger that was ridiculous, the dumbest thing I ever heard. The judge, he told me to please not answer questions when an objection was sustained. Then he struck my comments from the record. Right then, I felt like a helpless child in the company of powerful men—just like always, I guess . . .

"You controlled Dr. Don as well, didn't you?" Hydigger asked, as nice as if he were offering me candy.

"No. He was supposed to be helping me."

"But actually, you were helping yourself. You looked up to him."

"My sessions weren't helpful. I could tell he was out for himself."

"But you went back to him."

"For my daughter's sake. He thought I could be of assistance to her, if I understood her struggles better. She—"

"It was after hours, though, when nobody was in his office."

"That's when he said I should come."

"Three times. Nobody there. You knew you could find him alone, and seduce him."

"That's what he claims, but I did no such thing. He worked on me, made it seem like he cared, got me to open up, then put the moves on me."

"We're supposed to believe that, yet he has no record of your visits, he wasn't billing you, and no one saw you there."

"That's how it happened, though. It's the truth."

"The truth was you wanted him."

"No. Far from it."

"Your marriage was on the rocks, and here's a famous psychiatrist, a successful man, a caring individual, whom you thought you could seduce, by using your womanly wiles, your attractiveness. But when you failed, your husband sued him, and you ran scared. So you lied."

"Didn't happen that way, no, sir. He roped me back in, and when I got there, he used everything he knew about me to get at me. Everything from my past, all the stuff that made me the mess I am. It was him that used me."

"Mrs. Loberg, may I remind you that you took an oath—"

"Objection!" Ms. Aames said. "Argumentative. Counsel is lecturing the witness on the meaning of the truth."

"Your Honor, I didn't even get my question out before Ms. Aames here rudely—"

"Argumentative," she repeated, ignoring that weasel Hydigger.

"Sustained," the judge said, and wow, you'd think he was about to take a nap, that judge was so calm-looking.

I can't with any certainty recall the rest of Hydigger's questions, but the truth is, they didn't matter anyway; that's because, to my total surprise, it had dawned on me that this old gas-bag with the wicked boy eyes was doing the same age-old number on me that had worked so well for every man who'd ever controlled me, used me, hurt me, thrown me away like a piece of trash when he was done having his way with me.

First he did his best to make me feel bad about myself, like I was the one caused all the trouble. Next, he'd highlight my guilt by isolating me. I was the liar, making all this up, and I had nothing, no proof, no one to back up my story. Only my word. Then, the fact that he'd done his business on me was all my fault. Because I was bad. Evil.

Jesus spoke to me in that moment, the dark night of my soul.

I love you. You are Mine.

"Redirect," the judge said, and Bradlee Aames stood up. She seemed tired and a bit angry, and I wondered why until I saw the hungry pack-dog eyes at the table of lawyers to her left. I wanted to kiss her when she asked her first question.

"Defense counsel came at you with some tough stuff, Mrs. Loberg, but you seemed to settle in more, even when you were essentially called a liar. Why?"

"Because I'm not lying. I have no reason to tell any tall tales."

"May I ask why you're smiling?"

Soon as she said that, I got embarrassed and lost the smile.

"Well, because through all the ups and downs I've been through, all the mistakes I've made, I come to realize that when a man mistreats me, first he makes it out to be all my fault . . . "

That's when I started to cry. Suddenly, out of nowhere, I'd got to thinking about myself as a little girl, my first birthday party, how I wanted a pony 'cause I'd seen it in a magazine, some rich kid getting one for her birthday, all the guests, other kids, riding it around, having a high time. Back then we were still poor, so of course I didn't get one. But I knew I wasn't shedding tears over a birthday, I was crying over the loss of that little girl's hopes and dreams, how life and the people she trusted just crushed those hopes and dreams . . .

"Mrs. Loberg? Ma'am?" The judge was calling out to me, his gray eyebrows wrinkling.

"Sorry," I said. "Next, after I catch the blame, I get singled out, you know, to stand alone for my sins. All alone. Funny, how the men who use me, heaping their own shame upon me, they always stand close by, near enough to condemn me, but just far enough away to maintain a safe distance from their own wrongdoing."

I stopped and wiped the tears from my face again, blew my nose.

"It's not my problem," I muttered.

Ms. Aames heard me. "Please explain," she said.

I looked at her, at the nice judge, at that scum persecutor Hydigger, then Dr. Don, my true tormenter, before I spoke. Took a breath, privately thanking God I was still alive—miracle of miracles!

"I may be a sinner, but I'm a victim, too. These gentlemen here, they may sit back, at arms' length, and pretend otherwise. But there is a difference, and I—that man's victim—cling to it every day. Dr. Fallon, he's reaping what he has sown. Not me. This is not my doing."

"Nothing further," Ms. Aames said.

"Re-cross?" the judge asked Hydigger.

Hydigger smiled. "Briefly. So, Ms. Loberg, you say you are a victim. But you suffer from borderline personality disorder, don't you?"

"Yes."

"Dr. Fallon's diagnosis was correct, wasn't it?"

"Yes."

"You're mentally ill, aren't you?"

Ms. Aames seemed ready to object, but I shot her a discouraging glance.

"I'm damaged goods, Mr. Hydigger. And if that's all you got, I'll sit here all afternoon. Ask another question."

Hydigger wasn't expecting that. The judge, he was typing away. And Jesus? I knew He was smiling down on me, I just knew it.

18

ANDREW LOBERG

Three times I circled the block the state building was on, unsure of where to park, not even sure if I should stop. I'd taken a Softail Deluxe right off the showroom floor, a black beauty with cherry-red pinstripe that was stealthy silent, so quiet that when I banked off Olive and carved a right onto Fourth, I unintentionally gave quite a jolt to a shirtless guy . . . squatting in the gutter to do his business in the road. Wow—desperate people, but I guess that's the big city for you.

Why do I have to be here anyway? I was asking myself as I peeled off a twenty to a parking lot attendant with these funky white-framed shades and an accent I couldn't place, guy who promised to watch the Softail like a hawk while I was gone, yapping in another language on his cell phone the whole time he dealt with me. Yeah, I'll bet. Glad I didn't have to leave him the keys.

Rue, Dr. Don, my dead marriage—what was the point of rehashing such a tired old story?

An hour later I was on the stand, wishing I was anywhere else. That exotic lawyer, the brunette babe who knew how to ride, came to the showroom and stroked my ego before she more or less threatened me? Talk about an unseen detour, the bloom falling off the rose. She was hot, all right, but whatever sex-doll allure I'd responded to before was in serious remission. She still couldn't repress her babe-factor, even with her dressy lawyer look, but now she was focusing on only one thing: busting my balls. And with each question, I could feel my sack shriveling.

I did my best to resist.

Yes, I hired a private investigator when I suspected Rue was fooling around. Every Saturday at 4:00 p.m., always some excuse or another. Come on, something was up. Yes, I went with him to Dr. Don's office to see for myself. See what? Dr. Don and my wife, of course.

"What did you see?" Ms. Hot Number asked me, zeroing right in on my discomfort.

"Ms. Aames? I really don't want to get dragged into this thing."

"You are in it already, sir. I subpoenaed you to testify, and the judge gave you an oath."

The judge, a nice enough old man, sitting up front like Santa Claus until now, well . . . he turned up the heat on me with a simple, three-word command.

"Answer the question."

"Right. It's, uh . . . hard to say what I saw. I mean, late in the day, looking across from a parking structure. There was a lot of sunlight, and uh, glare."

"You told the medical board's investigator that you were alone. You said you told the private investigator to wait for you down below, in the parking lot, while you went up three flights of stairs to position yourself to see into the doctor's window, is that correct?"

"Yes."

"Why did you wish to be alone?"

"I don't recall."

"Please give us your best answer, your best recollection."

"Objection!" Fallon's nasty old dog attorney shouted. "Cumulative, asked and answered! Only Ms. Aames didn't like the answer she got, so she's trying it again. Your Honor—"

"Overruled," the judge shot back. Apparently, he didn't care for Fallon's choice of legal representation any more than I did.

Man, oh man, suddenly my head hurt like hell and my brow was dripping with sweat. The plan was to stay in a gray area, to say as little as possible, not get tied up in this thing. Then I made a huge mistake: as I was concocting a string of meaningless words, searching for a way to say I hadn't seen a thing, I looked up and saw, for the first time, Rue, sitting out there in the gallery with her hair done up and pinned back in a way that made her look younger by some years, like a cute flight attendant with that pantsuit, and all. Clean and sober, and alone, those sad eyes fixed on her gutless ex, not even blinking. Hoping I would have the spine to do the right thing, but tempering that hope with bitter past experience.

"What I saw?"

"Yes. You still haven't answered the question."

I shut my eyes, thinking: here goes nothing.

"Two people, half-naked from the waist down. My wife, and that man."

I pointed at Dr. Don, who was busy counting the weave in the carpet.

"Originally, I thought we could film them together. The investigator said he could come back next week with a rented cherry-picker, raise himself up with a video-cam and catch them in the act."

"Why didn't you?"

"Same reason I left the private eye downstairs. I thought I could take it, but I couldn't. Once I knew, all of a sudden, I didn't want any more to do with it. With her."

I could still see Rue sitting back there, her chin up. Thing is, she wasn't crying or falling apart and I've gotta say, it impressed me.

The defense attorney, Heidegger, he really let me have it when he got his chance. I'd sued Dr. Don, and agreed not to talk about the case again. Boy, the state attorney jumped out of her chair when she heard that, telling the judge there was no such thing as a civil-case gag order, I was bound by the law and my oath to tell the truth, and so on. The judge made Heidegger knock it off, but really, he never stopped ragging me with his cross-examination. Made me out as an opportunist out only for money—sure, I said sarcastically at one juncture, I *wanted* to wreck my marriage and blow up the family as part of a master plan to net some bucks in a stupid lawsuit. But no one, not even the judge, could save me from the beating I took. It was just before lunch when I limped out of there, not looking back, that tough bitch from the attorney general's office acting like she wanted me out of her sight anyway, which I didn't quite understand. I'd done my duty and gave her what she wanted in the first place. So I waited outside, in the hallway, till she came out.

"Well, so how'd I do?" I asked her.

"Thank you for coming," was all she said before she started to walk away.

"Hey, hey wait!" I grabbed her by the arm, and when she whirled on me, a sheet of that straight long hair fanned out over her head like a halo. Her cheeks were high and perfect, but her eyes were jumpy up close. I got the hell back instinctively.

"Doesn't matter what I think about how you did," she said. "All that matters is what the judge decides."

"You know, I almost didn't come," I said. "But I did. For Rue."

She waited for me to say more, and seemed disgusted when I didn't oblige her.

"For Rue," she said. "Uh-huh."

Without another word she started to walk away.

"What—that doesn't count for anything?" I asked with open palms.

"What do you want, a medal?"

"Well, hey," I said, trying to lighten things up, "if you've got one handy . . . "

Apparently she had no sense of humor, because that's when she stepped right up into my grill.

"I've got one more question for you."

"Sure. Shoot."

"When you saw them together, did the vic—did Rue appear to be enjoying herself?"

"Kiss my ass, lady."

"I'm serious," she said. "Put your feelings aside, and think: was she enjoying herself?"

"What's the damn difference?"

She leaned against the wall behind her. "Think about it."

And I did. The answer was there, right in front of me. I could see it all just like it was yesterday.

"She looked like a zombie. A robot."

"Your ex-wife is mentally ill. All her life, she's been a victim of men who want to dominate her. Almost all her life. You were the one good guy who didn't fuck her over. Until you did by bailing on her." She studied my face. "Oh, why bother? You can't even see it."

"See what? After all that, *I* was supposed to stick by *her* side? Who the hell are you to judge me?"

"Okay. You manned up and told the truth today. Stood by her for once."

"Damn right I did!" I sounded angry, but she'd knocked the wind out of me.

"I'm sorry, I didn't realize what a great accomplishment you thought this was. I'll look into getting that medal for you." She walked away before I could fire off another hollow protest.

Speechless, I staggered out of the place with my head down, and didn't look up until I was back at the pay lot, the Softail gleaming in the midday sunlight like a magic carpet designed just for me.

Rue was standing ten feet away from it. All I could think was to throw my leg over the tank and key the ignition. The Harley fired up with all the power and precision of a twenty-one-gun salute; it's a moment I always love, so filled with the promise of the open road stretched out ahead. Horns were honking and people were out walking the streets and a cool breeze was tunneling its way down through the old stone buildings, and boy, how I wished I could slide up the kickstand and tilt those handlebars toward the curb. But Rue, she'd come closer, near enough to rest her tiny hand on mine.

I sat there on twenty-five grand worth of gurgling chrome, my ex-wife silently patting my hand. Turns out I'd asked the wrong woman for an atta-boy I didn't really deserve anyway.

"Thanks for coming, Andy. Drive safe, and take care of yourself." Kissed me softly on the cheek.

My eyes were hot and scratchy—lotta dust blown in them, from off those dirty downtown streets, I guess. The Softail came to life in a clean, straight shot down Fourth, right past a busy street called Los Angeles. Rue was heavy on my mind, and as I glided along, gassing it as the road tilted left near Alameda, in my mind, I was back outside Dr. Don's office that one ugly day, but this time I played it differently and stormed inside the building, kicked down a door or two, and protected my woman from all harm. Righted a wrong still in its inception, instead of letting it fester and grow. I was so locked into this . . . alternate vision, that I forgot I was tooling a Harley in lanes of traffic. I snapped out of that weird sort of trance when I came up on a guy crossing Fourth, a tall, dark-haired guy with a deep tan and a . . . what? He was carrying, of all things, a big, old-time surfboard under his arm. A longboard. I just missed smashing him with my dual pipes blaring a *Kindly get the lead out* message when he caught my eye with what I can only describe as a nod of respect—like he was saying, *Finally, man, but you did it.* Maybe I was on the right track, at last, by taking ownership of my failure to act that day outside Dr. Don's place.

How could a stranger in the road with a surfboard know this? You'd have to ask God or Satan, but anyway you want to look at it, I felt better. Turned my head to check behind me, over my shoulder, even though I was doing fifty. Didn't see the guy with the surfboard anywhere—anywhere!

Ho! These old downtown streets always felt haunted to me, loaded down with the abandoned dreams of all the weak and foolhardy souls who have packed up their dreams and headed west and met only heartache and failure. *Enough with the sunshine voodoo, please!* I dropped down a gear and goosed the throttle.

Man, oh man, that rise onto the stone bridge over the LA River lifted me up, up so sweetly, such a carbon-blasting reawakening of the soul, it was, the Harley thundering beneath me like an apocalyptic cavalry. Moments like this usually make me feel like the king of the road, the cock of the walk. Instead, by the time I hit the 101 south, I was clinging to that Softail like it was the side of a lifeboat, the whole time thinking how wrong, how very wrong I'd been about my life. I always thought I'd been on the short end of the stick, how nothing seemed to work out in my favor. But I'd got out of it exactly what I'd put in—no more, no less—and now, I'd have to find a way to live with that forlorn, indisputable truth.

Southbound 101, you will kindly save my life now by carrying me home, posted speed limits be damned.

Air smashing me in the face and still I can't catch a breath. Softail sailing, RPM dreaming . . .

I loved you, Rue, I truly did, just not the right way, not like you needed. And not enough. No, not near enough, my poor mistreated darling. I know that now . . .

19

DESHAUN FELLOWS

My first problem with testifying had to do with walking into the state building downtown. Soon as I get in there I see two brothers in police outfits working security, a line of folks waiting to scoot through a metal scanner. Sign says ABSOLUTELY NO WEAPONS ALLOWED, and I know, it's a crime to even come through here with one. I'm like: Damn, forgot all about this government building security! That means I gotta go all the way back to my car, three blocks, lock my piece in the glove, and hope some hopped up 'baser making his nut around here slinging purple caps doesn't spy me parking the piece, and doesn't go pulling a smash-n'-grab with a crowbar while I'm gone, leave me without a strap when Bulldog comes for me.

Yeah, that's right, Bulldog. Word on the street is he knows I'm the one got his little lady Sadie on a plane out of LA—which is true, so it's not like I can hide from the truth. I know he'll be along soon enough to even the score, it's how a bad boy like Bulldog keeps score, it's how a young man with an eye-for-an-eye, street hoodlum's code would be thinking. Damn sad how you jus' know he's gonna wind up dead or in prison, that Bulldog. One more thing I know, though, is I don't want to be a clay pigeon.

But I can't get into court carryin,' not even with a license, can't slip in through a back door or climb up a fire escape, so I guess a clay pigeon I am. Jus' two blocks up, and two back, that's all I gotta worry about. Knowing jus' that same I must be suicidal to do this, Bulldog waiting out there somewhere and me not carryin,' but here goes nothing.

Light foot traffic on the street and I'm practically running down the sidewalk. No Bulldog yet. Then it hits me: I'm in no danger for now. If he's watching me, gettin' ready to move, he's smart enough to let me stash the piece first before confronting me.

Not that I can take any credit for showing up—it was Ida Mae who set me on my current course of personal responsibility. Ever since that lady lawyer came around with her subpoena, I've been making plans to leave with Ida Mae and Sadie, close up shop, look into the licensing regs for a state of Louisiana PI, concealed weapon applications, and assorted whatnot. Then once I get there, I'll look around for a quiet little parish needs an experienced PI, work something on a part-time basis, that's all I want to do. But I've been noticing little things? Tell's me something inside ain't right. Like, I'm losing my energy for doing tasks, simple jobs. Got roses to tend outside the kitchen window, bag of mulch needs spreadin', but all last weekend, I couldn't drag my butt out of my chair and out the door to do it. Eating less, too, because food jus' don't seem to taste as good, even a pulled pork sandwich from Meat n' Taters, a very fine southern barbecue place down the block. Can't hardly sleep either, not without waking up, every dog barking or car backfiring doin' a drumbeat right on the back of my skull. Haven't even looked at Ida Mae 'tween the sheets, meantime—and that's enough said about that. We talked about the situation plenty, me doing most of the talkin', giving the wife every good reason I can think of for us to get on outta town. You know, we can start fresh too, I say, jus' like Sadie.

Ida Mae, she listened quietly, thinking hard. Last night, she says: "I know, I know, honey, that's all fine, lover, you're making good sense."

"But what?" I say. "Go ahead, out with it."

"But you're leaving out a reason, the most important one, in fact."

"For staying put."

"Yes. You left out the main reason you gotta stay," she said.

Ida Mae told me straight, and I listened. Woman know me better than I know myself.

I got to my car, stashed the hardware, got back up the block to court in one piece, made it past the uniformed brothers easy enough.

Which meant that the time had arrived for me to speak like a licensed investigator with years of experience in commercial, professional, and domestic matters.

It's just how it is. When white people pony up a big retainer to a black man, have him look into an important issue, clean up an untimely mess, this is how they expect a black man to conduct himself when he reports back with his findings.

Anyhow, what I was building up to saying was the reason I showed up here today. You see, I try not to get involved in the personal business of my clients or their loved ones; seems to me a good investigator can't do his job right—can't maintain the objectivity necessary to make sound decisions—without keeping an emotional distance. But talking to Ida Mae, I discovered something right under the surface of all the work I'd done for Andrew Loberg. I really hated what that Dr. Don did to Mr. Loberg's wife, and his family. In my eyes, Dr. Don was just like Bulldog: a bully, an exploiter of the weak. Only real difference is Bulldog, a black man, carries large bore hardware, while Dr. Don, a white man, travels with a team of lawyers.

Sixth floor, some empty hallways with nice carpet, not a sound, not a soul . . . *where's the rock and where's the roll?* Guess I'll find that out soon enough. I take my time, follow the signs to the courtroom, look through the little glass window cut into the door, and see a judge in there, talking to a court reporter, a nicely dressed woman in the middle of changing the paper roll in her little black reporting machine. Kick around the idea, one more time, that maybe I should just leave, scoot, get on outta here before anyone sees me.

Ida Mae's with me in spirit, just like she said she'd be.

Ready to go inside, Deshaun?

Yeah, Ida Mae, I'm here, guess I might as well—and then, I get a surprise tap on the shoulder! I swing around, ready to rumble, all right, thinking: *How in hell did Bulldog found a way to get through security down below? How in hell—*

"Hello, Mister Fellows."

Oh, man, relief—not Bulldog. Instead, it's the possum-faced Mr. Leyes. I could've hugged him for not being Bulldog, but my dislike for him rushed in just as quick as my relief that I wasn't facing a killer unarmed. By the time Mr. Leyes reached out his little white hand to shake mine, I'd recovered.

"What're you doing here?" I said.

Mr. Leyes was in another nice suit, this one black like the other one he wore, but double-breasted. Smiling, but I could tell he was nervous, could smell the sweat and cologne and antiperspirant under his lapels. Last time I caught that scent that strong was in the tunnel at the Coliseum for an SC football game, Trojans losing their homecoming game against Arizona, a team they should've been putting a whipping on. Lotta nervous wealthy white men in attendance. Same smell.

Mr. Leyes, he looked at me like he noticed I had no pulse during our handshake.

"Interesting question," he said, "because I was just about to ask you the same thing."

I unfolded the subpoena from the pocket of my sport coat, showed it to him. He read it, shaking his head. Gave me a so-what kind of look.

"As you can see, it's what I've got to do," I say.

"Deshaun, please be reasonable. When I came to your office, I felt certain we'd worked out a mutually beneficial arrangement. Had a meeting of the minds, so to speak."

"I don't see any contract."

"A valid contract *can* be oral, Deshaun."

"I'm guessing you learned that in law school, am I right?"

"This is not a game."

"Yeah, well, here I am. The subpoena wasn't my idea, sir. You know that."

He frowned. Put his hand under his chin and propped up his elbow with the other hand, like he was the principal thinking about sending the upstart black boy home for the day. Or the week.

"We struck a bargain."

"So you're now saying.'"

"You do know this causes complications—"

Whatever complications he was coming to, I didn't care as I reached into the other side of my jacket. Leyes cringed when I did, and I felt just a tingle of pleasure at his expense, slowly pulling out my hand, which I shaped like a gun.

"Bang," I said, the man tilting back like he wanted to avoid the kick from my loaded index finger.

"Now you listen to me, Mr. Fellows—"

"I don't know what you take me for," I said, puffing up my chest as best I could.

"We had a *deal*."

"No, you just thought you had a deal. Now, I may not have looked exactly overjoyed to see you here today, but I am truly glad you came. You saved me a trip down Wilshire to see you."

I reached into my jacket again, this time pulling out the envelope with the money. I'd been carrying it around, on my person, ever since he'd first handed it to me that day he came to my office.

He acted like I'd hit him with a stun gun, Rodney King style. There had to be something witty and wise I could say, but the truth is, I wasn't prepared to part with all that money, not up until that minute. So many things I could do with that cash, for myself and my family. I'd been hoping there was some other way I hadn't thought of, some way to justify my keeping it. But I was stumped. Truth is, it hurt like hell to part with all that cabbage, even though I'd thought about it plenty before now. But I let it go, slapping the envelope against the man's lapel.

"Mr. Fellows. Your commitment to civic duty is inspirational, but actions do have consequences."

"Nothing left to talk about," I said as I turned to grab the knob on the courtroom's door.

"Did you hear me?" Leyes hissed like a snake who'd just been stepped on. "This isn't over."

I may be a little longer in the tooth these days, but my temper still fires up strong, under the right conditions; and this little man in the fine suit, with three little words, just kicked off a major storm inside me. His eyes got bigger as I stepped back to where he stood, the cords in my arm tightening like when I hit the bench press in my garage.

"I heard you fine, Mister Leyes. Now I'm gonna tell you something you need to hear. Anybody messes with my family, I'm coming right back to you and you alone. Understood?"

His breathing was tight, as if he was squeezing air through a straw, but he nodded.

"I told you before, I'm a former military policeman. But I don't think you listened, I don't think you understand what that means. No, that day you were too busy talking sports and barbecue and other shit you know nothin' about, Mr. Leyes."

"Now, Deshaun," he muttered, but I ignored him.

"When I was an MP, I used to go after AWOL Marines, badasses who were trained to use guns, trained in hand-to-hand combat and weaponry. Think that was an easy job?"

"I'm sure it wasn't."

"Damn right it wasn't. Now, that was a long time ago, but let me update you to the present, so listen carefully. I still carry a concealed weapon, Mr. Leyes. And make no mistake, I know how to use it. To you, that means if you send someone to do your dirty work for you, they'll wind up dead. You wouldn't want that on your conscience, would you?"

His "no" was barely a whisper, but it was good enough.

"And then I'll come back to deal with you. You do understand that."

The man's forehead was getting sweaty and the wisps of hair on his head had gone a little sideways, blowing like tiny frayed curtains when he exhaled.

"I don't take kindly to this treatment," he said.

"It's the hand you've been dealt. In time you'll come to accept it."

Man, my back hurt just from pumping myself up and my head hurt from thinking up all that tough-guy shit I just laid on him. Seemed to have the effect I was after, though. Mr. Leyes teetered back like the thought of making a run for it was making some sense.

"If you'll excuse me," he said.

Maybe the whole Bulldog thing was making me cranky, maybe the fear was chewing on my insides to the point where I was too ready to fight, just mix it up at the drop of a hat. But I couldn't resist messing with Mr. Leyes one more time, and as he backed away, checking to see if I was following him, I raised my big black hand, my thumb and forefinger at ninety-degree angles, just like a pistol, pointing right at him as he backed his ass down the hall.

*   *   *

Man, I'd kill a nun for a drink right now, I was thinking when I walked in. Three men in fine dark suits, looking like they buy their clothes where Mr. Leyes shops, were sitting next to a nervous-looking Dr. Don at a table on the left, and that state prosecutor who looks like she popped right out of a music video sat at a table opposite theirs. The prosecutor got up to shake my hand, smiled and thanked me for coming, but she was no-nonsense and before I could offer any chitchat, she pointed me right to the witness stand. The judge welcomed me, said he hoped the traffic and parking down here wasn't too much trouble for me.

No, judge, I wanted to say, *the parking and traffic were okay. Staying alive?*—now *that* might be a problem.

The man in the black robe, he took his time swearing me in, like he was making sure I could follow the concept of telling the truth. Well, yes, sir, I do know what is at stake here, I wanted to pop back, but I just nodded the way a man making a living in the service of others is expected to nod.

They started with my background. Always funny, how they act all impressed when they hear about my credentials, as if any man like me with a resume must have stolen it from a white person.

Ms. Aames ran the show. I started to tell her about Mr. Loberg hiring me to investigate his wife, and Mrs. Loberg's goings-on with the psychiatrist, but the defense lawyer, Mr. Heidegger, he jumped out of his seat and told the judge I couldn't say anything because my investigation was confidential, that he knew that from the civil case. I thought Ms. Aames would never get to speak, but she just chilled, let the judge get tired of hearing Heidegger. Then she told the judge Mr. Loberg had waived any confidentiality when he testified earlier in the case, this case.

Mr. Loberg? I was thinking.

I have to say, I was impressed that Andy Loberg had shown his face in here, because the last time I saw him, he wanted nothing to do with this business about Dr. Don. Must've had his own Ida Mae backing him.

Or that prosecutor. Fine-looking woman, Ms. Aames, I admit that's what's foremost on my mind whenever I look at her. But then, something about her was too wound up. Like, if she was armed, you'd best duck for cover.

The lawyers for Dr. Don, they just kept going on and on about how I shouldn't be here at all; and Ms. Aames, she stayed on my mind, her pretty face right across from me, where I was sitting, could see her tensing and twitching, like her insides were twisted up. Reminded me, Ms. Aames with that handsome troubled face, of the summer when I was a boy in Terrebonne Parish, got a job at the fairgrounds, cleaning out stalls where they had horse races. Backbreaking work at ten cents a stall, man, and I was standing in foot-deep horse dung. The stalls, they were supposed to be empty when I'd come round to clean them, but this one afternoon, a filly that got scrubbed from the card at the last minute because of an infected hoof got left behind and was probably sleeping off the meds they gave her when I came stumbling along. Anyway, I start pitching dirty hay out of that stall and that horse wakes up, bolt upright, and we see each other, eye to eye, both of us surprised as hell. Horse might've killed me if the kick it tried connected, but I got out of there, left that pitchfork right on the ground, didn't care. The filly, she ran out the open stall, ran free for fifteen, twenty minutes, bucking hard and nothing could calm her down. Turns out that horse was a little mad, and the hoof disease pushed it over the edge. Never ran another race; I think they put her down.

Maybe I'm wrong and I hope I am, but to me, Ms. Aames, she had the same look in her eyes as the filly did.

So, after a while longer the judge got tired of hearing, Heidegger complain about me and said my testimony was proper. Well, I thought, I'm not sure about proper, but at least I can hope to live up to that standard.

Ms. Aames questioned me, slow and steady, like she knew just how to get a witness to tell a story. And I did, told about how I got hired by Mr. Loberg, tailed Mrs. Loberg myself back to Dr. Don's office building, figured out his window blinds were open enough so I could see inside, took some pictures.

"No, I didn't see genitalia, I couldn't see that low, but I saw clothing coming off, Mrs. Loberg's bare breasts once, Dr. Don getting on top of her on a couch."

Mr. Heidegger asked me if I brought the photos with me, to show them to the court today.

"No, sir," I said. "I don't have them. I gave them, along with the negatives, to Mr. Loberg at his request."

Mr. Heidegger asked me if I wrote a report. I said no. He wanted to know why. I said Mr. Loberg told me his attorney in the lawsuit told him—

"Objection," Ms. Aames said. "That information is attorney-client privileged and confidential between Mr. Loberg and his counsel."

"Your Honor," Heidegger said, "if he told the investigator, he waived that privilege."

The judge agreed with Heidegger and told me to answer the question.

"Well, he said it's better not to have a report because that way, they wouldn't have to turn it over to the other side."

"You mean in discovery?"

"I don't know. I'm not a lawyer."

"So, they were already planning to sue my client, Dr. Fallon, when they hired you, isn't that true?"

"Objection, calls for speculation," Ms. Aames said.

"If you know the answer, go ahead," the judge told me.

"Yes," I said. "They wanted to sue."

There weren't too many other questions, but man, I felt like I blew it when I talked about not writing that report. I almost stopped at Ms. Aames's table to apologize to her when the judge excused me, but that would've looked terrible so I kept on walking. Back in that empty hallway, I got about halfway down to the elevators before I decided to stick around, wait for them to take a break. Honestly, I know what that Dr. Don did to the woman, how it wrecked their marriage, and she was a mess already. Now, I make it seem like I was part of a trap. Any fool could see that's where the defense was gonna take this thing—we were all ganging up on poor Dr. Don, trying to fleece money outta him. Damn, I could've handled those report questions better. Truth is, sometimes I don't write a report because they do take time to prepare, and sometimes a client doesn't want to pay for one. I could've said that! Damn, I felt like I should apologize to Ms. Aames so I found a spot along the wall, leaned against it, and waited.

A few minutes later, Ms. Aames came out, but she walked the other way without seeing me and went into a room farther down the hall in the other direction from me. I walked over and out she came, with a big, I mean very big, woman who looked like she'd seen a ghost or something. Ms. Aames was talking to her nice and soft, calming her down. Ms. Aames saw me and the thing about her eyes, the jumpiness, had changed—in fact, when I told her I wanted a brief word with her, it seemed like she was counting something, doing a math problem in her head. She asked me what it was, and man, I was too embarrassed to say right in front of that huge woman, a stranger and all. Last thing I wanted to do was say something stupid about myself testifying poorly and make this woman, who I was pretty sure by now was the state's next witness, feel even jumpier about testifying herself.

I told her not a problem, it could wait.

The huge woman called to Miss Aames to say she forgot something and ducked back into the room she just come out of. Then Ms. Aames seized the moment, walked up to me close as if to say thank you, put her hand on my forearm.

"Thanks for sticking around. We can walk out together when I'm done, if that's okay."

"Yes, ma'am. Sure. That'll be fine."

I could tell Miss Aames wanted to talk about something on her mind but she wasn't in a position to tell me what, not just then.

Man, that's when the thing that really bugged me about this case came right up to the surface, really got to me. A voice inside me said: *What's your hurry, man? Where you gotta be goin' to, anyways?*

All this courtroom stuff had me thinking, again, about the job I did for Mr. Loberg, how seriously messed up this shit with Dr. Don had been from the start. Kind of thing you take for granted in my business, but the reality, it's terrible just the same. Mrs. Loberg was a patient, lady with a lot of big problems that needed help, and the professional supposed to help her, a doctor at that, took a lot of her husband's money and took advantage. Helped himself to her naked body. Man, I know it was business that brought me into this thing but there was something else about it, something Ida Mae knew all along. And this lady prosecutor who looked like she was carrying around a medicine ball on her back? She was in there fighting three lawyers just so I could open my mouth to say what I saw, saw with my very own eyes. And do a damn poor job on that witness stand, I must admit.

The lady prosecutor knew, too.

She came out of that room where her next witness was waiting, saw me. I smiled.

"You look a little weary," she said.

"The truth shouldn't be so hard to get to, Miss Aames. They took what I said and tied it up in knots."

She looked at me a little funny, but her face was kind.

"It might seem that way, but that's just how the law works."

"Yes, ma'am."

She seemed okay with the lousy job I did on the stand and I wanted to say good luck or something light like that, but she said her next witness was waiting—and I knew it had to be the fat lady who forgot something. Door swung open on cue, the fat lady came out, looking ready to jump right out of her skin. *Man, Miss Aames, you got a full plate*, I was thinking.

Feeling tired, I leaned against the wall, closed my eyes, picturing Ida Mae in that champagne-colored dress she wore to the city hall the day we tied the knot, girl putting her dainty little hand in mine, giggling as she slid the gold band onto my finger.

So then, Ms. Aames, she's done whispering with the big lady in the dress so wide it looks like a bed sheet, lady looking more nervous than I was the day I got hitched to Ida Mae. They were ready, so they walked on by me, and I had to turn sideways a little jus' to make room. Truth is, the big lady's not jus' big, she's giant, and panting and sweatin' up a storm already, dabbing a hankie on her forehead while Ms. Aames is whispering something in her ear. Big lady turns quick and sees me looking her way, smiles at me and winks, like *Don't worry, my friend, this thing is in the bag*.

Well, how about that, she's gonna give it a go, and I hope she fares well. And like that, I recognized the benefit that came out of my testifying. You do battle, it's always better to have people around that have your back. The judge was getting a picture I couldn't quite see on my own, but maybe I provided a solid piece of it, a piece only I could supply.

Ida Mae was on my mind, her spirit telling me: *Deshaun, you married a damn smart woman, all right.*

Mighty big of you to point that out, Ida Mae.

Jus' listen to me, hardheaded black man. You ain't a bad fella yourself. You done right coming here today.

Thank you kindly.

Honest to God, I can't explain—no, that's a lie. Thing is, I wanted to hold on to that feeling longer. So I peeled myself off that wall, walked in behind them, and found a seat in the back of the courtroom to watch. Ms. Aames came over immediately, whispered she wanted me to sit with her at counsel table, if that was okay. She said it might help with the judge, he might see the state's case more as a team effort.

I said yes, yes—sure I will.

Got that feeling again.

20

WENDY GLICK, MEDICAL DOCTOR

Seventy-two. Yes, Wendy, seventy-two, and you're still alive and well.

Seventy-two hours—that's how long it was since I last ingested a benzodiazepine.

I knew that if I was going to testify, I couldn't get through it by having to admit I was under the influence of meds of any kind. According to Ms. Aames, that kind of revelation is an instant credibility killer. She ought to know. Girl was fighting some kind of a battle, and I don't mean the mostly civilized one happening in the courtroom. I mean, the Battle of Evermore going on inside her head.

Guess we were a pair, she and I. My nerves had been shot for the entire week leading up to this day. Last night was a decided low point. I didn't sleep a wink, finally giving up at 3:00 a.m.—just in time to turn on the tube and catch the weather report. *Oy—so very glad I don't live in the land of grain silos and cornhuskers.* That was my quite rational conclusion. In the Midwest, they've got their snowdrifts and icy roadways that kill people. Here, you drive too fast, about all you do is arrive where you're going sooner. Last night's update featured a deadly pile-up outside of Omaha, some poor schmuck plastered like a june bug on the grill of an eighteen-wheeler. When the subject turned to LA, the TV weatherman had no real weather to report on, so he cracked wise about whether the "stars" would be visible at the Hollywood Bowl for some benefit concert tonight.

Now that I can reflect on it, I think that weather report helped me, afforded me some perspective. Reminded me how lucky I actually am to be who I am, living where I live.

So okay, my life is what it is. I'm fat and ugly, but lovable, if only you take the time to get to know me! My typical therapy session, I'll listen to a reality-show producer kvetch about how his daughter is breaking the bank at Princeton, changing her major every time she brushes her teeth and charging Swedish massages to the credit card he gave her to buy groceries. So what? Boo-hoo. The kid's helping the economy in New Jersey, I could sassily point out; or I might try some therapeutic tough love and make him sit through one of the same shitty TV shows that's making him a mint, because I bet he doesn't get around to watching that junk, and if he did, maybe he'd recognize how meager a contribution to humanity his shows offer. Life in a body-piercing salon; hillbillies catching giant catfish using their own ham-hock forearms as bait; a doggie-wedding consultant. But because I'm a professional, I retain my dignity, sighing and nodding sympathetically until he hands me a check and leaves. And if you're inclined to call me a sellout of a therapist, I'll tell you I am not because if a patient is willing to change and do the hard work, I'm always, always there to help. But the bottom line is most people don't possess the will; they just want to talk, and they'll pay me just to listen. It's easy, doing what I do, listening mindfully to their often mindless chatter. So yeah, maybe I haven't got it so great; maybe I'm not changing the world a patient at a time, the way I once thought I would. But I'm also not in a pile-up outside Omaha, waiting for the Jaws of Life to pluck me like a chocolate wedged between the sofa cushions; I'm not on my meds and can still apparently function; and I'm not in Bradlee Aames's shoes.

In my line of work you hear a lot of talk, and much of it is gibberish, but you also see with your own eyes the signs of mental illness. And Ms. Aames, this dear girl who seemed genuinely concerned with how I'd hold up on the stand, well, she was showing some serious signs:

counting her steps as we walked, quietly conversing with herself about how she was *real*, the defense attorney's last objection was *real*, I was *real*, but that wall of water at the end of the hall, sweeping our way? No, dear, though God love her, she said she wished she'd brought her surfboard. I'd observed without judgment as she touched every one of the black rosary beads around her neck, sequentially, as if she was pushing buttons at a console, her taut game-face hiding the meaning of each gesture but her lower lip quivering with secret words. Not that I'm one for armchair diagnoses—they're unprofessional—but this girl was teetering on the brink of something deep and dark.

Then again, who is Wendy Glick to judge? I admit I got dressed about eight times this morning, couldn't decide what horrible, shape-less garment to drape over my horrible shapeless physique. I admit that when I saw how close the judge was from the witness stand, I thought he'd stare at my moles in revulsion before abruptly throwing up. But he didn't. The oath was, well, just an oath; his greeting, friendly and apropos. Still, my mind was raked with worry.

As lawyers go, Ms. Aames was brilliant, effortlessly walking me through the sexual exploitation scenario, every allegation. I had an easy time of it, starting with the Hippocratic Oath for every doctor, which is to do no harm, then breaking down the psychiatrist-patient dynamic, explaining how therapy is based on confidentiality and trust, how transference and countertransference—the natural strong feelings a patient can develop for her therapist, and the similarly natural recip-rocal feelings the therapist experiences in return—can work. And how sometimes, in a case such as this, those phenomena can get horribly out of hand.

"If the facts alleged are proven to be true," Ms. Aames asked, "would Dr. Fallon have committed a departure from the standard of care?"

"Yes," I told her, "an extreme departure. What Dr. Fallon did to Mrs. Loberg was not only criminal, but from a professional standpoint, it was grossly negligent."

"You discussed her diagnosis of borderline personality earlier. Doc-tor, I'm not suggesting that anyone can predict human behavior with absolute certainty, but would you say Mrs. Loberg had a higher chance of becoming a victim of exploitation from her psychiatrist?"

"Absolutely. Borderlines have more trouble delineating the parameters of their relationships with others. They also tend to be vulnerable to authority figures."

"Would Dr. Fallon, as a trained psychiatrist, know these weaknesses?"

I shot my best disdainful glare toward the well-dressed man half bent over his notepad. He didn't look up, though his flat-faced lawyer aimed a sourpuss face right back at me.

"If he was any good, he would."

I could hear the judge tapping away at his laptop as I spoke, which I took to be a positive sign. In terms of saying what I needed to say for the state to prove its case, my testimony was effectively over. But the defense hadn't taken their crack at me and I knew Ms. Aames would try to take the wind out of their sails by more gently having a go first-up.

What I wasn't ready for was how I'd react, minus any assistance from my meds. Funny—looking back, all I'm recalling about this part of my testimony is pieces, like a broken puzzle.

Anxiolytics.

Yes, I said. I'd taken them for years. Since my freshman year in high school.

And benzodiazepines, I discussed them freely as well. School problems . . .

You could call it a leave of absence. I was out all of one semester. They thought it was a breathing issue due to my, uh . . . weight problem. But I knew it wasn't.

Lorazepam.

My father, he was so disappointed in me. His only daughter, who'd surely never marry.

Sure, of course I tried all kinds of diets, stopped eating. Still didn't lose weight. An internal medicine specialist isolated my problem, a rare thyroid condition.

That's right, a medical condition, I'm not just a fatty by choice. Essentially I've got the world's worst metabolism . . .

Robby Valderi. He was in my homeroom. Big, handsome jock, on the football team of course, but he could be mean. Really mean. . .

Wendy Wideload.

  Wendy Ick.

    Wendy Glick-you-make-me-sick.

      Wendy I-wouldn't-even-do-you-with-Herbie-
      Eisenberg's-dick.

Symptoms? They abounded.

I started to pull my hair out a strand at a time. Had a quick enough wit with idiots like Robby, but when I was cornered, I'd get this horrible shortness of breath like I was choking.

The school psychologist, Mrs. Burns, hated the sight of me and would tuck in her elbows whenever I came into her office on a hall pass. In her warped mind, she was all about self-sacrifice. But she was horrifically out of touch. In fact, almost every time I saw her, she'd tell me the same old horrifically out of touch story, how, when she was a high school senior herself and getting ready for homecoming, her ball gown didn't quite fit right. So she'd taped her mouth shut at home to lose weight. And guess what? She was chosen as the class homecoming queen! Wow, what a heartwarming success story!

You see the connection, I'm sure; according to Mrs. Burns, I was fat and moley and undesirable because my will was flawed, too weak.

I didn't want to be beautiful *badly enough*!

All that unfeeling bitch gave me the will to do was die . . .

Alprazolam . . . banana stand. My secret password . . .

I hung in there pretty well at first under Ms. Aames's questioning, but the more I tried to explain myself, the more the walls in the courtroom started to shrink in on me, as if I was the trash in a trash compactor and had to be—deserved to be—crushed. By the time the cross-examination started, nausea was building in my throat and I was fighting to keep my breathing even.

Mr. Heidegger, a man whose jewels got squeezed in a vise every time Ms. Aames made a move, didn't scare me one bit. But he was smart enough to keep pushing me deeper into that trash compactor.

No, I did not steal this expert-witness assignment from Malcolm Flaherty. He bailed out on the state and went to Vienna. No, I did not read his expert report for this case. Was I supposed to?

Would I—open my bag? What? Were these people insane?

Ms. Aames was jumping up and down objecting, but the defense lawyer made an offer of proof—whatever that means—about how his associate had seen me in the witness room reading Malcolm's report and that this raises a serious issue of bias on my part. I can't read what I've never seen, I told the judge, but he looked at me as if he were stuck in a spot. So I agreed to open the bag . . . and there was Flaherty's damn report, right on top of all my things. Dammit—I'd gone across the room for a cup of water from the dispenser and left my bag and just when I did, some woman came in the witness room and started engaging me, asking me if I knew how to get to an IRS office, showing me some piece of paper with an address on it. When I came back I remember thinking: oh, my bag's zipped shut, not recalling it being closed like that.

"Someone must've put it there, Your Honor. I swear, I've never laid eyes on it before."

The judge said, "Doctor, just answer the questions the best you can."

Did I know what Doctor Flaherty concluded? No. But let me guess. Doctor Fallon was the world's greatest psychiatrist, bar none.

Nobody laughed.

They told me what Dr. Cut-n-Run said anyway. According to Malcolm, the patient appeared to be stalking Dr. Fallon after hours and the good doctor tried to befriend her, to be kind rather than report her to the police. She'd come onto him. His record-keeping was inadequate, as he'd failed to make notations describing this troubling development and he'd failed to refer her to another psychiatrist, someone who might help her with these obvious transference issues she was struggling with now.

Two simple departures from the standard of care.

Mashugana! What a bullshit finding! No wonder Malcolm was their man.

I remembered asking Bradlee Aames the day we first met and ate a box of candy together, why she'd ever wanted such a limp noodle as Flaherty as an expert in the first damn place. She had told me first of all, she hadn't chosen him, the board did. Somebody in Sacramento knew Dr. Don and was pulling strings for him, and Malcolm Flaherty was a marionette. But Ms. Aames said she'd figured out a way around the Malcolm problem. She was going to put him on the stand and then make him assume a different set of facts, one much closer to the truth about what happened. In that case, Malcolm would have to testify as I had, or look like a damn fool.

But he'd deserted the case, and here I was.

The one called Heidegger was staring at me.

"We're you just talking to yourself, Ms. Glick?"

"Uh, if I was, I wasn't aware of it."

"Did I just hear you say—forgive me your honor—that Doctor Flaherty's opinions were 'bullshit'?"

My throat tightened up and like that, I was breathing through a pinhole deep in my throat.

"I might have said that, yes. But only to myself."

"To yourself? I heard it too."

"Bully for you, sir."

"That doesn't seem like a very objective way to assess the opinion of a colleague, Ms. Glick. But you don't like Doctor Flaherty, do you?"

"It's not that I don't like the man. He's just—well, Malcolm."

"Didn't you, at a holiday party last year attended by several doctors in your practice—"

"We share suite space, Mister Heidegger. They're not my medical partners. I'm a sole practitioner."

Heidegger smiled as if I was entertaining him just by offering an answer.

"Yes, well, didn't you, at a party, call Doctor Flaherty a vulgar name and throw a glass of wine on him?"

"No. He came up behind me and made a tasteless joke."

"What kind of joke?"

"It doesn't matter."

"If you recall, please answer," the judge said.

"He made a joke about hiding out behind the barn. Me being the barn, that is."

The judge had stopped typing and was shaking his head as if to say: *Why do I have to listen to crap like this?*

"But he startled me," I said. "Bumped me in the elbow, and my wine spilled."

"Isn't it true that you physically attacked Doctor Flaherty?"

"No. Do I look to you like a person who routinely commits assaults?"

It sounded like a good counterpunch but I could barely breathe. The sweat was cascading off my forehead. I may as well have been hacking through a rainforest with a machete. Which is how I felt, trying to defend myself against this stupidity.

"What I mean is that I did nothing of the sort."

Lawyer Heidegger asked the judge if he could approach, and when the judge said yes, Heidegger glided over to Ms. Aames and handed her a document. Then he approached me with another piece of paper. Showed it to me. Told the judge it was a restraining order. Filed just days ago, before Malcolm had gone to Vienna.

I said I'd never seen it. The judge looked at me quizzically.

"You're not objective, Ms. Glick," Heidegger accused me.

"Sorry, I'm not following you, sir."

"You've got a vendetta against the state's other expert witness, their original expert."

"He's just a man to me, a colleague. Maybe one curiously lacking in moral fiber, but I really don't care, that's his problem."

"You'd do anything to show him up, to prove him wrong."

Then the lawyer held up a copy of Flaherty's report like he might swat a fly with it.

"Wrong. This isn't about Doctor Flaherty," I said.

The walls, they kept tightening, and all the air in the room began to corkscrew in on my temples, making me see stars.

"Let's discuss the medications you're taking."

"Wha . . . hold on."

"Currently."

"Nothing, nothing at all."

"—side effects."

"You're dirty tricksters," I practically yelled, but I couldn't breathe and barely a sound came out of my mouth. When that happened I started to get lightheaded and the air kept corkscrewing in on me, which made the room tilt and start to spin, and like *that* I was in a bad spell. I was in a black-and-white hell . . . Dorothy in that ratty old house, except I wasn't beautiful Judy Garland, I was Big Ballast, the gargoyle-ish Wendy Glick; that house kept on spinning, and it was only a time before it hit the ground, and I had to get out of it before it crashed.

They brought in paramedics, two nice young men who let me breathe from an oxygen bottle until I could sit up. About half an hour later, I told the judge I could continue. Insisted, despite his skepticism. Mr. Heidegger made a calculated goodwill gesture by saying he was finished with his questions.

"I think the witness has said quite enough," he told the judge. As if I'd been the one holding a shovel to dig the hole I'd fallen into.

"Redirect, Ms. Aames?" the judge asked. He seemed a touch intimidated by her physical presence just like all the other men, even from his privileged perch.

"Yes, thank you," she said. Then she smiled at me as if to say she trusted me enough, at least, that I could hold up under a little more scrutiny. Well, all right, I thought, my confidence suddenly spiking.

She asked me a few questions which I found easy to handle.

"You never saw the report, Mr. Flaherty's report, the one that was in your bag?"

"No, ma'am."

"Since you came to court, was there any time your bag was left unattended?"

"Yes, when I was in the witness waiting room. I went to get a drink of water and left it by the chair I'd been sitting in. I just remembered something, earlier, when I was being asked about this phantom report. As soon as I stepped away, this woman came sidling up to me, asking for directions to the IRS, sticking a piece of paper in my face so I couldn't see my purse."

"It was . . . a ruse?"

"Well, yeah. Even I know this is a State of California building, it says so all over the lobby downstairs. The IRS, they're federal."

I just couldn't help myself and glared at Dr. Don, that slimy defense lawyer and the other stiff suits at the table over there, the whole sorry bunch of schmucks.

"The woman wasn't even a good liar. They stuffed that report into my bag when I wasn't looking."

"Objection, speculation," said Heidegger.

"I'll allow it," the judge responded without looking up. He looked tired of the whole subject, and Ms. Aames took his cue and moved on, handing me a copy of the restraining order I'd never laid eyes on.

"No, I said, I'd never been served with this order."

"You have a suite on the same floor of the offices at 6220 Santa Monica Boulevard, correct?"

I looked right at the judge, with his natty gray beard, and answered yes.

"So, if this restraining order requires you to keep away, you wouldn't be able to access your office without violating the order, would you?"

"That's right. I'd be out of business. Which means, now that I've finally seen this, I'll have to retain legal counsel to get rid of it."

"Do you recall that first time I met you?"

"Yes, in my office."

"Do you know how that meeting came about?"

"Sure. Malcolm—Doctor Flaherty—he came to my office, trying to duck your visit with him."

"Pardon me?" the judge said.

"I mean, Your Honor, he was hiding from Ms. Aames here, said he didn't want to testify 'cause he was leaving for Europe—"

"Objection, hearsay, move to strike!" Mr. Heidegger shouted.

"I'll allow it," the judge said, and boy, did he look disgusted. He told me I could go ahead and finish my answer.

"So, I've actually done Doctor Flaherty a favor by substituting in on this case, since his sudden departure to a conference in Europe."

"Have you ever attacked Doctor Flaherty?"

"No, I am not a violent person. At all. I'm the type who gets bullied, not the other way around. I do, though, intend to call my lawyer, Mr. Abel Levine, to inquire about suing the pants off Doctor Flaherty."

"Why is that?"

"Because this declaration of his ought to be written on toilet paper. It's pure libel."

"Do you have anything to add to your testimony today?" Ms. Aames asked me.

I took a breath, resting my palms in my lap, thinking: *Wow, this was tougher than I imagined, dealing with the pressure of all this testy Q-and-A without any meds.* I saw my father's face back when I was a child, the way he wouldn't look at me when we were at Temple and he'd be talking with Rabbi Shenkman, bragging about his wonderful family, everyone except me. I'd become a doctor just to show him, just to prove my worth to him. Hah!—he didn't even come to the graduation. UCLA, way out west, on the coast, so far to fly on a plane, he always got cramps, sitting all those hours in one tight space, and the doc, his cardio specialist, he said it wasn't good for his circulation. And should we even discuss the parking in Westwood? Fuggedaboudit.

Robby Valderi was still inside my head, after all these years, taunting me.

Wendy Glick-you-make-me-sick.

Yeah? Well you can kiss my full-figured ass, Robby.

Given the final word, I knew what I had to do.

"One thing I didn't get to say, Ms. Aames, is how sorry I am, to you and—"

I nodded at the judge.

"—to you, Your Honor, about that, uh, little problem I had. Anxiety attacks are like relatives from out of town, they always come along at the most inopportune time."

The judge smiled, and a wave of relief hit me.

"And I want to apologize for making a spectacle in the courtroom. Not my intention."

"It was a medical emergency, Doctor Glick," the judge said graciously. "I'm relieved you're fine now."

Man, why can't I ever hook up with a guy like this: a professional man, smart, kind, successful, nice natty beard? Oh yeah, because I'm Wendy Glick, the scary chick . . .

"Thank you, Your Honor. One other thing, if I might. Just . . . people? I think we're all pretty vulnerable. My buttons got pushed and there I was, on the floor gasping for air. Mrs. Loberg? Now, she had a lot of buttons that could be pushed, quite a few, indeed."

I turned my gaze on Donald Fallon and pointed, no jabbed, a fat finger—bam! like I was poking him, and Robby Valderi, and Flaherty, and Mr. Heidegger, and every other prick who'd taken pleasure in picking on a fat moley Jewish girl who made just about the easiest target in the world, right in the eye.

"Her psychiatrist? He knew, he knew where every one of those buttons was located," I said. "If you decide that he did it, Your Honor, you know, that he sexually exploited that poor woman, well, I'm sure you'll never know the reason why, 'cause I'm also sure he'll deny the whole thing."

Heidegger started to object but I kept right on talking and he shut up.

"But if he did it, I can tell you as a psychiatrist myself, it was simple. I know life isn't fair. All I've gotta do is look in the mirror to remind myself of that. But some things ought to be very, very fair. Telling your problems, your deepest, darkest secrets to a therapist who's supposed to be looking out for your best interests, that has to be even-steven, fifty-fifty."

I leveled a long stare across the room one last time.

"I'm not here because a weak-willed colleague had to jet off to Vienna. I'm here because what that man did was wrong."

The judge typed quietly. Ms. Aames said she had nothing further—which was good, because I sure felt the same. Mr. Heidegger, he consulted a legal pad as if it were an oracle, and the rest of us waited, the sweat tingling down my many broad slopes and sliding into deep crevasses unseen by human eyes in decades. Apparently Mr. Heidegger had run out of mean-lawyer pills, but he scoffed, staring down the thin slope of his nose at me once more, for old time's sake, before he passed on asking any more questions.

I patted one hand in my lap with the other, sighing happily. The court-reporting gizmo was stone still, and I watched the gizmo-operator check the condition of a nail on her third finger. I smiled, and she smiled back. Sure, sure—I suspected the reporter, who'd done a bang-up job thus far of never making eye contact with the hideous blob on the witness stand was merely displaying a perfunctory courtroom courtesy; I get that, and I wasn't offended. See, I had reason, a real reason, to be happy: the courtroom wasn't spinning like that ratty old black-and-white house.

Hey, Wendy, I said to myself. *Hey, Big Ballast. Way to go. You are officially over the rainbow.*

Best day I've had in I don't know how long . . .

21

DeShaun Fellows

Dr. Glick had a handicap parking pass because of her weight most likely. So Ms. Aames and I got her out of the old Broadway building and over to her car pretty quick, nearest spot in the lot corner of Fourth and Hill. It was a white Honda minivan, almost new and as we helped Dr. Glick pile into the front seat, she explained how she'd picked this car because it had no center console and she could spill herself over toward the middle pretty easy and still be comfortable. Cheerful lady, thankful for the steadying hand I gave her—and leaning over at the last minute to me, asking in a whisper how'd I think she did, testifying and all, notwithstanding the "medical downturn."

Myself, still speaking in my most formal voice, being in a courtroom so many hours, I told her: "You did well, quite well, in my opinion. Judge was eating out of your hand, ma'am, any fool could see that. And there may have been a few of those in attendance, so there you have it."

She and Ms. Aames laughed. Then the doc got serious again, asked both of us what we thought, about the anxiety attack, the meltdown that came later. What it might've done to affect her credibility.

I lied first, told her it only made her more human. Ms. Aames said she agreed.

But in truth, it was a scary thing, seeing her laid out like that, couldn't even breathe, like a fish out of water. Lady had some fight in her, coming back the way she did, keep on keepin' on, like the Curtis Mayfield song goes. But that shit was scary.

"Thank you," she told me. "You're too much a gentleman to tell the unvarnished truth, but your discretion is much appreciated."

I had lied and right off, she knew it. Damn. Doesn't matter if the woman looks the way she does, she gets paid to observe people, to express her insights into the human mind. Of course she'd know I wasn't straight with her.

I was flush with shame and had to look away, down the block at a snarl of cars out in the intersection. This case, man, everything about it felt like being out to sea without a compass. I decided to play it straight from here on out.

The minivan fired right up, and Ms. Aames and I stepped back a foot or two. Right then, giving a tiny wave good-bye as we watched Dr. Glick pull out into traffic on Fourth, I should've said my good-byes to Ms. Aames, too. Wasn't safe, not with Bulldog out and about, because you never know where he might turn up. But truthfully, Bulldog wasn't much on my mind. Ms. Aames was onto something and just wouldn't let up. You could sense it ever since we left the courtroom. She wanted to talk.

We walked on down to Broadway and crossed on a green light without waiting. People were spilling out onto the streets, heading home from work at this hour, and every lane on Fourth was packed with cars and trucks and buses and scooters. A man with messy hair and a gut sticking out from a tee that was too small, looking like he crawled through a crack in the border fence about an hour ago, he came walking by pushing one of those white cooler carts with little pictures of ice cream plastered all over the sides. He smiled when Ms. Aames stopped him, and we saw that he had to be missing half his teeth.

I bought Ms. Aames a lime fruit bar and an ice cream sandwich for myself. We kept walking, going at our ice creams as the sunset start streaking the sky, turning the old brick and stone buildings down the block from gold and yellow to pink and ashy purple. Ms. Aames saw me looking south, a ways down Fourth.

"See that bank on the corner down there? One with the pillars as big as bridge supports?"

"Quite a beauty. Looks like an ancient temple."

"Imagine seeing it chasing you down the street."

"Say what?"

I had stopped walking altogether.

"That building. It chased me, but not really. You know, in my mind."

"No, ma'am. I don't follow."

She told me she had problems sometimes, with having visions, seeing things that weren't really there. Sometimes, but not all the time.

"How about in court."

"No," she said. "Well, rarely. Sad to say it, but most of the can't-believe-I'm-seeing-this bullshit I've witnessed in that place has been real."

"I'll bet. Don't they have medicine for that? Treatment?"

She said yeah, she'd tried a lot of different drugs, but most of them knocked her on her ass, to the point she couldn't work. "Or even feel like a normal person, Deshaun."

"Sounds pretty bad."

"It's worse than seeing things, not being able to outthink your opponent."

Some of the stuff she took didn't work at all, she said. Lately, she'd done better, found a way to keep sorting through what she sees, keep track of how her brain's working that way. Didn't sound like anything near a foolproof method of keeping your head on straight to me, but then, who am I to say? The young lady's a tiger in court, so it must be working.

Standing there, talking on the corner of Fourth and Spring now, we see some guy is walking a pair of dogs that look expensive, got these long noses and perfect fur, strutting with their heads up, tails straight like some dog-show judge is about to hand them a blue ribbon. Guy walking the dogs has tight jeans and a hairdo that looks windblown but I'd bet he spent an hour getting it to fall just so. Ms. Aames sees how I'm looking the dog-walker over.

"A lot of artist types live in lofts around here."

"This used to be wall-to-wall shitsville," I said. "It's something, how the times, and neighborhoods, keep on changing."

Ms. Aames said, "Yeah, but don't get too breathless about this place's transformation. You can score coke, pills, H, crystal meth, anything you want within a block or two from here."

I just stared at her again, same way I did when she told me the bank chased her down the street. She grinned, said that was just another way she coped with her brain being out of whack, but not so much anymore.

Finished my ice cream with one last, big bite. More poofy dogs passed on by. Ms. Aames said she was parked in an indoor garage another block away off Main. But first, something about the case was bothering her.

"It's how Rue Loberg found her way back to Dr. Fallon's office."

"What about it?"

"I can't bridge the gap from the time she left him as a patient, creeped out to the point that she'd have been happy if she never went back, to the following year when they're doing it on his couch. When I questioned her about that, um, transition, she seemed to hold back. Overall, her testimony was solid. I mean, to me she sounded highly credible throughout."

"I agree with you there, Ms. Aames."

"Please, it's Bradlee. But it was like she was skirting something, skipping over a step. I think the judge noticed it, too."

Right then I knew I had a problem, but I didn't realize it was written all over my face. Ms. Aames, she tilted up her dark shades and drilled those black licorice eyes right down on me.

"What's missing? And if you can't say, point me in the right direction. Tell me where to look."

I looked around, but on the street there was nobody but strangers around. "Thing is, that civil case I was hired to investigate on? Well, it paid real well, ma'am, and one of the things I had to agree to was, uh, not to talk about what I found."

She took a step back and hissed at the sky. "Please, not this shit again. What is up with these stupid civil settlements? It's not a fucking suicide pact, Deshaun. You're not cracking open the lost ark."

"I know, I know."

Ms. Aames pointed back up the street to where we come from, the big old, almond-color department store with the green trim on all the window frames and ledges.

"Then what was with the testimony I heard back there?"

"I probably said too much as it is, ma'am. My guess, Mister Heidegger's already been on the phone, making trouble for me."

She shrugged her shoulders, that big head of hair shakin' around. A man walking along in a gray suit on the sidewalk, he sees her and, boy howdy, needs a closer look, starts to stare so hard he almost trips over a hydrant.

"That asshole Heidegger can't find his way out of a paper bag, Deshaun. He tries to push your buttons, let me know. No—I'll make him cease and desist myself."

"You'd do that."

She looked at me, her perfectly shaped face a blank. "Hell yeah, with pleasure. I know a State Bar prosecutor, J. Shepard. He's a surfing buddy of mine. I make a professional misconduct complaint, J. will hand-carry that sucker through the system for me."

"You think this hush-hush stuff's against the rules for lawyers, huh?"

"I don't think so, I know it. He's suppressing evidence."

"I guess you're right."

"Listen, Heidegger approaches you with any money, let me know. He pulls that shit, I'll get his ass disbarred."

Her comment about money had me feeling lower than a legless skunk. The whole episode with Mr. Holmes was bringing me a mighty spell of shame, as you can imagine.

"Thank you, ma'am. You put my mind at ease."

"It's Bradlee, Deshaun. For a guy whose mind is at ease, you look like you've seen a ghost. You all right?"

"Long day. Lot on my mind."

I couldn't stand it anymore. Maybe I'd get sued by those people from the lawsuit, or maybe Ms. Aames could protect me by threatening them. Maybe the strong move I put on Mr. Leyes was enough. But I couldn't take it anymore. Standing there in a sea of foot-traffic, cars roaring down the cooling black asphalt, smell of piss rolling up from the gutters, I guess I made a decision.

"Now, that gap you were wondering about, between Mrs. Loberg's therapy, her quitting it, then coming back?"

She perked right up. "That's the part I just don't get, Deshaun."

"Their daughter. Mindy. They don't want to drag her into this mess. Girl was stuck in the middle, right in the part of the case you say you can't piece together."

"Why didn't Rue or Andy Loberg talk about her when they testified?"

"Because Mindy, she was stuck. Real bad. See, she used to see Doctor Don alone, and now and then, he wanted her mother and father to sit in too, even the messed-up son, so they could talk about problems they all were having, you know, within the family."

"Conjoint."

"That's right, ma'am. Mindy, she got this boyfriend, want to move in with him, and it causes this big fight with her parents, but Mindy has a mind of her own, she does it anyway. Meantime, both she and her mother had stopped seeing Doctor Don. But then, about a year later, things aren't going so hot for Mindy and the boy-friend, so she comes back to Doctor Don, to talk about it. What happens then is he uses Mindy as an excuse to get her mother back into his office."

Ms. Aames was stopped cold. "That's despicable."

"About how Mindy felt about it, too, ma'am. And when her mother and Dr. Don, um, got involved—"

"I'm sure she was blown away. Let me guess, by the time the lawsuit came along, she'd disowned her folks."

"Pretty much. And out of respect for her, because of the mess their family had become, they let her go her own way. But she did help with the lawsuit. At least long enough to see to it there'd be a settlement."

A tall guy lugging a rack of leather belts and purses slowed up like we might see something of interest and buy it. Ms. Aames gave him a look to rock him back on his heels.

"I'll bet Mindy Loberg was the key to the whole civil case."

"Yes, ma'am."

"They used her as the threat they needed to settle."

"You get the picture."

"Well, that's it, then. She has to testify."

"I thought your part of the case was over."

"Rebuttal," she said, a rack of bright white teeth shining confidently. Right then she stepped closer to me, near enough to put her hand around my wrist. "Thank you, Deshaun."

I shut my eyes, too ashamed to say you're welcome.

A steady flow of strange faces bent their way around us on the sidewalk. Homeless guy with a Lincoln beard, swearing and cussing at thin air. Hip young dude in a black suit and open collar, had a stare at Ms. Aames, of course, then me, probably wondering how a black man managed to break off such a fine piece.

"So, Mindy's done with her family."

"That's my understanding, ma'am."

"Can you find her for me?"

"I got a head start on all that already, Ms. Aames. When I investigated this thing, I left no stone unturned. Looked into the boyfriend's family when Mr. Loberg said he wanted to make sure Mindy would be okay. He paid me extra for that. Anyway, they run some concessions at swap meets, selling antiques and other valuables. Most of it legit, but a contact I got in LAPD, he ran a CII arrest report for me and come up with two burglary convictions, a grand theft, and a couple petty larcenies between Mom and Dad. Old stuff, a long time ago."

"What about the boyfriend?"

"He had an arrest for transporting stolen goods across state lines, but the AUSA who had the case didn't like it, so the kid walked. Some of the stuff the family sells, it's black market, for sure."

"Stolen."

"They're small-timers, but I'm pretty sure LAPD's still keepin' tabs on them. I'll make a call."

Ms. Aames smiled like she hadn't all day. "You are the *man*, Deshaun."

"Happy to help," I said.

"Help nothing, you're saving my ass."

I returned kind feelings, but inside, all I felt was torn up. I always thought I had my own business, a black man proud I didn't work for the Man. But what I failed to notice—or maybe just wouldn't admit to until now—was how easy it had become for me to let myself be bought. I held the key to the young lady's whole damn case here, and if I hadn't hung around to watch Ms. Glick testify, Ms. Aames would be in the soup.

That's when things got so strange that I didn't know if I was awake or in a dream.

We were just east of Spring, still on Fourth, heading down to the indoor parking structure, just past a sign that announced we were in the Old Bank District. Now, here, the block looks just like New York or Chicago, with brick and stone buildings hanging over you on both sides, these rows of carved lions' heads watching you pass from high above on these fancy, hand-carved ledges. Coming down this block is like walking among old castles the color of peaches and cream at this hour, and even though there's bums and winos and a rush of noisy cars going full-tilt down Fourth, it's gotta be one of the prettiest blocks in all of LA. They even got little white lights strung from side to side above the street like Christmas decorations.

On the opposite corner from us a bunch of guys in jeans and tees, some with headphones, others with radios, were working with coils of black cable and light stands up on poles. In the street, along the gutter, a camera was on a big rolling contraption, like a fancy cart, and two more men were crammed behind it, looking into monitors. Someone farther down the block yelled quiet. I felt a tug on my sleeve from Ms. Aames.

"They shoot a lot on this street," she said.

"Hollywood."

She didn't answer, but I saw her face had changed, like from curious to taking it really seriously. Seemed she was wrestling with ghosts, her back half to me and her lips tightened up, like she was gonna tell somebody on the edge of her wheelhouse to kindly step on back. I even looked behind me, just to check, but in all that street scrum, crew people around and regular dirty birds shuffling along, nobody was right there on us.

"What's wrong, Ms. Aames?"

"I'm feeling tired."

"You need to sit down?"

"—getting to a place where . . . my mind goes into a sort of . . . overload setting, Deshaun."

She reached out and I took her hand to steady her.

"I start to see things."

"Yes, ma'am."

"That's . . . that is the problem for me. Meds, they tamp down the action in my head, but it turns my thought processes to mud. It's like, I keep laying out a five-course meal and my brain keeps pouring oatmeal over it."

"Looks like they're shootin' some kind of scene, soon as they're done I'll get you to your car."

"*Deus ex machina.*"

"Pardon me, ma'am?"

"Dr. Don and his little posse, trying to play God in the Machine. Fuck a patient? No problem, we'll just make all the witnesses disappear at trial!"

"About that, ma'am, I—"

Her eyes were blazing, like a fire inside her was starting to flare up out of control.

"—pricks break into my apartment, jump me on the beach at Malibu, pack my expert off to Europe. Hey, you! Little girl lost!"

"They did all that?"

"Like a bad fucking episode of Scooby Doo. And they would've gotten away with it if it wasn't for . . . those pesky kids. Meaning us, of course. No, I'm not crazy, Deshaun, I see that look in your eyes."

"No, ma'am, I wasn't—"

"This may sound obvious, Deshaun, but you are my witness to the following revelation. I cannot be a lawyer if I'm stoned with shit for brains. So forgive me, but I'm making lists."

"Lists?"

She gave my hand a little squeeze, which got harder, till it hurt. But I was too unsure of what was happening to pull away.

"Let's get you to your car," I said with my best everything's-gonna-be-all-right tone."

"Into the abyss, Deshaun."

"Yes, ma'am."

A film guy not ten feet away from us with a black walkie-talkie looked up and said *quiet*, and all the people around him stopped moving. I noticed the people waiting behind him to go down the block. They looked normal enough, but almost too normal, like real life but too much of it in one place. Men in suits with briefcases; women in nice dresses carrying handbags; a lady walking a little white dog that looked like a perfectly shaped snowball; delivery guy on a twelve-speed bike; all of them standing by, looking ready to go.

"Two lists," Ms. Aames said. "One for what's real, the other for what's not real. All I've gotta do is adjust my behavior accordingly. And I swear, it's working better than any drug I've ever had the pleasure to ingest. Come on."

We started down Fourth again, but a blond gal with a clipboard standing next to the walkie-talkie man stepped in front of us just as someone yelled, "Action!" and all those perfectly normal but not normal people started moving along, natural as could be.

"That bank," Ms. Aames said to me quietly, pointing to the monument down on the end. "That bank chased me down the street."

"Yes, ma'am, so you said."

"And all this cops and robbers stuff coming at us? Fake, but real. Wrap your brain around that for a minute. That's LA for you."

A young man in black jeans and a tight black shirt—must be a bad guy, I thought—comes running down the block, porkpie hat flying off his head. Two guys are chasing him, the lead one young and good looking, a TV star I recognize, though I don't know his name. The older guy behind him, he drops back hard all of a sudden, bent over, huffing and puffing like he can't go on. I've seen the older one, too, but don't know his name either, saw him on late-night TV with a ridiculous beard last summer acting like he's Shakespeare with a dirty joke to tell in fancy old-time English.

"Not real," I say quietly to Ms. Aames. "Why I don't watch much TV."

"But you are. Thank God for that."

The lead guy chasing the bad guy reaches out and tackles him on the sidewalk, all the normal people in the scene jumping back like they've gone from having not a care in the world to dying of shock.

"Some mighty bad acting," I whisper.

The tussle on the sidewalk continues, the young cop having to tackle the man he's chasing again, then the old cop comes wheezing up at long last, staggering over to the crook his partner just collared. Says something mean and nasty right into the crook's face, growling like a mad dog.

"Who wrote this shit?" Ms. Aames whispers back. "Nobody talks like that."

Then things got stranger and for a time, I needed my own list of what's real and what's not real, because honestly, I lost track.

I'd seen this cop-show scene a thousand times on TV and in the movies, and when the cuffs come out for the bad guy, the squad car—backup, they call it—appears and a door opens. Then they stuff the bad guy in the back seat and tha's all folks! Scene over. But not this time.

Apparently the director got an itch he'd been wanting to scratch for a long time, or some writer was trying to win an award because instead of the squad car arriving to pack off the crook like usual, bright yellow muscle car, a Dodge Cobra I think, comes screeching up its tires smoking. The driver and passenger gotta be friends of the crook, because they jump out and start shooting at the cops while the crook on the pavement, he rolls away, trying to escape.

"Can you believe this?" I say to Ms. Aames, trying to sound tired of it, though I'm pretty damn excited because it really is quite a spectacle.

"There's a man with a gun," she says, calm but intense, like she's back in court again. "Coming your way, Deshaun."

They're shootin' it out, the actors, and in my head I'm still the tourist, having a ball just watchin' this crazy scene. So I don't connect what she's saying with anything else.

"Hooray for Hollywood," I say with a laugh.

Her face is tight with fear, a look I've never seen her wear in public. Now she's making me wonder, as she steps closer to me and suddenly swings her big black bag up over her shoulder like she's gonna throw it at me. I'm thinking: she's lost it, all this commotion too much for her, poor crazy girl gotta keep her lists to stay off meds, but the visions, they just keep coming. But my first order of business is to avoid taking a whack from that bag she's swinging, so I twist a little to my left, back toward the building and sidewalk, away from the gutter where the phony gun battle's going on—and I see the ugly, rock-like head of Bulldog, not five feet from me, gun in his hand and that silver cap on his front tooth flashing, his grin so blank it was downright evil, right as he takes aim on my chest.

Ms. Aames, her bag got there first—to Bulldog's gun, I mean—with her body following, her hips swiveling as she came in on him, and I can't say I heard it go off, there was too much Hollywood shoot-'em-up going on not twenty feet away, like fireworks popping in puffs of white smoke. But in about a second and a half, I put it all together.

Bulldog had been following me like I thought he might. Saw the Hollywood people working on this scene, who knows? Probably all afternoon while we were in court. Seeing the fake shooting, Bulldog figured he could cap me right on the street and no one would even hear it and if they did, they'd think it's part of the show anyhow, wouldn't even blink an eye. Hey, this is LA, a city chock full of weird, anything-goes happenings, more than any other city I can think of, and there's plenty of starry-eyed folks to go right along, hand in hand, with all the bizarre things that go down here every day. No one would even notice.

Then again, he may have planned nothing but to come looking for me down the street, coming out of the courtroom. Bulldog wouldn't know when I'd be coming out, because he wouldn't know when the trial would adjourn for the day. This all could've been nothing but dumb luck for him.

Either way, sure enough nobody noticed a thing out of place. Bulldog? He's just another gangster got a tilt of the head for a sexy black-haired lady, thinks he a mack daddy. Or is he an actor? Even when Ms. Aames fell down on the pavement, almost landing on Bulldog, nobody suspected a thing.

When he realized he shot her, not me, he took stock and tried to regroup, but I was a step ahead of him.

In my head, I took a step back, though, back into the only karate dojo in Inglewood, sparring with Grand Master Nuuhiwa, which I did almost every day for five years, back in the sixties. Before I became an MP. See, I took a beatin' during the Watts riots, just for asking some looter where he got a brand-new couch he was carrying down the road in broad daylight. I was just a kid who thought it was a funny thing to say but the looter didn't. He put down the couch right as three of his buddies come along, stood in a circle around me, and beat the stuffing outta me just for fun. I was in the county hospital ICU for a week, walked funny because of a busted kneecap the whole next year, a daily reminder I couldn't take care of myself the way I should've. So, I learned how to fight. Master Nuuhiwa taught me, all right, all the way through to a black belt. But he imparted a philosophy, too: how to seek peace in situations, how to avoid confrontations, defuse them before they escalate. Which I've been doing pretty well most of my life.

Not today.

I got at the gun first, prying it from Bulldog's hand. He swung his free hand up to my throat and clutched, but my other hand caught his elbow from underneath and popped it out of joint. He screamed as my foot slammed down on his toes. His head shot down, and as it did I met his face with a hard knee. Chopped his neck for good measure, but by then he was going down, folding into a pile of hurt and confusion.

A retired cop on a motorcycle providing security for the Hollywood shoot came running over as I rolled Ms. Aames on her back, and I think he figured I was trouble till he saw the blood oozing onto the sidewalk beneath her. I yelled in his face to get an ambulance. Bulldog, he stayed down, too. I told the retired cop he's a killer, shot the lady in cold blood, so get the police down here.

"You okay?" the cop asked me as I stared at a squirming Bulldog.

I was pumped out of my mind. "That boy comes around, I'm gonna deal with him with my bare hands, so please, get some backup."

Ms. Aames, she had a wound above her hip, and I stuck my hand right over it, pressed down, and prayed for those sirens down the street to get here fast. The back of her head was bleeding, too, so I did the same, my arms spread like wings. Her breath came and went in rough hiccups, but it was steady enough. Her eyes, they were open and blinking up at me, clear as day.

"I got him," I thought she said—although now, looking back on it, I think that may have been my own wishful thinking.

"Yes, ma'am," I told her, "you surely did."

22

Donald Fallon, Medical Doctor

"Terrence Heidegger!"

I had to stand up, wave, and bellow for my lawyer to see me, though I'd given him a ticket with the row and seat number. He sidestepped his way down the aisle, past a Staples Center usher and onto the hardwood floor, in shock, the only guy in wingtips to make this trip to the Golden Circle tonight. The courtside seats were filled as the game had started at least thirty minutes ago. Not that I was watching the young African American men and—ooh, look, for novelty, there's a Russian seven-footer on the other squad!—their opponents at play, so close that we could reach out and touch them as they grunted and grinded through sweaty set pieces foreign to my eyes. You don't come to a Lakers game to watch basketball unless you're a fan, and a fan I am not.

"Sorry, got detained at the office." He was out of breath from climbing over the well-heeled and street chic alike that flock to these Staples Center spectacles. "Wow. I think I just stepped on Adam Sandler's feet. They're . . . big."

"Terrence, this is my entertainment lawyer, Trey Fox." I was tickled as Heidegger sized up Trey, who's tops in his field but sports long hair and a scruffy beard, as if he hauls the amplifiers for a rock group.

"Terrence Heidegger. Thank you very much for having me."

Trey was cheering a basket or a steal or a jump ball—I don't know—and didn't remove his sunglasses, which were shaped like granny glasses from a bygone era. He was dressed like a pirate, as usual.

"Howzit, man? Glad you could make it. This is Chase from Insite Cable. Thank him, they're Insite's seats."

"Chase? A pleasure."

"Hiya."

Chase, the cable executive we'd met with to talk about my new show on their network, rolled out his meet-and-greet clasping handshake, which upon execution, looks like a giant clam snacking on fingers. Down here, in these floor seats, I'd seen the shake at least thirty times since we arrived. His suit was black with thin lapels and appeared as soft and body-fitting as a jumpsuit, the way he leaped to his feet to cheer and exulted with total strangers all around us when the Lakers were to be commended for their play. Custom, had to be worth thousands. No tie. Like a good teammate, Terrence was keeping up appearances but I could sense his discomfort with the general surroundings.

A glistening, chiseled hoop god swooshed past us, followed by two apt defenders. The god caught a pass, dropping his head in a fake charge but—no! Rearing back, forty feet from the goal, he lofted the ball toward the cavernous ceiling above where it arced gracefully into a perfect descent, splashing through the tiny orange hoop. The fans erupted. The cable exec and the pirate, who'd been snarling over some obscure term and condition an hour ago, high-fived each other like they'd just sacked an abundant port of call.

Sometimes I wish I didn't live in this silly sycophantic town.

"Yeah, baby!"

But the feeling quickly passes.

My palm was smarting from the skin Trey slapped on me. "We need to talk," I said quietly to Terrence, who was looking behind me, over my right shoulder. "I'm deeply concerned."

"Oh my goodness."

A wave of concern over my pending litigation with the state swept over me and I leaned closer, touching my legal counsel's shoulder.

"Tell me."

He regarded me quizzically for an instant, then smiled breathlessly.

"Salma Hayek is . . . wow, she's a stunner!"

Sycophant City, meet your newest resident.

"Terrence. Please. Get a grip."

"Sorry."

"I mean it. I'm worried."

"Mm-hmm."

His eyes beamed like a pair of glazed doughnuts. Okay, so maybe inviting him here was a bad idea—but enough of this.

"Stop acting like such a goddamn tourist. You're here to bring me up to date on—"

The last thing I needed was for Insite to get cold feet, so I lowered the volume and chose my words with care.

"—the uh, matter you've been working on." Then I leaned in close and whispered, "I'm this close to securing a deal with the cable company for the new show. Chase's staff apparently isn't so strong in the due diligence department. They've yet to visit the medical board's website. Or read the damn newspaper. Or, who knows? Perhaps they don't care, as long as the show will draw viewers. Maybe a little Dr. Don danger will spice things up."

"I wouldn't bet on that."

"At any rate, I'm sure as hell not going to bring it up. Remember, if he asks, you're—"

"Don, please," Heidegger interrupted. "I've got this. I'm your investment counselor."

"Correct." Despite the cacophony of applause, my mouth stayed so close to Terrence's ear that I could have bitten it off. "Let's begin with an obvious premise, shall we? The trial? Or should I say the 'walk in the park.'"

He glowered at me. "That wasn't necessary."

"I think it's apropos. We're losing."

"Not so fast. I say we're right where we need to be."

"How can that be? That lying bitch former patient told her side of things, more or less, and so did the former patient's gutless wimp husband."

"I roughed them both up good on cross. The judge gets the thrust of it now. She's a disturbed woman, an unreliable witness, bent on revenge. He got his settlement money, which cements his bias against you. They're far too compromised to be believed."

"You'd better be right."

"What I'm paid to do," he said, sneaking another peek at Salma. "We're golden."

His distracted brand of confidence was less than infectious. I snapped my fingers in front of his face. "Come on, you're killing me. What about Flaherty? You said he was out of the picture, and hence, so was the state's case. What happened, Terrence? How did that psycho-witch prosecutor get a replacement so damned easily?"

Heidegger snorted. Just then a pampered millionaire from the inner city soared across the purple-painted floor and dunked the ball, bringing the fans around us to their feet.

"Monster jam!" Trey reported with glee.

Heidegger wasn't used to having his chops busted. "Come on, Don," he groaned. "Look what she dragged in, right off the psychiatric community's garbage heap."

"Seemed to me that fat ugly broad hit all her marks."

"But that's assuming facts that they can't prove. It's like saying Swiss cheese from the moon makes for a tasty fondue."

I stared at him sideways.

"Don, if they don't establish an evidentiary basis, it doesn't matter what their expert says about outcomes."

"You said that little bitch—" I remembered EJ and the Pirate Boy were parked at my left elbow, "that prosecutor could be intimidated. 'Deterred.'"

"We tried. And we're not done. She might dwell on the outer limits, but that girl's resilient."

"Excuses."

"You're not being fair."

"I'm the client, Terrence. I don't have to be fair."

Sylvester Stallone breezed by, and my lawyer dutifully fell silent as if royalty was passing in an official pageant. God, I hate LA, but it feeds me, nourishes my sense of self in ways no other place can—or ever will.

"Not as tall as I thought he'd be," Terrence commented.

"You kidding, he's been Rocky in—what? Ten movies by now? In this town, he's a giant on stilts."

"These seats are amazing."

"The investigator, Fellows? Why is he still in my life, Terrence?"

"We supplied him with an optimal exit strategy, but—"

"Exit strategy? This is . . . right now you sound absurd. I mean it. Just like with Flaherty, you promised the investigator would be out of the picture, headed to—where was it?"

Terrence's shoulders slumped, which brought me no measure of comfort.

"Cajun country."

"But lo and behold, there he was, on the witness stand!"

"I know, I know!" Trey shouted to me. "Alice in Wonderland!"

Terrence seemed aghast. "The hell was that?"

"He's into the game," I said. "Misunderstood what he heard. What about you? Am I getting through with sufficient clarity?"

"We're still working on the investigator problem. Apparently he's being pursued by a very dangerous man who would like nothing more than to . . . share a private moment with Mister Fellows. My associate has located the man—"

"Associate? Terrence, at this juncture I have no trust in that simpering suit-wearing associate of yours. He's ineffective."

"Don, please. He located the gentleman who's looking for Fellows, did some fine work to that end. Supplied the man with some very useful information which should greatly aid him in his search."

"It's too late anyway. Fellows testified."

"I know, Don. Remember, the state's burden is high. They're nowhere near it, and you've yet to even take the stand. My team has prepped you and we all know you're going to give a stellar performance."

"I don't know. I've got to admit to compromising myself with the former patient."

"It's the best strategy. The AG and the board will be wishing they'd settled." He patted my knee. "And don't forget, our defense expert's a pro. He'll shred their case as well."

Perhaps his reassurances should have been enough, but I have a sense about impending danger. That ominous, oh-shit feeling that had descended on me when I'd undressed that little bitch Bradlee Aames with my eyes and she locked in and bore her black irises right back through me, well—it hadn't left me. Against my dominant Alpha Dog kick-ass-and-take-names persona's standard practice and better judgment and all my lawyer's verbal massaging, I was worried.

"Why are we at trial anyway?"

"Don, we've been over this part be—"

"I handed you a board insider, dammit, the president! How could you have botched the settlement?"

He glared at me. His face, with those giant liver spots on his forehead, resembled a worn-out frying pan.

"That one's not on me, Doctor. He's your 'contact,' and yet, he won't return your calls."

"Well, fix it. Call him yourself."

"I'm not Superman." He mulled in silence. Five feet away, a zebra-striped referee's jutting ass briefly invaded our space before tooling off toward a screaming, spitting, Italian-suited coach. "But I'll try."

"Good. Do it."

Heidegger gazed into the reflection of my sunglasses, which I'd absently put on as a shield of sorts when he was making excuses. "Say," he said, "why is it so damn bright in this place? The house lights are on all the way up to the rafters."

I didn't have to be a basketball fan to know the answer.

"You're in the land of the image-makers. People don't come here to sit in the dark. No one can see you in bad light."

That uneasy sense came over me again, and I pictured killing that bitch prosecutor, squeezing the life out of her, mangling her windpipe with my bare hands wrapped around her long lovely neck. Right after I'd tooled her within an inch of her feigned-rebel womanhood and she'd begged Dr. Donnie for more . . .

The home team did something noteworthy, bringing the crowd to its feet in roaring elation and foot-stomping ecstatic joy. A bevy of gorgeous young cheerleaders high-stepped and somersaulted into view. A sonorous announcer's voice boomed in tones of orgasmic glory. I leaped up, too, but I was rooting to win my case against the medical board.

Terrence's suit was a boardroom special too stiff for a sporting event, but he was up and jamming good with Trey and Chase and the best celebrity shrink in town, joining in the celebration.

"I can't believe this is preseason!" Trey exclaimed. I had no idea what he meant.

"You like basketball?" Terrence asked.

"Hell no. But I'm on the verge of hosting another show and this is a celebrity town. Face time is the lifeblood of success."

From across the court, Andy Garcia—yes, Andy Garcia, in 'preseason'—seemed to look right at me as he pumped his fist in the air. Like the swashbuckling counselor to my left, the Godfather Junior was sporting some custom, very eclectic shades with these small, reddish lenses. Oh, the meta-theatrical genius of it all: a genuine movie star taking in the kaleidoscopic unreality of the star-studded downtown hoop scene through *rose-colored glasses*! Good God. Some bastards have just got life completely by the balls.

"Yeah, baby!" I screamed in Andy's direction. Or something insipid like that.

No matter the vacant message, it felt good to be a part of something bigger than the both of us—and I mean Andy and me. Greater than the puny sum and substance of myself, beyond the facade, even if my participation was coldly, utterly fraudulent. I pumped my fist in solidarity.

Heidegger? Mildly appalled by my display, I'd say, and he poked me in the ribs with his program, pointing skyward. Above us, an electric scoreboard hovered above the court like a mother ship from outer space.

"You might want to save some for later," he said. "It's not even halftime."

23

RAUL MENDIBLES

Ten minutes after he'd somberly accepted my substitution in on the case, Shelby Drummond, the long-legged judge with the dusty gray beard and crinkled, nice-guy pink face, used that implacably pleasant demeanor of his to toy with me—no, make that *screw* with me—betraying no indication of how he might rule on my motion to continue the trial. He did sigh and make teepees of his fingers, expressing an appropriate level of concern for Bradlee Aames's outlook for recovery, which I couldn't discuss on the record anyway, not without violating her privacy rights at least. Good cause—the requirement for a continuance—was in abundance, am I right? Who knows? But why discuss it further? Why! Dammit, I was not at all prepared for the sharp-edged questions he zipped at me like flinty daggers and my responses, delivered like the dizzy pleas of a trusting assistant pinned to a spinning wheel, fell short.

To try a case, you've got to enter what I call The Zone—to live with that particular dispute every waking moment of your days and nights, to immerse yourself in every subtlety and detail of facts, law, and evidence. You brush your teeth anticipating defense objections and countering them with new offers of proof; you drive the highway reading in every road sign the script of likely and expected testimony of the next witness; you see the judge's face in the assessment the girl at the coffee bar makes of you as she hands your change to you. I hadn't been in court, on the record, since I'd been promoted to supervisor and the more the judge bore down on his purpose, which apparently was to get this trial over and done with here and now, the farther out of The Zone I found myself.

"Counsel, Ms. Aames very capably put on her entire case and rested. You have no other witnesses or evidence to present now, correct?"

A-bu-buh-bu-buh-

A curious spectator wandering in at this juncture might have thought I was channeling Porky Pig, for God's sake. I looked dumbly at the boxes of documents still under the counsel table, right where Bradlee had left them. I may as well have been staring up at a noontime sky, trying to guess the weight of the sun.

A la verga!

"Uh, technically that's correct, Your Honor, but—"

"'Technically?' Drummond barked. "The question calls for a yes-or-no answer. So, which is it?"

My managerial bullshit couldn't quite take flight in this guy's atmosphere. "Uh, yes, the board did rest its case. But Ms. Aames is the 'captain of the ship,' here, and in such cases, if that lead attorney is unavailable, it's pretty much a *prima facie* showing of good cause to—"

"Counsel, I've read that case and it has nothing to do with good cause or continuances, it has to do with the attorney's ability to decide who to call as witnesses, even over the client's objection."

Okay—it was an odious attempt to bamboozle him, I admit it, but I was desperate. The judge shook his head drearily, eyeballing me like he was examining a cheap watch I was desperate to unload.

"Sorry, Judge Drummond, I just haven't had time to prepare. Not in twenty-four hours. How could I?"

"You've heard Mr. Heidegger tell me he's ready to present his client's defense."

"Yes, I know that, but we thought—I thought, uh, that further discussions regarding settlement may be productive, and—"

"But, Counsel, my understanding is that your client contact for the board is unavailable."

"Uh, technically that's correct. However—"

"Please, not that again. Just give me straight talk."

Ay, Dios mio! I'd never been further off my game than right now. Management had made me soft—in the gut and in the head. What the hell made me think for a nanosecond that I could ever step in and competently finish this case?

"Counsel, you heard Mr. Heidegger when he just told me he was ready to proceed."

Looking sideways, I glanced at the defense table and caught the edge of Heidegger's smirk, a ripple of self-satisfied nods passing back and forth at the defense table. They knew where they had me and they were savoring it.

"Yes, Your Honor. I was hoping you might give the board more time—"

"I've heard this already, Counsel," the judge said as he constructed another finger-teepee. "Hope may spring eternal, but it doesn't amount to good cause for a continuance."

Heidegger dropped his chin and gave a tiny fist pump below the table's edge, where the judge couldn't see him. But I did.

A la verga!

I'd come in early this morning just to talk deal after a two-hour phone marathon last night with the Major during which, after calling me a painted lady with a briefcase, I'd received the repeated directive to make this case go away. I could tell that the Major had been back on his VO rocks regimen again for the first time since the near-DUI that had brought us together, hitting it hard—so hard I could hear the ice cubes clinking in the glass as he rambled on. I'd replayed for him from memory our previous conversation about the public menace that was Dr. Don. Unused to being impeached by his own words, the major got ugly—nasty in a way only a drunk can achieve, clawing a finger right into any open wounds within reach. Bradlee Aames was getting it done, and the defense knew it. That was yesterday, in the past. Now, with her out of the picture, I was back to being his water boy.

Ray-ool. Fool Raw-ool. Tool Raw-ool.

And man, was I ever sick of his shit. *I should've left your ass in the gutter, where I found you,* I'd shouted at one point in the argument, I think right after he'd accused me of being a self-important fraud. *Well, you didn't,* he'd growled back. *Which says it all about you, now doesn't it, Raw-ool?*

Very unproductive. Not that any of this tit-for-tat mattered a damn because when water-boy Raw-ool made the offer outside the courtroom first thing this morning, it was scoffed at with impunity. They knew about Bradlee's unavailability, knew I was in this jam, well outside of The Zone. Now I would pay for letting this proceed to trial.

As if I didn't have enough on my mind another complication reared up to block my path.

Hey, Lobo? You ask yourself yet how those dirtbags knew so quickly Bradlee Aames couldn't go? Mendibles! Pay attention! Look at the space on the table in front of Heidegger! See the blue-backed document? That's a typed opposition! Only it's sitting there, not submitted to the judge because you're crashing and burning so badly here—Heidegger doesn't even need it.

That can't be right. I called him last night. Left a message.

That she'd been shot? That she couldn't go?

No, I just said . . . call me back, we need to talk, there's been a new development and—

Right, you idiot! Standard Mendibles double-talk: heavy on the verbiage, light on the content.

"Mr. Mendibles," the judge continued.

Was I this bereft of conscience? They *knew.*

Which meant that in some clandestine, unsavory way, they were involved.

I think the judge was talking but I didn't hear the words as I turned, stood, and stepped aside to counsel table. Grabbed one of Heidegger's blue-backed documents before he could pull it away—

"Your Honor!" he shrieked. "Counsel is invading—"

Or some such nonsense; I can't recall for sure. I was too livid. It was an opposition all right, to the motion I'd launched ten minutes ago.

"Counsel, sit back down and do not make me—" The judge was jabbering, but I didn't care. I flipped the document back at Heidegger.

"Odious."

Heidegger brimmed with phony indignation. "You have no call to—"

"Reprehensible." One-word sentences were all I could muster, such was my level of disdain.

"—traipse over here and start lunging at my—"

"She could've died."

"Your Honor, I—"

"She could've died."

"—demand an apology! Counsel—"

I didn't hear the rest, but I can say for sure that I had no regrets.

It took the judge a few minutes to calm things down. "If you two should reach some kind of resolution," he said, "you're free to submit that to the court at any time. But that's not good cause for me to hold up the proceedings."

When I didn't respond—technically or otherwise—his cheeks twinkled.

"Motion denied."

Fine. If this was the price I'd pay for my ignoble deeds, so be it.

Not so fast, water boy. You won't get off that easily.

Don't I know it.

* * *

The defense wasted no time in calling Dr. Don to the witness stand. Heidegger was a weasel, but he was a smart weasel; he had his client decked out today not in the kind of bland gray business suit Dr. Don had worn since the start of trial, but in a classic charcoal slacks and navy blazer combo with a soft blue button-down shirt and repp tie. The impression was warmer and more casual, and the tortoise-shell glasses balanced on Dr. Don's smallish nose gave his thin-lipped, tightly wound face a softer, more professorial look. I still didn't like anything about him, and he couldn't hide, from me at least, the calculation that was always brewing behind those merciless eyes.

I nearly slept through the preliminary questions detailing his illustrious education and professional career. Why is it that major universities always seem to fall all over themselves for the biggest self-serving pricks? I, for one, cannot tell you. I mean, it's not enough that he did a PhD at UCLA, but they had to give him grants and awards and ass-kissing accolades along the way, as if a class-A education in and of itself wasn't enough of an ego boost. And how anyone could've stuck this get-happy sniveler on TV (albeit the late-night wasteland) was beyond my comprehension. By the time he started explaining away the supposed care and treatment he'd provided to an overly demanding, entirely fucked-up Rue Loberg, I was queasy.

Not the proper mind-set for a prosecutor who must remain cool and objective and strategic, I know, but I was way out of practice. The Zone eluded me.

Hey, Mendibles? Hello? Welcome back to the human race and all, but please, don't spoil the reclamation of your sorry soul with performance anxiety, eh?

Okay, okay, I'll find a way to deal.

How Bradlee Aames could handle this kind of pressure, the multiple witnesses, all the problems that crop up during trial, the attempted hijackings by the defense—how she could contend with all this and excel, with her messed-up head guiding the way? Well, I truly had no concept.

Dr. Don went on and on while carefully saying nothing. My thoughts drifted back to Bradlee's blank face, the placid closed-eyed ceiling stare she'd met me with last night, a stack of monitoring equipment blinking beside her hospital bed and tubes shooting out of her arms like translucent snakes feeding happily on a corpse. It slew me. Five minutes, maybe ten, was all I could manage. She was resting post-op, and the lights were dimmed. The floor nurse, a six-footer with ugly glasses and a faint brown cookie duster mustache, had made an exception, letting me in this way, but she stuck around—Nurse Ratched, hovering by the door, jaded eyes latching on to my every movement from the dark shiny-tiled hallway, encroaching on to the fringes of my dream state. *Oh, Bradlee!* She needed me, but there was nothing I could do. I needed her worse—practically, as a lawyer with a case to handle; shamefully, as a married man adrift—but there was nothing to be done either. I floated over her, impotent. Leaned close to say good night, heard her breathing so softly, each wisp seeming to catch the air, like a butterfly's transparent wings fighting for liftoff. And I'd wanted to say a prayer for the next breath, and the next, to come.

No, I was nowhere near my best self, not last night. The nurse, hovering nearby in her creaking shoes and crinkling starched polyester, she saw my knees wobble, I think, and the indignity of the situation made me shudder. I all but ran by her for the elevator.

A massive yawning attack struck me and I buried my face in my fist. Between my hospital visit and the phone call with Major Coughlin, I'd never even gone to bed. Might have slept a few hours before dawn on the family room couch, but it was fitful, dream-filled sleep at best. Great: the judge was going forward and I was shot to hell.

According to Dr. Don's predictably blameless viewpoint, it was his former patient, Rue Loberg, who threw herself at him and he did all he could to resist her.

Don't tell me what's coming next, I thought as I stared at the scuffed toes of my dress shoes. Practicing law has a million ways to make you cynical. One way is having to listen to a lot of lying, self-serving bullshit.

"But I was just a man," he said, his chin drooping like a little boy whose puppy had just been squashed by a Sherman tank, its brains squeezed out of its eye-sockets like toothpaste from a tube. Okay—my tired mind was blowing everything up into cartoonish dimensions. But still, my first impulse was to projectile vomit in the direction of the witness stand; my second was to shout something rude at the esteemed psychiatrist who'd so bravely revealed his human frailty. Yet I did neither. The import of his lying words was too great for any of that.

You see, by admitting to at least some sexual contact in the form of Rue Loberg's overtures, Dr. Donald Fallon had just moved the state's case a lot closer to being proven.

It was a complicated, delicate strategy by the defense, to portray the shrink as the victim. It was he, the professional, who'd needed to be in control at all times, to always act in the patient's best interest. He was now admitting that he hadn't done so when she'd made inappropriate advances. Fallon was almost admitting to negligence, but not quite.

Holy shit, Mendibles! You just might redeem yourself here.

Dr. Don's team of legal geniuses saw fit to make him concede a huge admission, because they felt he had to.

Which meant that Bradlee Aames had done an excellent job putting on her case.

The trial crawled along. Sitting alone at counsel table, reading her tightly looped, handwritten notes on a legal pad I'd found inside her file, stifling one gaping yawn after another, I began to miss her terribly. Yes, yes, I cop freely to my lust, my unprofessional, animal desire for Bradlee, which I know is a violation of the promise I made to God when I wed Myrna. But I'm in the company of a lot of men on that count, and for what little mitigation it may be worth, my thoughts have never translated into deeds. Or, at least I've never tried anything with her.

What overwhelmed me now, more than the weight of the cross this dishonorable husband and public servant must carry up his own Calvary every day, was a sense of awe for the power of a brilliant, troubled mind. She'd faced down their manipulations, string-pulling, and lies, and managed to establish a solid narrative as to what really happened. Like it or not, the defense was stuck with Bradlee's vision of the case and had to respond in kind by putting a gentle spin on the details.

This realization led to a terrible thought: Jesus Christ, this case is winnable—and it's all on me.

What I've been trying to tell you, Lobo!

I couldn't just show up and fill a seat for the state, yawning and mumbling passively through the rest of the proceedings. I'd truly have to perform.

My head felt light and my scuffed shoes seemed to swerve right up at me. Once again, projectile vomiting seemed in order. When Dr. Don had finished on direct, the judge asked me if I was ready to cross-examine. Heidegger interrupted quickly.

"May we take a short break first, Your Honor? I'm sure opposing counsel wouldn't mind having a few extra moments to prepare his questions."

Wouldn't mind, my ass. That Heidegger had some *juevos*, man, but there was another, well-hidden side of me he'd not yet seen. Raw-ool was about to get raw.

Really raw, brother!

Maybe it was the grace of God shining down upon my sinner's soul, or maybe I'd just been thinking, as I read her notes, about what Bradlee would do if she were here. But I was no longer in a conceding, conciliatory mood; now I had atonement on my mind. Whatever I did from here on out, I would do for her.

I thought of last night, way after the major and I had broken off, sitting on the couch, totally exhausted but my mind too occupied to think of sleep. I'd turned on the TV, keeping the volume low so Myrna and the kids wouldn't be disturbed. Not much on—must-buy deals on overpriced costume jewelry that looked like the real thing; a conspiracy show claiming that Fort Knox had no gold; a movie with French subtitles in which the actors, attending a masquerade party at some mansion, all seemed to be talking backward. Then I found it: that old surfer classic, *The Endless Summer*, with its aw-shucks narration and water-bound thrills and spills. Instantly I fell into its easygoing rhythm, and suddenly, I was nodding off. Before I lost consciousness . . . there was a segment on Malibu beach playing, the "best surfer ever," Mickey something or other, just slipping and sliding his way through an obstacle course of other surfers who kept popping up in front of him as he tore along this wave, as smooth and poised as Fred

Astaire. The way he navigated through the masses, so calm and confident—the guy's approach, the simple take-what-comes brilliance of it . . . the style. So classical, but so modern, and to think, he had it all worked out fifty years ago. I don't know . . . it had an effect on me. Put me at ease enough to sleep.

Put me at ease again, now, in the courtroom, in a way I'm at a loss to explain.

Give it up to a Higher Power, Mendibles. Then go about your business. Meaning: kick some ass and take some names.

"Mister Heidegger should speak for himself, Your Honor. I'm ready to go."

"Very well," the judge said. "Proceed."

I was out of practice and still operating outside The Zone, indeed; but I knew a few things about questioning witnesses on cross. One is that they've likely seen their share of TV shows and movies in which the confrontation is overblown and the attacks are vicious and demeaning. Opposing witnesses expect you to come at them hard, so their defenses are up. Way up.

But those defenses can be broken down simply by making the witness feel comfortable. You do this by asking easy questions, as many as necessary, and if you have to, you sugar-coat them. Get the witness talking until fielding your powder-puff queries becomes routine. Only then do you even think about making inroads.

The fact that these guys regarded me as something of a pussy didn't hurt me either. They didn't expect me to go hard because I wasn't capable of going hard. Wrong—but I could play the pushover a little bit longer.

An egomaniac like Dr. Don would enjoy nothing more than hearing the sound of his own voice. I obliged by kissing his ass, questioning him about his TV-host experience, his philosophy when it came to family therapy, the impressive scope of his private practice, some of the charitable work listed on his mile-long resume. He lapped up every question.

I took him into the realm of Rue Loberg's care with a discussion of the most routine part of any doctor's care: the charting. At least

I'd had the chance to read through the chart early this morning, sitting in my office as the sun cracked over the San Gabriel Mountains. There were blind spots in those records—holes that even I could see. A 6:00-a.m. call to Bradlee's last-minute expert, Dr. Glick, confirmed every problem I saw and revealed a few more I wouldn't have noticed.

Dr. Don took me through the cycle, from doing early intake and making a diagnosis to session notes, to cessation of therapy. I had him walk me through the beginning and middle first, and he never suspected a thing. After twenty-five minutes, I was finally poised to ask questions that meant something.

"The charting you've detailed for us is very thorough, Doctor. Is this the norm for you?"

"Yes, it is. As I said, I pride myself on keeping meticulous patient records."

"Now, Doctor, you've described the patient as a very troubled woman, whom you'd diagnosed with borderline personality disorder. Did you feel your care and treatment of Mrs. Loberg was successful?"

Dr. Don paused for the first time in half an hour before answering, and he cast a glance at his counsel. To my left, Heidegger shifted his butt in his seat, his pen poised as he studied his notes.

"I think 'successful' is a relative term. It's not as if we're curing cancer, it's not so black and white. I would say, however, that yes, yes, she did make significant progress with me."

"But you described her, in your testimony, Doctor, as quote, 'incapable of recognizing social and personal boundaries.'"

"Yes, but—"

"Isn't that a hallmark of borderline personality disorder?"

"Yes."

"You also noted, in the beginning, that the patient had unresolved guilt over being victimized by multiple male authority figures in her life. Doctor, do you recall testifying that Mrs. Loberg was still, as you put it, 'a woman wracked with guilt'?"

"Yes."

"So that didn't get resolved either, not while she was in your care, did it?"

He laughed without a sound. "Oh, I wouldn't say that."

"But you did. In so many words."

Heidegger made an objection that I was being argumentative. For the first time in an hour, the judge looked fully awake.

"Overruled. Please answer the question, Doctor."

"Heh. Yes, well—"

"Was she still wracked with guilt?" I asked.

"She was."

I directed the doctor to his last chart note, his final session with Rue Loberg.

"You had an opportunity to reflect on the patient's condition before writing the notes here, didn't you Doctor?"

"I don't recall. That's June, and June is usually a busy month for me, so I might have been rushed for time, with other patients and conferences I typically attend that time of year."

"Objection," I said, "move to strike. Nonresponsive. And the witness is speculating."

The judge sustained my objection and instructed the witness to answer. Dr. Don's thin smile was gone, and he glared at me through his smart-guy glasses.

"Yes, I wrote notes. I could've written more, I suppose."

"Isn't the standard of practice when you terminate with patient that you make a final assessment, Doctor?"

"Yes."

"But you didn't do that."

"No."

"For a patient with major unresolved problems."

"She had her challenges."

"And doesn't the standard of practice in the profession require that a psychiatrist in his last session with a patient make referrals for the patient to see other professionals as needed, should the patient still face significant problems and issues, and still require ongoing care?"

"Yes, but—"

I was nearing The Zone and was not about to let him talk his way out of this.

"—and isn't Mrs. Loberg, as you described her, just such a patient still struggling with some pretty difficult problems?"

"Yes."

"But you made no such referrals, did you?"

"Well, as I recall, we did talk about, uh, something to do with her insurance, or . . ."

I wasn't going to let him ramble.

"Doctor, why don't you just read for us the handwritten notes in their entirety, right now, into the record. The final comments you made."

He adjusted his glasses, the lapels in his blazer drooping. Then he wiped his brow inelegantly and started in.

"Patient wants to terminate treatment, unresolved issues re: male authority figs, can't open up at home w/ hub. Or w/ DF."

"That's all you wrote. There's no referral to another professional there, Doctor."

"No."

"And you are 'DF'—Donald Fallon?"

"Yes."

"She was your patient for over sixty sessions and she couldn't open up to you."

"Well, we did make some inroads that aren't captured by my chart notes, sir. Not everything that goes on between a patient and their psychiatrist is reflected in the records."

"Good thing for you," I said. "Very convenient, in this case."

"Objection!" Heidegger was unglued by my insinuation. Predictably, the judge chided me. But it was worth it. Dr. Don was stuck in his own charting contradictions and Heidegger was a long way away from his next fist pump.

"You were another authority figure in her life," I continued. "And she was supposed to be able to tell you anything, because you were her doctor, her therapist. But she couldn't do that, because she believed you were sexually attracted to her."

"I was not."

"You failed to note in the chart anything that would even suggest that, by that point in your interactions with Mrs. Loberg, you weren't solely acting as her therapist."

"Objection!" Heidegger shouted. "Argumentative!"

This time the judge calmly overruled the objection. He knew where I was going.

"You noted not a single problem between you and the patient."

"I don't know what you're getting at here," Dr. Don said innocently.

"You were, as you put it, just a man. That's normal for psychotherapy?"

"Objection!"

The judge's face was impassive. That kind of impenetrability was a good sign. Dr. Don's shtick was wearing on him.

"Overruled. Please answer."

"That's simply a characterization I made here, today."

"But you couldn't write about those feelings you had for her. That would be unprofessional. Point to your negligence. So you put it all onto her shoulders. It was her fault that she couldn't open up to you."

For the first time today, Dr. Don looked exasperated. A sweat stain was forming at the bottom of his shirt collar, and he tugged at his tie as if it were strangling him. Then defiantly, and without warning, he fired back.

"That's not how it happened. By the way, transference and counter-transference are common occurrences, Counselor. Your own expert even said so, but since you weren't even present, you wouldn't know that."

Well—the man had chutzpah, all right. *Juevos*. It was my time for a little theater. Standing up, I made my best face, like I couldn't believe what I'd heard. Dug a finger into my ear for good measure.

"Wait. Isn't it true that you characterized the patient's inability to open up to you as her fault?"

Before Fallon could answer, I spread my hand as if to cover the courtroom with one sweep.

"And now, Doctor, you're admitting to me, and to this court, that you had feelings for the patient, feelings that would raise issues of countertransference on your part?"

Donald Fallon, MD, was at a loss. The court reporter, a middle-aged brunette who rarely looked up except to adjust the white sweater she wore loosely over her shoulders, had stopped to stare at the witness. Heidegger tweaked his pen like a tiny propeller between his fingers, waiting. Fallon turned toward the bench and judge.

"Is . . . that's not what I said."

"Nothing further," I said, taking my seat.

"Re-cross?" the judge asked Heidegger.

Now it was the defense that wanted to take a break. Boo-hoo.

I objected. "The witness isn't finished testifying. His counsel shouldn't have a break now, to prep the witness any further."

"Let's keep going," said the judge. "Counsel?"

Fallon's arms were crossed as if he was about to have a tantrum. He was burning a stare at me, but the heat was easy to deflect. I was gliding along, so excited by being alive that I forgot to even breathe. A glum Heidegger rifled through his notes as the judge waited. Dr. Don seemed rattled in a way his lawyer dreaded—and feared. Heidegger seemed to feel my expansive satisfaction. I knew he'd never take me for granted as a lawyer again.

"No further questions, Your Honor."

24

DUKE P. WINSTON, MEDICAL DOCTOR, MS, PhD

Notes for my memoir, a work-in-progress with the rough working title: *Always on My Mind, A Psychiatrist's Journey* . . .

The staunch grandeur of the former Broadway department store building is a visual salve; that is, after witnessing a woman I surmise to be a drunken prostitute stoop behind the Lexus sedan two spaces over from where I've parked my car and urinate standing stark upright. She catches me staring back at her in revulsion and, apparently resenting the visual incursion, curses me first, branding me a dirty old man, as if all the world were a freelancer's potty and I'd forgot to knock before entering.

Verisimilitude, Duke; deliver the goods, by golly.

She is scruffy, her hair an unruly rat's nest, her sweaty rolls bulging in a tight pink skirt and skimpy white blouse and despite our mutual Caucasian status, she doesn't hesitate to verbally assail me as a rich honky pud-whacker that practices certain unmentionable sexual acts upon his mother.

Not bad with the first two assessments, I must say, as I am reasonably well-heeled and have, since the death of Glenda, my beloved wife of thirty-seven years, routinely engaged in acts of self-gratification (note: far too much verisimilitude; but one must go with the flow to make the writing go—edit later); yet the latter slur is merely invective that misses the mark. I scuttle away, formulating an over-the-shoulder assessment of this vulgar, verbose streetwalker:

Classic narcissistic behavior; poor impulse control; anger management issues; and, considering her line of work, a wealth of self-image issues to boot. Oh, yes—and let's not neglect to slap on a fashion violation for the tacky, ill-fitting couture.

Still got it, Dukester (note: edit out all self-aggrandizement).

I shouldn't have been smiling, but I must say, I enjoyed the rapidity with which I'd aggregated my observations, and when you're good, you're good (note: see previous note). My undisguised, sunny self-satisfaction, however, further perturbs the woman and she follows me toward the sidewalk, gaining on me as she continues to curse, having moved on from standard name-calling to some rather colorful descriptions of anatomical impossibilities involving foreign objects lodged in my rectum. Perhaps the parking attendant, a gaunt Latino thumbing a wad of bills as he hands out receipts, can help me. But he's disappeared into the recesses of the lot, leaving me as alone and forgotten as Gary Cooper in *High Noon*.

Like Coop, I too am a gunslinger of sorts, the hired gun riding into town to lay down the law. Not in any dusty, mean streets of yore, but in court today on this sexual misconduct dust-up, this pecker peccadillo of a case (nice alliteration!) brought forth by the medical board against one Donald Fallon, MD, a psychiatrist with flavor-of-the-month written all over his grinning, telegenic face. Should he lose his license, I feel certain he'll land on his feet as a political appointee on some corrupt commission whose unstated purpose is to stifle the will of the people; or perhaps, a manic pitchman touting miracle ointments on late-night infomercials. (Note: *Change all names!* These are private, go-with-the-flow impressions only—anticipate big cuts; openly seek legal advice from publisher's in-house counsel.) But unlike Coop, there is nothing heroic about the task I've been hired to fulfill. My intellect is my gun and words are my bullets. A check for services rendered is my reward.

How do I live with such a potentially unseemly trade-off? I tell you, without qualms: It's a job and somebody's got to do it. If not I, another medical savant whose integrity has been compromised by a pursuit of the almighty dollar would take my place in a heartbeat. (Note: locate softer place to land, so to speak.)

Somebody's got to do it, indeed. Oh, if my wife were to read this tripe. My dearly departed Glenda was a former literature professor and Virginia Woolf scholar at Loyola, and she despised the profligate over-use of clichés as the most flagrant of myriad offenses to the English language. My beloved Glenda abhorred the trite blandness of everyday howdy-doody American vernacular, and no doubt, she would judge this writer equally harshly for rendering yet another hackneyed justifi-cation. But here it is:—*and forgive me, my love*—if you can't beat 'em, join 'em. (Note: see previous note.)

I stand directly across the street from the stately old Broadway's entrance—which now bears the name of the Junipero Serra Building—and though the morning traffic is fairly dense, I waste no time wading into the one-way lanes, determined to pad the distance between myself and the angry harlot, who is presently assuring me of her intent to inflict bodily injury upon my person. Though I hardly dare to look back lest I further enrage her, I surreptitiously take note of her rather stocky build and the boldly depicted dragon tattoo on her right forearm, which con-torts whenever she shakes her fist, scarily animating the beast's whip-like tail. A bustle of pigeons takes flight from the pavement before me and in the same breath, a horn blasts—I've jaywalked straight into the path of a slow-moving delivery van. The driver can either brake maniacally or unceremoniously squash me like a bug on his front bumper and let his insurance company deal with the aftermath; yet, fortunately for me, he chooses the former. Shrugging an apology, I scurry to the other side of the street and bound over to the double doors, grateful to still be alive.

In the Broadway's wide glass front doors' reflection the distinguished gent in the black Hermes suit with the neatly trimmed gray hair, sharp nose and precision moustache comes face-to-face with himself, and though a tad out of breath, his faculties are well intact, the mind clicking along as incisive and alert as the sunshine banking down through these gorgeously appointed facades of yesteryear. The man in the thousand-dollar suit seems pleased to have survived his latest little adventure. (Note: exceptional man-on-the-street details—take care not to over-edit.) What else can I do but salute him with a wink and a thumbs-up?

Ten feet into the lobby my buoyancy takes a blow.

Up steps a security guard who—how to say it?—could be the malevolent tart's brother. Arms as thick as tree trunks, a bland scowl that betrays a tortured, impoverished childhood. My smile bounces off his mile-wide chest like a rubber ball off a brick wall. I'd chosen the open aisle of entry reserved for court personnel, eschewing the line of regular folk crowding in to be processed through a metal detector while their personal items were placed on a conveyor belt to be scanned. (Note: soften privileged tone.) Apparently, I've erred.

The guard blocks my path with a hollow stare that no doubt served him well traversing the mean streets and tragic back alleys from whence he's sprung. (Note: this detail's a keeper—gritty!)

"Badge," he mutters.

I bid him a good morning and ask him to step aside, as I am a subpoenaed witness scheduled to testify forthwith in a courtroom upstairs.

"Step to your right," he grunts, motioning toward the huddled souls lining the conveyor belt.

Seizing the advantage, I unhesitatingly follow his directions, doing so literally, which places me directly at the front of the line. The congregation of the routinely oppressed murmur complaints and charges of favorable treatment from my flanks, but I look forward singularly, refusing to even acknowledge their inarticulate protests.

"Belt," he adds. "Shoes."

With an affable nod, I assure the young man that indeed, I possess both.

*   *   *

Six floors up, I promptly arrive at my destination but am informed by one of Counselor Heidegger's associates that a motion is being argued and I'd best return in twenty minutes. So I ride the elevator back downstairs and venture into the ground-floor cafeteria, where I procure a cup of tasteless coffee and a blueberry muffin so hard that it warrants a geological study. (Note: witty, tone-setting turn of phrase—another keeper.) The woman behind the cash register smiles humbly. Perusing the hundred I've handed her, she frets in silence, digs under the black money tray, unearths a stack of twenties, and grudgingly makes change, counting the bills into my open palm with a shake of her head that only partly disguises her disdain. Reflexively thanking her—for no matter the circumstances, I never abandon the manners prerequisite to good breeding—I am given pause, and find myself wondering if somehow she knows about the task I am here today to perform. How many smartly attired elder statesmen of their professions, how many learned experts with mile-long curricula vitae—how many hired guns—has she laid those saucer-like eyes upon?

Enough, perhaps, to peg me as easily as she's just done while counting out my change. What kind of customer whips out a hundred to settle a five-dollar tab? (Note: On rewrite, let's spin something more soul-searching into the mix.)

Who could say? Certainly not I. But the cashier's nose-wrinkling consternation annoys me, as I am reminded of the one woman in my life that I could never, ever please: my mother.

Ah. Mum.

Sipping my bland coffee, I absently make review of my written credentials, twenty-six pages of blood, sweat, toil, and tears, little of which came and went with a single acknowledgment from the one woman on this earth I most sought to impress and make proud. Mum—dead and buried now for nearly a decade, yet she still so effortlessly, readily invades my psyche. . .

Berkeley? A state institution?

Their medical school is excellent, Mum. Indeed, it's ranking—

I suppose your grandfather's endowment to Stanford means nothing to you.

No, of course it—

—and to study medicine is all well and good, son, since your father is the chief of neurosurgery at the city's finest hospital, but psychiatry? I simply don't understand.

It's . . . what interests me, Mum. I'm fascinated by human behavior, by—

Tell me, what "interests" you about a world gone mad, dear boy? I really must know . . .

Alas, there was no telling my mother anything she did not wish to hear. (Note: too confessional by half; consider cutting.)

Two tables away a pant-suited woman with a pile of blond hair and glasses with tiny gems sparkling in the frames erupts at something her lawyer has just said.

"Admit it, when I . . . why? I didn't do anything wrong!"

The lawyer attempts to calm her with a soothing directive, but she refuses to make eye contact. As she fumes, her counsel, a reddish, puffy-necked man with the posture of a garden slug, reclines in his plastic chair and folds his hands on his lap, waiting. Of course he has all day, he's billing her hourly. To him, observing a client's tantrum is no different than filing a brief—and significantly less work for him.

Blast it, I say to myself; rubbing elbows with the accused is no fun and makes for a miserable milieu. (Note: cut if tone is too whiny.) Duty calls. I take a final sour gulp of coffee and trudge upstairs once more.

The courtroom is more compact than I'd imagined; the judge, a gray-haired papa-bear type, greets me as if he's reserved the best seat in the house just for me. Settling in, I glance at Fallon, who peeks out from the opposite end of the defense table, shielded in part by Heidegger and his two grunts. Fallon's eyes are watering like a hound dog that's lost and needs to find its master, and he searches my face, beseeching me for a nod of acknowledgment, a wink—anything. Which, of course, I cautiously withhold. Good God, the man is pathetic, so driven is he to gain acceptance. To be liked.

I am more than mildly disappointed to learn that the state's attorney, a female with a family history of schizophrenia who'd become a major thorn in Heidegger's side, is not in attendance. Quite a knockout, Heidegger had raved, but icy toward any friendly come-ons and all business in the courtroom. He'd paid me an extra fifteen-hundred—cash, no invoice or paper trail whatsoever, please—to read an old autopsy report on her dead father and render an opinion as to how her effectiveness could be effectively neutralized. I'd offered to refund the money, a response far more polite than my first reaction, which was to laugh in his face. But he held out for enlightenment, so I told him what he needed to know.

That brilliant people the world over live with mental illnesses every day.

Oh, it's hardly a secret. Had he not heard of John Nash, the Nobel Prize–winning mathematician? Nijinsky, the spellbinding dance man? Kerouac? Granted, *On the Road* was a mess, but a stupefying, wondrous mess. Perhaps, I proffered, this young lady was simply very good at what she did for a living. (Note: a valid perspective, but won't make the cut due to attorney-expert confidentiality; also suggestive of underhanded attorney-expert behavior. DELETE!)

I can still easily recall her oddball name: Bradlee Aames. And I'd looked forward—even as a truck down in the street threatened to wipe me from the face of the planet—to coming face-to-face with her today, to matching wits. I must admit, not seeing her here, deprived of the chance to engage in intellectual combat with a worthy adversary, is more than mildly disappointing; it is a full-fledged letdown.

Damn it all.

And who, pray tell, is this unimpressive replacement sitting in for the fearsome, formidable Bradlee Aames? A haggard-looking man of perhaps forty, still young but fighting a losing battle against the bulging sag of middle age. His hair is curly and greasy, and so are his dark Hispanic eyes. (Note: nice detail, but may have to delete racial reference—let's keep the tone PC throughout.) The rumpled suit looks slept in. Goodness, I've seen better-dressed valets at Trader Vic's.

My testimony proceeds relatively easily, although to lay the groundwork, lead counsel Heidegger has me first assume the preposterous narrative supplied by the amoral psychiatrist seated to his far left. (Note: scrub clean to protect the culpable.)

"In such a case," I tell the court, "when the former patient pursues the therapist, he must do what he can to dissuade the patient from such a course of action. Although he owes no formal duty to the former patient to do so, professional ethics and simple human decency would compel a compassionate, patient-first response."

"Any other duties for the therapist to consider?" Heidegger asks.

"Well," I say, rubbing my chin precisely as I'd rehearsed the night before, "there is something more." (Note: true, but too revealing—cut.)

"Go on, Doctor," Heidegger coaxes me, as if the king's ransom they were paying me wasn't motivation enough.

"Although I believe Doctor Fallon did his best under trying conditions, the standard of practice would require him to have made a patient referral for Ms. Loberg to see another therapist, since obviously her personal advances on her former therapist raised significant issues pertaining to her inability to comprehend, and respect, social boundaries."

"Yet, he didn't make such a referral, Doctor."

"No," I concede gravely. "He did not, and I would consider that omission to be a simple departure from the standard of practice for a California psychiatrist."

I sit back, the issue settled, my goal achieved. This is because the negligence statutes for doctors require at least two acts of simple negligence for the charges to stick. Therefore, by my final assessment offered herein, Donald Fallon is legally blameless.

"Now, Doctor, did you find any other instances in which Doctor Fallon departed from the standard of practice?"

"I did not," I say, as if I've been thirty years on horseback searching for the Holy Grail itself, but have come up short. (Note: colorful image, but a mite too cynical—consider cutting.)

Heidegger thanks me genteelly. Now for the verbal fisticuffs of cross-examination . . .

I shift in my chair, suddenly gratified to have run the gauntlet I'd run earlier downstairs. The hot-blooded, hot-footing harlot; the screech of smoking tires in the roadway; the grumpy guard keening for his next strip-search; the deplorable coffee—these tribulations, one and all, have served to gird my loins for battle and I feel ready to match wits with anyone. Even the rumpled replacement lawyer, this . . . Mr. Man-dee-bless . . .

He begins by having me admit that my opinions are based on the facts as presented by Dr. Fallon. "Yes, of course," I say.

Then he provides me with the story as told from the perspective of the patient, Mrs. Loberg. Instead, this story features an opportunistic psychiatrist lying in wait for the troubled former patient, whom he lured back to his office after hours. Would that change my opinion, the rumpled lawyer asks, and how so?

"Yes," I say, "if indeed Doctor Fallon took advantage of this former patient, such behavior would be . . . frowned upon by the professional community, but not a standard-of-practice violation per se."

Goodness, what initially seemed a delightfully nimble phrase— "frowned upon"—I can now tell has fallen on deaf ears. (Note: smells defeatist—cut.)

"'Frowned upon?'" the judge repeats as if not quite believing what he's heard.

"Uh, yes, Your Honor. In the general neighborhood of negligent behavior, but not quite there."

Ms. Aames's replacement pipes up: "You were paid a lot of money to come up with excuses like this 'frowned upon' business, weren't you, Doctor?"

"Objection! Argumentative!" Heidegger booms.

"I'll allow it," the judge croaks with an edge of hostility. "Please answer the question, Doctor."

"My fees aside, this is my honest, unvarnished opinion," I say too meekly. (Note: re-state this in a more dignified exchange, somehow.)

"How much per hour are you being paid to testify today?"

I tell them $1,000—but quickly clarify that I've only charged $750 for review of documents, meet-and-confer discussions, and the like. One would think such a distinction would soften the tone of this inquisition, but no one seems the least bit impressed by the reasonableness of my fees. (Note: eschew whininess.)

The replacement lawyer is practically laughing at me.

"How do you know behavior would be 'frowned upon,' Doctor? Did you take a poll of your colleagues' facial muscles when confronting them with a sordid tale of sexual misconduct, similar to what the board has alleged here?"

Again Heidegger objects; again, to no effect.

"You made that up, didn't you, Doctor?"

I do my best to appear offended, which I am. Yet, I'm also acutely aware that I cannot plausibly bolster my comment with any empirical evidence, let alone peer review articles, research, or recognizable data of any sort. "Frowned upon?" Please, it was horse-pucky, tripe, doggeral . . . all right, then: pure bullshit. And I—and they—knew it. (Note: CUT CUT CUT!)

But the worst is yet to come, because now the state lawyer grows wily.

For the next several minutes he asks me easy questions about the extensive professional-practice history detailed in my curriculum vitae. Questions about how many patients I've seen weekly, monthly, and yearly in various settings over the course of my career. Hundreds of patients, thousands of visits. How many patients I've terminated from treatment. Hundreds. Impressive totals, stretched over a thirty-four-year career.

I'm feeling much better now, reinvigorated, the blood filling back into my cheeks. Reflecting pleasantly on the overarching accomplishment, the achievement inherent with claiming such a long, distinguished body of work and time of service. Duly gratified, and duly satisfied—such that I walk right into the next few questions without even noticing how ensnared by my narcissism I've become. (Note: rework, excluding deleterious personal insights.)

"So, Doctor, you've treated countless female patients, have you not?"

"Why yes, I have."

"And some of those patients have had feelings of what you psychiatry specialists would call 'transference,' that is, strong personal feelings of affection toward you, the therapist?"

"Yes. Again, it's a common occurrence."

"And in your training and experience in psychiatry, are you aware that for the therapist on the receiving end of such affection, feelings of what is called 'countertransference' may occur?"

Hmmm. The replacement lawyer apparently knows his stuff.

"Yes, of course," I say too eagerly. "But one must act appropriately."

Rats. I have just broken one of the rules of cross-examination: never to freely offer information which was not specifically requested.

"And do what?" the prosecutor asks.

"Well, you must discuss the patient's feelings, the phenomenon of transference, explain what she's feeling, and why. You must emphasize that there's nothing wrong with having those feelings, they're natural, but that they can take away from the patient's therapeutic process, and indeed, she may now need to be referred to another doctor."

"That is the standard of practice when a patient demonstrates or expresses strong personal feelings for the therapist, correct?"

"More or less, that is correct, Counselor."

"But what I just asked you about was what a therapist does when he, the therapist, experiences strong feelings for the patient. In other words, I want to know what you, Doctor Winston, would do when countertransference occurs."

"I'm sorry," I say, offering the judge a beseeching pair of eyes.

But the judge looks away, refusing to rescue me.

"I thought I'd answered the question," I explain.

The saggy prosecutor bears down briefly on his notes, then slowly looks up with large, sleepy-brown eyes, his serenity sending a jolt of terror down my spine.

"I'll say it again. What do you do yourself, Doctor, to deal with countertransference? Do you talk with the patient about it?"

"Oh no," I say, too eagerly yet again. "That would be too easy to misconstrue, not to mention disorienting to her, so you can say nothing to the patient, nothing."

"Is that because the psychiatrist is there to always act in the patient's best interest, and talking about his feelings for her wouldn't fit that model?"

"Yes."

"Then, what does a conscientious therapist do?"

"Doctor," the judge asks, "I'd like you to tell the court what *you* would do."

For the first time in this claustrophobic little setting I become aware of the electrical hum emanating from the metal clock on the wall, the seal of the State of California hovering like a Roman gladiator's shield behind the judge's chair. The court reporter, a middle-aged bespectacled woman with rope-like red hair and a double chin, appears pained; her lumpy bosom is tightly wrapped in a sweater, and I note that the air conditioning vents are lodged in the ceiling almost directly above her, in the room's center. Mutely, she awaits my next utterance, her fingers curled above the odd black keyboard of her instrument of recordation.

I attempt to formulate the perfect statement, keeping track of my testimony thus far and its multiple objectives, the most paramount of which is to render Donald Fallon professionally blameless. Yet all I can think of with pounding clarity is: *What would Mum say if she could see me now?*

The answer to that one I know with equal clarity.

What a farce, a grand, comical farce this is, this game of made-up facts and conjured standards of duties owed to hypothetical patients. This is the sum total of your education and experience, son? To this you have aspired?

"Doctor?"

"Uh, yes, so sorry," I say, still rattled by the ubiquitous specter of Mum. (Note: cut, cut, cut!)

"Please answer the question," the judge insists.

"I . . . suppose I would discuss with a colleague, a mentor, an experienced psychiatrist whose opinion I trust, any feelings I'd have of countertransference, probe the root of those feelings that way."

Suppose? I am inwardly horrified. Good God, I've surmised instead of speaking from experience. My job is to empathize with the plight of Donald Fallon, and good God, I've just distanced myself—naturally, of course, but there it is.

Absently I accentuate my misstatement by sliding a finger inside my collar, thinking: Just breathe, and this will pass. Heidegger is stock still, but his glare is arctic and accounts for the burning sensation on my neck and forehead. I swallow dryly, awaiting the inevitable. Should I ask for water? No—supplication is tantamount to weakness.

The rumpled replacement for the formidable Ms. Aames, this Men-dee-bless, he may not look like much, but he hones right in on my tragically poor choice of words.

"Doctor, do you feel the kind of transference and countertransference that seems to have occurred between Rue Loberg and Doctor Fallon is normal?"

"Yes, I believe I've said so already."

"But your answer was speculative. Doctor Winston, with all the thousands of patient visits you've had, including your encounters with female patients who you believed were experiencing feelings of transference toward you, you've never experienced feelings of countertransference toward them, have you? That's why you just had to 'suppose' what you'd do in a situation like Dr. Fallon was in with Mrs. Loberg, isn't it?"

I've trapped myself.

"Well, I'd have to consider that carefully . . ."

"You've never become embroiled in something romantic, or sexual, with a female patient."

"No."

"And how many times have you testified as an expert witness?"

"Fifty, maybe sixty times."

The sleepy brown eyes hone in further.

"How many times on behalf of a psychiatrist who allegedly slept with his patient?"

"I . . . don't recall."

"Ms. Aames, my colleague, had an investigator for the board look into that. Her notes say this is the *first* time you've testified in a sexual misconduct case. Is that correct, or should I call the investigator to testify on rebuttal?"

"That's correct," I say.

"That's because this kind of thing is way out of bounds for a practicing psychiatrist, Doctor, isn't it?"

"It does present a rare, and unusual, challenge for all involved."

"Just a few more questions, Doctor. You've found a single instance of negligence in Doctor Fallon's behavior with his former patient Rue Loberg, a single simple departure from the standard of care a psychiatrist must adhere to, isn't that right?"

"Yes."

The prosecutor has straightened his spine, and the sleepy eyes seem poised for mischief.

"I'm curious. Are you here to 'frown upon' the rest of what he did to her?"

Heidegger lets fly another objection, which the judge swiftly discards. I nod before another directive to answer issues from the bench. I've held this battered beachhead long enough. The truth is, Donald Fallon has done a despicable deed to a troubled woman. Too bad the state can't prove it.

"Yes," I say with a decisive air. "I do frown upon the rest. But that doesn't change my findings."

The prosecutor allows himself a silent chuckle.

"No, Doctor, I suppose that wouldn't be possible. Not at your prices."

I look at Heidegger, who opens his mouth to object, but he coolly regards his high-priced expert with ambivalence, then disdain, and says nothing.

25

RAUL MENDIBLES

I never should have let Myrna come to the hospital with me tonight, but the events of the evening sort of conspired against me. First, her little sister, Lenore, was in town on leave from ROTC, crashing at our place, as usual, so she offered to babysit—just to burn my ass, too, that damn Lenore. Second, Myrna was keeping tabs. She's got this radar, it tells her how far I'm on or off the marital grid. And since I took over the Fallon case for Bradlee, I've been mostly off.

Excuse me for whining, but these days, I don't even feel alive when I'm home. Paying bills, doing dishes, taking out the trash, trying to find the reset button on the garage-door opener without getting electrocuted, lying in bed mute, listening but not hearing the numbing details of her day. Why the fat in peanut butter is beneficial; infant inoculations that may cause autism; thirty delicious new recipes for gluten-free Mexican dishes. My life at home is all about waiting; waiting for the other shoe to drop, for the next silly argument to kick up, for Myrn's post-partum depression—at half a decade, one of the longest-term cases in modern medical history, I suspect—to fade away. When it's lights out, I'm thanking God for the void of sleep, diving straight down to the bottom of sweet nothingness. Unless it's time for weekly maintenance sex, with the lights way low and the fantasy meter way high, and Myrna so rag-doll tired she doesn't even try to fake it anymore.

But before seeing Bradlee, I've got to survive dinner at home. Myrn, I can handle with my usual husbandly deflection shield, yet I'm raw and dry-throated from court and full-up with shaky doubt, so I'm less prepared to deal with Lenore. She's a younger, cuter version of my wife, a thick-boned girl the boys in her neighborhood used to call Fat Betty because she was plump, but in a good way. When I see Lenore, I see a part of Myrna that's less visible to me every day—the sexual, animalistic element—and that recognition smarts. My wife, she knows me so well that she can sense the disquiet stirring in me.

So I've got Bradlee on my mind tonight, especially since I'll be seeing her later; and Fat Betty's over there on the living room couch, unwittingly prodding my libido every time she kicks up a bare leg on the couch, or slinks to the fridge for a snack, her Botticelli backside half hanging out of her cut-off army fatigues as she bends over and peeks in. Feeling whipped already, I can hardly believe my ears when the doorbell starts ringing: Lucita Valdez. Verna De La Cruz. Rhynna Ortiz and her half sister, Felice. Beatriz Peña.

No, not tonight. Myrna's goddamn Barrio Babes book club.

I always have seconds on Myrna's *enchiladas espinacas*, but tonight, eating off a paper plate, surrounded by hefty thighs and even heftier opinions, the scent of aerosol hairspray fouling the air, I could barely taste them.

Ten minutes at the sink, scrubbing pots and loading the dishwasher, and I'd be free. That is, if they'd ever leave me alone. The last time Myrna hosted, the group's monthly selection was *The Scarlet Letter*, and not a lot was said about the text beyond the obvious—

"*Ay, mierda,* that Hester had it rough, first with that gutless preacher, knocks her up, but he's too ashamed—"

"Didn't have the *juevos, m'ija.*"

"—to be seen with her?"

"*Puritano pendejos, estan loco!*"

"That's thoroughly fu—messed up, dude."

"Es un mojon!"

"And then, that kid of hers turns out to be crazy."

"Like, evil, a bad seed."

"You seen that movie? *Coño,* it's scary as hell."

"Betty Davis and Joan Crawford, first when they were kids, then later—"

"No, *mira, muchacha,* that's not the one, you're thinking of *Whatever Happened to Baby Jane.*"

"Ay, que estupido . . ."

"In *The Bad Seed,* the little *bruja* goes around murdering everybody, but you don't see it, they just talk about it later."

"Don't see the murder, that's the best part."

"What kind of movie leaves out all the good stuff? You ask me, *that's* what's stupid."

"Ask me, that Baby Jane was way scarier than the kid."

"That bitch was crazy, and she didn't even know it!"

"That's how crazy people are, *m'ija,* I mean, if that's your world, you wouldn't know otherwise . . ."

The rest of that evening was spent this way, on pretty much any topic other than Nathaniel Hawthorne. But tonight, the ladies were intently discussing a sensational new piece of chick-lit tripe with a plotline bordering on soft-core porn, and because I was the only male in the house, my opinions were highly valued.

"Raul, *m'ijo,* close your eyes and imagine, if you was a single guy and some rich bitch was makin' a play for you, and she said she wanted to tie you up and spank your butt to get her jollies, would you do it?"

"Hey, his eyes ain't closed!"

"They should be burning from that Liz Taylor perfume o' yours, Lucita—what'd you do, take a bath in it?" I said.

"Carajo!"

"Just to be clear, the dominatrix, she's loaded?" I asked, straining to be funny.

"Stinky rich."

"How good-looking?"

"*Carajo!*"

"Don't forget, boy, you're a married man."

"No, he ain't, not fo' this; this is just like, high poetical—"

"Girl, you mean hypo-thetical."

"What I said."

"Never mind that, this rich girl's fine, Raul. Killer body, dressed to the nines all the time."

"Hot sauce. C'mon, *señor abogado,* do you or don't you?"

I throw the dish towel over my shoulder for effect, giving the group my best innocent shrug.

"Ladies, please, you can call me a stick in the mud, but *en mi puta vida . . .*"

"Liar, liar!"

"His stick's in the mud, all right!"

"*Coño!*"

Several pairs of false eyelashes fan the circle in unison. More wine cooler flows.

And so I'd thought my participation in the club's Q and As would have scored me enough brownie points with Myrn to make an easy exit, but I'd rattled the car keys when I pulled them off the wooden hook near the door, and—dammit!—as soon as she heard me, she buzzed over, grabbed her purse, apologized for cutting out as she thanked the ladies for coming, and asked Lenore to cover at home for a couple of hours.

Inside, I executed a silent scream.

Coño!

Lenore regarded me sideways, as if I was only marginally present, a ghost in my own home. "On it, girl," she told Myrna.

"I'm ready," Myrna told me, pulling on her stand-by black wool coat.

I said no, not necessary.

She aimed her best serious stare at my forehead. "Well, I say it *is.*"

"Myrn, don't be silly. Bradlee's my coworker, I'm handling her case, I'm obligated to—"

"Stop it, Raul."

I leaned in closer, so Lenore and the others couldn't eavesdrop.

"Myrn, you're being ridiculous."

"Then why are you blushing?"

"You are, dude!" Lenore chipped in helpfully.

If Myrna took exception to her sister's nosiness, she wasn't letting on. Instead, she calmly dropped a set of handwritten baby-care notes on the dining table, came back to the front door, and took the keys right out of my hand.

"Have fun, you two," Lenore called out.

I said good night to the book club ladies, who were now debating whether loneliness naturally makes a woman hornier.

"What you think, Raul?" Rhynna called to me as Lenore passed around hunks of marble Bundt cake.

"Nah, leave the boy alone."

"Yeah, boy got his stick stuck in the mud, remember?" Lenore said acidly, drawing one of the biggest laughs of the evening.

"Girl, that is cold!"

"She's mocking me," I said as Myrn snapped the front door shut. "Your own sister."

Myrna didn't look at me.

"I know who you're talking about. But, Raul? Leo's right."

"My foot! She should keep her damn—"

"You asked for it."

I dropped the argument, stood back as the house key slid into the lock. Myrna paused before turning the dead bolt. She regarded the lightly swaying porch swing, its white paint crinkled like shattered glass.

"This house needs tending, Raul. It's been neglected."

"Myrn, I—we should talk about this."

"Can we just go?"

I didn't know what I was saying anyway, but it would have made me sound guilty, so I played it smart for once and shut my mouth.

We climbed into a station wagon smelling of potting soil, snack crackers, and years-old baby vomit. I drove, the corroded tail end on the muffler purring loudly whenever I accelerated with the least bit of urgency. My thoughts returned to grade school, the stern, wrinkled nuns who yanked on fresh young earlobes with bony iron-clawed fingers, tattle-tale nuns with thin blue lips that could shush entire pews of squirming, evil boys with a literal promise that there'd be hell to pay. With clear-eyed aplomb they'd laid down the concept of the guilty mind, the sin that is desire alone, even free-standing desire without action.

Repeat after me, boys: I must not think bad thoughts.

Jimmie Guerra, my best friend in second grade, stood next to me and smiled.

All nuns have stinky twats.

I'd giggle, then recite it the correct way.

I know it's mumbo jumbo, Catholic mind control. But the lesson stuck.

Not for Jimmie Guerra; he left the church as soon as he could legally drive. He's a sculptor in New Mexico now, lives on a five-acre ranch with his beautiful Puerto Rican wife, Celia, a playwright barely half his age. Jimmie rode sacrilege as far as he could, I guess. Got himself free and never looked back.

Not me. Like a chump, I married a younger version of my mother and live daily with the guilt of having had my way with Bradlee Aames too many times to count—adding up, of course, to an actual sum total of zero.

The night traffic on the 101 freeway dusted our eyes with white glitter, the river of headlights merging seamlessly into a four-level interchange engineered by men with a confidence that had me near tears. They'd mastered the functions and forms of concrete and steel, their designs built to last. What was I but an also-ran who could not even begin to contribute, let alone compete? My moments of truth were filed away in folders that lay dormant for all time, stacked into cardboard boxes with the forgotten names of past offenders scrawled in black marker.

Myrna sat a mile away, as cold and broken as an outdated timepiece in the bottom of a sock drawer. I drove on, muttering street names on passing signs like a child greeting strangers.

I must not think bad thoughts. I must not think bad thoughts. I must not think bad thoughts.

*   *   *

The doctor, a tall, wrinkle-thin man named Levi—just like the jeans, he said blandly—had these papery shoulders that hunched forward and made him resemble an insect awaiting a meal. He'd just finished his round with Bradlee when we got to her room, and I caught him at the door, announcing myself too formally, as if I knew I didn't belong here. Dr. Levi pushed his glasses up his nose a little farther to get a better look at me.

"Another lawyer who works for the medical board," he quipped. "Better watch my step."

I thought of Major Coughlin and instantly felt unclean.

"I'm not checking up on you. Just my colleague."

"Yes, of course," he said with a glance at Myrna.

"I'm Mrs. Mendibles," she said.

Dr. Levi bowed. "Yes, hello."

He seemed to pause as if to decide what to say, or to wait for me to excuse my wife, but man, I was fine with letting her stay. Maybe if the wife heard about Bradlee's condition, Bradlee would seem like less of an abstraction, less a touchstone for all this unspoken tension between Myrn and me.

I told him how concerned everybody at the Attorney General's office was about her well-being. He said yes, yes, the short white hairs on his head glowing like whiskers. Betraying little emotion was part of his skill set; it probably had to be for him to function day to day and not go mad. But then . . . I thought I saw a barely perceptible grin light the corners of his mouth. *He can't know*, I told myself as he tapped his clipboard. *Am I that obvious? No, he can't know . . .*

"—recovering well from the gunshots," he was saying. "Her wounds are healing, and no sign of infections, knock on wood. Now, my—"

Myrna's eyes were on me the whole time the doc was talking.

"—greater concern is that the brain injury from her fall to the sidewalk was difficult to measure. We're certainly encouraged, her eyes are open and she's sitting up."

"Jesus!" I eased back a few feet and for the first time, allowed myself a look inside the room. A young man in a tight black v-neck shirt and jeans was seated by the bed, reading an open book. The bed was creased by a folding elbow, and Bradlee was cranked up at about thirty degrees. That is, a version of Bradlee was sitting up, the face and eyes perfectly bland, her hair straighter and more cleaned-up than usual, a long arm resting across her midsection like in an arranged portrait. Even without makeup, the face retained its beauty, but the look was one of joyless imprisonment. I imagined her thinking: *Someone, anyone, kindly get me the fuck out of here.* Whis is exactly how she'd have put it.

And damn, did I wish I could be that someone.

I nodded at Myrna, who'd ducked in behind me to look in on Bradlee, too. Myrna's face was the same as when she'd caught me staring at Lenore coming out of the bathroom in her undies last Saturday morning.

"—can't speak or move as yet," the doc rambled on. "An MRI showed minor fluid build-up, so the neurosurgeon drilled a tiny hole in the back of her skull to allow for drainage and lessen the swelling, which proved effective. Otherwise—"

Dr. Levi hedged his bets a while longer, though the message remained upbeat. My thoughts drifted away, back to the Fallon case and my latest involvement, which was having the unexpected effect of reviving my passion for practicing law. The only better result would be to impress Bradlee while I was in action, but obviously, that wasn't a possibility at this juncture . . .

"So tell us, what's the outlook, Doctor Levi?" I was tired of his equivocations.

The doctor paused long enough to regard the patient as if her blank stare might somehow change if she were to hear his next pronouncement.

"Physically, she's on the mend. Very resilient young lady."

"Don't I know it," I said as Myrna studied my demeanor.

"As for the mental, just give it time," he said. "There's simply no telling when she may come around, but she should."

I thanked him in the customary fashion, although the man was only doing his job and, to me, had showed no special passion for his work. He turned and began to leave the room, but apparently thought of something more.

"Oh. And you could pray, if you believe in that sort of thing."

To my shame, Myrna had bent over Bradlee, and with exquisite tenderness she squeezed her hand.

"We do believe, Doctor. And we will."

26

Rue Loberg

I'm used to being the one that comes into the room and everybody goes quiet. They see me and they think: *well, look what the cat dragged in*. Whisper things that aren't true, or at least are only half true—which is probably worse than an outright lie, 'cause half-truths tend to stick on a person even worse than lies. I've got a lot of those half truths stuck to me, like a bad rash I can't ever scrub off. Not ever.

I've heard a few doozies these last few weeks, what with this case and all. Turns out that because Dr. Don is still a name, and some cable TV network apparently had plans to give him a new show, right after the show about those old-time Vegas hoodlums, the news people saw an angle for a new story. So the case made the newspaper and got reported on TV and naturally, people are talking. Like they always have. Try as I might to tune them out, I can't help but be torn by the hateful words of those who don't know me but think they do.

Lookie there, it's the home-wrecker.

Yeah? That one?

Oh, hell yeah. She's the one who enticed a holy man, made him do evil things; brought such grief upon his wife, a fine, upstanding woman in her own right, such grief that she lost touch with the Lord's loving embrace altogether, left the church and her husband. Mm-mm—girl went and drove her own mother away from God.

That one, huh? Oh yes, indeed. Destroyed her high school's varsity football season. Yeah, she's the one who met that popular boy, the star quarterback, behind the bleachers, janitor comes along and sees them, quarterback on top of her, his pants down around his ankles—

Well, boys will be boys . . .

—and they both get suspended from school, he misses the big game. So much for the team's chances that season.

Out of the playoffs.

That's a damn shame.

Ha—no, this woman's got no shame. Career-wrecker, too, this one. She's the one threw herself at a top-drawer shrink, had his own TV show. Came to his office, sneaking in after-hours so no one would see her, made a spectacle of herself to get him in her clutches.

Dirty damn slut.

You got that right.

Family-wrecker.

Got a brown thumb, eh? Everything she touches turns to—

What else can you say? And I'm just sayin', here.

Oh, I know, she is what she is.

You said she's a family-wrecker.

Damn straight. She drags her very own family through a lawsuit against the shrink, just to cash in. Then she spearheads this medical board case? More like a witch hunt to strip the poor guy of his medical license. And you'd never guess who the star witness is for the state.

Good God, not the slut. Well, that's government for you, I guess.

Yup. Husband divorces her for cheating on him; son can't stand the sight of her; daughter disowns her, and the family . . .

That's how they talk about me. How they've always talked.

That's the special blend of insecurity and grief that echoes inside my head wherever I go, and will probably follow me to my grave. I can't always hear the voices clearly, can't always catch every word, but I've pieced together my share of what's been said, and it's not hard to fill in the rest. I can also see with my own two eyes the snickering faces, disbelieving shrugs and shakes of the head, those you-disgusting-piece-of-trash stares. I know they don't know the real me; they can't grasp how I came to be so helpless at times that I honestly can't think my way through a problem and stop myself from being a victim before it happens all over again. They shun me—but because they can't see my side of the story, I tell myself it doesn't matter. They don't matter.

Except, that is, when the people looking down on me are my family. Then it hurts. Cuts me deep, right to the core.

The divorce should've been predictable enough, but it rolled over me like an avalanche. Made me want to end my life and if I'd had the courage to face my maker, I'd have done it. Andy had some painkillers left over from when he got banged up a couple years ago, took a spill test-riding one of his custom hogs, raspberried up his side. He tried a couple of those pills but didn't care for the way they made him sleepy during the day. When Andy split on me, he was pretty mad and in a hurry to clear his stuff out. Forgot to take inventory of what he left in the bathroom, including that little red bottle on a glass shelf in the medicine cabinet. That first night he was gone I nerved up to do it, and it was like every word printed on that bottle's white label was egging me on.

Acetaminophen and oxycodone, for moderate to severe pain. Schedule II narcotic analgesic.

It seemed the time had come, so I lit some candles, shook the bottle, and counted out sixteen little white capsules on my pillow.

Take two per day, as needed. Use only as directed. Not to be taken with alcohol; when combined with alcohol may lead to respiratory depression and death.

Sixteen, I counted—once and then a second time to be sure. More than enough, if mixed with alcohol, to do the job. I'd been hitting the grape all day, but just in case, I poured a big glass of chablis, brought it back to bed, and drank it down to the last drop. Sat back, the candlelight pulsing so pretty, these dripping sheets of gold sliding down the walls; having a good last cry, basking in the false glory of self-pity, my darkest hour coming forth with an empty wineglass and a fistful of pills intended to ease the pain of knowing my life partner despised me. Maybe these little white gems would serve that purpose . . .

Closing my eyes so tight it hurt, I searched the blackness. Time passed, and soon enough, I wound up saying a prayer—though I wondered if I even believed anymore. I said: *If you are there, Jesus, please tell me You are ready to take me. Show me.*

It was, indeed, the strangest moment in my life. My fist, it had a crushing grip on those pills, but my hand would not open, and I do not know if Jesus spoke to me, or if it was just my fear doing the talking, but all I could say, the only word coming to my lips, was no. *Hell no!*

Now Jesus, in his time, was never known to curse. But looking back, I must conclude that I did feel His presence, like a soft, healing touch upon me in that moment, for I arose, rolled off the bed, stumbled into the bathroom, and flushed those sixteen pills down the toilet.

So yes, I may be a pitiful loser, may have trashed the best years of my life, but then, my time has not yet come. There's more to do. I don't know my precise purpose, have no true bead on the future, but I do believe with conviction that He has a plan for me.

Why else would I be here tonight, in a big LA hospital I never even knew existed, come to see Miss Bradlee Aames, the lawyer that took it to Dr. Don for what he did to me? I'm thinking there has to be a reason, there's just gotta be a reason . . .

* * *

Listen to me, going on about myself! Poor thing, Miss Aames, she's fallen on major hardship of her own, shot in the street by a man they say was gunning for that private investigator Andy hired, Deshaun Fellows. Happened right down the block from the courthouse. And to think, I could've been there to save her.

That's right, Dr. Craig Weaver and me, we were going to go together—back to court, that is, to watch more of the proceedings. Continue to face down my demons, you know, same way as what you do if you come across a bear, you run right at it instead of away from it. Talk about a taking a different tack; this is a groundbreaking change for me, all right, and I owe it all to Dr. Weaver. Wish I could've stopped that shooter. Now why, I thought, couldn't *that* have been God's plan?

But I had a meeting this afternoon and couldn't get ahold of my AA sponsor to get her okay to miss. My sponsor, Gwen, she's a no-nonsense type; Gwen did six years in prison for killing her no-account wife-beater bum of a husband, and ever since the day she came out of solitary confinement swearing she'd been graced with God's forgiveness, she's not keen on people telling her they can't do something. Dr. Weaver offered to call her, to get permission, but even though his intentions are good, there're parts of my life I just don't want to expose to him. It's like, if he knew every last thing about me, then what would I do if he were to reject me? I'd just shrivel up into a ball and blow away in the wind like a tumbleweed. Silly for me to think that way, I know, because a therapist is supposed to act in my best interest at all times—but obviously, that hasn't always been the case in my experience. Anyway, I went to my meeting and Dr. Weaver said he understood.

Miss Aames—ho! It was awful! She just lay there helpless. She did seem peaceful, though, like an angel. Her eyes were open, but there was nothing behind them, none of that sharpness, that gunfighter's glint in her eyes that's a thrill to see when she's in court. There was a crowd of people around her tonight.

Mr. Fellows, the investigator, smiled and said hello first. I thought he looked a little lost or sad about something he couldn't find the words to express.

"Heard you testified real well, ma'am," he said.

I could only shrug. I was too scared to remember much.

Miss Aames's boss at work, Mr. Mendibles, was here too, with his wife, a big-boned lady with a knee-length jacket over jeans and a turtleneck sweater. She was very polite, but with that jacket still on, she seemed ready to be anywhere else. Her handshake was like a ghost's, and that smiling face was verging on cracking into a million pieces.

"I just want you to know the trial is going well," Mr. Mendibles told me.

Do I thank him? I was thinking, but before I could come up with a dumb pleasantry, Mr. Mendibles tilted his head toward Miss Aames, as if to attend to her. And even though it was just a split second, that look of his had longing written all over it. So that was what his wife already knew: that Mr. Mendibles couldn't hide how torn up he felt about Miss Aames.

And I don't mean as a concerned boss for an employee; I mean: as a man feels for a woman.

Another guy, young handsome fellow named Reeves, was seated bedside with Miss Aames, patting her hand as he said hello to me. Guy resembled an ad in a magazine: nice face, great smile, this perfectly groomed brown hair cut short around the sides and back but longer-looking somehow. His shirt had these curvy white dolphins jumping around and the silver watch he wore had a cluster of tiny gears exposed right in the watch's face. His waist was skinnier than mine, and his arms were toned like he put in regular time at the gym.

"Call me Reevesy," he said. "Everyone else does."

Gay as a three-dollar bill, was my private assessment, but I liked his friendly manner and the way his eyes held mine without judgment when we talked.

"I'm Bradlee's roomie, a bona fide computer geek. I also happen to be a pro bono cosmetologist and an unpaid fashion consultant for all my hopelessly ungrateful friends, not necessarily in that order."

"Sounds pretty rough," I said.

"Oh, it is. But don't mind me! I've made an art form out of bitching and whining. Ask Bradlee, now that girl has heard it all . . ."

He stopped as if he just remembered she was here, laid up beside us. Next thing, his handsome face wasn't so handsome.

"It's okay," I said.

"Is it? Look at her."

We both did together. Honestly, she hadn't changed a whit since I walked in here, but I still felt a little surprised and let down to see her laid out like a living statue.

"Let me tell you, Rue, if I wasn't a pacifist, I'd kill the social reject who did this with my bare hands."

"Me too," I said.

"You're a pacifist?"

"Nah. It just sounded good. Given the chance, I think I'd waste the bastard."

I covered my mouth, not quite believing what had just come out of it. That made Mr. Reevesy hoot.

"Rue, we may have just met, but somehow I believe you'd do the same yourself. So no guilt-tripping, please."

"Fair enough."

Across the bed, Dr. Weaver was leaning over Miss Aames, searching her face as if by force of will he might bring her back from her coma. Mendibles, the lawyer, seemed to be keeping pace with Dr. Weaver's intentions. Mrs. Mendibles? She was at the foot of the bed, soaking in all this . . . scene. God, all you could call it is male yearning, and I could tell she'd about had enough. Right about then she clutched her throat like she couldn't breathe, spun toward Reevesy and me and stamped her foot.

"*Coño!*" she said quietly—some curse word in Spanish.

Mr. Reevesy nodded to me to slide closer to her, and I did. My guess was the best thing to do was to offer a little female companionship.

"Coffee?"

"I'd love some," she said.

I took her hand and got her out of there. Men, they can be so insensitive, but women don't miss a beat. And Reevesy, too, he was right on the beam.

Ten minutes later we returned to Miss Aames and the circle of men at her bedside. Downstairs, I'd learned from Mrs. Mendibles, whose given name is Myrna, that the brain doctor here said the more mental stimulation Miss Aames gets, the better. Which was good. What I learned that was *not* as good was that she suspected her husband was in love with Miss Aames. She was so concerned—and so deeply hurting over it—that I couldn't help but lie on instinct, and spectacularly so.

"Forgive me if I sound too forward," I said. "But I doubt it's anything."

"Back there," she said. "You saw him. The recognition was all over your face."

"Listen, dear, a lot of men respond to Miss Aames 'cause of her looks. But that's a far cry from being in love. You're his wife. That puts you on a whole different level."

Which was *true*. Maybe I was making more sense than I give myself credit for. Where I'd got the confidence to talk to a total stranger like that, I have no idea. But it worked, and she seemed comforted.

Heading back upstairs to Miss Aames's room, I had a realization.

I'm changing. Not so much the victim anymore. Now, I'm more of a helper. And darn, it feels good . . .

Miss Aames's black eyes were open, but she was still unresponsive. That didn't stop attorney Mendibles, Dr. Weaver, and investigator Fellows from carrying on this big conversation, like she was a part of it all.

"I don't know," Mr. Mendibles said. "Duke Winston is as credentialed as they come."

"Man was lying every time he opened his mouth," said Mr. Fellows. "Said he'd never done a thing like Doctor Don did, not with anyone. Not even close."

"Doesn't matter," said Attorney Mendibles, "what the defense expert admitted. The burden of proof is mine, and it's steep. I have no clue whether our case has reached that high a plateau."

He looked right at me. Instinctively, I shrunk.

What could I tell them? That I knew the signs of losing better than just about anyone? That, like a dog, I can smell it coming down the block before anyone else even blinks? My heart felt hard and unfamiliar to me, like a foreign object, a lump of stone buried in my chest. I'd forgotten how to breathe, too. The tears, they sneaked up on me this time—a flash flood, no warning. I couldn't face the others, but there was nowhere to run or hide. I shielded my eyes with a bare hand, sniffling horribly.

"I knew it," I told them in a choked voice. "Good old Doctor Don, way cooler and way more credible than me. He's gonna get away with it, isn't he?"

Mendibles stepped closer to me near the end of the bed, but said nothing. Which, of course, said everything. The whole thing was depressing beyond words.

"Right," I said, still too raw to fully show my face. "Sure. None of this is any different than what always happens. Why am I even surprised?"

"You were a very brave witness, Mrs. Loberg. And credible. But . . . nevermind."

"But what?"

The lawyer looked at the others, then Ms. Aames, like he was taking an invisible vote, then me. "When you get down to it, it's still Doctor Fallon's word against yours."

"Honestly, I don't know what I was thinking," I said.

"It doesn't have to go that way, ma'am," Mr. Fellows said quietly to me. "Because of the settlement, I can't go around making disclosures, nor can Mister Loberg. But not you. As I recall, you didn't sign the agreement, or take any money."

"How could I?" I replied way too loudly. "My family was ruined, and it was all my fault!"

Next thing, Myrna Mendibles had her arm around me and was easing me up from the floor. Guess my knees gave out and I went down.

Breathe deeply, they told me, so I did. Sat in a chair by the end of the bed. Someone handed me a cup of water, which I drank down fast.

"We should go," I heard Craig Weaver say. This was my idea, and what can I say?—it was a mistake.

He'd been pretty invisible until now, hanging back on purpose to let me have my experience. Now he squatted in front of my chair, his face on the level with me. His skin was a pale yellow in the fluorescent light.

"Are you well enough to walk out of here yourself?"

"I think so."

"I can get a wheelchair from the nurse if you like."

"No thanks, I got a little woozy but I'm all right now."

"I'm terribly sorry I upset you, ma'am," Deshaun Fellows said. "Truly, I am."

"Mrs. Loberg's been through a lot the last couple days," Dr. Craig said. "She needs to take it easy."

Suddenly, it was like the rest of my life had always turned out: another unhappy ending, everybody disappointed, and me, right at the center of the latest failure. The fly in the ointment, the crack in the dam—that's me.

Until I remember my darkest hour, the prayer had said. Well, I'd remembered. And then, by God's mysterious grace, an answer came to me.

Waving off my dear-heart therapist, I sat up straighter. Ouch—the curved plastic made me feel like cereal poured into a bowl.

"My daughter hates me," I told the whole room. "Swears she'll never speak to me again. And so far, ever since my husband's lawsuit settled, she's kept her promise."

No one said a word, so I kept going.

"Now, Mister Fellows remembers correctly what happened when the lawsuit ended. I took no part in any deal of theirs. I'm free to do as I please. And I intend to, if it'll help the case."

"Mindy was there," Mr. Fellows said. "I told Ms. Aames that much, right before she was injured."

"Mindy could help us big-time," Mr. Mendibles said to me.

"I can't guarantee a thing," I said. "But I'll talk to her. And if she grants me the courtesy of listening, I will ask her, from the very bottom of my heart, to help right this wrong."

The men were quietly excited and thanked me. Even Reevesy the roommate privately informed me that in his book, I "kicked ass." But I felt tired and hollowed-out, as if the task I'd committed to had already taken a toll—in advance. My next thought scared the holy heck out of me.

You're already sick and depleted. The stress of all this will only speed your downfall.

I wanted a drink so bad that if I didn't have one, I would surely die. But due to all the extenuating circumstances, I stuck with coffee.

27

DONALD FALLON, MD

For me, as a meeting place the House of Chai Tanya really fits the bill. Its upscale Thai menu offers pleasant intrigues, the bartender knows how to mix a whiskey sour that goes down smooth but with a kick, and the nighttime lighting is dramatically aglow, generating notions of intrigue and romance in the heads of the women I like to pair up with in such a setting. No—it's not a meeting spot; Chai Tanya suggests more of an incognito rendezvous. And best of all, it's just a hop and a skip down Larchmont from my office, so for my rendezvous partner, there's a sense of familiarity with this neighborhood that helps offset the newness of seeing her therapist for drinks and a late dinner.

Former therapist, that is.

I usually start out at the bar downstairs, so I can make easy eye contact with my date the instant she walks into the restaurant, and wave her over—the last thing I want is for her to step inside, look around, and get hit over the head by the sense that getting together with me off-site just has to be wrong. On more than one occasion I've had to leap from my barstool to intercept a doubtful fretter when her conscience intervened and caused her to do an about-face and flee. But once I've got her inside the lovely, semi-dark lounge, and the flickering light and welcoming ambient restaurant noise begins to soothe her senses, my first order of business is to gently put her at ease, so I ask her what she'll be drinking. This little cordiality serves a second purpose in that it commits my lady to the concept of meeting me here socially, which she acclimates to quickly as I call in her drink with the bartender. She'll be sticking around now, at least long enough to be polite and sip her libation. Later, we'll move upstairs to a table for dinner. Dining upstairs is another feature I love about this place, as it signifies a passage to a zone of greater elevation and enhanced privacy. I needn't be so crass or condescending as to explain here the psychological advantages of such a run-up to sexual intimacy, so I will leave that to your imagination.

Upstairs, the Asian kewpie-doll waitresses that work the handful of small, square tables know me as Doctor, and I've tipped them heavily in the past while giving the gentle instruction that they please consistently refer to me as such when I dine. This simple greeting is personal enough to convey that I am in full control here, while injecting more openness and normalcy into the setting. Yes, I take a chance by identifying myself as a doctor, but I always pay in cash and, hell—scads of MDs are running around Los Angeles at night anyway. The staff here is discreet in that wonderfully subservient manner that Orientals in the service industry so effortlessly convey, so I don't fret much about exposure.

Did I say "Orientals"? Jiminy, I mean Asians. Gotta be so damned careful not to offend anyone these days.

Control and normalcy—I won't deliver a lecture here on these elements either, but suffice it to say, control and normalcy are at the heart of virtually every male sexual conquest. Your every move and gesture and comment subtly lets her know that you are in command of your realm; and since she is within that realm, subservient to your power and authority, naturally you are going to take her, business as usual. Then you do.

My date tonight was almost too easy, but after days and days and weeks and months of sweating every detail of this blasted medical board trial, I needed a made-to-order conquest, not a leery, co-dependent challenge. I was tired of being pursued and ready, again, to be the pursuer. A re-establishment of the realm was in the offing, twenty milligrams of Viagra were coursing through my veins, and I was primed for action.

I'd spoken with Terrence Heidegger late this afternoon, walking back to our cars following court; he'd tucked me into my Mercedes with a wink and a devilish grin.

"Go home," he said. "Have a nice meal, a glass of wine. Get some rest."

"One question: is it over?"

He squinted into a shaft of sun. "Well, Don, let me see. The dragon lady's lying in a hospital bed—drooling, or so I am told. Her sorry excuse for a supervisor—"

"The Mexican doughboy?"

"Hah! Good one. Yes, the Mexican doughboy still wants to settle with us, even though we're kicking their asses, and their burden of proof's a mile high."

Heidegger clapped me on the shoulder through my open window. The Northwestern class ring on his big, spotted paw of a hand stung my clavicle, but I stifled the wince. Terrence plays his own complicated game with me. Yes, he's a type-A personality all the way, and despite the fact that I'm the one paying him and concomitantly, it is he who serves me, he cannot resist the impulse to wield his physical superiority over me. As if to say: *I'm the lawyer and you, as the client, are the man of the hour, but if we were to meet in a dark alley under different circumstances, you'd be saying your Goddamn prayers.*

"Go home," he'd said again. "And stay out of trouble."

As part of my own equally complicated response to being squeezed by a type-A ball-buster like Terrence, I'd done neither.

Getting back to my date, her name is Sheila Mullany, and she's best described as a homesick Bostonian professional student, thirty-six and still trying to figure out what she wants to do with her life. Comes from a family of overachieving freaks, including a mathematician patriarch on the faculty at MIT, a book-editor mom who makes more money than the old man, a Harvard MBA brother currently designing a new monetary system for a struggling African country, and a kid sister with a new techno-pop CD that entered the Billboard Top 100 at number 15 last month. Understandably, Sheila feels she can't measure up.

No shit, I wish I could simply say. But then, we'd have forty-five minutes left in a fifty-minute session and that wouldn't do.

I knew Sheila's family had money, but she was too proud to take it anymore, what with her having pursued a higher education on the family dime pushing two decades, now. She had no medical insurance and little ability to pay when she came to me on a trusted referral. She also had a huge pair of creamy white jugs and a pile of curly auburn hair, both of which I wanted to bury my face in the moment I first saw Sheila. By that point in time my civil lawsuit with the Lobergs was taking a turn for the worse, so I decided to be cautious. Then I thought: why not let her pay a small sum in cash, and not create a billing record? Or a medical chart? She was broke, so she'd take the low-cost cash part of the deal—which she did—and it was unlikely she'd ever ask for a copy of her chart anyway. That way if I got caught fooling around with her, I could just deny, deny, deny, and it would be near-impossible for anyone to establish a doctor-patient relationship—except, perhaps, that pillar of arrogance, Duke Winston. (To think that royal jackass picked up eight grand for that absolute blather!)

That's right: Dr. Don is evolving, polishing his act.

Sheila was fifteen minutes late, but that merely gave the bourbon time to lubricate my brain. A light dining crowd tonight at a quarter past eight: three stout, not very athletic-looking men in striped tennis outfits at the bar, half falling off their stools as they strained too hard to yuk it up; an older married couple living out their mutual death sentences at a table near the window facing Larchmont, absently nursing their white wines; a handsome older brunette in a shiny black dress farther down the bar, leaning over a martini glass as if a fly were in it. Say, not bad, the brunette loner—lovely hair and nice body-tone. If I didn't have a date I'd inquire immediately.

Should've ordered an appetizer while I waited, I thought. I'd passed on lunch today, as I was not inclined to sit through another hour of lawyer-talk with Heidegger and the Brooks Brothers boys, so I was famished. When Sheila popped in, her tits barely arrested by a low-cut white blouse that had me instantly conjuring a nifty landowner/peasant-girl fantasy, I was ready to eat a bear. But first she wanted a drink and since we were in the lounge, I had to buy her one.

A "cool breeze"? Well, it was what she wanted. Jesus, wasn't this the favorite drink of barely legal sorority girls in Westwood? Oh, Sheila, I thought, when will you ever grow up? But, since at present I was picturing my rigid member nestled in her spectacular cleavage like a hot dog in a bun, I thought it best not to pass judgment on her relative maturity and made no comment.

I strolled up to the bar, pleased with my expanding fair-mindedness. It seemed I was on the verge of a new era of higher enlightenment. Or maybe that was just a damned good first whiskey sour.

"Hit me again, maestro. And a . . . cool breeze for my guest."

I'd leaned over a barstool to half mutter my date's ridiculous request. The bartender, a muscular guy whose ancestors probably paddled a canoe between continents, must've thought I'd lost my mind with the latter request, but he played it straight and said, "Yessir. But I'm out of tangerine juice. Will OJ do?"

"Sure, damn right—and make it a double," I said quietly.

"A double, sir? That kind of drink, it sort of defeats the purpose."

I raised an eyebrow. "Precisely."

The bartender got my meaning. I had some serious realm-building to do if I was going to reach the Promised Land with Sheila tonight. Her froufrou drinks would require a serious boost.

But before I could even commence construction, the realm's tenuous foundation crumbled and collapsed.

"Excuse me, little boy," came a gravelly female voice from a few barstools away. "Are you lost and looking for your mommy?"

The handsome brunette in the shiny black dress. My wife, to be precise.

My mind blanked, just before my tongue tried to nose-dive down the back of my throat.

"Hilary." I stumbled toward her, if only to lessen the chance that she might raise her voice and embarrass me further. "Why, uh, aren't you—"

"What?—At home? Darning your socks?"

I did my best to seem sincerely mystified. "You're not . . . following me."

"Oh, you are a hoot, Donnie."

"Is, uh, something the matter?"

She snickered, crossing her legs. In the forgiving light, she looked ten years younger, and dressed in black from head to toe, ten pounds lighter.

"Donnie, you are a prize."

I chanced a backward glance at Sheila, who, fortunately for me, was playing with her cell phone, oblivious to my current plight.

"Hil, I know how this may look, but this is actually a therapeutic exercise."

"You don't say."

"And I shouldn't, because patient care is confidential, of course."

She seemed bemused by my fast-talking—and not to be buying a word of it. "Oh, of course. Now you're a medical ethicist."

I leaned in closer to add a tone of secrecy. "You see, I'm meeting that young woman here, in this place, to guide her through a social situation safely in a controlled manner, so that her fear of social situations will diminish."

"Aah. Always the clinical innovator."

"She's got a first date tomorrow night with a crackerjack guy she really likes, but her . . . her debilitating anxiety threatens to—"

Splat! That was the sound Hilary's drink, a martini, made as it hit me in the face, the gin burning my eyes as I rubbed them ineffectually.

"Those breasts she's showcasing don't look too debilitated, Donald, they look pretty revved up and ready to go."

"Please, Hilary—"

"Don't Hilary me, you prick, just look at her. Debilitating anxiety, indeed—she doesn't need a bra for those pointers, she needs a missile silo."

"Darling, I swear—"

"Oh, I wish you wouldn't. I'm so . . . you don't know how tired I am of your nonsense."

Reverting to old habits, I reached across and grabbed her wrist so hard I could have snapped it. "That's enough, naughty girl."

Her speed and strength surprised me. First off, she bent forward and sunk her teeth into my gripping fingers until I released in agony. Then she grabbed my earlobe so hard that I couldn't breathe. Or think.

"You cannot touch me, intimidate me, threaten or control me, ever again, you sadomasochist fuck," she hissed. "Three years of therapy and four belts in Aikido have freed me from your uniquely loving husbandly touch."

Years? I'd not even noticed her absences. She always seemed to be out shopping, which was well enough with me as long as I could pay her credit card balances.

"Leggo," I quietly begged, until she released my ear.

She ordered herself another martini from the bartender, who silently offered me a small white towel to dry my face, a flicker of respectful disappointment in his eyes. I declined.

"But you wouldn't . . . you can't even know that," she went on. "You're too oblivious. You love the sound of your own voice too much to even notice."

"Um—Doctor Don?"

Sheila stood behind us, those hooters jutting spectacularly, and at exactly the wrong moment.

"Hello, dear," Hilary said with an evil calm. "I'm Hilary Fallon, the esteemed doctor's wife, though not for long. I've come to save you from his clutches tonight."

Sheila said she didn't understand—until Hilary made her.

"You're not, um, mad at me for leaving?" Sheila asked me, twenty minutes later, her cool breeze double untouched and utterly windless.

"No, no," I said.

Hilary cackled. "Darling, his madness is of another stripe."

That silly little dope Sheila actually thanked Hilary. Then she gathered her purse and sweater and fled without looking back. I downed her drink without thinking, then my own.

"You're the one who should be thanking me," Hilary said when Sheila had gone.

"Is that so?"

"Because I'm saving you. From yourself."

She said it with enough declarative force that two of the three drinking pals just down the bar from us pulled back and took a gander our way.

"Always drink responsibly," one of them declared before throwing back a shot—as if to suggest I was an alkie and this business with the wife was an intervention. I was seething, but when I looked down at my icy palm I saw that I'd been gripping my glass like my life depended on it.

"Y-you don't know what you're doing," I said, my whole body shaking uncontrollably.

"Easy, tiger."

"You think you can j-just walk in here—"

"Put down that glass before you smash it and cut yourself."

"—and . . . instantly assess what's happening at a mere glance, drawing your f-false, outlandish conclusions—"

"Save it, Donnie. I've got your number." Her newest martini was delivered on a fresh napkin. "Honestly," she said. "I didn't come here to torpedo your latest conquest. Then again, that did turn out better than I expected."

"Oh, sure." I could've grabbed up a handful of those pearls hanging from her neck and strangled her with them. No, I'm here because—"

"You really should go."

"Not until I announce the inception of your professional demise."

My fist came down on the bar. "What—do—you—want, dammit?"

Hilary smirked at me the way the rest of those smug Coughlins did the day I married into the family.

"Such poor impulse control."

"I'm warning you, don't push me, Hil."

"You should enroll in the same kind of anger management courses you so sanctimoniously recommend for your patients. And by the way, I've got a gun and I know how to shoot it, so don't get any ideas. You will never brutalize me again."

My head felt like it would explode, which is probably why the bartender walked over and camped himself across from us.

"Everything's okay," he said, more as a statement than a question.

Hilary smiled like she had all night, just to turn the screw deeper between my ribs.

"The gentleman here is irritatingly obtuse. Then again, he is my husband, so I suppose I've signed on for this."

The bartender nodded and walked away. Damn—now Hilary was messing with my Chai Tanya mojo. I sat there, letting time pass if only to show I was in control.

"My brother called," she said at last.

"Bet he was drunk."

"He has his demons. Now, don't get bitchy, Don. In what's left of our marriage, that remains my department."

She sipped her martini as if it were the libation of the gods, and as she did, I remembered why I'd married her. A smart, fine-looking graduate student with a bubbly, upbeat outlook that put me at ease whenever I was at her side. A family name known here and in Sacramento, a prominent surgeon father heading up a well-respected cardio-vascular department at Huntington Memorial, two uncles in the state senate. Good connections among the USC and UCLA families of alumni. She'd raised my game for twenty years, until we'd tried every fertility clinic and method and placement of furniture and given up the quest for proliferation. Slowly she'd gone sour from loneliness and the bitter singular failure of an empty crib in the soft yellow room at the end of the upstairs hallway. My weak sperm, my weak chin, my weak jokes at cocktail parties. The more I did to advance my career, the less impressed she seemed. Nothing was good enough.

It didn't help that the more I personally asserted my dominance, the more she apparently recoiled.

Bad girl. Very bad girl!

"Major called to tell me he'd resigned from his position with the medical board," Hilary said.

"No major loss," I quipped. "One less hack in Sacramento."

"He asked me to tell you one thing."

She was grinning like the alley cat she can be when she wants to scratch my eyes out. I finished my drink, belched inelegantly on purpose, and waited.

"What do you want, Hil, a drumroll?"

She shrugged and polished the rim of her martini with smiling lips.

"So, I'm enjoying myself a little, so have a cow. Know what he said?"

"Jesus, Hil, knock it off already."

"He had a message for you: you're on your own."

I wanted to smack that cocky grin right off her gently lined but still pretty face. I half raised an open palm, which she eyed with prejudice.

"Touch me, and I'll break your arm at the elbow."

My hand slid back down in defeat. "I'm going to win this case. My lawyer says we've got 'em right where we want 'em."

She laughed as if only she knew what a dunce I'd been, but I was now about to find out. I felt a sudden urge to turn and run, and had I not run up a bar tab that was yet to be settled, I'd have bolted.

"Perhaps your lawyer is merely telling you what you want to hear, Donnie." Her brow had wrinkled and her dark eyes were shiny with hate. "I look at you, Doctor, I see a man who doesn't even know that everything he's gotten wasn't earned, it was handed to him. Even that little tootsie tonight. She was here based on entirely false pretenses, a grand, skillfully executed artifice. You couldn't attract a girl like that on your own merits, not in a million years. Not even a screwed-up freak, the likes of which you cherry-pick from your practice, you goddamn heel. No, Donnie, you've got to cheat your way in. It's your signature move, your métier."

"You're drunk, Hilary."

"I like a martini, so what? But you! You are a bamboozler and a confidence man. A limp-dick. A fraud."

She pushed away from the bar and stood up, surveying me like I was excrement lying in her path, to be skirted cautiously. For all the bluster she'd issued, her eyes were rimmed with tears. I grabbed her before she could walk away. She turned on me viciously.

"Let go of me. Now!"

"Do as the lady says," the beefy bartender told me. Apparently he'd been shadowing our confrontation the entire time. I let go of Hilary.

"Such a bully," she said. "Right to the bitter end. When they expose you for what you are, toss you out of the medical profession on your ear, I won't be there to dust you off. By God, I rehearsed a good line or two for this moment, but . . . I think my dear brother put it best. Donnie, at long last you are on your own."

Ten minutes later I was upstairs, fulfilling Hilary's angry prophecy. Dining alone at a nice little table. *Not so bad, not so bad at all . . .* I'd had another drink in transition and needed sustenance to absorb the alcohol sloshing around my gut, so I ordered an appetizer the description of which I didn't even hear. No matter—the mood of this place, so warm and calming, was like an embrace, keeping my spirits from bottoming out entirely. My waitress, Kim, was bright and sexy and cute as a button. I chatted her up vigorously, feigning endless fascination with her pursuit of a degree in fashion design, her part-time work in some crummy little Koreatown clothing mill. Her skin, those flawless cheeks, and that perfect nose, now this was where my true interest lay! The quiet dignity of this soft-spoken daughter of boat people, this exotic, delicate flower of femininity! The industriousness, to hold down two jobs while putting herself through school! Swooning, I finished that fateful appetizer—a dish so fishy and spicy I may as well have eaten a box of thumbtacks, because my system never had a chance of processing it. God—could it be? I was in love, in love again, locked in waitress Kim's thrall . . .!

What they told me later, the two policemen, was that I'd lost my balance, passed out, and fallen onto my food server, briefly subduing her on impact. Mr. Chee, the bartender, had helped me back to my feet and taken me outside to cool off. Although another patron had a differing account, describing a swift, punishing scuffle, Mr. Chee insisted that everything was fine and the waitress involved was still working her shift. Customers faint. Heat rises, and the air upstairs can get too warm. No trouble tonight, no trouble at all.

My left cheekbone and eyebrow were mildly swollen and tender to the touch. My rib cage felt funny, too. I took a deep breath, crying out in pain.

Thankfully the police seemed indifferent to the travails of a lonely psychiatrist. One of them, a mouse-eared redheaded guy that recognized me from TV, even said it was a pleasure meeting me. Offered to call a cab, but I said I could do that myself. When they left, I checked my pants pocket and fished out my wallet. I always put receipts inside, just behind the bills. But there was no Chai Tanya receipt for dinner or drinks tonight.

Mr. Chee was waiting for me at the door when I tried to re-enter.

"I want to square my debt."

Mr. Chee remained immovable. "We do not want your money, sir."

"But . . . please, it wouldn't be right."

Carved into his big, black war mask of a face was a frown grim and unyielding. "You Americans think it's always about money. You are wrong. Go home."

"But—"

"Go home. Do not return." He folded his muscular arms like a noble sentinel.

What could I say—that he'd suggested an impossibility? That I had no real home to return to? He turned and melted back inside, enveloped by the ambient dining splendor I'd utilized to my advantage so many times, it was like a part of me, a valuable working component of the devastating Dr. Don persona. Losing it was like experiencing a death, and I don't know if it was that sense of loss, plus the booze, my internal injuries and the wingding appetizer that hit me so hard all at once, but I crumbled.

A turban-wearing cabbie with bushy black eyebrows came to scoop me up. Retching on the street curb, I hid my face from him.

"Sir!"

"No, no, please." I was not yet done with my tragic wallowing and waved aside his strong helping hands.

"Sir—"

"My tears are cried for no one but myself," I explained.

The cabbie stood back and posted himself beside his car, politely waiting, but I could sense his confusion. I took a deep, painful breath and straightened up in search of a scrap of dignity. Used my palms to wipe away the tears—of which . . . there were none. *What the hell?* My eyes, my cheeks, my face . . . all bone dry. What could this mean? I tilted back, sucking in a deep breath of night. The sky above was vast and indifferent to my miniscule problems, and studying its black expanse was like staring into the bottomless, uncharted riddles of the mind.

A single thought came to me.

No, no, it couldn't be . . .

Persisted.

No tears. No real emotion. No kidding, Donnie . . .

Jiminy—I'd faked myself out.

28

RUE LOBERG

The place had only one entrance and exit, so I marched right up, my feet working fine but my head in a fog; wondering about what my daughter was doing in here, how I was going to approach her, what she might say—that is, if she decided to start speaking to me again.

The doorman was easily as wide as the door he guarded. He had a braid of dark hair, sunglasses, and an earpiece, and he stuck a hand the size of a catcher's glove out to halt my passage. It worked.

"Step back, please."

I hadn't even noticed he was there, to be honest. That's how long it's been since I went out to have fun at a night spot like this. A searchlight twisted in the dark parking lot behind a murmur of voices, bunch of young people no doubt wondering what the middle-aged lady with the lumpy curls and flat heels was doing, trying to push her way in without waiting like the rest.

"Ma'am, I said step back."

That line over there had to be half a block long, but it was midnight and I was dead on my feet. Worse than that, the pain in my abdomen was coming on again. It had started two months ago, a tightness I felt leaning over as I made the bed. For a week or so I just ignored it, but then, the tightness changed, like a closing hand scrunching into a fist.

Knew it was trouble when my primary care doc got on the phone as I sat on the high table in my gown, made a call to have me scheduled for a ton of tests that same day. Seems if medical people decide they got to rule out cancer, you go to the front of the line.

No such luck with the line here, tonight.

I held up the slip of paper my daughter Mindy's boyfriend, Ian, gave me an hour ago. My head still hurt from all the begging and borrowing I had to do to get Ian to even tell me where I could find Mindy tonight. Like almost everybody else in my life, Ian had his own special list of grievances, and he took his sweet time trotting them out, one by one. My regrets were listed in kind.

Sorry about that time I was tipsy at your parents' barbecue, Ian. And that, uh, stuff about using Mindy's ID when mine was suspended and then getting pulled over? No excuses, and I do thank you for paying her fines, you're such a kind, generous young man. I'll ask Mindy's father to send you a check right away. Oh, and, uh, the birthday dinner at that Japanese steakhouse? I know I was wrong, dead wrong, to party crash, I just missed her so, and sure hope you can understand how I . . . .

That teeny piece of paper tingling between my fingers cost me what little dignity I might have had left, but I'm not sure what's the difference there, anyway. That well is pretty empty these days.

I told the doorman the God's-honest truth: I wasn't feeling well, had a recent medical setback, and didn't think I could stand in line. He suggested that would be a waste of time at this hour anyway, that as of now maybe the front half of the line would make it in before last call. Everyone else would be asked to disperse.

Again I implored him that I had to see my Mindy. His shades were only semi-dark, so I could see his eyes travel down to the cold concrete I was standing on, then back up.

"You got another problem, ma'am. We have a dress code."

I surveyed my attire with dread, like when you're in a dream and forget you're naked. Glad there was something there, but he was right: I wasn't exactly turned out for a night on the town. Then again, those kids in line were hardly decked out. Torn jeans. Scooped blouses with bra straps showing. Spiky jewelry. But they were all young and good-looking and able to strike up cool poses there behind a red velvet rope, for one thing, making like this little delay didn't faze them at all. And here comes the ex-housewife divorcee, alone and none too hip and smelling of desperation. It was dawning on me that I cut a ridiculous figure in more than one regard—and that this refusal had nothing to do with my clothing.

"My daughter works here," I said. "See the paper her boyfriend gave me?"

The paper I handed him said two words: the Factory. The man read it and shook his head no.

"Those are the rules. I don't make 'em up, I just see that they get followed. Step back, please."

"But I have to talk to her. It's . . . urgent."

"Ma'am—"

Urgent. The word gave me pause. For a person in my condition, everything ought to feel that way; but since I got the news, the hurry-up mode I expected to kick in really hadn't. I was still dealing with the day-to-day matters of living more or less the same way. If anything, time seemed to be slowing down. What it was, I think, was that for the first time ever, I was noticing the world, paying it full attention. Not stopping to smell the roses, or any such nonsense—not hardly, because these days my life isn't exactly a rose garden, nor has it ever been. What I mean is, I'd started losing my self-consciousness and finding a new perspective, taking a view of my life far enough outside of my petty worries and fears to really see things and people for what they truly were. I guess mortality has a way of waking you up to cold realities.

But more and more, my body was sucking me the other way, away from clarity. My insides hurt, my abdomen felt bloated, the treatment was sapping my energy, and the pain just grew and grew.

"I j-just need . . . a minute please."

My head got fuzzed-up and woozy and I shut my eyes to block the sensation, which instead made the ground tilt sideways, so I opened them again quickly. The man was guarding a door painted black, and as we stood there, a thick hum of voices floated through space and slid in through my ears, settling in me like a colony of bees building a new hive. And then came the music, thumping and pounding away so hard, I could feel it in the soles of my aching feet, a vibration, bum-ba-bum, coming up through my knees and thighs, punching at my half-eaten organs until I was bent over, staring at my crooked shadow. Nausea gripped me and I tasted bile behind my teeth, had to suck in a breath and hold it to fight off the urge to throw up. That long line of young people was barely of drinking age, I bet, and the thought of the watered-down liquor they'd soon be chugging down made me sicker. Talking and laughing, some of them staring right through me with those who-the-hell-are-you look kids practice all through their teen years just for moments like this. I wanted to die, would have welcomed the relief from this pain, but I had to see Mindy. Somehow, I found my balance again and straightened back up.

The doorman had put up two fingers like making a peace sign and another stout gentleman in dark slacks and a sport coat pulled aside the rope. Two girls in slinky tops and short skirts at the front of the line strode right on by me, slowing a bit as they passed and giggling, like I was a joke they just heard and, ha-ha, they just got it.

Guess I should feel ashamed, I thought, if I had a reason to even care.

I thought back on the night they gave me the news. The oncology team, a collection of specialists, coming together like they were planning my funeral. Very professional. Took their time showing me the slides, explaining the pathology reports on the multiple biopsies, the x-rays, MRI results, white blood cell counts, and all that stuff that led to the same conclusion. "It began here, Mrs. Loberg, in the ovaries. They have to come out, later tonight. If cells break off and invade other organs in the abdomen, the chest, possibly the liver . . . it would not be good."

They took out the ovaries, thought they got it but couldn't be sure. It's not like they could just keep removing my insides to check. All I could do was pray it wouldn't spread. Then . . . well, a trouble zone popped up in the lower abdomen. When they made a pitch for chemo,

I had to laugh. Why be sick as a dog with whatever time was left? I asked. Makes no sense. They told me this was my decision, of course, but I might want to talk it over with my family. A 40 percent chance of full recovery wasn't so bleak; with luck, I'd make it all the way back.

Luck—me? When I laughed at the notion of me being lucky, they stared at me as if I was crazy.

Seemed it was easier for me to deal with the question of my mortality then, several weeks ago. I was still worried about the trial and having to testify, couldn't really wrap my brain around dying. It didn't seem real. The thickness I felt down below, the lack of appetite, it was different and a little uncomfortable, but not even painful. Like feeling bloated after eating too much. So what? The doctors asked me again, and I said no, again, to more chemo. Didn't want to go through all that just to tack on a few more months. Especially if there wasn't any hope.

But there is hope, they kept telling me. You've made strides already. Still, I would not believe it. I'm just not lucky that way.

But now, tonight, at the worst time possible, this thing I'd pushed out of my mind had decided to push back, and hard. How I got back over to the doorman I can't even say, but my jaw felt like melting wax as I worked him a second time.

You see, here's the thing. I didn't know this was a nightclub. I was told my daughter worked at the factory down on Pine Avenue. So, what do you know? I thought she had the night shift in an *actual* factory. Isn't that funny?

He failed to see the humor.

"Otherwise I'd have buzzed on home to change into something more, um, appropriate than these old rags."

My brightest smile didn't crack his shield.

"Please, ma'am. The fire marshal won't allow persons to congregate where you're standing. It's the law. You have to step back."

A foghorn moaned somewhere in the LA Harbor. The beehive in my head buzzed louder. The man was paid to be cold and hard and turn folks away when he had to, and I hadn't given him a reason to make an exception. I started to go into my purse, to dig for a picture of Mindy;

maybe if he knew her, or thought she was cute and wanted to know her, he'd make an exception. But as my hand went down, the whole right side of my body followed, like diving down a rabbit hole. It was dark in there, but quiet and still, so maybe it wouldn't be so bad to duck in for a rest, I thought. My eyes slammed shut, and a peaceful calm came over me, and when I opened them again, I was staring up at the doorman and five or six other faces framed by a night sky. One of those faces was Mindy's.

The doorman reached into his pocket and handed me a tissue, which I used to wipe my mess of a face and blow my nose. Sitting up, I concentrated on breathing slowly, normally. That line of snotty kids may have been back there, behind us, but I chose to imagine that they had relocated to a floating glacier in Antarctica.

I came around in time to talk them out of calling an ambulance. Food poisoning. Too little sleep. I'd have said anything to talk to Mindy.

The doorman's bear chest heaved as he helped me up. We went inside, down a hall and into a tiny room with a table and two plastic chairs and a bunch of electronic equipment and speakers and lights piled in the corner, covered in a film of dust, like someone spilled milk all over the pile. He handed me a plastic water bottle. I thanked him profusely before he shut the door behind him.

"You okay?" Mindy asked. "You look like death."

Her outfit was flesh-toned and revealing; almost made her look nude, in fact. The logo of a popular brand of tequila was stamped across her very low-cut top. Maybe I was staring at it the way a concerned mother would.

"I'm better now."

She looked over her shoulder at the door, then at me with a jaded, unbelieving expression. Her skin was whiter than I remembered, but her soft nose and doll's eyes were the same as when I pushed her on the swing out back, when she was a little girl full of fear and wonderment.

"I'm really pissed at you for showing up like this, Mom."

"And I am so, so very sorry for—"

"Last call's not for half an hour, and if I don't get back, they'll fire me."

I apologized again and told her to go do her thing. When she left, I sat around for a minute or two before deciding to check out the rest of the place. Might as well, now that I was finally inside the castle walls.

Turns out Ian's directions were right on the button. The place was one big open space hemmed in by four walls—probably used to be a factory. On one side was a bar packed to the gills with young people. In the middle, more bodies bounced to the beat, which was pretty deafening—rap, I think. Kids dancing like their souls were on fire. The last couple weeks, as my predicament sank in, I'd started to wonder whether my drinking during low times had taken a toll on my body, made me weaker and more open to illness, a breakdown. I'd never know, and though the oncology team steadfastly maintained that this is a random affliction, it bothered me more and more now. History always seems to catch up to me and run me over. My certainty of one sad truth was growing.

I'd done this to myself. I deserved to die.

In two corners were dancing girls on lighted pedestals, grinding to the beat. In the other corner a DJ wearing a head-set commanded a panel full of electronic equipment. Just below the DJ was a pack of men, laughing and jostling and holding folded bills over their heads. I pushed through the tangle of bodies on the dance floor and came in closer to the pack.

Mindy was in the center, balancing a tray full of shot glasses and cups of colored Jell-O as she doled out drinks and made change. "Hey, Worm Girl!" a happy guy with a crew cut shouted. "Take a picture with me! I'm going into the Army in six hours!"

It dawned on me that her outfit was supposed to make her resemble the worm in the bottle.

"Worm Girl, I love you!"

She was raking in the cash hand over fist, a plastic smile glued on her face. I stepped back, content to order a six-dollar club soda and wait near the bar. A joint like this would thin out before closing, same way they always do. This crowd was here to see and be seen. Once the feeling of a happening passed, they'd lack the loyalty to stick around.

Ten minutes later, the place was a ghost town.

"You shouldn't be here," Mindy said, setting her empty tray on the bar. "At the very least, I thought you'd respect my wishes. Why am I not surprised you didn't?"

"Honey, I'm sorry. I have to talk to you."

"I wouldn't care if it was twenty years. Fifty. Nothing's changed."

Her arms were crossed and her head was turned, as if the DJ was doing something worth watching. But he was wrapping cables over one arm and closing up shop, his head buried in his work. She huffed with frustration when I didn't budge, and her brown bangs ruffled when she exhaled. On instinct, I reached out to brush them.

"My sweet little—"

Her hand came up and flicked mine away. "Don't."

"Mindy, I am so, so sorry. For everything. Much as I want to respect your wishes—"

"I don't want to hear it."

She stepped back and pointed past my shoulder, across the emptying dance floor and down that same dark, fun-house passage I'd come in through an hour ago.

"I am truly sorry, but I gotta do this, honey."

"Yes, you can do it. It's easy. Just put one foot in front of the other and start walking. Okay, do it."

She may have been full of righteous anger, but I was still her mother.

"No. And if you deny me the five minutes I need with you, I'll just show up at Ian's place, and we'll do this little dance all over again." Her body coiled like a cornered snake ready to strike. I knew she wanted to get rid of me whatever way she could. But she was still just a kid, Worm Girl outfit or not. My kid. And I was determined.

"Bye."

"Please listen, then I'll be gone. Completely gone, like you want."

She looked a bit tired and defeated. What girl wouldn't, with a job like hers?

Even in the weak light, she read my disappointment.

"What now? You don't like the club?"

"No, no, it's great. I just think . . . it looks like hard work. Maybe you can do better than this."

"No lectures, Mom, or I swear, I'll . . . okay, that's it. You win! Just say whatever it is you have to say, and then leave."

The bones in my body ached like dry, brittle twigs about to snap. I imagined pushing all the pain into my pinkie finger, which I then bit on, hard. Snapped my eyes open and shut to clear the fuzz in my head.

"What is *wrong* with you, Mother?"

"Huh? Oh. Not feeling well is all."

"Your face is white. Go home and get in bed."

I worked on some slow and normal breathing. Then I told her why I'd come, told her about the trial against Dr. Don, what he'd said, how he'd put it all on me, as if I seduced him. Mindy's face got tighter and crankier as I went on.

"That's your business," she said. "Not mine."

"He's gonna get away with it if you let him, Mindy. You're the only one in the whole world who was there, can set the judge straight on what really happened."

She seemed to be thinking it over, but for me, the option of waiting on her decision was fading fast. The floor kept moving and swaying, an earthquake rumbling through my body. I reached for the brass edge on the bar but missed. The barstool behind me clattered. Mindy grabbed my arm and held me up long enough to slide me onto the stool proper.

"You're clammy," she said.

Again the floor rushed up to greet me, but my daughter got an arm around my waist before I went down.

"Jesus, Mom, your scaring me!"

"Please, honey, don't take the Lord's name in vain."

"Is that blood in your mouth?"

No, no, lemme . . . I'll just sit down again, rest—"

"Mom! What is *wrong* with you?"

"I can't say. You'll think I'm taking advantage."

Gently, she held my head in her arms and stroked my head. "Come on, Mom, how bad could it be?"

Her words, they had the effect of lifting my spirit like the Grace of God. My heart, it nearly burst with loving joy, and it seemed those 40 percent odds should not be ignored, but rather deserved to be embraced.

29

BRADLEE AAMES

Floating, drifting, face-down, I see nothing. Or is this even sight?

Thought—yes, because I've composed the question of whether I can see. One question: is this a beginning?

Now a second question: is this the edge of consciousness?

Possibly; and yet, it seems too well-defined, like a higher state of nothingness . . . .

Sensation—not merely the suggestion, but the sensation of floating remains. Instinct, antiquity, a relic of unseeing life . . . that first echo of feeling from the womb itself, trailed by an outline of . . . nothing, a wisp, then a thread, then a string of thoughts, unspooling slowly.

Next question: Dreaming? I could be, locked in my imagination, or—worse—deluded. God knows, my mind loves to play tricks on me.

Or not.

Again, a thought constructed and considered. A . . . yearning, the ache for control—yes, that's what I need, what I want: control.

Of my thoughts.

Imagine? Why not? It's a step toward regaining control and besides, wherever I am, I don't seem to be in any hurry to leave. Experiment with it; set parameters; make it a mental exercise.

Exercise; stimulate; do something!

A prerogative emerging from the deadened space, breaking off from a stifling inertia, even if the act is . . . as benign as floating . . .

Imagine: myself in the outline of a leaf, or a surfboard—yes, better yet, a vintage longboard, a foam and fiberglass airbrushed work of art at rest, but ready to be put to use on a down-the-line mission, a point-break missile poised to glide and carve and swoop and slash, and all I need is a wave.

A wave!

But then, there is no wave without an ocean, and a homing instinct for waves that, among the twisted, heaping piles of bad wiring in my head, still works perfectly well, and that instinct tells me one thing: Wherever this is, I'm nowhere near the sea.

Pragmatism—a good sign: one step closer to control.

So, no waves, no surf, no ocean. I want to curse but have forgotten how, or even the meaning of the word. Fullness, bursting without relief. Oh, to . . . curse.

Back to the beginning. Backward, boring into a . . . black hole. Shall we wait? Why, yes, we shall. Waiting I-don't-know-how-long, no sense that time even exists, except for the distant blunted frustration of the wait.

A thought: Curse. Do it—no one will hear you anyway. Do it.

Curse!

Not a word presents, not a single word.

Goddammit, curse already, you, you . . . assbite!

Haven't said assbite since the third grade.

Failure, defeat.

But wait . . . a detail emerges from a past—which means I *have* a past, therefore . . . my existence precedes my essence.

But that I took from Sartre, and . . . he believes I have no creator. Which cuts against my belief, leading to . . .

—not one, but two details: pigtails, and shiny black leather shoes, in the third grade. Before a memory can build, the rest fades, and Sartre . . . rhymes with fart. Not why he was called on, no . . .

I curse the concave void of nothing at all, curse the erasures on the clean blackboard before me. Time is the backdrop of emptiness, and therefore, cannot be measured, and hence, cannot be recognized or quantified or calculated . . . and therefore, ceases to exist.

Magnanimously uncomplicated silence—the universe condescending to my insignificance. I . . . am left alone without excuse—no, Sartre doesn't just rhyme with fart. The cosmos yawns at my presence, but even if I know this, I feel my insignificance. I exist, with or without time.

But Sartre says I have no creator, and thereby no nature, which means I bear full responsibility for my actions . . . . Full responsibility, moral ownership—a satisfying notion deeply tied to a struggle I can't recall, a scrum I've engaged in, a fight I can still taste.

But godlessness? Not me.

What I lack is an . . . exit strategy.

Exit strategy?

Terminology; no, trendy jargon, more like. Where does this crap come from?

My sole exit strategy is imagination. Work it . . .

No waves, no ocean. Instead, the longboard's rails lie still, inert, as if the water all around is black and perfectly stock still, frozen, and I have no momentum, nothing to move me, zero traction. Imagine! . . .

But . . . is this water, into which I cannot even dip in a finger? Or is it empty, unlit space in some receded, tucked-away corner of my brain now holding me prisoner? Trapped. Calcified, awaiting more thoughts to give details and distinguish . . . nothing at all.

Just imagine, dammit! Lie face-down—at least that's how it feels, how the memory chooses to categorize this.

Not that it's real. Saddened, without tears or a means of self-expression, I wait, wait for what could be hours, days, weeks. *Hey, assbite, it could be years.*

Did I just curse? I did. Ooh—that's so much better . . . .

I could be dead; this could be God's rejection of a soul unworthy. (Yes, Sartre, I said God.) A forever-loop of endless nothing, of knowing nothing. And this teasing Q and A? No game show, no grand prize, no winning to be had from any of this. Just shards and junk and garbage, a dive into the Dumpster out back of the thought factory. No break-throughs here . . . .

Just an eternity spent chasing trash blown down the alley behind a shut-down brain.

Third-grade highlights.

Fearing the unknown. Guilty about my behavior.

No tears in hell.

Say what?

Still a Catholic, wrapping this guilt up tight. Yeah, so I cursed, said a bad word, however incoherently. The guilt dies out over an eon . . . or passes in a minute.

I pray, now, remembering the concept. Pray for an exit strategy. An escape. Then light. Then insight. Then acceptance. And finally—*what the assbite hell took you so long?*—Ah, cursing again, gotta stop that.

Or keep doing it, if it kick-starts a process . . .

I pray for forgiveness.

Seconds, minutes, generations pass. No way to know anything; uncertainty is the only certainty. I could be dead, but that could be wrong. Dead wrong. Maybe hell is the place where bad puns go to die.

Again, I am floating, but there seems to be no bottom beneath me. Which means I can go even lower than this. Better brace for the worst—why they call it hell . . .

Then it happens: a ping, a flick of movement as miniscule as a fly rubbing its legs, or dust floating onto the spine of an old law book in the back row of that outdated county library downtown, a silent updraft tickling an eyelash. Barely anything at all, but I feel it, a brush against not my person but my psyche.

A wave?

With me, even in death, or nonexistence, or heaven or hell, it's always about a wave.

Not the kind you can ride, but more like . . . the world's smallest wave, a vibration lapping against my being, then another, just before another age of maddening stillness settles in again. But then, a third, a ping followed by the shape of a sound.

Muffled.

A word.

Keblang.

Floating, taking seventeen years to unscramble the letters, I arrive at:

Blanket.

Rishp tishion.

Floating, wishing I could put this inert wave-riding plank to its intended use, picturing the puzzle:

Prescription.

If I'm dead already, maybe I'm seeing God, and He's a linguist . . . .

Durrolesttvledred.

Challenging, though a vague familiarity suggests it will not be impossible to unravel. Not worth the effort, or food for my withered, overused, underfed brain? My imagination is cold and overrun with doubt. I resolve to wait here in the dark till the end of time, when the answer to that question will be long since moot. But . . . the sounds do have contours, an outline, like a row of soldiers marching. Or a rhythmic song. A chant.

I lie flat, or I float . . . or not. Two years, or the blink of a blind eye staring at that empty blackboard. *Nothing to see here, folks, move along.*

Humor—black humor, my favorite kind.

Progress. But what kind? I've got a board, but there's no ocean, no wave to ride.

Defiance. Feels good, even in these dire straits. *Assbiting assbite, man, assbitish assbite.*

Assbitish assbite?

Hey, at least I'm cursing again—got all the time in the world to sharpen those very useful skills.

Therrode lustrovll.

As usual, my assbite brain won't leave me well enough alone. Okay, do something, please, be productive, assbite brain . . .

Lemme see: it's a rhythm, da-duh da-duh; a chant. No, the hard consonants don't roll out with enough pop. Rap music? Can't be—not without the underlying, cage-rattling beat. The fit is tighter, more precise, as if planned with great precision.

Five minutes, or five hours, or five days later, please go ahead and place your bets, ladies and gentlemen, 'cause I don't know. Pick the time—any time—but know that *in time* an answer comes.

Poetry.

In another instant, or God, felt like a month, the words find their contours.

The road less traveled.

My biggest win thus far—not an ocean, not a wave, but . . . a poem from high school honors English? A ten-page paper, an A-plus effort. My theory? A gentle death wish, expressed so politely, you wouldn't know it was there unless you thought . . . subversively. In high school, nobody's thinking much about death, except maybe a tall skinny friendless girl no one talks to because she looks scary, especially when she's content to chat with thin air. Nobody but the teacher, who read the paper to class, saw that old poem as a meditation on dying. So why do these sidewinding thoughts make this detour, to this creaky old poem, now?

Chew on it; (all the time in the world anyway); deduce.

I am unconscious—which is likely, since I can't see a damn thing.

But . . . someone is . . . talking . . . about blankets.

Prescriptions.

And . . . reading poetry . . .

To me.

And I am hearing it.

Three years, the time it took to go to law school, just to figure out this last part.

Law school—I went to law school? Am I a lawyer? A flunk-out, maybe, but . . . somehow, the law seems familiar but shapeless. Vague.

Floating free—and assbite tired of it, to be frank. But no, I'm no longer a surfboard kissing a sea of empty space. Up meets down in a more logical fashion as slowly . . . a room, the kitchen in my parents' house, appears. I cannot feel a thing, but my body, or my thoughts alone, are traveling through a warm, dull mist silently, like . . . a bare-foot child tiptoeing through the shapes of a dining room lost in shadows to the flood of yellow light and shining white tiles and a fridge that will hold something to drink for a girl awakened by a dry throat and a bedroom coat rack that turns into a strung-up zombie as soon as the lights go out.

Full-blown scene, back home: and I am here. In the kitchen, my father is working at the breakfast table surrounded by those ugly wooden chairs with the beveled spokes I used to grip like motorcycle handlebars whenever Mom stepped up with an after-school snack, a reheated wedge of some smoldering creation from last night's dinner. Jesus, Mom, not that ghastly tuna casserole again, I'd want to protest, though I always opted, in the end, for the silent hunger strike. Skinny girl, she'd say with accusing eyes, you should eat some real food once in a while—and listen, you'd better watch out for those boys, they'll be after you, never leave you alone if you don't fatten up.

But Mom is not here now, in the kitchen—nor do any slabs of congealed pasta, or tuna surprise, await my reprove. I sense only a hole, an absence of energy, where she should be.

God rest your soul, Mom, I do miss you . . . .

My dad the lawyer is here, not looking up as he bears down on a document. Working on a case late at night, just as always.

Here is the law in my life, in the form of my father, the lawyer. A great one, or so I believe for no reason I can articulate here. But it is so, I'd stake my life on this man's reputation for . . . I don't know, but I can tell I'd die for the principles he embodies in his work . . . whatever they may be . . . .

Daddy, I say expectantly, like a child with a question, my voice soundless and tranquil as a bamboo shoot.

His eyes dare not blink, so locked down tight they are beneath a brow dense with concentration, but oh, the head, that large head is calm and regal, like a lion surveying the bustling plain. More than a lawyer, a crusader, this man, and a great one at that. His starched white shirt, severed by a slash of red tie, it holds a pair of hands that could snap that bamboo shoot of a sound—which has just, heaven forbid, interrupted a delicate, intricate thought-process.

The moment irretrievably punctured, the child backpedals, but a force field of momentum walls up from behind, pushing her closer, heel-dragging but closer yet, to the center of the room and certain doom.

Yet memory—if that's what this is—fails me, because behind the lawyer's intellectual drive and dogged intensity is . . . wait . . . a kind-hearted patient soul who will rise up from his tornado-blown pile of papers to fetch a glass of ice water and soothe the wandering girl with deft words of understanding and a soft, lion's kiss atop the head.

Daddy.

The road less traveled, he says, though his gray eyes cannot find mine. Hah—you and I are quite a pair!

That was you, reading the poem, I say.

His voice has the soothing sound of tires on fine gravel.

We share two paths, you and I. One lit by God, the other by demons.

The devil?

He shakes his head, pointing at his temple. *Our demons. Trick is—*

You need only know which path you're on, I blurt.

He smiles, regarding the work spread out before him again. Doesn't give me the answer I'm hoping for.

My little girl, he says.

His little girl feels a powerful urge to come to his side, to touch him, kiss his cheek, as if this is a good-bye she didn't see coming until it was here, now. Instead, the force field burns off like midmorning beach fog, pushing her away and back out the kitchen and down another unlit corridor of . . . aching nothingness.

The . . . *aloneness*—I couldn't feel that before, but it hits home now. Like a punch in the eye. And it hurts. A lot.

*   *   *

God kisses my forehead; my vision returns . . .

Nighttime and the room is dark. Light slides across a slick floor from a hallway outside the cracked door. I'm not face-down, but facing up in a large bed. A plastic alien with a thin metal body gazes down, as if studying me. I stare back, blinking into kind, benign eyes for I don't know how long, but eventually the alien reveals himself to be a suspended IV drip. I am in a hospital bed, unable to move, as yet, yearning for some kind of understanding but recalling nothing of how I got here.

A pair of hard-edged, glowing red eyes glare at me. With some effort I tilt my head to the left, staring back at those eyes until they reveal themselves to be numbers in a digital clock.

5–0–5

5:05 a.m.

I lie there, fixing on objects around the room, all of which transform themselves, upon closer study, metamorphosing like flowers I have willed into blooming. An aircraft carrier turns into a plastic tray; a foamy white waterfall becomes curtains. Enjoying the sensation of power this exercise brings me, I engage in shape-changing until the dawn cracks in along the windowsills.

Out in the hall, an alarm sounds, bringing a hail of pounding feet. The voices are calm and technical, but urgent.

Crash cart.

Prep.

Stat.

Clear.

More voices, more urgency. An alarm drones in the background.

Clear.

No voices now, only a murmur, the creak of wheels on waxed floors, a silence—respect for the dead.

Down on the end of Lonely Street, the Heartbreak Hotel, I say to myself.

I am so outta here.

Six hours, five arguments, two grand rounds, one private consultation, four conflicting opinions, a discharge doctor with taped glasses and an Indian accent, and about twenty consent forms later, I'm walking gingerly to the elevator doors, turning down the offer of a wheelchair ride just to show them I'm not crazy, I can do this. Or . . . just to show myself. A short black nurse with a halo of cornrows jogs toward the elevator and shoves her hand in before the doors can snap shut.

"Whoa! You forgot this," she says, handing me a book. "Found it on the nightstand."

The Collected Poems of Robert Frost.

I open it and read the name inside the cover.

"Thanks," I say. "Thank you. For everything, I mean."

"God bless."

God bless.

Yes—true, this is so, I tell myself on the ride down to the lobby.

*   *   *

Mendibles was at counsel table when I arrived in court. So shocked to see me, he dropped half the contents of his trial notebook on the floor as if to prove it.

"Bradlee? Oh my God, you . . . how—"

"Nice to see you too, boss."

"H-how'd you even get discharged?"

"I'm fine," I said, which qualified as half a lie, and half a leap of faith.

"But the doc, your doctor—"

"Nice guy. That is, for someone who has to split skulls open like coconuts when the situation presents, I thought he was a remarkably centered dude."

Mendibles's face constricted. "He . . . told you that?"

"Uses a high-speed saw, titanium. Could cut through a diamond."

"That's . . . terrible."

"Shop talk," I said. "He was trying to be nice. Asked me what I do, I told him, so I asked him the same thing."

"But . . . I don't get it. He said you'd, uh, you know."

"Suffered a head trauma? I did. So? I'm better."

"He, uh, said it might take a while before you, uh, recovered, if at all."

"Don't worry, I'm not a ghost."

"It's just . . . he thought it would take, um, longer."

I shrugged as if, hey, baby, I was feeling no pain, good to go! In truth, I had two wounds oozing blood under the dressings and my head felt as thick and loaded with untamed momentum as a wrecking ball. All I could do was keep lying to my supervisor, acting as if this was all part of the plan.

Mendibles had not yet moved from his first-chair position, and he wanted more details.

"Fine," I said. "Woke up early Saturday morning, more or less fully cognizant. And my progress was great after that. Miraculous, even."

"Hmm. I see."

Strange: when you're gone from the world you know for a while, even a few days like I was, your perspective shifts, and you see things more clearly upon your return. To me, Mendibles looked like a dog sniffing around, trying to catch a snootful of my female scent.

"Well, I'm, uh . . . relieved you're better, Bradlee. This is so . . . yeah, great, really."

Less than entirely won over, his gaze turned to a stare, which in turn put me on edge. Making my head hurt more.

"What is it?" I asked when I saw him staring.

"Um, your uh—"

"Jesus, Mendibles, just say it."

He pointed down. "Your hand. It's shaking."

Shit. I reached down and corralled the twitchy appendage, which seemed about to scramble right off the table.

"It's frigid in here," I said casually. "Building maintenance needs to dial down the AC."

After a moment of nothing to say between us, I made my way into a chair and sat down, my supervisor silently mirroring my movements. It was still upon me to explain my way back into the Fallon case.

"I'll be honest with you, Mendibles. The neuro guy didn't want to let me go, but I signed myself out AMA—"

"Against medical advice? Oh, great, so you just—"

"—and they knew they couldn't stop me."

"That's just great."

His face was too grave for my liking. At that moment I realized that the trial notebook he'd spilled all over the place when he'd turned to see me walk in the courtroom was my own.

"I'm here to finish this case, if you're wondering."

"You must be joking," he said bitterly.

I didn't think he had even that soft-spoken level of fight in him.

"Listen—"

"No, Bradlee, you listen. You can sit here with me, but that's it. You're not well."

"Bullshit, Mendibles. This is my case."

"Excuse me?"

Just like that I was breathless, struggling to hold back a raft of rage.

"I had a lot of time to think this weekend, sitting in a bed as my mind came back online, bit by bit, and . . . you want to know what I've concluded about this case?"

He folded his arms the way a husband does just before his wife lets him have it. "Go ahead, say it. I can't stop you."

"You never wanted me to try this thing from the get-go."

"That's—lemme use your word: bullshit. Not true. *I'm* the one who assigned *you*."

"You knew I'd be the best reason to settle this thing from our perspective because I'm so obviously a mess."

"Oh, please."

"You pushed me to do the sweetheart deal, but then, when that fell apart, you found a different way to push me."

"I pushed *you*?"

His air of easygoing denial was pissing me off, and for reasons I didn't understand, my hand began to shake again.

"Right off a goddamn cliff would've suited you fine."

"Bradlee—"

"You sat back and did nothing while that cretin's lawyers tried to dismantle my case."

"That's absurd."

"Intimidated Deshaun Fellows."

"Oh? That's why he testified and stuck around throughout the case?"

"Sent my expert packing."

"And you got another one."

"Yeah, by hook or by crook, and she suffered an anxiety attack on the stand."

"No matter. She testified well."

I'd reached the outer edge of my patience with my supervisor and his lack of accountability.

"You may be my superior, but you're a coward and a primo jerk."

"Bradlee, let's be calm."

"With a wife you don't deserve."

"Hey, that was below the belt."

"Don't push it, Mendibles. The only thing below the belt is that bulge you get when you stare at me too long. I'm sick of looking up to see you leering back at me, like a stalker."

His face flushed as he sputtered for words. "I can't believe you just accused me of—"

"Don't even try to deny it. I have half a mind to make a sexual harassment complaint, and if I did? I'd have, oh, seven or eight of our secretaries lined up to back me."

He was silent, staring at the bench, right where the judge would soon be seated.

"You're wrong," he said with some finality.

I didn't care. "No, I'm right."

"You can't prove—"

"Mendibles, I'm a lawyer. A litigator. Do not talk to me about proof."

"You're . . . angry."

"I know I can't prove what you did to harpoon this case. But I don't care. All I want is to finish it. The right way."

He was back to staring, his shoulders slumped.

"You know what, Mendibles?"

"What."

"Your posture's shitty."

He chuckled silently. "Among other things." His palms went up as if to reason with me.

"You're not well, Bradlee. You can't handle this case effectively in your condition."

"Yes, I can," I said. "And you're going to let me. As a private gesture of gratitude."

"For not—"

"Don't even say it," I said quickly. "Give me the case back, and that shit is in the past."

"Fine."

"But you leave me alone from here on. I mean it."

He'd finished stuffing the papers back into my trial notebook and pushed it over to me.

"All yours. Have fun."

I was suddenly lightheaded. "Thanks."

Another gallows laugh from Mendibles. "Well, here comes a final reality check, so get ready. We're losing."

Then, in a low, sober voice, he filled me in on what I'd missed. When he was done, I was without any comebacks. For the first time since I'd left that hospital, I felt as if I was without a distinctive purpose, a first order of business. The thought scared me—unreasonably. More than the sight of buildings chasing me down the block, or that gangbanging prick with the gun slinking out of the gutter to hunt me.

"Okay," I mumbled as Mendibles went on. "Okay, got it, no problem . . ."

I was still shaky as hell; what I needed was a big, broad goal, a plain objective. Step one, baby, please! An objective was my gateway to sanity. Two paths, in my mind, two paths to be delineated with great care along the way. The time was now; my moment had arrived. Find an objective and grab hold, girl!

Then the door to the courtroom swung open, and for the second time in these last few short, eventful days, the hand of God touched me on the forehead, calming my frenetic, defective mind. I felt like kneeling and reciting a prayer of thanks, but instead I stood up and smiled as if this was nothing to me, nothing at all. Ha ha!—just another day in the life, in court, at trial . . .

"Morning, Ms. Aames," Deshaun Fellows said.

Swaying like strands of sea grass in the sand, I caught my balance and gasped.

"You were there, by my bedside."

"Yes, ma'am. So glad to see you up and about."

He touched me on the shoulder and I reached up and squeezed his large hand. I felt like crying, crying until I might melt into a puddle.

Then Rue Loberg came in the door behind Deshaun Fellows.

"Brought you some friends this morning," Deshaun Fellows said.

Rue Loberg gasped herself at the sight of me and started to cry.

"Miss Aames! You're here! Oh, thank God!"

I traded glances with Mendibles. "Well, sure," I said. "I wouldn't miss this for anything."

A girl, a young woman of maybe twenty, with the same rounded features and oversize doll-eyes as Rue Loberg, trailed in behind her.

"This is my daughter," Rue said proudly.

"Of course," I said. "Hello."

Mindy Loberg, my lone rebuttal witness—and about the finest first objective any lawyer with my kind of injuries could ever dream up—came closer until she stood beside her mother.

"So, where's the party?" she asked.

I shot a false glare at Rue, who giggled. "What did your mom tell you?" I said.

"Whatever I could think of," Rue said.

Mindy and her mother regarded each other silently. They'd been through some kind of private process but didn't seem diminished by it. Not to my view, at least.

"Doesn't matter," Mindy said. "It worked, 'cause I'm here."

My head rang with hurt and soreness, but I nodded as if to show her my thanks. "So you are, indeed."

30

BRADLEE AAMES

Rebuttal evidence is a gift to the prosecution, coming along late but just in time, like giving mouth-to-mouth to a case flat on its back. I was so damn grateful for my rebuttal that my hand kept clenching into a fist under counsel table—which, in turn made my head hurt. Jesus, even thinking was making my skull throb. The fist-pumping wasn't helping, but on the emotional side of the equation, it felt sublime.

The equally delicious flip-side on rebuttal? It's the bane of the defense attorney's existence, a calling of bullshit on the Spell of the Lie—that carefully crafted counter-narrative concocted solely to undermine a case's core truths, to explain away any unpleasant facts, or at the very least to distort the known into something questionable and unreliable.

I looked at the row of black wing-tips poking out from the other table and thought: *Well, too bad, guys, you're about to endure a little suffering.* The Dr. Don Trio had shown me no courtesies and dealt nothing but dirt behind my back. They had it coming.

By my act of walking in here, I'd already given them a beating. Deshaun is a thoughtful, detail-oriented man who thinks things through from every angle, and the shooting had troubled him on a number of levels. The young man who shot me was being held for murder so he was not in a talkative place, but Deshaun said the man had a history of violence dating back to his middle school years and a reputation for hitting his targets. He had personal business with Deshaun, but he may have started with me because that business took precedence.

I couldn't argue with his logic. I'd lost an expert witness for the first time in my career on the eve of trial, had the shit beaten out of me for no good reason surfing Malibu alone. Deshaun also seemed vaguely guilt-ridden. I'm sure the defense team did what they could to keep him from testifying, but he had come through, which was all that mattered. Fighting these battles in my head alone for all this time had left me feeling hard-edged and isolated. Homeless—though I was fortunate enough to have a roof over my head. I'd lost contact with the people around me and had little motivation for reaching out. Deshaun was within my reach; I was not inclined to push him away.

Fallon seems to enjoy hurting people, even indirectly. Before we went back on the record, I caught a glimpse of him on the far side of his minions; he was studying my bandages with a smirk, digging my pain.

Back to the poetic beauty of rebuttal: Right at nine, as I asked my witness to step inside, the door cracked open and all heads turned. Heidegger's twitchy face was the first to fall. I soaked in his air of surprise with such pleasure, it was almost as good as getting high.

Her mother—that is, the victim—and Craig Weaver filed into the gallery behind Mindy. I took their presence as a hopeful sign, a show of strength. But I had no idea how Deshaun had arranged all this. I'd accepted his help, no questions asked.

I gestured to Mindy Loberg to split the space between counsel tables and head right up to the witness stand, which she did without hesitation, lifting her right hand to take the oath the instant she got there. Heidegger studied her as if trying to place her in his memory, then frowned and passed a note to Fallon when he did. I imagined the note to say "WE'RE HOSED!" I savored the moment so much my head hurt worse.

My eyes were stuck again on Donald Fallon. By the way he dug in, burrowing under Heidegger's wing with a blast of whispering even I could hear—*can't be testifying . . . the terms of the agreement you wrote, Terrence . . . of* course *she's unstable, but*—it seemed a solid bet that Mindy Loberg would be as good as advertised. Right now, Rue Loberg and Dr. Don were more or less in a standoff. If anyone could tilt things back toward the real and the true and break that Spell of the Lie, it was Mindy. She was there when the shit got heavy between Fallon and his victim.

Heidegger was quick to insist that the judge bar her testimony. Prejudicial. Unfair surprise. Whatever else he could think of, he let it fly.

The defense will have a full and fair opportunity to cross-examine, the judge pointed out, rubbing his short gray beard. Shelby Drummond was a tall man already, but in my overworked mind's eye, he grew another foot as he made his latest ruling.

"Overruled."

After another round of hush-hush strategizing, Heidegger piped up with another objection, claiming that Mindy was part of a civil settlement that, in exchange for the money damages she'd received, barred her from testifying.

"You see, this has already been decided, Your Honor."

Please. Not this again.

I was ready for that bogus sidestep; it's a self-important ploy civil litigators pull all the time, an arrogant fiction that once the money changes hands in a stipulated settlement, none of the parties to the lawsuit can ever speak of the facts and circumstances of the case again—even in a criminal, administrative, or disciplinary case involving separate allegations of legal violations, breaches of different laws than those at issue in the settled civil matter. They work their grubby little deal, the filthy lucre changes hands; then later, when someone is subpoenaed in another case, they proclaim the witness out of bounds. It's a bit like telling the IRS you won't pay taxes because you had a formal agreement via a stipulated settlement with your next-door neighbor not to pay.

But the law doesn't recognize or uphold private pacts of silence, bargained for as part of a final dollar settlement. Good civil lawyers know what these gag-order deals are worth down the line.

Shits and giggles.

"Pardon me, Ms. Aames?" I heard the judge say.

Whoa—I may have muttered that last thought aloud without knowing it.

With an innocent shrug, I apologized for sneezing. Then I asked the judge if I might respond to the objection. He cast a fatherly gaze on me, as if he knew there was a battle being fought between my ears and there was little he could do to assist, except to make his rulings fairly.

"Please do."

I cited the Rules of Professional Conduct for California attorneys, in particular the rule prohibiting lawyers from entering into agreements that would serve to gag future witnesses in other proceedings.

"That rule applies here, Your Honor. Mr. Heidegger was legal counsel on that civil case. Therefore, with this objection, he's effectively admitting now to having committed unprofessional conduct when he made that deal. Is that what he proposes to do now?"

I tilted my head to the left, a fistful of needles pricking the base of my neck. My body was so bumpy and bruised it seemed there were whole new vistas of pain I was stumbling upon moment by moment, and with each different movement or gesture or response, I paid a price I hadn't expected. But oh, to look square upon the schoolboy row of grimacing, agog faces lining the left-side table, the poison-pills poised on the tips of their tongues! A sight to savor, and it made me think, pray, meditate on one singular sentiment.

Thank you, God; how lucky I am to be a public servant whose job is to protect the public from the vipers and exploiters and phonies and rip-offs and slap-dash incompetents.

The Dr. Dons.

Even sitting down, I felt a wobble.

Come down from your soapbox, a voice in my head told me. *Your sweet melon will split wide open should you become overly emotional.*

Hearing no further protest from Heidegger, the judge tuned in on the witness, thanking her again for coming.

The way I dress, I should be the last to judge another female's attire, but Mindy's choice of outfit was a bit unusual for court: black spandex pants tucked into cute calf-high leather boots with chrome buckles on the sides, a cool-mint silky blouse through which her bra straps were faintly showing, and two streaks of eyeliner in the same shade of green as the blouse. A touch of cleavage, and resting above her breasts was a gold necklace with a charm that stated her given name in fancy calligraphy. She'd taken some time to put herself together, probably thinking she needed to look more adult, somehow, but the effect was like a girl playing dress-up.

Damn. This girl would be less effective if she came off as too eager to impress. I decided to go slow-lane with her, just put her at ease and let the facts roll along naturally. We'd had all of ten minutes together down the hall before the judge took the bench. I only knew the most basic outline of her narrative. Mindy would have to fill in the rest as we proceeded.

I got her talking about how she'd seen Dr. Fallon for two years for individual therapy.

"Starting when?"

"My junior year at Loma Vista high."

"What did you see him for?"

She paused and gave me a girl-to-girl look, as if to say: you gotta ask me about *that*? I ignored the protest, my fist balling beneath the table and my head pounding above it.

"I was having some problems in my classes," Mindy said.

"Tell us, what kind of problems?"

"Well, um, I guess the first, uh, problem was getting to class. I got caught cutting. Smoking cloves. I mean, cigarettes. Me and one of my girlfriends that got caught, uh, she also had stash. It was in her purse."

"Stash?"

Mindy gave me the stare again. Then she pinched two fingers together.

"Crack. A teeny little bit. And a roach."

"Marijuana?" the judge asked.

"Uh-huh."

"You have to answer yes or no."

"Oh, sorry! Yes."

So far, I liked her demeanor, and so did the judge. But all the discomfort for my witness lay ahead. I had no other choice.

Jesus, I thought. *I'm sensing the emotions of others, buying into their experiences. The chemicals inside my head are an unpredictable, unreliable mix, but—can it be? Is it possible that when I'm not mixing in booze and pharma, I'm becoming more capable of not just doing my work, but showing up to be counted in the human race?*

Fine—long as I don't walk in front of a fucking bus while reflecting deeply on the Meaning of Life . . .

"Were you two under the influence?"

"That's what they said, but I hardly had any, and that was hours earlier, at Janelle's—I mean, at my friend's house that morning, before we were gonna walk to school. It was stupid. I never did anything like that again."

"What else did you come to see Doctor Fallon about?" I asked.

"I, uh, wouldn't go out on weekends anymore with my dad, the people from his church. You know. To 'fish for souls.' As in, bothering total strangers."

"You mean to proselytize?"

She seemed nicked by my intrusion. Then she glared at her mother, who was seated behind me in the gallery.

"I prefer to call it bothering people, 'cause that's all it is. Nobody wanted to see us parked on their porch uninvited."

"Why did you stop proselytizing?"

She looked sideways, like she was searching for a hidden camera. "Are you kidding? Sorry, I didn't mean that."

"You may answer the question," the judge reminded her.

"Well, I had my reasons. Like, always missing birthday parties, Girl Scouts. My troop kicked me out 'cause of bad attendance. I dunno, I just got sick of it, got to the point where it was like, that's it. I'm done, I can't take this shit—" Mindy's hand shot up to cover her mouth. "Oops. I'm sorry, judge! I meant stuff."

The judge was stern, playing the authoritarian with a law-and-order face to match the flowing black robe, but he gave a small nod, I think, to take the pressure off her.

"All right," he said, "we'll strike the witness's last sentence from the record, following the words 'I'm done, I can't take this,' but please, keep it clean."

Mindy played with her hands in her lap and adjusted her necklace.

"Well, I . . . anyway, I'd just had it. So I was talking to Doctor Don about all that stuff. And we had sessions, a few, where he had my parents come in so I could tell 'em what was bugging me, and we could talk about the problems as a . . ."

Her eyes got teary, and we all waited.

"Family."

"How did that conjoint therapy go, in your view, Mindy?"

"OK, I guess. They were mad about a lot of the—the, uh, bad stuff I pulled. I don't really blame 'em for that. But they listened. I tried to hear their side of it, too."

Briefly she gazed at Fallon.

"Are you puzzled about something?" I asked.

"Well, um. Yeah. One thing's always bugged me. I just . . . just, what I couldn't understand, was how Doctor Don could use things I'd told him when we were talking in private, tell my parents during the conjoint."

"You mean your secrets?"

"Yeah. I mean, yes. He told 'em about me and Ian, a few things I definitely didn't want them to know, not yet, but he came right out with it. I was pretty shocked."

"Like what other issues?"

"Well, this time me and Ian got into an argument at a ballgame. Angel game, traffic was bad getting there, on the radio the game was already in the second inning. Ian locked himself out of the car, with his cap and wallet still inside. Said it was my fault, I distracted him. He got mad, then I got mad, we started shoving each other. Got outta control."

"Ian hit you?"

She nodded. "Not with a fist or anything, but he slapped me once across the face and tried to hold my arms. I lost it and hit him back. Someone called stadium security. They ended up holding us till the fifth inning. Whole day was kind've lost at that point, 'cause we were both still mad."

"Did that make you feel you could trust Doctor Don with your secrets?"

"No, it made me feel like I couldn't say stuff to him I didn't want my parents to know, 'cause he might use it behind my back. It's one of the reasons I stopped going to him."

"But you came back."

"I did."

"When?"

"About six months or so after I moved out of my parents' house and in with Ian. His family has this place, big two-story corner house, with a guest house out back, next to the garage. That's where me and Ian lived when I first moved in. We got a one-room apartment now, it's really nice."

"So, what was going on in your life that made you want to go back to Doctor Fallon for counseling?"

"Well, when I moved in, there were all these relatives, some of 'em living there, others would stop by. Aunts and uncles, a cousin here or there. Ian's mom, she's really, um, outspoken, doesn't beat around the bush. Has her opinions, and once I started living with Ian, I heard just about all of 'em, too, whether I wanted to or not."

Mindy seemed to falter. My instinct told me she could use a little empathy.

"His mother was critical of you."

Mindy's eyes were leaking. In a minute her mascara would turn to mud.

"She doesn't like me much. Thinks Ian . . . can do better."

"She told you that."

"No, ma'am. I heard her say it when she thought I wasn't listening."

"So, you wanted to sort out these problems with Ian and his family, you living situation, when you returned to Doctor Fallon's care?"

"Yes, I did."

"Why go back to him? Couldn't you have found another therapist, someone who might keep your secrets?"

"I was hoping my dad's insurance was still in their system. But I got a lot of, I dunno, history. Stuff I've done that I regret. And honestly, I didn't much feel like plowing through all that stuff again, you know, which I would've had to do if I started over with someone else. At least Doctor Don knew most of my problems already. I thought it'd be faster, too, I guess. And since the things that were bugging me were about Ian and his family, and not mine, I figured at least I wouldn't have to worry about him spilling secrets. Unless he decided to bring Ian's mother in, but that wasn't ever gonna happen."

"Why not?"

"She doesn't take me seriously. I mean, as a person."

"So, you came in to talk about you and Ian, and living with him and his family."

Mindy straightened up, her shoulders clicking back. "Yeah, and here's the crazy part. You wanna know what Doctor Don says? He says, 'Your mother's gotta come in, Mindy, for me to be able to help you at all.' I said, 'What? What's my mother got to do with it? I mean, things weren't exactly great between Mom and me either, but she had nothing to do with Ian and me living together.' I told him that, what I just said, told him it made no sense. What was the point?"

"How did he respond?"

"He wouldn't hear it. He just kept on insisting, 'This won't work without you mother, gotta involve her.' I kept asking why, but he wouldn't budge. So I felt I had no choice but to ask her to do it."

"Did she agree?"

Mindy met her mother's eyes in the back of the gallery. "Honestly . . . you know? I forgot this part." She paused to cry a little. The judge handed her a tissue box. We waited. "Mom thought it sounded nuts, too. I could tell she didn't want to see him again, so I asked her why. She said—"

"Objection, hearsay!" Heidegger shouted.

"Sustained," the judge said.

The judge was right. I had to take a different approach, to have Mindy do more of the talking and not rely on what her mother once said.

"Mindy, did your mother agree to come back in when you asked her?" I said.

"No. Not at first."

"Did you say anything to finally persuade her?"

"Objection, calls for hearsay!"

"I asked the witness what she said. Whatever she testifies to now is not inherently unreliable, because Mr. Heidegger can cross-examine."

"Overruled," the judge said. "The witness may answer."

"I told my mom it would mean a lot to me. And it did, 'cause I knew she didn't want to go back."

"Objection, hearsay!"

"Overruled."

It seemed the judge was tiring of Heidegger's efforts to obscure the Loberg family history with Dr. Don.

"Mindy, back when your mom was seeing Doctor Don for individual therapy, or coming in for conjoint sessions with you and your brother and dad, did you ever observe how Doctor Fallon behaved around her?"

She glared at Dr. Don, who was locked in a bad impression of Bartleby the Scrivener, too busy and bent over his laptop—and too chickenshit by a mile—to even look up at the witness.

"Truth is, he was like a puppy dog. A boy with a crush. You know, feeding her all these compliments on how nice she looked, super smiley, jumping up to get the door for her, hustling around like she was a little queen or something. Made me uncomfortable."

"How about your mom? Did you ever observe how she'd react to his attentions?"

"Objection, calls for hearsay!"

The judge was calm of demeanor, but I could tell he was really chafing at Heidegger's tactics. All Heidegger was doing now was trying to break my stride, and distract the witness. His desperation fueled me with a cautious sense of encouragement.

Maybe this isn't another Bradlee Aames delusion. Maybe this case is actually coming together.

"The question calls for her observations, not Mrs. Loberg's statements. Overruled. You may answer."

"Thank you," the witness said, regarding counsel table for the defense with a tired, wish-you'd-stop-screwing-with-me face. "She always looked embarrassed. But . . . it kind of bothered me that she took it without complaining, or telling him to back off."

"That upset you."

Mindy rubbed her eyes and tried not to look into the gallery. "Yeah, I mean yes. Typical Mom. Always the victim. It made a lot of sense, now that I look back."

"What did?" I asked.

"Why she stopped seeing him back then. You should've seen the way he acted when I got her to come back in for my latest therapy. The next week, before our next session, he must've called me five or six times. 'Is she coming, is she coming?' Then, the day of our session, my mom's not there when we were supposed to start, and Doctor Don, he's like, pacing around, freaking out. 'Where is she? Do you think something happened? Can you call her?'"

"What did you do?"

"I was paying for the session out of my pocket, so I started talking." She threw a deadpan stare at Dr. Don, who continued to hide his face in his note-taking.

"What about?" I asked her.

"About *me*. You know, my issues, things, you know, that were on my mind. But what he did? He kept peeking back over his shoulder, through the blinds in that big office window. Like he was obsessed."

"What happened next?"

"Oh, I'm still talking away, even though he didn't even seem to be listening, but I'm giving it my best anyway, feelin' like an idiot, and he says 'Oh, oh, there, there she is!' Like it was Madonna or the pope out there."

"So, she came into the session while it was in progress?"

Mindy rolled her eyes as if still irked by her mom's encroachment. "Yeah. And that's when things really got weird."

"How do you mean?"

"Minute she walks in, he's fawning all over her, telling her how great she looks, her outfit, her hair, 'is that a new hairstyle, I really love it on you!' Oh, and he announces to her, 'Now that you aren't a patient any more, we can be friends.'"

"And how did your mother react to the attention?"

"She had that confused face she gets, like when she's driving and suddenly realizes she doesn't know where she's going."

"Lost."

Mindy nodded in commiseration. "I've seen the look. So has every man who ever took advantage of her, I guess."

"Did she participate in the rest of the session?"

"Truth is, I can hardly remember what we even talked about after she came in. I can say it wasn't about me, that much I do recall."

"Did you and your mother meet for further conjoint sessions with Doctor Fallon after that?"

"No. No way was I gonna go through that sh—that stuff again. I didn't care what he said about my mom having to be there, I wasn't going for it."

"Why didn't you think it would work?"

Mindy gave me that incredulous stare again. She was right where I wanted her to be, and all I needed was for her to finish this thing—which she did.

"Because it was a scam. Any woman with two eyes and a pulse could see Doctor Don had the hots for her. He didn't want to listen to my problems, he wanted to get down my mother's pants."

That last comment got Heidegger going with a hot objection, calling for speculation—which sounded funny to me, at the time. As

I watched Heidegger wind down, his neck as white and veiny as a jellyfish, I looked back to see how Rue Loberg was doing. She'd just absorbed a blast of resentment from her daughter, but I saw no signs of distress. The woman had been through plenty, losing her family and her dignity. If she wanted to feel sad and weepy and victimized, she had a right. But for now, she wasn't exercising any such prerogative.

Just then, as I was reflecting on Rue Loberg's apparent newfound poise, things got a little strange . . . for, seated in the row behind Rue and Deshaun Fellows was a beige, concrete, winged creature. One of several gargoyles that guard the Water Department tower on the corner of Third and Broadway. His face was elfin but fierce, with wolflike teeth that seemed even hungrier when he cackled at me. Which he did, just before he spoke, his voice a quiet hiss.

Bradlee Aames, you're a painted fraud, a flimsy fabrication of faulty metaphysics, a—

I turned back toward the bench and the judge, who was in the process of calming down Heidegger before telling him he was going to allow Mindy's observation to stand with the caveat that it was noted by the court that she could not know what Dr. Fallon was actually thinking.

—charlatan, a phony, a fraud, a sick-in-the-head poser—

I closed my eyes to concentrate on rescuing my soul from my troubled mind.

Stone gothic beast, with your curled tongue and fans of folded wings, you may sit there forever and a day, if you want, but you do not impress. This is a public proceeding, and the gallery is open to all comers, be they occupants of flesh-and-blood reality, or trick-of-the-mind fiction. So sit over there, sit there and watch a very good lawyer put on rebuttal evidence you wouldn't even understand, but I don't care. Compared to young men in the street armed with loaded guns and twisted personal agendas, a hand-carved relic faux monster like you is overrated and not the least bit intimidating.

He didn't care or my impertinence.

Bradlee Aames, crazy psycho-bitch hack liar-lawyer! You dare to—

My right hand remained under the table, the palm down but the index finger pointing like a large-bore rifle at the gallery.

I place you, hunched leering gargoyle, on another path, file you in the drawer marked Phantasmagoric Comic Book Figures. Make no mistake: we say our good-byes as I shut your mouth, fold your wings, place you in the file, and slide the fucker shut.

Which I did.

The judge asked if I had any more questions on direct. I told him I had just a few.

"You never saw your mother having sexual relations with Doctor Fallon."

"No," Mindy said.

"But you gave a statement in the civil lawsuit your father brought against him?"

"That's right. Pretty much what I said this morning."

"Is it true that you and your mother are no longer close as a result of what happened between her and Doctor Fallon?"

"I guess. I don't really talk to her anymore."

"Is that because you think she's responsible for what happened?"

Mindy was not happy I'd put the question to her, and for a second I thought she'd bolt from the stand, but it was done. Mindy opened her mouth, then hesitated, then began again. Nothing but a strangled noise came out. Then a gush of tears.

The judge patiently sat by, offering Mindy a tissue, then another, telling her to take her time. Two rows back of me, Rue Loberg was as much a wreck as her daughter.

"I do partly blame her," Mindy said finally.

"Why?"

"'Cause she's a woman. Maybe one with a lot of problems, God knows she had a hard life growing up, I get that. But any woman in her right mind should've been able to see what that man"—Mindy pointed a straight arm at Dr. Don—"had in mind."

I had one fairly risky question left for my rebuttal witness. She was raw, but I had to push her a step further.

"Did you ever consider that perhaps your mom is not in her right mind, which is why she'd been a patient of Doctor Fallon's in the first place?"

Mindy wept again quietly. Then she looked past me at her mother. "In my anger I might've forgotten that. I forgive you, Mom. And I . . . hope you can forgive me."

Rue was losing it back in the gallery, and the judge had no choice but to sit through another stretch of tearful acknowledgment. Maybe two more minutes passed like this.

"Cross-examination?" the judge asked Heidegger, who smiled like he hadn't in days. Mindy shifted her weight in her seat as if to hang on tighter before the ride got bumpy. I turned to check on the gargoyle, who was still in graceful repose, his batwings framing his peaceful grin. Was ready to tuck him right back into the phantasm drawer when another shock jolted me—a million or so volts right to the forehead.

Another spectator, a man, was shuffling into the back row a few chairs over from the gargoyle. My father, taking a seat, a nice gray suit and thin navy foulard tie suiting the formalized surroundings perfectly. He winked at me like: *look at the two of us—government shit-kickers, half-mad but righteously backed by the power of the law and fully arrayed to fight whatever evil may otherwise put asunder on another sunshiny feel-good morning in this, the greatest fault-ridden broken-down overdeveloped teeming gorgeously ruined city the world has ever seen . . .*

I was knocked back, flattened by a blast of pure love and sadness and longing for the past, my irrepressible energies bursting every which way.

Oh, Dad—why now?

Shut my eyes hard, I did. Still, I knew Dad was pointing at Dr. Don.

This one is bad news, like a black hole sucking up inside himself, inverting back, back through the past and decades of denial and near misses and mind tricks and diversion and subterfuge. I've glimpsed his force field, and it's black on the inside, inside and out, like a dead wound—

Thanks, but not now. Two paths, Dad.

Angel.

So sorry, but I've got a trial to tend to here.

Another phantasmagoric beast filed away—different cabinet—and I was back.

But then the courtroom tilted, and I gripped the table, certain my skull cracking open from the base of my neck on up, until a faint, icy breeze escaped just above my eyebrows. Coming here was a mistake, I thought, quite sure I'd never make it to the next break. I closed my eyes, which were sore and still swollen from my yearning to see something, anything, those protracted days and nights I lay passed out in a hospital bed.

Opened them . . . and by some miracle, the room leveled off. I turned and sneaked a peak behind me. My father—my psychological grounding wire—was there, his huge feet planted wide, knees slightly bent, long arms spread, holding the entire courtroom steady for me, grinning because we were both in on the joke that is my frayed mental circuitry. With a nod toward the nighttime wandering girl in the kitchen, he held up two fingers like a hippie making a peace sign.

Two paths.

"Thank you," I whispered.

I'll be going now.

Love you, Dad.

He'd let go of the courtroom, handing off the task of leveler to me.

As a surfer, I rely on instinct and a ten-thousand-wave history to locate balance; so closing my eyes, I sighted a perfect swell roping along a cobbled point, swiveled my board toward shore, stroked once or twice, and was up and gliding in perfect harmony with the elements.

When I opened my eyes, Mindy Loberg was alone on the witness stand, clinging to her sliver of a toehold in the universe as if the Earth's rotation might knock her clean off. Heidegger was thanking her for coming in to testify, ingratiating her like a hunter making friendly with the hunted as he adjusted his rifle scope. An overwhelming urge came over me to look behind me and take another inventory of the gallery.

Surfing my way down the point a minute ago, I'd sensed Dora's presence in the lineup. Had he, too, stopped into the court for a gander?

Don't turn around.

Hell no, why should I?

I kept my eyes on Mindy, who would no doubt need rescuing when Heidegger was done.

"How old are you?" he asked.

"Twenty-one."

"You just had a birthday three weeks ago, didn't you?"

Mindy looked at me as if she knew where this was going to go. I hadn't a clue, but Heidegger was a good enough lawyer to always have a direction in mind. I studied the blank sheet of legal pad on my desk, careful not to make eye contact with the witness. For now, she was on her own.

31

CRAIG WEAVER, MD

She was Lazarus, back from the dead, out of the crypt and straight into the courtroom.

How Bradlee Aames did what she did, navigating an unreliable mindscape without chemical assistance, overcoming head and bullet wounds in a few days' time, surely defying the expectations, recommendations, and dictates of any number of huddled, white-coated disciples of modern western medicine at her hospital, well . . . I have no explanation. Personally? She is . . . well, unpredictably extraordinary. Psychiatrically? Defiant of, and ever-resistant to, every established empirical carefully catalogued categorization. Historically? Utterly unique and—

Cut the rambling! Honesty, man, even if only with yourself—

Okay, right, this isn't a dictated note to chart.

Just admit it. . . .

I—okay, yes, back off, I'll say it. I think I'm in love.

You "think." Really going out on a limb there, aren't you, Mama's Boy—

I—am—in—love. There—happy?

Not quite. Mildly satisfied, for the time being. For a head-shrinker, that was way too much heavy lifting to accomplish so little. But hey, you do have to bill hourly for this wonderful service to mankind you provide. It's not like you're used to setting any speed records. . . .

So there you go—I've got a few of my own internal struggles. Every minute of every day, to be precise. Psychiatrists may be highly trained in the study and understanding of human consciousness, but mastery of one's own interior life is not a built-in fringe benefit.

Back to the state prosecutor on my mind. She should have been lying down, resting in bed, under medical observation. Not in court, duking it out with the most destructive psychiatric practitioner I'd ever seen.

Was this just me being protective of a woman who, but for her arm's-length attitude and my lack of professional resolve—but for that kiss we shared on PCH—should probably be my patient? Hard to say. Yet I could scarcely believe she was here this morning, jawing with the slick-suited row of Dr. Don legal advocates across from her, the judge's eyes flitting from side to side as if he were officiating a noisy tennis match marred by one disputed call after another. The argument flew back and forth; I spectated in awe. She was more banged-up than she appeared; the staples the doctors had used to close the gash in the back of Bradlee's head were invisible under the thick sheath of hair. She'd devised a way to brush it more from front to back to provide more coverage. An inch of white bandage could not be hidden, though, and the sight of it brought me down. This should not be happening. If only I could step forward and address the judge myself, make him call this thing off.

Sure, cowboy. Do it and she'll never speak to you again.

I know, I know, not in this lifetime . . .

Her voice cut like a razor; her logic marched from point to point inevitably, as if the conclusion was ours to claim. The pitifully inert frame I'd seen crimped into a hospital bed a few days ago now displayed perfect posture, the shoulders squared for battle. Her demeanor: Don't-mess-with-my-success—and I'm putting it nicely. Reclining briefly behind a table papered over with files and documents and legal pads as the other side took their turn with the judge, Bradlee executed a teeny, tiny hair flip, her back arched in a brief flash of curvy-girl fluidity.

I was dumbfounded by her allure.

Is it possible to be turned on by the way a woman sends a pen slip-sliding between her fingers before jotting a note?

Yes. So there you have it: she's not your patient.

Thank God for that.

Back and forth the arguments flew, careening off the walls, the court reporter taking it all down with no visible emotion—just another contentious day in paradise. Back and forth I looked on in wonder, an MD—and a red-blooded man with a thundering pulse—comprehending the basics but nothing more.

The defense attorney with the big head and liver spots was aggressive as always, but he seemed . . . worried somehow, and I could tell it was galling him.

Bradlee gave it right back to the man. The last time I'd seen her she'd looked like a mannequin, propped up like a peaceful dark princess felled by a poisoned apple. I'd wanted to lean in and kiss her lightly, soothingly on the lips—which, beyond the creep factor that goes with kissing an unconscious patient—

Yo, Craig, we're creeping ourselves out, here.

—would have also set a god-awful precedent as my first intimate gesture toward her. I chided myself to even think it.

Nice, Weaver, always the smooth operator with the ladies. Good thing you lacked the spine to do something that stupidly impulsive.

Yeah, good thing. I'd been miserable last weekend, seeing her that way—so helpless and vulnerable and incapable of receiving any of the care or support that I so badly wanted to provide. Nothing I could do to aid her, no gift to give but my presence; so I stayed, hung out, sniffed around like a friendly puppy, persisted by her side until visiting hours were long over and a beefy nurse in creaky rubber soles came along, staring me down for the trespasser the clock had made me.

Oh, so you're a doctor yourself? Uh-huh, I see. And you think the rules don't apply to you, is that right?

Maybe I shouldn't have played the MD trump card with the nurse, but quite often that one card wins the whole game, so what the hell, no regrets. She'd escorted me to the elevators, warning that next time,

I could bet security was going to be involved. Fair enough. I wanted to see Bradlee, and if all I could do to help was sit at her bedside, talking or reading or humming a song to provide the stimulation her neurologist swore she needed most, then I'd check right back in the next morning, knowing the beefy nurse would be home by then, sleeping off her late-night power trip.

I did—on four hours sleep, a quick shower, and a shave. Oh, and a cup of coffee from the cafeteria downstairs that tasted like used motor oil. I got past the nursing staff, but my timing wasn't altogether good, as I was told that a specialist was in with the patient.

Has she recovered? I asked, but the morning nurse, as whip-thin as her nighttime counterpart was barrel-thick, told me nothing.

So I played the doctor card again.

The morning nurse folded her arms with a practiced toughness, as if she'd spent years fending off countless well-meaning friends, siblings, boyfriends, girlfriends, priests, executors, and trustees alike.

Sorry, Doctor Weaver. Unless you're her personal physician—which you don't claim to be—patient confidentiality prevents me from telling you anything.

I stopped her before she could retreat to her fortress of files arrayed behind the long front desk.

"Would you please just tell me whether she's improved? I am a friend. A good friend, and I . . . think you know, she's got no immediate family."

The nurse softened her stance and came closer again. "Young lady's got a strong constitution."

"So, she's improving?"

The nurse gave me a nice-try shake of the head. "You said it. Not me."

I reached out and thankfully shook her hand, I was so relieved. And . . . happy.

"Now you go."

Right. It was back to the elevators, but with a click in my step.

Wow, Craig, a spontaneous gesture with the nurse, and apropos at that. You surprise me.

Yeah, thanks, I surprise myself, too . . . .

By then, I was ready to give in to that wonderful expansive feeling you get when your ego boundaries extend beyond your own sense of self, the id's recognition that—

Please, man, cut the psychobabble!

I know I know—trust me, I can hear it myself.

—I was ready to welcome the euphoric ache that comes from being in love, but duty and responsibility intervened.

Saturday, noon, I got a distress call from the mother of Evie, one of my most troubled patients, a twenty-year-old Filipina with suicidal tendencies who'd gone to visit her auntie and stepped out onto the apartment's tenth-floor balcony, straddling the railings as she wept. They talked her back down, but the police came, and when she told them—in Tagalog, which they mistook as her speaking in tongues— she wanted to fly away from her mistake of a life, they put a 5150 hold on her and routed her to a county hospital. No competent psychiatrist would allow his patient to endure such an ordeal without being present to provide input to the medical staff and support to the patient. I spent the balance of the afternoon and evening with Evie, counseling and assessing and reassuring her, conferring with county staff as they titrated her meds with my previous prescriptions.

The funny thing is, I never once thought of Bradlee the whole time. I'd never been in love with a woman and at the same time, recognized that I truly love my work.

So this was quite the weekend for us, eh?

Fuckin-A.

Edgy!

Knock it off.

I didn't get home Saturday until 9:30 p.m. Sunday, my schedule was shot—for months I'd been signed up for a mandatory continuing medical education course on prescribing practices and had to attend to keep my privileges—so I couldn't make it over during visiting hours. Then last night, Rue Loberg phoned and asked if I could meet her in court. Her daughter Mindy was coming in to testify, and Rue thought it might get ugly, due to Mindy's close proximity to ground zero when the Loberg family had been blown all to hell. Rue wanted to be there for Mindy, but she didn't want to get overwhelmed and say or do anything she'd regret. Especially with Dr. Don right across the courtroom.

I rescheduled two Monday appointments and said yes, I'd be there. Had no idea Bradlee would be up at that table when I walked in.

Happiest day of my life as yet? Eh. . . .

She didn't turn around once to see me, which I admit made me feel unimportant, like a silly boy nursing an obsession. To rid myself of that unpleasant indicator of my emotional fragility, I consciously analyzed her as a physician would a patient.

Okay, her other wounds could not have fully healed, not in such a short time, which meant she must be in a fit of pain to even sit upright—in a tumultuous courtroom setting, at that. So, how could she do it? The average patient, brain-cramped by the pounding, ever-present, drumbeat pain of serious head trauma and multiple bullet wounds would be more than happy to go the maximum-meds route, camping out on the couch in front of the tube with a half gallon of ice cream and far greater enthusiasm for penguin documentaries than discretion would normally allow.

Not Bradlee Aames.

Honestly, I couldn't think straight.

I'd silently slid into the seat next to Rue Loberg, whispering a hello to Deshaun Fellows, as if everything was oh so under control. But the tangle inside me had settled in my chest, and I could barely breathe. So who does a psychiatrist turn to when he has an anxiety attack?

How about yourself, genius. Physician, heal thyself.

That much I could attempt.

I was secretly heartsick and bereft and, after all these years, had still yet to wash the blood of an adulterous girlfriend from my hands.

Fine—there you have it. So deal, already, Craig. Deal.

Now, if I knew anything as a therapist, I knew it was time to ask myself the question I ask patients the most in-session: how do you feel about that?

How about accepting, *Craig. So you're a person with flaws. What it is, man. Congratulations, you're human. Forgive yourself, and any others you've wronged. Atone.*

Guess I can do that, too. Don't think I've got a choice any longer . . .

Very perceptive, Dr. Weaver.

No need to patronize. I'm ready . . .

Good-bye, Deb.

No—not now. Not ready.

With my eyes closed, the lawyers' vocal jousting was just a hum. There was peace in staring at nothing, and from that calm a link was formed to my slow, mechanical breathing until the in, the out, the in-again, the out-again became an abstraction, governed not by thought but by an instinct blessedly requiring zero maintenance.

Aah, yeah, so much easier to just be, just be, man . . . I could have gone on this way for a much longer spell, floating gently downstream in unthinking quietude . . .

But no, it should not and could not last. I was here for my patient. That meant I should be alert and aware, unselfishly so. Focused on her daughter's testimony.

Recalibrating my senses, I sat up and rubbed my eyes, my deadened ass-cheeks prickling. The arguments were winding down now, and Fallon's lead attorney—Mr. Heidegger—the supercilious jerk, old spotted guy whose every word carried a hint of bitterness and holier-than-thou condescension, old Heidegger seemed to have the floor. He started by smarmily thanking Rue's girl, Mindy, commending her for coming in to testify today, for doing her duty. (Shit—it felt like my duty to sock the self-satisfied smoothie right in the mouth.) Then he told her that even though she was a patient who'd come to Dr. Don with plenty of problems to discuss, he didn't want to delve into those problems here and now, trampling all over her privacy.

What a great guy, respecting Mindy's secrets.

I was suddenly furious. Not the usual Craig Weaver, the calm, even-handed therapist. I wanted to beat butts and take names. I wanted this pale, slightly google-eyed girl on the witness stand to hold steady under fire; for Dr. Don to lose his license, and access to unwit-ting victims, forever.

More than anything, I wanted Bradlee Aames to prevail.

"Is that all right," the old lawyer asked, "that we simply leave the subject matter of your therapy be, Miss Loberg?"

Gaining her trust, the jackass.

"Fine with me," Mindy said warily.

"To me, the issue of your truthfulness, what we lawyers would call your credibility, that's what I'm more interested in, Miss Loberg."

"Your call," Mindy agreed—but she looked puzzled.

"Now, in reviewing your patient file, I noticed your birthday, and let's see, you just had one about three weeks ago, correct?"

"You already asked me that. Yeah, I did, earlier this month, on the second. A Tuesday, I think. Yeah, a Tuesday."

"Now, Miss Loberg, you're currently employed at a dance club called the X-Factory, is that right?"

"Well, yes and no."

"Really? Please explain the 'no' part of your answer."

"That's what it used to be called when it was a sports bar. You know, like, how they'll call one special player on a team, could be the difference between winning and losing, the 'x-factor'?"

"Yes, I've heard the expression."

Mindy smiled a little, pleased to have displayed a depth of knowl-edge on the subject.

"But now that it's become a dance club, with guest djs and all, nobody really calls it that anymore. It's just 'The Factory.'"

"Oh, I see."

Mr. Heidegger, he took his time being hammy, nodding as if he'd just absorbed a great truth. Then he attacked.

"And, what is your position there, at the Factory, Miss Loberg?"

"I'm a 'shooter girl.'"

"And what is a 'shooter girl'?"

"What it sounds like. I walk around the club serving shooters, you know, from a tray full of shot glasses."

"I see. And how many months ago were you hired?"

Mindy did some mental math as her round blue eyes studied the ceiling. "Oh, about two—no, three months ago."

The old lawyer was hamming again, his face overwrought with consternation. "But, Miss Loberg, you only reached the legal drinking age three weeks ago."

"Well, yeah, but I don't *drink* on the job, I just serve shots to customers."

Mindy searched the judge's face, but from where I was sitting, I think she got nothing in return. The judge, who to me resembled Freud, seemed intent on observing everything while betraying zero emotion. Like a very good therapist—or a champion poker player.

The air in this entire space seemed to have gone flat, as if punctured by the old lawyer's sharp-edged little questions. I hated him, but he was good.

"But, you do know that in this state it's unlawful for anyone under the legal drinking age to serve alcoholic beverages, don't you, Miss Loberg?"

"Yeah, I guess that's true."

"So, what I'm wondering is how you got yourself hired three months ago to be a so-called 'shot girl' when you were still legally under age."

"I, uh, dunno. I just applied."

"Miss Loberg, I want you to be aware that I can find out by using this court's subpoena power. I can make your employer turn over your job application, so we can see what you wrote on it."

Mindy shrugged. Bradlee seemed to wince when she saw her witness's glib expression.

"Do what you gotta do, I guess."

"But we'll have to continue this trial, put it over to another date, so that I can bring you back into this courtroom to answer questions about that job application. I promise you, that won't be pleasant."

Mindy turned to the judge. "He can do that?"

"Yes, he can," the judge told her.

The old lawyer was in full control now, taking his time. "I'd much rather have you simply answer a few questions now, Miss Loberg, and answer them honestly, as you swore you would when you took that oath this morning."

"Okay. I don't want to come back here again. Let's get it over with."

"Did you lie about our age on your job application?"

"I, uh, may have made myself a year older. But—"

"Thank you. Tell me, how many days a week have you been working since you were hired at the Factory, Miss Loberg?"

"The first month or so, two weeknights, and Sunday nights. You know, they gave me the slower shifts, 'cause I was new and at the bottom of the totem pole. Then I got another weeknight, and every other week a Friday night, too, a little upgrade in shifts. So, um, overall, I guess I've been at it about four nights a week, give or take."

The ornery attorney scratched out a few numbers, then sat back in awe, like Einstein on the brink of an epiphany. I hated his guts all over again.

Wow, Craig, really getting in touch with your feral side—

Yeah? Get used to it.

"That means, if your birthday was a mere three weeks ago, Miss Loberg, you worked anywhere between thirty and forty-five shifts as an underage person, serving alcohol."

"I, uh, guess so."

"Did you know that if you were found out, your employer could have faced legal ramifications including fines, and perhaps even being ordered to shut down?"

"Objection," Bradlee Aames said. "Calls for a legal conclusion, speculation, and argumentative."

"Sustained," the judge said, but his heart didn't seem committed to defending Mindy. That damn Heidegger's smile conveyed the power of ownership: this witness belonged to him.

"So. You misled your employer, didn't you?"

"I needed the job. Really bad. Ian's mom was on my case about—"

"Thank you, you've answered the question. Now, Miss Loberg, isn't it fair to say that you lied because you felt you had to?"

She shook her head as if this was all a joke. "Guess that's about the size of it."

"Now, getting back to the allegations in this case, if I might, you never saw Doctor Fallon touch your mother, did you?"

"Oh, please. He had the total hots for her. Anyone with two eyes could see—"

"Objection," Heidegger said. "Move to strike as nonresponsive."

"Sustained. The answer is stricken from the record. Please answer the question, Ms. Loberg."

"No, I never saw them in the act or anything, thank God."

"And now that your mother's story has been questioned, I would dare say refuted, you feel again compelled to lie, to lie on her behalf, don't you?"

"No. I would never do that. No way."

Attorney Heidegger held up his fingers to as if to count off points on his fingertips. "You needed a job, so you lied. Now your mother needs you to lie, so—"

"We don't even talk anymore, or see each other. I told her off, called her a . . . well, some awful names. How would I know what she needed, huh? How?"

"You are lying for her now, aren't you?"

"Dream on, mister. I told the truth."

Fallon's lawyer never even raised his voice, but Mindy Loberg had been brought to tears, her nose rubbed in her shortcomings, her mother's weaknesses, and the rotting carcass of the Loberg family. I was spellbound with professional—and admittedly prurient—interest.

"Thank you. Nothing further."

"I told the god's-honest truth today!"

"No further questions."

"But I did!"

Bradlee Aames was asked for re-direct, but she passed. The judge thanked Mindy, and it was over.

At that moment, to my view the law was as cold and hard and cruel as an ice pick to the base of the cranium, and I despised its brutal methods. But then . . . what else is there? Lie detectors are worthless, from a scientific standpoint—any first-year doctoral candidate would know that. And last time I checked, a reliable truth serum has yet to be developed. So this is it: a witness stand, an oath, some questions, and a whole lot of verbal jujitsu. And oh my God, talk about a dramatic confrontation! I was angry and exhilarated at the same time. As Mindy shrank back to the gallery, I noticed my hands were shaking.

Leaning over toward Rue, I thought to whisper a few kind words of consolation. But I knew I was full of shit, speaking only for myself. I had no skin in the game. Quickly, Rue was up and out of her seat for Mindy, and the two shared a long hug before . . . they both shocked me by not fleeing the courtroom.

"Hey, Doctor Weaver," Mindy whispered, settling into the row behind me with her mother. "I do okay?"

"Y-yes, you did great," I mumbled.

Jesus, I thought. Every woman associated with this case has twice the backbone I could ever dream of having.

There was a pause in the action. My heart was leaping. I had a powerful impulse to step outside the courtroom, where hopefully, I could be alone with Deb. My former love, Deb. My head, my heart, my entire being were so overfilled that if I couldn't shed some of the load I'd been carrying all these years, I'd be no good to myself, my patients . . . or Bradlee.

I excused myself and went outside. Looked both ways, up and down the long carpeted hallway and saw no one.

"Deb?" I said quietly. Leaning back, I closed my eyes, exhausted by the events of the last few weeks.

So you're tired, so what? You're young. Keep pushing, you're on a roll . . .

"I'll forever be sorry for what I did."

That was true. In fact, this case has made me think a lot about victimization of women; mostly, how easy it can be for a man so wrapped up in what he thinks he needs or wants to take a woman down that path, and not even notice until it's too late and the damage is done.

"To a certain extent I did use you, sexually—the time we rented a motel room in Laguna, and the parking-lot episode behind the triple-X theater come to mind—and emotionally, when I'd be insecure and say mean things; and as for getting too physical, I'll always regret bear-hugging you onto the couch the night of that mall shooting when we had that stupid argument about gun control and I wouldn't let you up till you admitted your statistics were just reiterated from your dad's bogus rants."

I was a jerk. A loser. Rambling away in an empty government hallway.

What the hell—here goes . . .

"But, Deb, I did not kill you, I did not pull that trigger."

Whoa! About time, buddy!

I know—I know. That was way too long in coming.

Hanging on the walls, here in administrative court, are some beautiful reproductions of modern art. I'd barely noticed them before, but when I opened my eyes, a Jasper Johns abstract beauty filled my head with lines and shapes and textures so seemingly random but so powerfully linked, it was like my irises were flooded with light, temporarily blind. Blinking twice, three times, I rubbed my eyes hard, shut them, sunspots exploding inside my eyelids. Looked again—past the artwork, way down the hall, where a tall athletic figure, a man as tanned and virile and sunkissed as a Tahitian warrior, tipped his sunglasses—indoors?—*Ah, you're probably seeing things, so just go with it, man . . .* in my direction, as if to acknowledge my progress with Bradlee. And Deb. And what—my life?

Thank you, man, I wanted to say. *I'm trying—really, really hard.*

I'd seen that guy's casual stance before, but couldn't place it. A magazine article? Could be . . . . A piece on California cool? Mocking it while acknowledging its powerful allure? Something like that, just out of reach to me now . . . . Everybody wanting a piece of the same thing, which this guy knew he had. In spades.

An attitude. A stance. Like . . .

Surfing.

A surfer. World famous. A surfer at the top of his game, in perfect balance. Like the streaking figure by the pier at Malibu . . .

Blinked my eyes again to get a better look, to fix my compass. But he was gone.

32

BRADLEE AAMES

Oh, God, my head is buried in burning coals! Face?—attached, I can pinch my cheeks. Hands, fingers—icicles! Another chill and my smallest quiver tugs at the bandages . . .

The judge is back on the bench, so sit up. Ouch!—not that far, that fast.

He says he's making a tentative ruling. Breathe!

A tentative can mean only one thing: I proved my case.

Breathe; even if it hurts, just breathe . . .

Here's how the dominoes fall: Because I proved my case, the judge sees Dr. Don as a menace to his patients and the public, and with public protection in mind, he'll have his proposed decision written and ready for the medical board to sign off on and order as soon as possible; the order will revoke Dr. Don's medical license, ending his career as a psychiatrist; hence the tentative—fair warning to both parties that this process will move quickly.

It's over. But then, it isn't.

I'd better watch my mail at work, because the minute the order hits, the defense will file an appeal. They'll rush off to superior court to get a stay of the board's order, claiming the board abused its discretion by taking away Dr. Don's license and livelihood without a basis of sufficient evidence.

Across from me, the firing line of tight-ass grimaces—courtesy of the chief bagman Heidegger, his stiffs, and a semi-hunchbacked Dr. Don at the far end—is truly photo-worthy. But damn, wouldn't you know! I don't have a camera.

Sons of bitches! Yeah, you, boys! All of you!

Silently, Heidegger mimics a tiny snake-hiss at me. Silently, I respond with my patented barely there, tough-titties-on-you smile. The judge keeps on, his every word perfuming the air on this glorious afternoon.

They can fight on all they want; hey, it's a free country. But a stay of the board's order is unlikely. So is a successful appeal. Cases like this rise and fall on the strength of the evidence, and that evidence came from three witnesses, Rue and Mindy Loberg, and Dr. Don. The wise, wonderful Judge Drummond essentially believed Rue and Mindy, and found Dr. Don's testimony not credible. Because later on, appellate judges reviewing the case cannot observe the demeanor of witnesses who have previously testified, they must adopt the lower-court judge's findings on credibility.

Therefore, an appellate court would not upset this wise and wonderful judge's determinations on who told the truth and who lied.

The judge's tentative is also intended to give unspoken, informal advance warning to Dr. Don that he'd better make some final arrangements for his patients, help refer them to other professionals as necessary. As for Fallon's office staff, they're about to get pink slips. The sooner they know, the better for them to start making other plans.

With the relief that the case is won, I unclench—only to be sucker punched by another hot blast of pain. I cautiously touch the back of my skull, can feel the throbbing bruised bone beneath my fingertips. The bullet wounds below are still tender, and I imagine them as open holes, leaking and draining away my strength, my essence. Touch my hip, expecting to dip into bloody wetness. No—nothing soaking through the skirt . . .

Paranoia?

Oh, please—how would a girl blessed with such a labyrinthine mind set ever puzzle her way through that one?

Could be, though: I'm still afraid to grope further, beneath my clothing, to check the wounds, assess their true status, lest I poke the wrong spot and spring a serious leak. Drain away. Better to become a silent freeze-frame of myself, not to tempt fate. But who am I kidding? Playing it safe doesn't work for me.

So I sit very still, become stillness itself, but not like a mill pond; no, my version of still conjures a vision of a house of cards in a wind tunnel. Always doing it the hard way, the only way I know.

Fragile, yes, but alive, and damned satisfied.

Yes, yes, *yes*: I proved my case.

People in the gallery are watching me; some are present, and some not. I wish my not-present father was really here, wish I could turn and exchange a wordless glance with him, enjoy the nod of approval I know I've earned from the wise and savvy senior prosecutor warrior. So, a bit of madness runs in the family, so what? Good genes for the courtroom are equally undeniable as a genetic trait.

"Thank you for that," I whisper barely audibly, though the belief that he can hear me is all that matters.

Yes, yes, *hell yes*! I proved my case.

"Pardon me?"

It's Heidegger, and I have nothing to say to him. But he keeps staring implausibly.

"What?"

"You said something to me which I didn't quite hear." He sounded tired and dismayed by fate.

Had I just babbled unawares? So what if I did, he'd get over it. Then I had a thought, a reminder of an important piece of business.

"I want my stuff back."

He stared blankly, betraying nothing, but I didn't buy it. I turned to Mendibles and leveled the same look on him, then went back to Heidegger. "My documents, lifted from my apartment."

They both began to protest, but I held up my hand to halt the bullshit before it started sliding downhill. "Enough said."

*   *   *

MINDY LOBERG

The judge said he found my testimony 'credible,' even though I lied on that job application. He mentioned some other court case he read about before, a case that says a judge can accept some parts of a witness's testimony even if he can't rely on other parts. As for me, he said I displayed honesty in admitting what I did, and I credibly explained the pressure I was under to get a job. The same pressure, he said, that had brought me back to see Dr. Don for more therapy. That connection he found to be very believable. I guess my troubles with Ian and his family had a familiar ring to the judge.

My mom? All over the place. Mostly, she was crying—but what else could anyone expect? Held my hand so tight I thought my fingers would break off. Mouthed the words: Thank you, baby. Thank you, Sugar.

Sugar. Mom used to call me that when I was a toddler, because every time she'd turn her back on me, I'd race over to the sugar bowl on the kitchen table, wet a finger, and stick it in the bowl.

Sugar—dammit.

I had no interest in crying, but that one got me going. We sat there, holding hands and sniffling while the judge went on about who told the truth and who didn't. Reminded me of what they taught us in Sunday school, that stuff about the rapture. When all will be revealed and we are judged before our Creator. This judge, he surely wasn't God, but sitting there with my mom, it felt good hearing him laying down the law he could manage.

*   *   *

RUE LOBERG

Honestly, the decision didn't surprise me. I admit, I was taken with the way Miss Aames summed up her case, and I knew the judge was, too. But there was one other difference between her summation and Mr. Heidegger's, and I just happened to notice it. You see, the whole time Ms. Aames was talking—reeling off point after point about the evidence, the witness testimony, the law, her expert's findings of gross negligence and boundary violations and sexual misconduct, and Dr. Don's lying ways and his not-credible overpaid hired gun of an expert—the judge, he sat there typing like crazy into that laptop of his. And then, when Mr. Heidegger took his turn, the judge's typing? It slowed way down to an occasional tippy-tap, at best.

God, I was so proud of Mindy the words simply escaped me. Out of all this ugly, unhappy, embarrassing awful mess, she'd been lost to me, and like Jesus's parable of the prodigal son from the gospel according to Luke, chapter 15, now she was found. Funny—as much as I've been messed over in the name of religion, those stories from the Bible never faded away.

Thank you, Lord.

Proud of myself, too, I am. Maybe I couldn't right all the wrongs I've done, but I righted one big wrong in my life, and it felt . . . well, downright glorious. Gave me the strength to walk across that courtroom and come up behind Dr. Don, who looked like he'd been run over by a truck. I startled him, and one of his legal goons tensed up like something bad was gonna happen, but I did what I came to do quick.

"I forgive you."

He looked at me with the eye of a reptile waiting to strike. Made my heart freeze right in my throat.

"How convenient," he replied. "But I've done nothing wrong."

How about that? The man was beyond help, without a conscience. Kind of person who could never fess up to anything, too wrapped up in himself to even see anybody else. Least of all someone like me—a bloody pile of road kill, psychologically speaking, but with a flat tummy and a nice enough pair of legs. That's about what that little weasel sees when I stand before him.

No more—I got out of there before his lawyers could start crying foul.

*   *   *

DONALD FALLON, MD

Oh, really, Mister Know-it-all? Hiding behind a cheap wooden edifice, in your cheap black flammable robe, you fat phony King Solomon, you!

So, these are your "findings," eh, fool? The . . . delusions of a failed attorney paid a pauper's wages to play the part of rent-a-judge? Bad actor—and you know I see your shallow performance for the sham it is, because not once have you dared to even look at me, you fake phony Solomon! Abominable coward, spewing legal gibberish like dressing up a pig in a top hat and tails—well the show's a bust, because the pig can't dance!

And a hey-ho to you, Bradlee fucking Aames! I have a tool that will split you in half, steal the breath right out of your lungs the way you've stolen my medical license, you dirty slutty bleeding little bitch, I'll make you REALLY bleed, all right! Bend over, and ye shall receive your due penance, little bitch Bradlee Aames!

Lawyers—costly, blood-sucking blabbermouth lawyers! Do NOT lean over for one more whisper or make one more goddamn hand signal to me, Terrence Heidegger, because so help me, I will chew off your ear and your there-there fingers, all of them! Go ahead, talk to me again about the retainer you'll be requiring "in the unlikely event that we'd have to appeal," and I'll give you another unlikely event, you slimy cocksucker! Oh, you'll see how it feels to be utterly dominated by your superior, and you'll finally know why I do what must be done to the likes of walking stupid fuck-dolls like Rue white-trash Loberg. When you're bent over and bleeding, you will be grateful, Counselor, because at last you will see that your put-upon client, Donald Fallon, MD, the man you have betrayed by rendering such consistently underwhelmingly substandard legal services, is merely maintaining the natural social order in this world full of victims and fuck-ups . . .

* * *

RAUL MENDIBLES

For a long time, I just sat behind her, closest to the door, listening to the judge, rehearsing what I'd say when the moment arrived. Congratulations were in order, of course, but what more then, I could not decide. An admission from me? She might not accept it; she'd instantly calculate the damage I'd knowingly inflicted on the board's case and demand to know why. And I didn't have the heart to lie anymore, not now. Another, even more personal admission was arguably called for—and impossible to deliver now, quite possibly for all time. I know I'm not enough of a man to take on any of that.

These things are hard to even admit to myself. But I must.

I know I'm not a special talent as a lawyer, so I've sought to distinguish myself as a leader, a supervisor. Among Mexicans born to immigrants—to simple people who view a college education as miraculous, and a professional, an *abogado,* as worthy to bow down to—I am an enormous, unqualified success. But a supervisor, at that? *Ay Dios mio . . . .* Since I've met the major and been promoted, at every family get-together and holiday celebration, I'm treated like a deity, the best seat at the table reserved for Raul, *El Jefe,* while tray after bowl after platter of greasy fried confections roll up to me in endless succession.

And yes, I enjoy the attention. Revel in it.

Despite my frequent bouts of self-delusion, I nonetheless know the difference between right and wrong; and the fact that I've done wrong, many times, never escapes me. For now, I'm too weak to share that shame with others, and certainly, not with Bradlee Aames. She has a distinctive spirit, a fire inside, a glow that flat-out mesmerizes me. I mistook that allure for sexual intensity. Yes, she's very fine and, in the eyes of a married man, dangerous; but that isn't the real attraction. Not until I saw her lying in a hospital bed did I realize that what drew me to her was her level of engagement, her willingness to fight instead of run away, both in the real world and inside her head—equally badass places, in her case. She's as brave as I am fearful.

Oh, she might explode on me if I listed my misdeeds now, and considering her medical condition, that wouldn't be good for her . . .

So how's that for avoidance technique? I fail to confess my sins to her not due to cowardice; no—instead, I'm simply being considerate.

The judge is wrapping up. He thanks the parties for their cooperation, declares the record closed. Then he exits the bench, leaving me to my conundrum.

Bradlee begins to pack up her papers and pads. For now, I tell her she did a wonderful job, which is the truth. I promise myself to tell her more, in due time.

She leans closer and fixes her eyes on mine.

"I want you to know that I'll never work for you again."

"Wha—excuse me?"

"And if you fight me, I'll expose you for what you did."

"Bradlee, wait, can we just—"

"See that man over there?"

I turn to see Deshaun Fellows, the investigator. He is standing with his back turned, chatting with Rue and Mindy Loberg, smiles all around.

"That man knows a few things, firsthand, about the shit you pulled, and how that scum Heidegger was working the other side of this case the whole damn time."

"Bradlee, I never—"

"Deshaun's a good guy, Raul. He thinks I took a few bullets for him, which isn't quite accurate, but that's how he sees it. As far as he's concerned, we're down with each other, like blood. Friends for life. And that's fine with me. I could certainly use more friends."

"Hey, I'm on your side too, I—"

"Because here it is, boss. I ask him to scare up the dirty details on what you did? He'll go to work, and he won't stop until I get what I need. Then he'll put it in a report. And testify, if I ask him to. You want to go there?"

"No, of course not! But this . . . wait! This isn't necessary! Let me explain, let me—"

"No! Too late. Here's how I see it. You're transferring. I don't care where, as long as you're out of our section, A - S - A - P."

My shoulders slumped. I rubbed my forehead as if to coax out the truth with just the right words. Instead, I came up just shy of blubbering.

"If I do that, I'll lose my supervisor status."

"How tragic."

"I . . . please, let's talk about this."

"We have, Raul, and I really don't care. I'll never work for you again."

"I can explain—"

"Too late. Transfer out. You do, and this shit you stepped in will be over."

"Bradlee," I said quietly. "I can fix this, I—"

"I'm done with you. We are done."

Mutely I watched her pack her big black bag. My mind spun, racing to string together an explanation, a justification . . . God—even a pathetic plea would do, if it worked. Not a single word would rush forth to save me.

El Jefe esta muerto.

I am done.

* * *

CRAIG WEAVER, MD

Rue didn't need me, but it was good to be there. She'd done it, facing down her fears by confronting her tormentor. Quite by surprise, she'd been rewarded with the chance to start over with her daughter. I hadn't seen that coming.

Nor had I prepared myself for what my life would be like without Bradlee Aames, now that the case was over. Suddenly, it was happening. The judge disappeared out a rear security door, the court reporter wheeled her contraption right by us, and we were on our feet, smiling and milling about in the warm afterglow of victory. Dr. Fallon seemed angry as hell, swatting at one of his chief lawyer's wannabe assistants when the guy tried to console him. I rather enjoyed that little tableau, but it didn't last. An odd thing happened: from the gallery, the investigator, Deshaun Fellows, stepped forward toward the defense table. He first regarded Bradlee, who gave him some kind of a signal, I suppose.

Then he swiveled between her table and the defense's table, squaring his broad shoulders.

"Time to go," I thought I heard him say with just a hint of menace. Stood tall, like a well-placed wall between Bradlee and Team Fallon as the parties packed up. Fallon, an arch manipulator to the bitter end, seemed particularly peeved, as he'd been shooting nasty glances Bradlee's way. For his part, Fellows had what you might call a certain male intensity on full display and he put an instant stop to that nonsense. As in: game over, Dr. Don. Oh, man, was I ever digging that spectacle!

Within seconds the defense team had decamped, their hushed, finger-pointing exchanges echoing down the hallway with the chafing bite of sandpaper.

You're a disgrace, Fallon, I wish I'd have told the doctor before he'd gone. But even though they'd tried to get at my treatment records for my care of Rue, I never felt enough a part of this case to intervene like that—not firsthand. Maybe if I see him on the street . . . or in an alleyway. Ah, forget the creep, the psychiatric community surely will . . . .

It was in that moment of rapturous *schadenfreude* that I received a tap on the shoulder, and there before me stood the object of my most intense affection. She reached into an oversize leather bag and pulled out a small book, a slightly frayed, faded-red hardbound volume of poetry.

"You left your book at the hospital, Doctor."

I stood there, waiting for a plan. Close-up like this, her face was a picture of exhaustion suppressed or even altogether denied. But her eyes were quick and bright, and when she smiled, I lost all contact with the rational part of my brain.

I shrugged. "You're supposed to call me Craig. Remember?"

"Right," she said, seemingly enjoying my discomfort. "May I ask you something?"

"Sure."

"Which poems did you choose to read?"

I hefted the compact little volume, which nonetheless felt substantial.

"I didn't really choose. They were all good."

"You read the whole thing."

"Classics. I figured I couldn't go wrong."

"I see. How long did that take you, Craig?"

My face got warm when she called me by my first name. My primary objective now was not to humiliate myself by saying something hopelessly stupid.

"It didn't seem like very long. I like poetry."

Like a teenager, I stuck my hands in my pocket and rocked. As a guy I was pathetic. We're talking no moves whatsoever.

Bradlee Aames came up close and kissed me on the cheek.

"I put a new bookmark in your beautiful little book. Bye."

Then she turned to Mr. Fellows, the investigator. I watched dumbly as he snapped open the door for her. As she walked through, Fellows turned back and gave me a belt-high, crushing handshake.

"Doctor."

Nodding, I took back my aching hand, vaguely jealous of her new friend and bodyguard. Then again, I'd have paid money to see Dr. Don or Heidegger try to get in Bradlee's face as she left the building. Almost hoped they'd try something. Fellows would gladly break any pipsqueak professional in two if they even thought about it.

Then I opened the anthology and pulled out the bookmark. It was a business card: Bradlee Aames, Deputy Attorney General, Department of Justice, Office of the Attorney General. Beside her name was a big, blue DOJ seal featuring the blindfolded maiden of justice, her scales dangling in perfect balance. On the back of the card, in black ink, Bradlee had written her personal phone number, with the following note beneath it:

Call me!

I began to replace the card in the pages of the anthology, but then . . . what was I, stupid? It wasn't a bookmark. I put it in my wallet. Took it out, in the elevator, read it again. Held it in the palm of my hand the rest of the way down. No one else could see it, but like a magician, I knew it was right there, where it should be.

* * *

DeShaun Fellows

We got ourselves out of the building and I thought Miss Bradlee would want to go home, get some rest, considering all she'd been through. But she had other ideas. I got her in the car, and she gave me directions to a restaurant jus' a few blocks away, over on Second, called the Fox Inn. No sign of any foxes anywhere, jus' a lot of old nautical junk on the walls—you know, old ships' wheels, diving helmets, and giant seashells stuck in fishing nets. Place did have food cooking—you could smell the fish frying in back—but the eatin' part seemed like more an excuse for people come on in here and get to drinking. Middle of the afternoon and there must've been thirty, forty folks all dressed up for court like us, getting good and tanked.

Exactly what Miss Bradlee had in mind.

I wondered which of the other folks here were celebrating victory and which were drowning their sorrows. No way to tell, of course.

She ordered a couple of gin and tonics, made them both disappear before the waitress even walked away. Then she ordered an ice tea for me, plate of appetizers.

"Sorry, Deshaun," she said. "But if I didn't send in reinforcements, you'd have been cutting me out of those cheesy fishnets."

"Don't have to explain a thing, Ms. Aames."

"Don't I know it. You're the best."

One more gin and tonic and she seemed all set. It was like, her eyes stopped dancing around—like a pool of water's bubbling and gurgling as it fills up, but when it gets near full, it gets real calm and you can't hear the gurgle anymore.

"I'm switching to ice water," she tells me. "Don't let me order another real drink."

"No, ma'am."

Food comes, and it wasn't bad, but let's just say it didn't hold a candle to the kind of Southern cookin' you can get down in South Central, or even over on Crenshaw, Leimert Park by the mall. But I was hungry, and the company was good.

"When are you moving, Deshaun?" Bradlee Aames asked me after the plates were cleared. "Reevesy and I expect a guided tour of Bourbon Street."

"Soon," I said. "Gotta wrap up some business, first. But come see me, you'll get the A-one N'awlins tour to beat all tours.'"

What I don't say is: I know Bulldog's got homies, and if they come for me, I don't want Ida Mae or any other family anywhere in the vicinity.

"Listen, Deshaun," Miss Aames says. "I've got a college girlfriend who's been a deputy DA her whole career. She heard about the shooting and called, left a message on my work phone. You know, the anything-you-need kind of message."

I stare at her, hard, thinking: how you reading my mind?

"I already called her back, during a court break this morning. Told her about our good buddy Bulldog. She said she'd make a few calls, look into what happened. Guess what? She called back; we talked during the lunch break. He's already under arrest."

"For the shooting?"

"Not that. That little shit's a person of interest in two bank robberies. The feds are all over his ass."

"You don't say!"

Hmm—young Lester had more nerve than I ever gave him credit for.

"LAPD's got a detective on the shooting. We'll have to give statements tonight or tomorrow. Maybe we can go to Parker Center together."

"Sure, sure thing," I say, still surprised. And relieved.

I sit back, fiddling with my iced tea. Thinking: wow. Sometimes I forget how powerful the government is, compared to the little old man-on-the-street, like Deshaun.

"Anyway," she says, "after the shooting, about ten people on that movie set ID'd his ass, and he still got away. Got picked up two days later in Inglewood, right around the corner from your place."

"You think he came looking for Ida Mae?" My jaw is hanging open like a busted gate.

Miss Aames's face, it changes. "Oh my God, Deshaun." She reaches across the table and takes my hand in hers. "I didn't even think of that."

"Maybe we should go," I say.

"Wait. There's more. Those two robberies? Apparently he was part of a three-man crew."

"I know that, ma'am. Heard it on the street. That's what's worrying me."

"Well, don't you worry, Deshaun. He was busted at one of their houses. All three of them were in the garage. And they had guns. Automatic weapons. A box of grenades. They didn't find the gun he used on me, but it sort of doesn't matter. Three felons, in possession of illegal firearms. You know what that means."

"I . . . think so," I say, the blood—and feeling—coming back to my face again.

"Gone, baby, gone."

Bradlee Aames took a long, deep swig from her ice water.

A steaming plate came floating by our table, a delicious fried-shell-fish smell I knew by heart.

"I've never had crayfish," she says. "I typically don't eat meals that can stare back at me while I'm eating them."

"Well, I can understand that. Though I have seen you in action in a courtroom. Seems like your appetite's workin' fine."

She liked that. "But I'm willing to make an exception, if you think I should."

"I know the prime spot in the entire state of Louisiana for crayfish, ma'am. Fresh caught. Served any way you like. Be glad to take you and your friend there myself."

"Tell me all about it, Deshaun," she says, sitting back as her tired eyes rolled closed. "Paint me a pretty picture . . ."

33

BRADLEE AAMES

Once the trial was over, time seemed to accelerate, and with it, a settling of accounts past due, as if the universe refused to withhold any longer a backlog of relative karma, good and bad. Like most people I know, change makes me uncomfortable, especially too much at once. Yet, despite my instinctive resistance, I did what I could to keep pace.

My wounds were healing well enough, leaving little trace of the shooting beyond a few dime-sized pink scars, one above my hip and another beneath my ribs. The blunt-force trauma I'd suffered when the back of my skull rapped the pavement downtown wasn't manifesting itself in any of the medical images the doctors studied, nor was I experiencing any side effects, aside from having to dispel an intense impulse to pick at the crusty scab beneath my hairline. But the sticky stuff back there fell off within a few weeks, which to me, was fittingly symbolic, because by then I was more or less back to my hard-headed ways.

Inside my head, however, I was evolving—at least in my approach to coping with the world. For one thing, I was no longer willing to write off medications and just go it alone forever-after. Obviously, there are times when narcotics do nothing but hopelessly obscure my perspective—such as in a courtroom, during trial. Drugs stunt my rational-thought processes. I can't practice law that way, and won't. So for now, even if I'm seeing monsters, I'm otherwise straight. But Craig—Dr. Weaver, I mean—thinks there may be lower-dose combinations that could help me without zapping my brain into a lethargic stupor. He helped sign me up for a trial program with a leading neurologist at UCLA that's focused on treating high-functioning schizoid and delusional patients with meds designed to tread more lightly on the brain's executive-decision-making abilities.

Not that I trust modern pharmacology, but it's worth a shot.

I've also had to acknowledge the fact that my list-making system of discerning reality from unreality has its limits, especially in bizarro LA, where recently, what I believed was an intense, deeply personal vision of Justitia came calling on me to—I don't know, gauge my true commitment to fairness, truth, and equity under the law, or some other deeply meaningful bullshit. Well, the supposed vision, which had me in tears befitting a career prosecutor, turned out to be real and involved an unemployed actor in a Statue of Liberty get-up pimping sandwich specials for a New York deli down the street. Sometimes reality dishes harder and crazier than my sketchy brain, and documenting the disparities can seem like a self-defeating waste of time.

Another simple truth that hit me in the face is that my condition sometimes affects other aspects of how I function. I was reminded of this on a three-day weekend during which I was consumed with cleaning out my closet and rereading *Siddhartha*. Yes, I am aware that becoming obsessed with a task long neglected while simultaneously binge-reading is nothing clinically abnormal—but then, failing to bathe, eat, sleep, or even brush my hair or teeth for seventy-two hours straight is yet another. Poor Reevesy, he didn't know what to say or do, and it wasn't until he slid onto the far end of the couch to watch his favorite Mexican soap opera with a clothespin on his nose that my shame propelled me to rediscover the essentials of good personal hygiene.

In hindsight, I think I hadn't bathed because that function of rational judgment lay dormant, like a loose wire in my head. The intense concurrent desires to clean and organize and read voraciously served to eclipse any simple acts of personal maintenance that would otherwise demand due attention. Not normal; but not alarming, either. Even mild bouts of mania have their signs, and I'm learning to be more watchful.

Which is hard to do when I'm sauced on JD. I know—this hardly qualifies as a news flash; but if I'm going to live better, and longer, I've got to examine the whole of my coping behavior. My hospital stay included a liver panel and an eye-opening set of results. I won't bore you with the details, but let me just say that drinking to self-medicate is like ridding your house from termites by burning the fucker down.

As I mentioned, time seemed to fly by, especially at work. The board revoked Donald Fallon, MD's medical license on a Tuesday. His attorneys filed an appeal in Superior Court that Wednesday, asking a judge to find that the revocation was an abuse of the board's discretion, and to issue a writ of mandate ordering the board to reverse its decision. They also asked the court to issue an *ex parte*—or immediate— order staying the board's revocation. Because of this last request, I had to fly to Sacramento, where the appeal had been filed, to argue the stay that Thursday.

Why Sacramento, for a case tried in LA against an LA psychiatrist? Well, because the court-venue rules allow the defense to choose to file either in the county where the case was tried, or the county where the opposing party is located—and since the medical board's headquarters is in the state's capital, Sacramento is a proper venue. Defense lawyers choose Sacramento over LA because the courts up north are far less busy and, in turn, may be more amenable to giving a case a closer, more detailed review. Or so they hope.

The courtroom I attended that Thursday for the Fallon appeal bore out the less-is-better theory to a tee, as the place was empty. Heidegger was there in a double-breasted glen plaid suit, looking a lot like an old geezer that hawks gourmet popcorn on television. When I walked in, he was busting a gut to ingratiate himself with the judge's clerk, a middle-aged woman in a simply cut navy cotton dress with a chiffon sweater draped over her shoulders. Though the clerk paused to take in my standard black ensemble, by the time I handed her my card she'd recovered and actually complimented me on my handbag.

"Prada?"

I smiled and said no. "Melrose."

"It's lovely. In a hellfire kind of way."

"I love that description. Thank you."

I also complimented her pearl-inlaid silver brooch. We chatted like women do about fashion, and that rusty old buzz saw Heidegger was forced first into silence, then a retreat to the bailiff's desk, where a uniformed man the size of a weightlifter sat at a tiny desk perusing a fly-fishing magazine.

The judge, a bald, stooped man with horn-rimmed glasses and a big nose, had a brief sideways gander at me the way men sometimes will, but his voice was gentle and his manner was welcoming. He listened first to Heidegger's strident plea—"Your Honor, this case is a travesty of justice!"—with an eye-roll that told me to take a more low-key path, which I did when I responded.

To get a stay of the board's revocation order, Heidegger had to convince the judge that they'd likely win this case on appeal. I pointed out that the state had proven what had happened with credible witness testimony from the victim and multiple corroborating witnesses, and that on appeal, those witnesses' credibility could not be reassessed, since their testimony could not be observed.

The judge agreed, sending Heidegger, whom he judged to be far less than a sure winner in this review, back to LA with a denial.

Of course, Dr. Don's appeal could continue even without the stay, but the evidence in the trial record suggested that a win was unlikely. In the meantime, his license was revoked. He'd have to relinquish his office lease and let go his support staff. His patient base would disintegrate, cutting off the supply of sad, damaged, unsuspecting women willing to place their mental well-being in his hands.

That Thursday up in Sacramento was a good day, so good that I felt the desire to slow down at some point in order to reflect upon my . . . okay, my fortunate circumstances. That moment came on the flight home in a half-empty jet at thirty-six-thousand feet. I'd taken a window seat and, twenty minutes aloft, found myself gazing east toward the deep green mighty tumbling folds of the Sierras and beyond, where great dormant pastel high-desert plains rolled silently toward Nevada. Late-afternoon high clouds raked over the tree-spiked mountaintops like roaring whipped cream freight trains. My breathing slowed as my mind settled into a sublime quietude. So peaceful, to skim the world's gentle curvature at this elevation, above all the confusion and messiness and lies and contradictions and human failings.

Way high, where the plum-colored rim of the sky bled into the infinite backdrop of deep space, I glimpsed a shape, a ghost moon, an orb, a dark planet—I don't know, some far-off place not so distant as to go unseen; but it was floating there, close enough, indeed, to serve as a receptacle of space explorers or telescope dreamers or souls untethered to the physical world but aching, still, to find a home. The jet engines hummed beneath my seat and the arid canvas scrolled by, turning twenty shades of parched brown against the odd finger-pointing scrawl of highway here and there. A distant reservoir shone like a lost nickel at the foot of a worn-out mountain. The cabin was as quiet and still as the landscape below.

I kept my gaze aloft, studying the planet's shape, readying to transport myself, conjuring the kind of dumb wonder necessary to power any great leap of faith. *This must be the place*, I told myself. My destiny was to be the dark planet's first leader, ruler, its moral arbiter, its heralded leather-clad skull-and-crossbones-bejeweled taste-maker—

Then the plane hit a bump, jarring me—and the planet . . . which, I instantly realized, was a reflection on the surface of the glass I'd been peering through. It was one of those startling moments of consciousness-shifting recognition, like when you're staring at a butterfly's silhouette and realize that instead, those are two faces kissing.

I'd been studying myself, constructing a world within my unblinking eye.

I was already there, where I wanted to go.

The jet banked right like a knife-blade descending, and through my little porthole LA's limitless gonzo freaky-deaky light show took over. The flight attendant who'd brought me a cranberry juice earlier stood by on the aisle like a dumbfounded freckle-cheeked kid in orange polyester, dipping her head to take in the view over my shoulder. Said she was from Turlock, a small-town San Joaquin Valley girl. No matter how many times she flew into LAX, she couldn't quite wrap her head around the colossal scale of the place.

"Neither can I," I admitted.

What I didn't say was that there's a vastness that, coupled with the impersonal vibe that comes with living among nine million strangers, makes this city feel overcrowded and at the same time, as lonely as the moon.

"You from here?" she asked.

I told her yes, I was, just as the jet wheels chirped, shaking the fuselage. Her Turlock-girl smile was genuine, and thus, incapable of masking heartbreak.

"Then welcome home."

I nodded, then turned to peer into the window, thinking: my planet is gone.

* 　 * 　 *

I'd promised to mail a copy of the judge's decision to Rue Loberg, which I usually do with any key witness in my cases; but when the time came, just dropping a document into an envelope seemed way too impersonal. Considering how much Rue had been through, such a mechanical gesture was damned near insulting.

Why, I wondered, hadn't I thought of this before? I've had plenty witnesses put their asses on the line for me in court, and I never blinked when walking to the mailbox to fire off the final verdict without any cover letter or even a personal note of thanks, as impersonally as you please. In truth, I'd been too enamored of my singular prosecutorial bent, content to see the push and pull of legal battle only in terms of my winning or losing on points of facts, law and evidence. My witnesses' moments of suffering, discomfort, confrontation, and humiliation were to me . . . just moments. My lawyer's perspective was alarmingly inadequate.

I wasn't an ice queen, as some suspected. I merely lacked the tools to express my humanity.

For the first time in my career, I hated the part of myself that I'd always considered to be an advantage. It's one thing to think you're being tough; it's another to treat people who are on your side with insensitivity.

At work you can't help but hear the talk, and a few of the secretaries have described me behind my back as a stuck-up bitch. That I am not. But my personal touch is lacking, to say the least.

I stuffed Rue Loberg's envelope into my desk and went home early, got a little shaky, the nerve-endings raw and exposed, as if I'd shed a layer of skin . . .

Oh, I thought—another little breakthrough: so *this* is how it feels to get in the game.

Went home feeling tired and defeated, and those walls seemed to come creeping, closing in. Had to see Mr. Daniels right away, in a tall glass, four, maybe five times. (So much for my rehabilitation project, the success of which I will have to measure like the AA people do: one day at a time.) Passed out on the bed fully clothed, woke up, and lay there, inert, until dawn, watching my thoughts scramble and dart across the ceiling like a pack of mongrels hunting for food.

These personal revelations come with a price. Put another way, my recovery is an ongoing process.

The next day, I closed my office door and called Rue Loberg. Instead, her daughter, my star rebuttal witness, Mindy, picked up. I told her why I was calling. She instantly shamed me by thanking me for thinking of her mom that way, by calling.

Yeah, I said to myself. Wasn't I the considerate one?

Then Mindy stammered and stopped altogether.

My wall of defenses shot up. The call was a bad idea, an intrusion, a mistake. What was I thinking? This kind of shit just didn't come naturally to me. Maybe I'd still mail that decision—

"My mom wants to see you," Mindy said.

"She does?"

"Yeah. But she's, uh, having a bad morning. The day after she has treatment is always like this."

She said it with such a matter-of-fact tone that I stumbled right into one of the all-time greatest stupid one-word responses ever conceived.

"Treatment."

Jesus—when Mindy told me her mother had cancer, it was like another set of blinders was torn off my thick head. All through the trial I'd seen Rue only as a victim coming to terms with her injuries by facing down the culprit. I'd missed any indication that for her, this may have been a last stand of an altogether different sort.

In a fumbled mess of words I can't fully recall, I offered an apology.

Mindy brushed it off, said hold the line, went away from the phone for a moment, then came back.

My mom wants to know if she can see you.

Yes, sure, I said before even contemplating what I might be getting into.

I hung up the phone, constrained as I was by the four walls and big desk. What was I doing? Though I felt more alive than I had in I don't know how long, I was afraid of what I was attempting. Reaching out only made me want to pull back to the familiar.

Which I found in the view outside my windowsill: another day, a dull, ubiquitous smog rendering the sky as a bland, flat blue brushed over dirty cardboard. High sunlight dominating the scene, bullying the street hawkers and parking attendants into any corners of shade they might find.

Down on the corner of Main and Third, a little tree-shaded spot with concrete planters and benches offers respite on hot days to Skid Row wanderers and junk collectors and crackheads. Always something going on. I glimpsed down through the branches to where a congregation of crumpled half-bent bodies nursed their cigarettes down to the nubs and clutched beer cans sheathed in brown paper bags that fool no one. Some waved their hands, and I knew they were arguing points no one in the real world would ever give a shit about. I'd knew because I'd heard the talk down on the street, times when I'd been out and about, looking to quell my mental dysfunction with a score. Even behind the double-paned glass eight floors up, I could hear every word they were saying.

Dis high! I was dis high when my daddy died. What I say, don't need nobody no-how take care a me. I kin take care a myssef.

The snakes? Yeah, sure, they live down underground. Huge, like a cross between a boa an' a anaconda, like this dude up inna Hollywood Hills, rock star? He breeds 'em that way, totally illegal.

Das pure bullshit, man!

Bullshit nothin, I seen 'em! Seen one come up from a storm gutter n' snatch a fat little Mexican baby.

Don' know what you seen!

Baby's momma tried to stop it, had the kid by the leg, like a tug-o'-war, but then the snake, it's like it gets bored, just opens its mouth real wide, swallows the momma right up, too. Swear to God!

You got shit for brains, man!

I tell ya, he's right! I can't walk near those storm drains, no, no, 'cause the snakes are callin' to me, whispering to me just like in the Garden of Eden, man . . .

A shock went up my spine. This could have been me—my life—I knew. I could be down there, fishing through fast-food wrappers in the gutter for something to eat and guarding a cart full of recyclable trash with my life. All it would have taken was a tiny downward tweak on my internal chemistry set, resulting in a deeper, more profound imbalance. I'd have been born with it, would have had no choice but to live zombiefied in a sterile lifeless Shady Acres hell on earth, or go it alone on the street with all the other thieves and crazies and drunks and dope fiends. If I'd been stuck with that lovely set of non-options, I knew exactly where my stubbornness would have landed me.

Down there, on Third and Main.

My father? With a tad more volatile chemistry, he, too, would not have been a lawyer. In his day, wandering the city with a more high-brow patter than the usual shuffling loony, he'd have been called a bum or a hobo, written off as an eccentric.

And so, I must conclude that I am lucky. And if visiting a woman with cancer is my idea of a supposed . . . *hardship*? Well . . . no, the task does not measure up to the word.

I retreated from the window and the sun's assault, blinking away the huge blotches of shadow obscuring my office. Tripped over a file box, but found my purse and got out of there before the weird sense of gratitude I was feeling could wear off.

* * *

Rue Loberg told me to wipe the long look off my face. But I had to ask my questions anyway. I'm a lawyer—sometimes even when I don't want to be one.

She'd been shying away from treatment, but the trial, and Mindy's example of courage, inspired her to be brave. The chemotherapy was a sickening pain, but it was more or less improving her medical outlook. Her doctors were encouraged. Guardedly optimistic. Those were the two words she was hanging on, of late.

Fifty-fifty got her attention, too. Decent betting odds.

She was feeling well enough to want to go out.

"Did you say you live in Venice?"

"That's right."

"How about the boardwalk? It's a nice day—"

"Kind of a scene down there," I said. "Lot of tourists, crazies, every kind of goofball. You know, LA at the beach."

She smiled and pulled down the brim of the gray tweed train-conductors hat that hid her recent hair loss.

"Jeans and tennies okay?"

"Sure," I said. "Anything goes down there."

"That's what I thought. Perfect."

So we piled into my Chevelle and rumbled down to the Venice boardwalk, where Mindy, Rue, and I spent the better part of the afternoon walking and talking and soaking in the scene, with its street performers and superheroes posing for photos and stilt-walkers and buskers pouring their guts out on bongos and guitars and tenor saxophones and even a kazoo. Mindy's big moment came when a magician with an African accent and a charming wit chose her from the crowd to help demonstrate several card tricks. He concluded his act with a bended-knee proposal to Mindy.

At a handmade jewelry display, Rue saw a glittering silver pair of skull-and-bones earrings and insisted on buying them for me. I reciprocated by picking up lunch: hot dogs and fries and soft-serve ice cream cones that we ate on a Mexican blanket I'd spread out on the sand as seagulls hopped around like little beggars. Rue said she was tired, so we sat a while longer, watching the wind-blown swells dump and explode near shore. In the deeper green water offshore, sailboats tacked in and out of the harbor against a steady breeze. An older man in a sweatsuit and mini-fedora swept a scanner across the lumpy sand, searching for loose quarters and other treasures. We fell into a deep, girls-only conversation, touching on everything from the high price of weddings to whether high heels are worth the arch pain to men who can't commit to whether all women fake orgasms (an informal poll suggested the answer was yes). Had such a good time that I totally forgot Rue's illness. That is, until she leaned forward on her elbows and smiled at Mindy and me, the sun lighting her tired face pink.

"There is nothing else I'd rather do than compare notes on the state of womanhood with you two fine ladies," she said. "But my body is telling me I've gotta rest."

Her sense of self-preservation gave me such a charge it's hard to put it into words—I won't even try.

Mindy and I scooped her up and walked her back to the car, our arms slung over one another's shoulders.

* * *

A few mornings ago, I surfed Malibu. That's right: in the morning. Daytime.

Craig Weaver made me do it. We'd been talking about having a paddle together, making a date of it. He'd called and stammered and asked me out not long ago, and we'd tried the usual dinner-and-a-movie thing, but I'm not inclined to sit in a dark auditorium and wait for startling images to be hurled at my consciousness—no thanks, that shit is too close to the way the less rational part of my brain functions. So then it was just dinner without the movie. He's smart, and a good conversationalist, if too shy by half. Last weekend we were going to give a new sushi place in the marina a try, but when he rang my doorbell looking lean and mean in these tight black jeans and cool-guy boots, I yanked him off the porch and imprisoned him in my bedroom. We called the sushi place for takeout and ate from white cartons on the couch; sat in front of the TV watching *High Noon* with Gary Cooper, a hero just as brave as he was terrified, one man striding down an empty street alone in a wild-west town full of cowards. Best dinner and a movie I'd ever had.

Surfing-wise, Craig is a kook—that is, a barney, a tourist, a rank beginner. But he's learning and becoming avid, and every time he feels the surge of a swell lifting him, he's buzzed. Amped. Stoked. As a surfer, I've got to respect that stoke, even though Craig possesses all the style of a drunken cockroach when he's up on a wave. But he'll improve if he stays with it. Weaver's never ridden Malibu, never harnessed the pure peeling down-the-line speed of a premier point wave. All he knows is the short dumpy beach break experience that spots like El Porto and Venice offer up, to be shared among a cast of thousands on sunny Saturday mornings. I like Craig, and I wouldn't mind surfing with him, but I won't lower my standards enough to stoop to that crappy-ass South Bay version of the modern surf-experience. Malibu is still my first love.

Yet he refuses to surf there at night. And I get that. If I were a beginner, I wouldn't dream of it. Too rocky; too cold; too fast-moving and incomprehensible in the dark.

So I compromised; waited for a foggy morning when the visibility was so poor, you couldn't even see the ocean from PCH. Couldn't even see the surf from the odd patches of sand edging into the wet cobblestones along the point.

"But you can hear it," I told Craig.

"I suppose," he said, less than convinced.

"No soul-sucking monster crowd clogging the lineup."

"Yeah," he muttered. "For good reason."

"You think I'm nuts."

He shrugged. "That's not really a fair question."

"Because you're a psychiatrist?"

He toed the wet sand, squinting into the drab mist.

"I'll, uh—what do you attorneys like to say?—take that one under submission."

I socked him in the arm.

"Weaver? We're going out."

In surfing, especially in So-Cal, where the conditions are often junky and every guy and his brother are out there groveling like hungry dogs for every scrap of open face, that's how it is a lot of the time. You've just got to throw yourself into what the ocean's offering up that day and not look back. Otherwise you'll spend your life talking bullshit over the back fence, waiting for the perfect day that never comes.

Weaver bear-hugged me.

"If you say so, Malibu guru. We're on it."

We turned back up the sand to get our boards and wetsuits. In the mist, a pile of black rags on the beach turned into a grizzled figure on closer inspection. A vagrant with black stringy hair and a short beard that looked like asphalt pebbles pocking his jaw line. His eyes were fearful, then resentful; we'd stumbled into his space, surprising him.

Weaver read the situation perfectly and squeezed my hand a little tighter, redirecting our path to create plenty of clearance.

"You!" the man grunted, pointing at me. "It's you!"

"Easy, bud," Weaver said.

"Know this! I never hit a girl! Not since my sister, and don'tcha know, that was back in the second grade!"

Just as abruptly he stared up into the fog as if in prayer. "Oh, Emily, forgive me, but you were a god-awful bitch!"

I stopped walking. He looked like a thousand other homeless men shuffling around the city, the kind you see so often that in time they become almost invisible: dark, weather-beaten skin; grimy pants; layers of holey, filthy shirts up top; laceless rumpled shoes; blackened fingernails; fearful, doleful, unhinged eyes. Still young, still big and strong and potentially dangerous. Wild, vaguely scary losers you cut a wide swath around to avoid. There was something familiar about this one. His . . . I couldn't place it.

"Never hit a girl, you gotta know!" His lip trembled as his arms tightened like straps lashed around his chest.

"You hit *me*. I remember."

"Nothing to eat, not a thing for days!" he said. "A hunnert bones! Right here, right in my hand! That's a lotta money!"

The wind shifted, and for an instant I caught a whiff of his uniquely foul body odor. He'd attacked me in the sand, that late night I'd been surfing the point alone, with Miki Dora. Those pricks working for Dr. Don—those pricks had paid a homeless guy to jump me.

"It's all right. Hey, a hundred bones is a hundred bones."

"Emily?"

"I'm not your sister," I said.

"I don't hit girls! Pull a few pigtails, maybe, yeah, I've been known to do that, but—"

I nodded to Weaver, and we pushed on through the primer-gray mist.

The surf that morning wasn't more than waist-high, but by Malibu standards, it was uncrowded. I guided Weaver into two pretty long ones, which he rode in his distinctive Quasimodo posture. But he managed to put some turns together, to build momentum with a continuity that the sand-bottom dumpers he was used to riding had never allowed for. The fog stubbornly sat on the point, and just before we came in, Weaver spun and nabbed an inside wave on his own, and we lost track of each other. Later, in the parking lot, he told me he'd been paddling back up the point, buzzing from his ride but chilled and ready to call it a session, when he saw the shape of a trim black figure streaking along, the rider's right arm up and bent at the elbow, the hand and fingers cocked as if holding an invisible teacup. He knew by the delicate expression that it was me, and he said he'd quit paddling, sitting up just to watch me go by, somehow sharing the feeling.

"I know it sounds silly."

I shook my head. "Not to me."

* * *

That's not to say I've quit night-surfing Malibu; I still get out there now and again, but not on those blackout nights I used to prefer. I'll wait until a decent swell coincides with a new moon and tolerate the presence of the handful of others who have the same idea. I must admit, I was mildly surprised—and relieved—to find that no one hassles much for waves at two in the morning. It's as if the shared obsession of having to surf when the rest of the world wouldn't even dream of it creates a bond, a cooperative pact between strangers that this experience is special and requires a different, more highly evolved approach. All the usual excessive jockeying and aggressive tactics, the kind of no-conscience water crimes routinely committed in broad daylight at every popular spot on the planet—well, that crap doesn't cut it in this peaceful, ethereal setting.

A few weeks ago, I somehow totally misread the weather report and pulled up on PCH to a black night sky and zero visibility out on the point. I was feeling unusually turned-around that evening because I'd come home from work earlier to find a box—my stolen box of documents—sitting on the front porch. I popped the top off, my car keys still in hand, and peeked in sheepishly, but there was no surprise: everything appeared to be there, in the exact same order I'd remembered, and for a moment I almost thought I'd imagined the whole break-in episode. No. It was real, as was a simple fact hammered home with this box's reappearance, the fact that they knew right where to find me and could slip in and out any time they wanted. I was equal parts angered and chilled by this reality.

Damn, I was thinking on that black night out at Malibu, *a half-hour drive from the pad in Venice for nothing*. Almost fired up the Chevy and peeled out of there; but then, the stars were out and a faint offshore breeze was seeping through the canyon passes and the surf forecast was tracking a small southern hemisphere swell for two days now. It sounds corny, but when you surf for a lot of years, sometimes you can sense when there are waves to be ridden. Sometimes, you just get a feeling.

I suited up, yanked the nine-six off the racks, and jogged down to the water.

The shorepound was more of a sound than a sight and rushed up like a linebacker, dunking me twice before I glided into slack water. Weaver would kill me if he knew, I thought; but he'd understand. He was turning out to be a very patient guy, willing to let me take my time shedding my lonely-girl ways.

The first wave I rode on instinct alone, as my eyes were still adjusting to the myriad shadings of night. I paddled back up the point, reflecting on Dora. By now, I'd deciphered a pattern in my manic visions. Mostly I'd been chased by the present, in the form of buildings; and chased by the past, by my father's ghost. Past or present, the visions had the same effect: to compel me to seek an escape.

Weaver's assessment that night at the fifties diner was essentially correct. Dora had fled this place long ago; my visions of him therefore fit the pattern. Only now, my desire to escape was diminishing daily.

Seemed I had it all figured out.

Until just before I came in, when on my paddle back up the line, I saw him swing into a jet-black insider, click his feet and dance and arch and stall and toy and power his way through a series of falling sections, right by me, both of us feeling the moment more than seeing—well, the electricity, the exquisite delicate celebratory buzz, the stoke that permeated our cynical defensive fears and told us to live this life no matter the rest, just take off and glide in . . . it was all too much, too perfect beyond imagining—even for me.

Which led me to reassess the true depth of my understanding of this phenomena, boiling it down to more subtle, durable essence.

Dora lives.

*   *   *

They brought in a cake for Mendibles to celebrate his last day in our section, sent an e-mail to everybody on staff to come to the conference room at three. I thought about leaving, just going home early to avoid the whole awkward spectacle, but I was behind on a brief that had to be filed the next day and had to keep typing.

About five minutes past three, I heard a knock on my door.

"I'm busy," I called out.

The door rattled open a few feet and Raul's secretary, Virginia, wedged her head in. I know she thinks I'm quite insane—her description—because I overheard her once in the ladies' room when I was occupying the end stall. At the time I hated her guts for it. Now, I don't even seem to care anymore.

"We're cutting the cake," she said. She'd worn a soft gold tapestry dress and put her blonde hair up for the occasion and I was reminded that for all I knew, Mendibles may have been a completely different person when he was with her. But none of that mattered enough to change my mind about today.

"I'm really tied up with this motion."

Her hand stuck fast to the doorknob, as if holding back the frustration and disdain she had for me. I feigned deep concentration, bearing down on my computer screen with the hope that she'd just leave me alone. Instead, she stayed put.

"*What?*" I said finally.

Virginia sighed. "He's . . . asking for you."

I took my hands off the keypad, concocting an apropos excuse, a suitable white lie. "Tell him . . ."

Not a damn thing came to mind. At first, I felt tangled up; frustrated, as if I could do better to conjure something, anything to get rid of this lady, to help her conclude this fool's errand she so plainly loathed. Yet . . . I had to give myself credit, for my thinking was perfectly clear: the answer lay in the nothingness of my response.

"Uh, excuse me, but . . . you were saying?"

I smiled.

"Sorry. I can't think. Tell him anything you want."

She sighed and shook her head. "Anything?"

"Just, don't hurt his feelings. No need for that."

Virginia's demeanor seemed to soften as she stood in my doorway, mulling a private decision. "I'll take care of it."

"Thank you." I had an impulse to say something out of character. "Hey, that dress? Gold is your color."

"Thanks." She looked at me as if considering me anew. Reassessing, I almost hoped. But not quite getting there. "Okay—um, gotta go."

After all, I am still the Warrior Queen.

The door closed, but the future—my future—seemed to crack open a little wider. My hands slid off the keyboard and I sat back, pinpointing the calm welcoming quiet and pulling it in until I was centered in the broadest possibility of the moment, which in that instant, revealed a gift: to be alone again, alone to dance freely within the crystal palace of my thoughts.

THE END

ACKNOWLEDGMENTS

My thanks go out to Fatemah Abooterab, MD, Josh Naqvi, MD, Paul S. Levine, Alexandra Hess, and my sister Suzanne for their thoughtful and timely guidance. Special thanks to my wife, Cynthia, for her support and encouragement. I am also grateful to Elyn R. Saks, JD, PhD, whose memoir, *The Center Cannot Hold*, casts an unsparing light on living—and thriving—with mental illness.